Praise for
TART

'A heartwarming story, bursting with queer joy, which explores the beauty of finding yourself and your people. *Tart* tackles big themes with real heart, which is sure to resonate with YA readers in this knockout debut'
Simon James Green, bestselling and award-winning author of *Noah Can't Even* and *Boy Like Me*

'Bold, unapologetic and often laced with sweetness, *Tart* deftly explores self-acceptance and the pressures of being a teenager in the twenty-first century. I dare you not to fall in love with Libby and her journey!'
Anika Hussain, author of *Heartbreaker* and *This Is How You Fall in Love*

'An explosive, twisting, thrilling, witty and fresh story full of heart'
Ian Eagleton, author of *Glitter Boy* and *The Boy Who Cried Ghost*

'Becki Jayne Crossley is the British Becky Albertalli. I absolutely adored *Tart*, a truly unputdownable YA novel with all the drama and chaos of teenage life blended seamlessly with small-town queerness. Total perfection'
Lizzie Huxley-Jones, author of *Under the Mistletoe with You* and *Make You Mine This Christmas*

TART

BECKI JAYNE CROSSLEY

BLOOMSBURY
LONDON OXFORD NEW YORK NEW DELHI SYDNEY

BLOOMSBURY YA
Bloomsbury Publishing Plc
50 Bedford Square, London WC1B 3DP, UK
Bloomsbury Publishing Ireland Limited
29 Earlsfort Terrace, Dublin 2, D02 AY28, Ireland

BLOOMSBURY, BLOOMSBURY YA and the Diana logo
are trademarks of Bloomsbury Publishing Plc

First published in Great Britain in 2025 by Bloomsbury Publishing Plc

Copyright © Becki Jayne Crossley, 2025

Becki Jayne Crossley has asserted her right under the Copyright, Designs
and Patents Act, 1988, to be identified as Author of this work

All rights reserved. No part of this publication may be: i) reproduced or transmitted
in any form, electronic or mechanical, including photocopying, recording or by
means of any information storage or retrieval system without prior permission
in writing from the publishers; or ii) used or reproduced in any way for the training,
development or operation of artificial intelligence (AI) technologies, including
generative AI technologies. The rights holders expressly reserve this publication
from the text and data mining exception as per Article 4(3) of the Digital Single
Market Directive (EU) 2019/790

A catalogue record for this book is available from the British Library

ISBN: PB: 978-1-5266-8445-5; eBook: 978-1-5266-8444-8;
ePDF: 978-1-5266-9667-0

2 4 6 8 10 9 7 5 3 1

Typeset by RefineCatch Limited, Bungay, Suffolk

Printed and bound in Great Britain by CPI Group (UK) Ltd, Croydon CR0 4YY

To find out more about our authors and books visit www.bloomsbury.com and
sign up for our newsletters
For product safety related questions contact productsafety@bloomsbury.com

For Mum,
my first and forever champion

And for Gill Hardiker,
my favourite teacher and
first champion who wasn't my mother

The Night It Happened

I don't remember the last time I needed to talk to someone this badly – I feel as though I could burst before I have the chance to get it out.

I pump the pedals of my bike faster and lean forward as if that might get me there a microsecond earlier. I know from living here my entire life that it takes ten minutes to get from mine to Libby's, but the ride across Chipping Hollow has never felt so long. It's dark out, and not just because the nights are starting to draw in now that we're into October. It was already late when Aaron dropped me home after our gig in the city, but this couldn't wait until morning. I grabbed my bike and headed off before I even went inside, so I hope I make it back before my parents start to worry about where I am. I probably should have just sent Libby a text, but this is a conversation I want to have face to face.

The vague smell of stale beer from the basement venue still clings to my hoodie. It was a great set, possibly one of our best. Lewis was buzzing when we came offstage, convinced it's only a matter of time until we're 'discovered'. I can't help but shake my head at the memory – it's true we don't sound half bad, and it's a lot of fun. But we've no lofty expectations about the prospects of what is essentially a bunch of seventeen-year-olds smashing away on their instruments to crowds that just happen to be there.

But that's not what I'm dwelling on right now. It's what came after we got offstage that has me hurtling through the night air to talk to Libby. My mind is spinning, and it occurs to me mid-pedal that I never got around to fixing my bike lights – I never needed them during the long, lazy days of summer.

The thought enters and exits my head in a heartbeat. *I'll fix them tomorrow*, I idly promise myself.

I reach the crest of a shallow hill and freewheel a little on the other side, weaving the handlebars back and forth as I turn things over in my mind. If anyone was to catch sight of me right now, I'd look like a madman. But there is no one about on this long, winding country road in the dark of encroaching autumn.

No one, until very suddenly there is.

The headlights burst from the night with a ferocity that, at first, is the only thing that scares me. On instinct I squeeze my eyes shut just as it occurs to me that, oh yes, there's a 3,000-pound hunk of metal on wheels behind those lights. And then the air is screeching and everything hurts all at once and someone is screaming and it might be me …

And then, nothing.

OCTOBER

LIBBY

I quickly learned that it doesn't matter if I can't remember a thing about the crime I committed, people will still blame me for it. In a tiny village like ours, your business is automatically everyone else's business. When I woke up that morning two weeks ago, head pounding, feeling like my brain had been turned inside out, I had absolutely no idea that half the population of Chipping Hollow already hated me.

'Almighty God, our heavenly father, graciously comfort your child in his suffering.'

I was never really what you'd call 'popular'; I don't think I was ever attractive or funny or talented enough to stand out. I've always held a sort of happy middle ground – my classmates are perfectly friendly to me when they bump into me at some party, but otherwise, they don't give me a second thought.

That's not necessarily a complaint. It's not the worst place to be in the social hierarchy. Especially as no one misses you if you decide to skip something to stay home and eat ice cream in your pyjamas.

'Bless the means used for his cure.'

I shift uncomfortably on the wooden assembly bench as I try to tune out the reverend's prayers. Not because I don't care, but because it's getting more and more painful to hear.

Dan was what you might call my first 'proper' boyfriend, if you don't count the two-week primary-school romance with Jason Pratt, which I generally don't. *He* only got me to agree to go out with him by following me around all lunchtime break, singing 'We Go Together' from *Grease*.

Dan was a little different. Then again, Dan was always going to be different.

In the first week of nursery school, a four-year-old Daniel King saved me from an attack by the biggest spider my young eyes had ever seen. It had crawled on to my Polly Pocket backpack and was staging a siege between me and my cheese sandwiches.

Dan was standing next to me at the row of coat pegs and saw me recoil in horror. He scooped the spider up between his pudgy hands and threw it from the nearest open window without so much as a flinch. It was nothing short of heroic.

I decided there and then that I wanted Daniel King to be my boyfriend.

He spent primary school singing in the church choir, and was the kind of kid that always got picked to do the best reading at harvest festival, or play his guitar at the Easter service. After we hit high school and most guys were still making crude jokes and terrible haircut decisions, Dan got hot. The dark curls and bright blue eyes he'd always had were now paired with broad shoulders and an extra foot of height, seemingly overnight. When your community is this small, it's hard not to notice that kind of thing.

'Fill his heart with confidence that he may put his trust in you.'

The desire for Dan to be my boyfriend never really went away, though it did evolve as we grew up. What started off as wanting us to hold hands and share our snacks at playtime developed into a full-blown crush, the kind that leaves you listening to a lot of early Taylor Swift.

When we finally became a couple at the start of the summer, I hadn't considered that my status would go up purely by association. I was the Libby half of Dan-and-Libby, and people I'd known all my life but barely spoken to now wanted to be my friend. It was as though I'd just bloomed into existence. There was some thinly veiled jealousy from a few of the other girls in our year, but nothing that ever came to anything. Until now.

I'd quite enjoyed my brief stint as a member of the 'in' crowd, as much as I always pretended I didn't care about such trivial things as popularity. And things didn't change too much – I still had Mona, my best friend since the first day of Year 1 when we turned up with the same Scooby-Doo lunch box. Bonds like that last forever, or at least, they're supposed to. Nearly a whole summer apart while she was away with her family was bad enough, but after what happened …

'Through Jesus Christ our Lord. Amen.'

Reverend Wallace finally finishes his prayer, and an unusually audible ripple of '*amens*' runs through the assembly hall, pulling me back to the present. Very few of us normally pay attention to morning prayers, more occupied with trying to stealthily check our Instagram notifications, slipping phones back up our blazer sleeves when a teacher turns towards us. But today, not a single person's face is under-lit by the telltale glow of a phone screen.

Today, the prayer is for Dan.

I can feel someone's eyes on me, something I seem to have developed a talent for picking up on recently. I glance down the row and spot Katie West staring daggers at me, a look of pure disgust on her face. The girls around her – every single one of them with me on the night that it happened – start to notice and join in, until the force of their collective gaze makes my skin prickle and burn.

I force myself to sit there, as still as if I was carved out of stone, until we're finally dismissed. I leap from my seat, shouldering my way through the crowd to get out into the corridor, heart hammering as I remind myself to breathe.

'*Slut!*'

I cringe as I scoop egg goop and broken shell from the bottom of my locker, pushing it with a wet *slop* into a plastic bag. My whole body is poised to gag but I hold it back, determined to keep my expression blank. It's enough that I have to do this in front of a corridor of sniggering onlookers; they're not having the satisfaction of knowing it's making me want to bring up my breakfast.

I wonder idly who did it. You've got to admire their dedication to tormenting me, really. Holding on to their on-the-turn eggs especially for me. I mean, that's effort right there.

Having a locker is supposedly a special privilege, something you're only bestowed when you reach the upper echelons of St Hilda's C of E School and Sixth Form. In our younger years we coveted the older kids, something as exotically American as *lockers* was seen as a badge of honour for the day you hit sixth form. Even the ancient, rusting things that line the walls of St Hilda's. It's an honour I'm not particularly grateful for right now.

A knot sticks in the back of my throat as I lift out a ruined notebook and hold it gingerly between my finger and thumb. Beneath a layer of gunk is a Polaroid I'd glued to the front cover; Mona with her burst of dark curls is grinning up at me. I'm tucked under her arm, my face so luminously red with laughter that you can't see my freckles. It's my favourite photo of us.

I drop the whole thing into the bag with the eggs.

From the corner of my eye I can see Lewis leaning against a noticeboard further down the corridor, scrolling on his phone with blatant disregard for St Hilda's 'phones off during school hours' rule. He doesn't look my way, but I duck my head back into the locker just in case. As one of Dan's best friends and his band mate, he's not my biggest fan right now.

Maybe he's the one that defiled my locker. I picture him coming into school early, jimmying open the metal door and pouring the stinking eggs all over my textbooks. It feels like the kind of thing he might do.

The slimy mixture seeps on to my hands and it feels pointless to try and figure out who did it. I suppose it doesn't matter.

At least all Aaron, Dan's other best friend, has done is give me is the silent treatment. Although every time he sees me in the corridor, the pain and betrayal in his eyes hurts more than anything Lewis may or may not have done to my locker. Aaron was always so friendly at their band rehearsals, the only one of their group to actually make me feel welcome.

Katie West is an entirely different matter, though she'd never do something as obvious as egging my locker. Her cruelty was always more subtle, clouded in a sweetness that couldn't quite overpower its bitter aftertaste. Even before the incident I knew she didn't like me. She's Lewis's girlfriend but grew up with Dan, the pair of them practically inseparable since birth, and she made it clear, if only to me, that I wasn't a welcome addition to their close-knit circle.

I wipe the last of the gunk from my locker and drop another ruined book into the bag. I close the door slowly, careful not to slam it, and walk with my chin up along the row. The soggy bag goes straight into the first bin I pass, tossed as casually as an empty food wrapper.

I pass Lewis, whose eyes finally drift up from his phone and land on me.

It's only a whisper, but I still hear the word that escapes his lips as I pass.

'Whore.'

I walk through the corridors ahead of a free period, feeling rather than seeing the burning stares that come my way and praying for the relative peace that will come after the bell rings and most people go into lessons. Lewis isn't the only student to throw some kind of derogatory term in my direction. Even the Year 9s are at it, my indiscretion evidently school-wide knowledge.

I duck into the library, hoping for a moment of peace, and disappear quickly behind the shelves, losing myself in P through R.

If we lived anywhere else, I would be attending a school full of people who hadn't known me since the age of three. I could have got away with being at least a little inconspicuous, despite my might-as-well-be-neon red hair announcing my identity. But no, we live in Chipping Hollow. And everyone in Chipping Hollow has known you since you were 'this high'.

Dan and I only started going out in June. At the end of our exams, Craig Shaw threw a party to mark the beginning of the end of our sixth-form careers, and I promised myself I was finally going to tell Dan how I felt about him. How I *had* felt about him for years, having never quite let go of the spider incident. I was going to tell him and then deal with whatever came next, good or bad.

Being Dan's girlfriend was almost like being royalty – not quite the King and Queen, but maybe a well-known duke and duchess. We sat just outside the centre of attention – close enough to feel its warmth but without too much pressure or expectation. All you had to do was avoid some major slip-up and you'd be golden.

I guess I failed there.

I browse my way through the bell signalling the start of

second period, and the library empties out a little. I tell myself to go to Psychology, but Lewis is in Psychology and I can't quite bring myself to suffer any more abuse this morning. The eggs were plenty to deal with before lunch.

I pluck a book at random from the shelves. Mrs Emerson, the school librarian, who by all laws of nature should be dead by now, gives me a measured look with her cloudy eyes before going back to her laminating machine. She knows I'm skipping lessons. I don't care. She doesn't care. We've been getting on just fine.

In fact, I think she's been leaving books out for me. Those cloudy eyes see all and she's definitely noticed that my peers have been giving me hell, so I think she's been trying to cheer me up a bit. The silver lining of living in a village with a rapidly ageing population is that most of them don't pay the slightest bit of attention to social media, so she doesn't know why I'm currently a pariah. Which works in my favour.

Sure enough, when I drop down into my favourite comfy chair by the windows, there's a photography book placed casually on the side table. I glance over to her, but she's pretending not to notice.

I open the book but I don't read it. My mind floats away from the library, across the village to the hospital where Dan is. Lying motionless, connected to half a dozen machines that I couldn't name even if I tried. Suspended somewhere between life and not life.

I can't believe it's already been two weeks since Mr King called me to tell me about the accident. At first, I thought it was one of Dan's friends playing some sort of sick joke. I was barely awake, still nursing my hangover from the night before, and hadn't yet realised what I'd done.

It took his dad a good few minutes to convince me that what he was saying was real. Once it finally sank in I dropped the phone and screamed at Mum to get the car keys. I didn't even listen long enough to hear all the details, just that Dan was in the hospital and it wasn't looking good.

I learned the specifics later as I sat hugging my knees to my chest on a lumpy armchair in the hospital waiting room. My eyes and nose were sore from the scratchy pieces of toilet paper I'd been rubbing them with, although by that point I'd cried all the moisture out of my body. I did that the moment I saw Dan, looking so tiny on a hospital bed with his face obscured by an oxygen mask.

They told Dan's parents the full extent of his injuries in a family room off the side of the ward – I could hear Mrs King's sobs all the way down the corridor. But just looking at him was enough to know it was bad. Any visible skin was covered in violent, angry bruises, one leg was encased in plaster, and his neck was supported by a brace. I didn't dare ask if it was just a precaution or something more.

Eventually Dan's dad came out, looking half in a trance, and explained what had happened. Mum had to hold my hands down to try and stop them shaking as I stared without seeing at the faded posters on the walls, Mr King's words washing over me. Thank god she was there. Her job as a social worker keeps her busy most of the time, buried in paperwork even when she *is* in the house. If she hadn't been there grounding me, I might have lost my mind.

There were a lot of complicated words that my mind was too addled to translate into English, but I pieced together that Dan had been knocked from his bike by a driver that they were still looking for. I told him – I *told* him – to fix the lights on his damn bike, or at least take the long route by the church. Not the dark, winding country road he'd been on when a car came hurtling through the night.

The road that he always took from his house to mine. When I lie in bed unable to sleep, guilt swirling around me like a toxic fog, that's what I think of – that he had been on his way to confront me, and his last conscious thoughts were of the awful thing that I did. Thank god for Mr Pine and his insomnia – he found Dan lying in the road while walking his dog, out far later than the rest of the village ever is. And of course, as everyone knows everyone in Chipping Hollow, he was able to call Dan's parents immediately after summoning an ambulance. I don't want to think about what state he might have been in if he hadn't been found until the morning.

The doctor told us that they'd be taking him in for surgery soon, assuring us that they would do everything they could. The way he said it suggested that it might not be enough.

Dan's parents were allowed to sleep fitfully on the sofa in the family room, but as a non-family member I was asked to leave. Mr King hugged me before I left, squeezing me so hard I thought my shoulders might pop. Mrs King had passed out by this time. I've not been able to face them since, too wracked with guilt about not only betraying Dan but being the reason he was on the road that late in the first place.

I shake myself out of the memory, closing my eyes and resting my head on the book I'm not reading. The sound of the library, pages turning and the occasional whisper of students working through a free period, lulls me into a half-sleep.

The relative peace is broken when I hear my name.

'Are you Olivia Dixon?'

I raise my head and squint at a younger girl with a 'Student Assistant' badge pinned to the front of her school jumper.

'I guess I have to be. What?'

The girl draws herself up with importance. 'I've got a note here to say you've got to go to your head of year's office, straight away.'

I groan, and tell myself that I knew I probably wasn't going to get away with skipping lessons forever. If she's found me this easily, then my library sanctuary isn't the well-kept secret I thought it was.

'You've got to go right now—'

'Yes, yes, I'm going,' I snap, snatching up my bag and stalking away. As I leave the library, someone coughs '*slut*'.

It's getting old, fast.

I squirm in my seat outside Mr Harper's office, watching the clock tick and realising that I'm going to miss English next period. Seems ironic that they'd keep me out of lessons to give me a telling off about skipping lessons, but in the grand scheme of things they've probably done me a favour. Just by being here I've avoided about three spitballs, several slurs and a can of Diet Coke poured in my bag.

The door to Mr Harper's office jerks open and he steps out, eyes boring into me. He nods curtly and goes back inside.

I suppose that's my cue.

The office smells of photocopier toner and an unpleasantly strong aftershave. It's empty of personal touches, save for a silver-framed photograph of a smiling blonde lady on a shelf behind the desk. I try to imagine Mr Harper with a wife, a family. The imposing figure in the grey suit across the room doesn't really lend itself to that image.

Dominating the room, on the wall above the desk, is a large wooden cross, on which a disturbingly detailed figure of Christ is splayed. We've got crosses in most of our classrooms, but Mr Harper has the only crucifix. Personally I think he put it there specifically so Jesus can stare down at those of us summoned to receive punishments.

I sit down in the uncomfortable chair opposite Mr Harper's desk before he invites me to, which earns me another hard stare.

'Miss Dixon,' he starts, lowering himself into his smart leather chair. He stares at me through thick-lensed glasses and I wonder if he's waiting for me to respond.

'Mr Harper.'

His eyes narrow. It's not what he was looking for.

'Do you know why I've asked you to come and see me today?'

I make an uncommitted noise and shrug. Judgemental Jesus looks on silently.

'I want you to explain to me why you've been missing your lessons.' He pulls a piece of paper from a cardboard folder that's been carefully placed on the desk, directly in front of where I'm sitting. 'Your teachers have reported five separate instances of unexplained absences in the past week.'

I wonder if every other truancy gets treated this way, as though I've been caught spray-painting the corridors instead of hiding out in the library. I focus on the lady in the photograph just above his head, a scrap of humanity in this void of a room.

'I've been having a rough time.' I try to keep my voice bland and uninterested, but I can tell it's not fooling him so I just go for it. 'My boyfriend is in a coma.'

There's a very awkward pause, and when I look up I'm surprised to see that he has the good grace to look uncomfortable for a second.

'Yes, well,' he says gruffly, seemingly not prepared for me to bring it up directly. 'Our thoughts and prayers are all with Daniel of course.'

I only get to enjoy his squirming for a moment before his gaze turns cold and steady again.

'However, I also understand there's been some talk amongst your year. Regarding a video of yourself that's been circulating.'

I say nothing, momentarily stunned into silence that the teachers are privy to idle teenage gossip. He knows about the *video*. Has he *seen* it? My stomach lurches worse than it did when clearing the eggs out of my locker – an incident I imagine he won't be concerning himself with, along with the other various hells my classmates have been putting me through.

Mr Harper drums his fingers on the desk. 'I hope you understand, Olivia, that St Hilda's has a reputation for excellence and self-respect.' He stands so I have to tilt my head back to stare up at him. 'As sixth-form students, your year is held as an example to the younger pupils. We don't want the *wrong* example being set. Especially when it comes to underage drinking.'

OK, he's just talking about the drinking. My pulse slows a little, but my hands clench and unclench in my lap. I shouldn't be surprised after all my time at St Hilda's that this man is more bothered about the school's reputation than bullying happening right under his nose.

He continues, my incredulity ignored. 'If you do not keep your head down, and that includes attending all your scheduled lessons, we will have to take further action on the matter. We don't take things like this lightly at this school.' He pauses, his eyes roaming over me in a way that makes me suppress a shudder. 'You may leave.'

He sits back down and turns to his computer. I've been dismissed.

I rise to my feet and start to walk towards the door.

'And tuck your shirt in, for goodness sake.'

I stop to look back at him in shock.

Mr Harper doesn't look up. Neither does Jesus.

I can't believe this is happening.

Neha

My new room, although I suppose I should really just start calling it 'my room' after nearly a year, is significantly smaller than my old one. I have to bend awkwardly to see my whole body in the oddly angled mirror that's wedged between the chest of drawers and the window.

If I stay here much longer I'll be late for school, but Jas is on an early shift at the hospital so there's no one to chivvy me along. Since I was tiny she's always been more like my big sister than my aunt, and has always *despised* being referred to as such, says it makes her feel ancient. So, despite my parents' thinly veiled displeasure, she always insisted I call her 'Jas' rather than 'Auntie'. But when it comes to getting out of the door on time, she has no qualms about pulling the age rank and any associated titles.

I tug at the end of my ponytail, wondering if I should try something different today, as if that would even make a difference. It might help if I was able to wear my regular clothes and convey at least an ounce of personality. Unlike my old school, St Hilda's insists the sixth-formers still wear the uniform. Something about 'modesty' and 'preparing you for dress codes in the workplace'. I just think the teachers want to maintain the privilege of snapping at us for not having our top buttons done up.

I look back at my wardrobe wistfully, wishing I could wear one of my colourful sweatshirts or patterned dungarees instead of this ugly maroon jumper, itchy blazer and gender-mandated skirt. My uniform had to come second-hand from the shop in town as I joined a couple of months into the last school year and they had no new stock in. The jumper is too baggy in the sleeves and the blazer is shiny on the elbows, but I didn't want to ask Jas to fork out for new stuff at the beginning of this year.

Apart from the unsightly uniform, there's nothing particularly *wrong* with St Hilda's. Not really. But after eleven months it still doesn't feel like mine. Nothing in Chipping Hollow does, and even though I visited Jas here plenty of times before moving, it's still not home.

Even my bedroom doesn't feel like it belongs to me, despite my and Jas's best efforts. We put up all my crinkly theatre posters over the dodgy wallpaper, covering up the gaudy pattern with flash promos for *Heathers*, *Phantom of the Opera* and *SIX*. We strung fairy lights around the metal bed frame, stuffed the limited shelves with my books, and even stuck the glow-in-the-dark stars from my childhood bedroom to the ceiling. The glue is old and they fall down sometimes in the middle of the night, but they're too comforting for me to get rid of.

I heave a sigh (the kind that Jas calls 'theatrical') even though there's no one here to witness it, and flip my ponytail back over my shoulder. I suppose it'll have to do. I doubt a radical new hairstyle would transform my new life anyway.

I'm on the way out of my bedroom when I pause and turn back towards my dresser. From a box of pins on top I pluck out a small rainbow pride flag and fasten it to the strap of my rucksack. A tiny act of colourful rebellion.

I wander towards school, taking the long way through the village green despite already cutting it a bit fine time-wise – there's honestly nothing worse than standing around outside of school waiting for the first bell with no one to talk to and nothing to occupy you.

The village looks as it always does – like something from a postcard, or perhaps an episode of one of those old cosy mystery TV shows that my nan used to love. Everything feels like it's been here forever, the people just as permanent a feature as the jumbled rows of stone-built cottages that line the green.

Moving to Chipping Hollow was like stepping back in time. The kids my age might have the latest phones and use modern slang, but it feels so out of place here – like spotting a smartwatch on the wrist of an actor in a period drama. This village is a time capsule of how things used to be, and I still haven't figured out how far that affects people's attitudes towards such radical modern concepts as 'being openly gay'.

The racism I can't avoid – there's no hiding that part of myself even if I wanted to, so I have to contend with being brightly told how good my English is every time I go into the village shop, or one of the other kids asking where I'm 'really' from. But I do feel a bit weird about how easily and automatically I slipped back into the closet after I moved, for the sake of an easier life.

Maybe I shouldn't be so hard on myself about it. It's hard enough being the new kid halfway through the school year, but throw in being the new, queer, Brown kid halfway through the year in an extremely white Christian school in a weird little village where everyone has known each other since birth, and it's way worse. Not to mention having left behind a group of beautifully supportive friends you miss like crazy, or the reason for the move in the first place ... but I know if I dwell on it too long I'll ruin the entire day for myself. I've already lost too many to self-pity spirals.

I concentrate instead on the morning activity of the village green, predicting what I'm going to see before it happens. It's not a hard game to win. Mr Taylor leans in the doorway of his tea shop holding a huge steaming mug as he chats with Mrs Bramley, out for her usual morning walk. I glance at the time on my phone and can't help but smirk: 8.42 a.m. She's right on time.

I look across the green to see – yep, there's Mr Norman, the postman, in his khaki shorts despite the chilly October breeze, wheeling his bike along the pavement. I don't think

I've ever seen him ride that thing. It fits with the cosy village aesthetic so well it seems that no one has ever thought to question it.

I suppose this level of consistency is comforting to some people, but as someone from a place bigger than Chipping Hollow, it's a bit eerie. Making it into a game helps a little towards alleviating the Stepford vibes.

I cross the road as Mr Norman approaches, wanting to stay out of his way. Even after nearly a year, I haven't quite nailed the same code switch that the other kids my age have perfected when it comes to interacting with the older people in the village. All I ever manage is an awkward smile as they frown and try to figure out who the hell I am.

I make it to school on time, passing under the stone archway above the entrance doors just as the bell rings. My last school was a flat, boxy concrete construction from the 80s. St Hilda's is a different beast, solid brick and stone that's been worn smooth by the years. It even has the old 'Girls' and 'Boys' entrances from decades ago, the words etched deep into the stone above the doors as unmoving as the school's rigid ideas on gender identity. I suspect more than one of the teachers still wishes the separate entrances were in use, the way they glare at students who get too close to one another in the halls.

Adjusting to the religious overtones at St Hilda's was way more jarring than the building itself though. Market Stepton Academy was resolutely non-denominational, so having to recite a prayer every morning in assembly took a while to get used to. Especially as all the other kids in my year knew them off by heart, having been trotting them out every day since they were six.

I was raised without religion. I know just enough to mumble 'amen' at the end of whatever the teacher or visiting reverend had reeled off, always a second or two behind everyone else. Every time I feel like someone is going to turn and call me out for it, but as with everything I do, no one notices or cares. Even so, it's hard to not feel scrutinised within such a tiny school population. At my old school, I could be surrounded by a sea of students and still feel less claustrophobic than I do in a classroom of only fifteen others here.

I make it to the assembly hall, shuffling along the bench of already seated students until I reach a gap. I sit down, the wood creaking and reminding me of just how bloody old everything in this school is. I glance at the person next to me, someone I recognise from Biology. I hitch a cheery smile on to my face.

'Morning, Kayleigh!'

Kayleigh takes a second to respond as she clearly grasps to remember my name. 'Umm. Morning, Neha.' She turns back to her conversation with whoever is sitting on her other side. I hear her ask her friend: 'Where's she from again?'

My smile fades, and I try to convince myself she's asking what school I used to go to. It's certainly plausible. I do wonder why I'm still bothering though. I'm an alien to these people, they've known each other all their lives. I sometimes think it would hurt less if they hadn't really learned who I was yet, but the sad fact is they do know – they just don't care.

Reverend Wallace is back again today. He used to run assembly about once a week, but since Dan King had his accident he's been coming in more frequently to lead us in a prayer for the sick.

The day the school got the news was horrible. By Chipping Hollow standards Dan is like a minor celebrity, but when I heard he'd been hurt I wasn't thinking of him as the popular boy. I was thinking of the boy who sat next to me in assembly on my very first day at St Hilda's. He welcomed me to the school with such warmth I couldn't for a second think it was anything other than genuine. He asked me questions about myself, and actually listened when I answered.

I wish we'd had the chance to become better friends, but he was the type that's always in demand – by teachers and students alike. Not to mention his friend Katie seemed to guard him like a pit bull, something I'm not even sure he noticed himself. He did always make an effort to smile at me when we passed in the corridors though. It went a small way to making me feel less invisible.

My mind is still wandering as the reverend finishes his prayer and our head of year starts delivering announcements. I tune it all out, rousing only when everyone is standing up and moving for the door. I shoulder my bag and join the throngs of students jostling around as everyone tries to escape the stuffiness of the hall.

'*Slut!*'

The shout makes me jump, and I immediately start looking around to see where it came from. I know it wasn't directed at me – there's only one person it could have been directed at – but I've been making a mental list of the people so quick to use that word and others like it.

Right now though, there's too many people and the shout could have come from anywhere. I do however spot a flash of red hair as the recipient of the abuse pushes faster through the crowd. Not for the first time I feel the urge to go after her, but we've never spoken two words to each other before. It feels too weird to do it now.

The crowd thins as everyone peels off to head to their first lessons, and before long I'm perched on an uncomfortable lab stool pulling out my Biology books. Kayleigh is at the workbench in front of me, and my heart does a sad little flop as I think about how she struggled to remember my name. It used to make me angry, but it seems I don't have the energy for that any more.

I switch my attention to the front of the classroom, where the Biology teacher, Mrs Rawlinson, is starting the lesson, and try to put everything but cell structure out of my mind. At least for the next hour.

I've found that the issue with being invisible means you end up with a lot of time alone with your own thoughts, whether you like it or not.

During lessons it's not too bad. I'm pretty good at focusing on the subject in front of me, with no pesky friends to distract me from whatever the teacher is saying. I scribble down notes, answer the occasional question put to the class, and generally fulfil the role of Model Student. I'm sure I'll be grateful for my loneliness when it comes time to take our exams, which I need to smash if I'm going to get in for Paramedic Science at university.

By lunchtime though, I've reached the point where I'd swap a glittering future career for just a scrap of friendly conversation.

I step into the canteen, scanning the tables for a group that might offer me a seat. Occasionally I'll find someone who'll give me a nod of approval to join their table, but once I'm there the chat washes over me, too full of unfamiliar references for me to attempt to chip in. And by the next lunchtime, it's like I was never there. I'm cautiously hopeful that one day I might find a group that wants to keep me.

Today though, I find myself sitting at the edge of the room by myself, and have only my sandwiches and cluttered thoughts for company.

I pull out my phone and jam my headphones in, choosing to soundtrack my lunch with *Everybody's Talking About Jamie*, and imagine I'm the main character on the cusp of a social breakthrough. I start scrolling through group chat messages from my friends in Market Stepton.

ZOE
Beanz after college?

SAM
What so you can torment me at my place of work?

ROBYN
Why else would we go there

SAM
Vibes

ZOE
Bold of you to assert that a coffee shop called 'Beanz' with a z has 'vibes'

SAM
Sorry. 'Vibez'

ZOE
I can drive us after last lessons

ZOE
Sorry Neha should have used the other chat!! Love you

I feel a pang that they now have a separate group chat to make these kinds of last-minute plans. I can't even drive to see them myself – I passed my test months ago, but obviously can't afford a car. I see them as much as I can, but in between times I don't half miss them.

I think about how easy it was to come out to them a couple of years ago – easier still because my best friend, Sam, has been out since we were twelve, and Robyn has always been so open about their relationship with gender. That kind of stuff just wasn't a big deal in my old life.

It's different here. I don't know of a single kid at St Hilda's that's out, although sometimes I wonder if that's because nobody really talks to me.

Almost as if on cue, from the table next to me I hear Grace Chapman ask her friends, 'Does this haircut make me look like a lesbian?'

Her words are loud enough to cut through the music from my headphones, and as casually as I can, I slip one out so I can hear the rest of the conversation, a mix of hope and fear curdling in my stomach.

'No, babe!' squeaks one of the other girls, my misguided hope fizzling away as disappointment settles in. 'Of course it doesn't!'

There's a cacophony of shushing and reassuring that no, of course Grace's new short haircut is not homosexual, don't worry. I stuff the headphone back in. It's not the first time I've overheard such effortlessly casual homophobia, and I conclude that it probably isn't just that nobody talks to me – it's that this doesn't feel like a particularly safe space to come out.

Still, I often feel that the half-secret of my sexuality is like an unplayed poker chip – it could make me even more of an outcast, or it could make people finally pay a bit of attention to me. I've kept it so close to my chest over the past year, not only out of fear of the former but the uncomfortable tackiness of the latter.

Remembering the pin on my rucksack, I self-consciously nudge my bag further under the table with my foot.

I give myself a mental shake and try to remember how lucky I am to have the friends I do have, even if they're further away than I'd like. It seems impossible that there are no queer kids in this village, small as it is, and I can't imagine what it would be like to need to keep something like that a total secret from everyone.

As if the universe wants to remind me that blending into the background isn't the worst place to be, the first thing I see when I tap into Instagram is another post of that damn video.

The first time I saw it I didn't even realise it was footage of someone I knew, or at least knew of. By the time I did understand what I was watching, it was already too late, and the image of Libby Dixon cheating on Dan King was burned into my brain. I haven't been able to work out if he was already in a coma at that point – from what I can gather, only the people who were there that night know for sure.

I can't pretend I'd never noticed Libby before. Even though I knew she was in a happy, very public (and very straight) relationship, something about the way she crinkled her freckled nose when she laughed, or the way the sunlight caught on her red curls, had captured my attention since I arrived in Chipping Hollow. But it was something I'd kept in a mental box labelled *Never gonna happen*, and I tried my best to just ignore her.

I remember the flare of fury when I first saw her in that video, mob mentality creeping in without permission. But then I looked closer and saw how unsteady on her feet she was, how hard this stranger seemed to be gripping her. I don't want to presume and I don't want to get involved, but that paired with the onslaught of slut-shaming directed at her makes me quietly uncomfortable with the whole thing.

The bell rings, signalling the end of lunch period, and I snap out of my jumbled thoughts. I look back down at my phone, Zoe's last message still unanswered – I assume everyone has remembered I can see their plans but not join in and is feeling awkward. Desperate not to ruin the mood, I fire off a quick message.

NEHA
Don't worry about it! Have a great time vibing/bothering Sam later :)

ZOE
We'll bother him extra for you babe. Let's sort something out for this weekend? I can drive us down and you can take us to that tiny cinema you were on about?

Warmth blooms in my chest. Things could certainly be a lot worse.

Four Weeks Before It Happened

The rumble of thunder rolls through my open bedroom window, a fresh wave of that glorious rain smell coming with it. Libby, perched on the end of my bed, heaves in a lungful of it.

'I hate to sound like an old lady,' she says, 'but, God, we needed this.'

I grin and nod. 'Feels like a good way to bookend the summer.'

'Oh, don't remind me it's ending,' Libby groans. 'I can't believe it's already back-to-school day. Feels like we only just broke up for the holidays.'

'Time flies when you're having fun,' I say with a wink, and she laughs.

She's right though, the summer has gone by in a blink. It feels like barely last week that we got together at Craig Shaw's end-of-exams party, but at the same time I feel like we've been together for years. I'm more comfortable around her than I ever was with some of my other friends.

I peer at myself in the mirror on the back of my bedroom door, running a hand through my dark curls and wondering if I should do something with them. I think I've got an ancient tin of hair gel in the back of a drawer somewhere. I check my watch and realise I don't really have time to be experimenting.

'It's weird being back in the blazer after a summer off, isn't it?' I say, rolling my shoulders and turning back towards Libby. 'I wish they let sixth-formers wear what they want.'

'Fat chance,' scoffs Libby. 'Show some individuality? Allow the girls to wear *trousers*? Mr Harper would go spare.'

'You're not wrong,' I say, lifting my fresh new rucksack off the floor and hitching one strap over my shoulder. 'Ready?'

'Aye aye,' says Libby with a mock salute, hopping up off the bed just as the door to my room swings open with unnecessary force.

'I thought I said door open when there's company round, Daniel!' says Mum, eyes darting over the both of us. Her shoulders relax a little seeing that we are of course fully dressed. Even so, I see Libby's cheeks start to burn at the obvious implication.

I roll my eyes. 'Mum, she's been up here for about three minutes. What are we going to get up to in three minutes?'

Mum raises her eyebrows at me and now it's my turn to blush. I grab Libby's hand and drag her from the room before anything else can be said to send me to an early grave by sheer humiliation.

'Have a good first day!' Mum shouts from the landing as we head through the front door. 'Study hard!'

'Will do!' I shout back, snatching an umbrella from the hallway before pulling the door shut behind us.

The rain has only got heavier, and I hold the umbrella up to keep us sheltered. Libby links her arm with mine as we head down the footpath that weaves through the fields towards the centre of the village. I live a little way out, so the walk is quiet except for the drum of raindrops on top of the umbrella.

As we round a bend we pass the church and the vicarage. I can see Reverend Wallace on the front step, wearing a very sensible jumper and holding a steaming mug of tea as he looks out at the rain from under the shelter of the porch roof. He spots us walking past and raises a friendly hand in silent greeting, and we wave back.

'Ready for final year?' asks Libby as we step out on to the village green and make our way towards school.

'Not particularly.' I keep my tone light, but a pit of worry has formed in my stomach. We're going to start getting badgered about university applications fairly soon, and I still haven't really decided what it is I want to do, or thought about what happens if I don't get the grades everyone expects me to. 'You?'

'Are you kidding?' Libby looks at me with wide, comical eyes. 'It's my first day as part of the sixth-form in-crowd. I'm gonna get torn to pieces.'

'Oh, shush.' I grin at her and bump her shoulder a little

with mine. '"In-crowd". You make us sound like some sort of high-school clique on a Netflix show.'

'You kind of are,' Libby laughs. 'We had it easy over the summer, now we'll really get scrutinised.'

'If you can survive Katie, you can survive anything,' I say, and she can't argue with that.

Watching Katie 'befriend' (if you can call it that) Libby over the summer has been an interesting experience. Katie and I never really had that awkward 'getting to know each other' phase. Our parents have been sitting together in church and sharing Sunday lunch since before we were born, so we've been friends practically since the womb.

We've been a part of each other's social landscapes for so long that I hadn't fully realised that what started as a tendency to be a little pushy had sharpened over the years. It was only after dragging Libby into the situation that I noticed how consistent the current was.

But even in the sharp teenage Katie the rest of the world sees, I still see the strong-willed but sweet Katie from our childhood. I know Libby doesn't get our friendship, even if she's never said anything explicit about it. I guess those years spent sitting next to each other at Sunday school, sharing sweets under the table until the teacher inevitably caught us, has bonded us in a way only the two of us can understand.

We reach the centre of the village and wave at Mr Taylor and Mrs Bramley, standing chatting under the awning of his tea room, sprinkles of rain pattering down on their sleeves. Mr Norman gives us a cheery 'hello!' as he passes by, wheeling his bike along, the back wheel squeaking slightly – as it has for as long as I can remember.

As we get closer to the school, we spot more of our classmates all headed in the same direction, huddled under their hoods and umbrellas. A few people wave at us, and although Libby was joking about it a moment ago, I sense her shoulders tense up at the new sets of eyes on us. I throw an arm around her and give her a reassuring squeeze. She smiles up at me, then goes back to peering through the rain at the different faces as we head through the school gates.

'Looking for me?'

Another head bobs under our umbrella, shaking her hair and sprinkling us with rainwater as it flies off her dark curls.

'Oh my god, you're *soaking*!' Libby laughs, but immediately links arms with Mona, pulling her closer under the umbrella.

'Well, hello to you too, sausage,' says Mona, before turning around to me with a wide smile. 'Hey, Dan! A very merry first day back to you.'

'Very merry indeed.' I smile.

'We should get in out of this,' says Libby, peering up at the sky, which shows no signs of letting up on its downpour. I nod, realising that in trying to cover three people with one umbrella we're all getting pretty wet. We make a dash for the entrance, stepping into the foyer and letting the water pool at our feet as we shake ourselves off.

'I suppose nothing says "welcome back to school" like a torrential downpour,' says Mona, shivering a little. 'I knew I should have accepted a lift off Mum this morning.'

'How is she … ?' Libby starts to ask, but Mona shoots her a look and shakes her head just a tiny bit. I busy myself rustling the umbrella to get off the worst of the raindrops, rolling it up into a damp lump and politely pretending not to have noticed.

We meander through the crowd of soggy students towards the lockers so we can unload some of our books. I'm stopped a few times by people I haven't seen since we broke up for the summer, buffeted from small talk to small talk as we head down the corridor. We reach the bank of lockers that Libby and Mona have been assigned first, and I step to the side to wait for them.

'Mr King!'

I turn at the sound of my (very formal) name. Striding towards me is Mr Dean, my A-level Maths teacher. He grins widely at me and claps a hand on my shoulder. 'How's my star mathematician? Hope everything didn't fall out of your head over the summer?'

'No, sir,' I laugh nervously, winding the loose straps of my rucksack between my fingers. I try not to show that Mr Dean has just voiced the very fear I had myself.

'Good lad, good lad.' He nods sagely, putting his hands in his pockets and jingling the coins he inexplicably always carries – seems that some things never change. 'Give me a shout when it comes time to do your uni applications, we'll see that you get into the right place.'

'Oh, yeah, thanks, Mr Dean,' I say, without conviction. He doesn't appear to notice though, and instead claps me on the back again and wanders off down the corridor, cutting his way easily through the crowd.

I stand marooned for a moment, the pit in my stomach growing a tiny bit more. I knew it would be quick, but I wasn't expecting the university talk to start within five minutes of stepping back through the school doors.

I'm saved the agony of dwelling on this by the arrival of Katie and Lewis, swanning down the hall as if it's their own personal catwalk. As they approach, Katie breaks away from Lewis and flings her arms around my shoulders as if we didn't see each other just a couple of days ago.

'Heeey, Dan!' she squeals, swinging slightly on my neck so that I have to wrap my arms around her and take some of the weight. 'Isn't it *so* weird being back?'

'We've barely been back yet,' I snort, setting her down and taking a small step back. Lewis lazily slings his arm around Katie again, pulling her back towards him – it's not *not* a show of ownership. He knows that I don't need the reminder, but anyone looking on might.

Katie and I make eye contact and she smirks, having succeeded in pushing Lewis just enough that he reacted but doesn't realise. I raise my eyebrows ever so slightly, and her smirk grows wider. Sometimes I think my and Katie's friendship is like that of a cat knocking over a vase for fun, the person trying to stop her but knowing it's somewhat inevitable and, if I'm honest, finding it a little funny.

Libby appears again at my side, shrugging her bag back on to her shoulder. I slip my hand into hers and smile down at her. As always, she blushes, and I almost feel guilty for knowing that's exactly how she'd react.

'Hey, Libby!' Katie trills. 'And … oh …' She looks Mona up and down – a person she has shared a school with since birth and whose name she definitely knows.

'Mona,' says Mona, raising an eyebrow. She and Libby exchange a look, which unfortunately Katie catches. Her eyes flash.

'God, I had to get up so early this morning to try and make myself look good in this uniform.' Katie flicks a curtain of blonde hair over her shoulder. She lasers in on Libby. 'Babe, you're *so* lucky your boyfriend doesn't care so much about looks.'

She digs Lewis in the ribs as if this is a jab at him. Mona gives Libby another look, and I suck in a breath waiting for one of them to say something, my mind fast-forwarding through at least six cutting remarks Katie will make in response. But thankfully Libby just shakes her head a little. Good call – it's too early in the day to start picking battles, especially with Katie.

'What've you got first, mate?' Lewis asks, completely oblivious to the non-verbal conversations happening around him. I rummage through my bag for the email Mum insisted I print off with our first-term timetables.

'Uhh, looks like Business Studies,' I say. 'After assembly.'

'Let's get it over with then,' Katie sighs dramatically again, starting off down the corridor with Lewis in tow.

'After you,' says Mona pointedly once Katie is out of earshot, and Libby snorts. I shift my bag on my shoulder again as we follow them down the corridor, unease settling heavy in my stomach. It's not the smoothest start to what was always going to be an interesting year.

LiBBy

I'm making my way to my first lesson, dawdling along the corridors for as long as I think I can get away with after another morning assembly. It's become my signature way of moving through time – sleepwalking through the days after lying awake all through the night.

As I slip through the door to my English classroom I pass the empty seat beside Mona, risking a glance at her. She's staring intently at the desk, and I know my usual seat isn't an option. I keep walking and sit by myself at a table at the back.

Mr Grahams is late as usual, so the classroom is noisy, all but for my lonely little island of solitude. For now, I'm blissfully ignored. I pull out my books, arrange them by title, then by author, and then I've run out of things to do. I feel like I should be occupied constantly with guilt and grief, but within it all I find myself bored out of my skull.

I stare mournfully at the back of Mona's head, her curls bouncing as she shakes her head and laughs at something someone has said. Maybe it was about me. If it was, do I really care?

A small voice at the back of my mind tells me that I do. Of course I do.

Mona and I were always a come-as-a-pair deal. We muddled through our teenage awkwardness together for years, from the first time we tried shaving our legs (blood everywhere) to the first time one of us kissed a boy (Mona, Ben Thompson, Year 8). Since we were eight I don't think we've gone more than twenty-four hours without calling or messaging each other.

The last time we spoke was over a fortnight ago. I didn't even get the opportunity to talk to her before she had inevitably seen the video, the morning after Dan's accident. I cling to the small and useless hope that, if I'd got to her first, maybe she'd have been more sympathetic. Deep down, I know that after the summer she'd had, it wouldn't have really made much difference.

I feel a surge of misplaced anger towards Mona's father. It would have been bad however it came out, but it was Mona who found the emails revealing his infidelity when she borrowed his laptop one night and he'd forgotten to log out of his emails. By the time her dad came down to breakfast the next morning, she'd printed out every incriminating message and was sitting with a stack of papers in front of her on the kitchen table.

Her family fractured beyond repair that day. Her mother took Mona and her little sister to their grandparents' in France the very next day, and we spent the summer video-calling each other after her family had gone to bed and she could cry to me in private. She was distraught. After that, it would be naive to expect her to have any tolerance for cheating, no matter the circumstances.

Maybe things would have unfolded differently if Mona had made it out with us that night. She'd have seen I was too drunk and bundled me away, taken me back to hers for crisp sandwiches and a natter. But she wasn't, and she didn't, and I'm exhausted from going over the what-could-have-beens.

Katie's laughter reaches me at the back of the room, a sharp sound that feels like biting into a lemon. Misery is replaced by a flash of anger towards those who seem to have forgotten it wasn't *my* idea to borrow someone's older sister's ID, which looked nothing like me. That was all Katie's plan. The mess I'm in now is a direct result of *that* plan.

But in the social hierarchy of small village schools, your standing is set early on by the age-old tradition of the nativity play. And while Dan was always Joseph, furiously determined to nail every line, Katie was perpetually Mary with her halo of blonde hair and angelic smile. I of course was always Third Shepherd or Innkeeper Two – or something else with no lines. Which is to say, not important. No one gave a second thought to following Katie's lead when she turned on me.

I used to think that Katie had a thing for Dan, even after she got with Lewis. But watching them more closely over the summer I realised it was more like she *owned* him – romantically or not, she was the most important girl in his life and was determined for it to stay that way. And I never planned to come between that lifelong friendship – if my relationship with Dan was going to work, I knew I had to somehow bond with Katie. I thought her 'girls' night out' might be my chance to understand what had kept Dan tethered to her his entire life.

I force myself to look away from the back of Katie's perfectly blonde head and count the ceiling tiles to distract myself. Mr Grahams strolls in while I'm halfway through my second count (one hundred and sixteen the first time, one hundred and seventeen the second). Before I can start my third count, Grahams says something that snags my attention.

'As you'll all know by now, Dan King is currently in Chipping Hollow ICU,' he says, the room falling silent. 'Katie has suggested that we all sign a card for him.' Here he nods in the direction of Katie, who throws a sickeningly sweet smile round the classroom. I suppress a gagging noise. 'Something for when he wakes up.'

There's a murmur of agreement. My gut clenches at his definitive use of the word *when*. With every day that passes it's beginning to feel a lot more like an *if*.

The card starts moving from desk to desk as Mr Grahams launches into the role of Ariel in Shakespeare's *The Tempest*. I'm only half listening.

What in god's name am I going to write on the damn card.

Words that Dan might never get to read. Words he might get to read, and then what? The knot in my stomach grows tighter as my guilty mind wanders back to that night on the dance floor. A face almost swims into view, but I push the half-formed memory away.

The card is finally tossed on to my desk. I ignore the illustration on the front and open it with trembling fingers, scanning the expanse of Biro scribble for a tiny patch of white. I pick up my pen ... and the card is whipped from under my poised hand. I look up to see Abby Lenton's ponytail bobbing away from me, her hands deftly slotting the card into its envelope.

'That's everyone, Mr Grahams,' Abby says firmly. She plants the card on his desk. I think I see Mr Grahams' eyes dart over to my corner of the room, just for a second, and then he nods.

'Thank you, Abby. I'll make sure it gets to him.'

I feel as though something heavy has been placed on my chest, the knot blooming upwards and tightening around my heart. There isn't enough air in the room, in the whole world. My hands are gripping the edge of the desk so hard that they hurt. I can't breathe. I can't *breathe*.

I half fall from my chair and stagger towards the front of the classroom, heads turning my way in alarm.

'Libby?' A voice, probably Mr Grahams's, swims through the soupy fog that is my brain. 'Are you all right?'

'Fine!' I gasp, hands fumbling the door handle. 'Just ... air ... outside ...' I burst through into the corridor and stumble down it, heaving air into my protesting lungs.

No one follows me out.

I reach the hospital, a huge stitch in my side from having run all the way over from school. My shirt is sticking to my back with sweat, and I finally tear off my tie and struggle out of my blazer. I lean against a dirty brick wall outside the entrance, begging my lungs to allow some oxygen back into my bloodstream. My legs finally buckle and I let myself slip down and land with a thump on the ground below me, hoping for it to just swallow me whole. I make a weak attempt to steady myself by watching a lady in a faded pink towelling robe a little further down the wall, hooked up to an IV, smoking a cigarette so desperately it's as if she believes it contains more medicine than her drip.

I look away as my heart starts to throb – an after-effect of the panic attack. It's not the first I've had since Dan's accident.

As I try to steady my breathing, I look up at the imposing red-brick building. Sitting on the outskirts of the village, the Chipping Hollow Hospital is one of the more impressive structures we can boast. The hospital's tall clock tower reaches out into the sky from its roof and can be seen over the tops of the trees no matter where you are in the village. It's the place where most of the people I know were born, and the sight of that clock tower has always felt comforting, like home.

Since Dan's accident, though, it's an ever-present reminder of what I'd rather forget.

After my heartbeat has returned almost to normal, I make my way inside. My footsteps automatically trace the route through the hospital to Dan's room, down the long corridors decorated in a sickly-green tile. The smell of the disinfectant feels sharp in my nostrils after the tang of the cigarette smoke. I duck past the nurses' station on his ward, not feeling up to explaining who I am or why I'm here. The nurse on duty is busy on the phone, his voice agitated and distracted.

My steps quicken the nearer I get, and finally out of sight I let the tears I've held back all day spill on to my cheeks. I sniff loudly and rub my eyes with my sleeve as I gently push on the door marked '14C'.

That's not how Dan sleeps.

I step up to his bed, my breath hitching at the sight of him. I try to look past the unnatural way he lies, the various unidentifiable tubes, the bulk of his right leg wrapped in plaster cast. The way his face is still and expressionless.

He'd be furious if he saw how they'd combed his hair back like that.

I miss the way his face lights up when he's excited about something. He's always so animated, constantly fidgeting or drumming a beat on his knees. I try to imagine that behind those bruised eyelids, his blue eyes are still sparkling with life even though the rest of him is lifeless.

If I whispered in his ear, would he hear me?

I reach out my hand and run it up the over-starched sheet that covers his body. He looks as though someone has ironed him in. My hand finds his and I squeeze, begging him to squeeze back. Even just a little.

Come on, Dan.

I feel the rough skin on his fingertips, built up over years of plucking at guitar strings. 'Hey, Dan,' I whisper. 'I miss you. I hope you're coming up with some good songs while you're just lying around all day.'

Silence, apart from the steady beep of the heart monitor by his bed.

'I think the band is suffering without their frontman. I saw on Instagram that Lewis even cancelled a gig, and you know how he feels about that, so you really should hurry up and get better.'

More silence.

'It would also be pretty nice to get a hug, I guess.'

Nothing.

'That is, if you even wanted to hug me. You might not feel like it when you wake up.'

His chest rises and falls rhythmically, but he doesn't respond. I don't really know what I was expecting.

I check back at the closed door, then slowly lower myself to sit beside his bed and rest my head on his hand, being careful not to disturb any of the medical apparatus. I close my eyes, but no matter how tightly I squeeze them shut, I can't quite make everything else go away. An image of Abby snatching that card away from me flashes through my mind. I've still not worked out what I would have written in it.

'I did a bad thing, Dan,' I sob quietly on to his bedsheets. 'I've ruined everything. I'm so, so sorry.' I find his hand again with mine and hold on like it's the only thing stopping him from floating away. 'And now everybody hates me, and I don't know how to make it better. I don't know how to fix it.' My voice is getting progressively higher, but I can't rein it back in.

Dan would know what to do, if he was awake. He'd sort it all out. If he wanted to. If he could.

I block out the sound of the machines whirring and beeping, tuning into the sound of Dan's breathing. I imagine hard that we're hanging out in his back garden, lying on a blanket in the sun. Dan strumming on his guitar, testing new chords and lyrics on me. Lyrics that he might now never sing in front of an audience bigger than one.

I think about all the times we ran down our phone batteries talking all night, whether we were sending each other videos we thought would make the other laugh or spilling all the things we felt we couldn't tell anyone else.

I remember how my stomach would flip every time he smiled at me, how every time he held my hand I felt the touch vibrate all the way up my arm. How much I miss the feeling of everyone knowing that he'd picked me.

'I can't do this alone,' I breathe.

There's the sound of footsteps passing in the corridor, reminding me that the rest of the world still exists just outside the door. I struggle back to my feet, hurriedly smoothing the rumpled sheets on Dan's bed.

I rummage in my bag and pull out my ancient iPod, a relic from my mum that I've grown strangely attached to, engraved on the back with a message of love from my grandma. I bring up a playlist, setting it to play on low, and gently arrange the earphones to sit in Dan's ears.

I pray that somewhere in the recesses of his dormant mind, he can hear the music and knows what I'm trying to say.

'I'll come back soon,' I whisper as I slip out of the door.

LiBBy

I stare dismally at my empty locker. I've got cross-country in five minutes and my kit has seemingly vanished into thin air. It's a good job we don't need to store anything more important in these things, as apparently the locks are ridiculously easy to break. Or maybe I'm just worth the effort.

I close the locker, resigning myself to the fact that pure concentration will not return my shorts and trainers. There's no way I can ask to sit out – once you hit sixth form most teachers usually don't care as much if you try and dodge the mandatory hour of physical education per week, but Ms Henson is particularly enthusiastic about the 'mental-health benefits' of us all trudging around a muddy track for cross-country. And that means the lost-property PE kit. I swear to god, the lost-property box should have been outlawed after Year 5.

I groan and head towards the changing rooms, telling myself that I need the run. I'm typically much more of a tortoise than a hare, but cross-country does mean solitary running, which might help towards burning up the bubble of anger that's been growing inside of me.

I'm late, so the room's almost empty – just a few stragglers left behind, reluctant to give themselves up to exercise. They watch me as I cross over to the wooden crate outside Ms Henson's office and begin sifting through the grey polo shirts and elasticated shorts. We're told all this stuff gets washed before being thrown in but I have my doubts. I shudder, finally extracting a T-shirt and shorts that look at least vaguely clean. To complete my outfit, I pick out a pair of trainers one size too big. They appear to have been chewed.

Marvellous.

I change quickly and head out on to the track.

Pulling the chilly air into my lungs, I start up a slow jog. Even the stragglers are now way out in front, already past the first corner that loops around the tennis courts to circle the school grounds. I don't hurry to catch up. I'm more thankful than I've ever been in my life for cross-country. Any other PE class and I'd have had to do something excruciating, like find an unwilling partner or risk life and limb in a game of hockey where my classmates play 'who can hit Libby the hardest without getting caught' instead of focusing on the goal.

A slow burn begins to build in my calf muscles and I lean harder into the jog, allowing myself a bit more speed as the rest of the class pulls away ahead of me. My feet slip a bit in the oversized trainers but I try not to care. I'm alone, away from the glares and whispers.

It's what I've been longing for all day.

I lose track of how long I've been running, my mind blissfully blank for the first time in weeks.

So blank that when my feet catch on a tuft of grass and are whipped from under me, I don't have the chance to even think about catching myself. One second I'm blithely running along the track, the next I find myself face down on the ground, spitting mud and gravel from my mouth. I scrabble for a second to right myself, slip again, and choose to lie defiantly half on, half off the running track. Whatever. I give up. I'll just lie here.

I'm so lost in my own misery that I don't hear someone approach from behind until they almost trip over me.

'What the—?' A girl stumbles into my legs, toppling over me precariously as if she might land right on top of me. But she catches herself at the last second, skidding to a halt. She peers down at me. 'Are you ... are you OK?' She extends a hand to help me up, clearly not realising who I am yet.

'I fell,' I say, somewhat unnecessarily. She pulls me to my feet and I see that it's Neha Gill. I don't share any other lessons with her but she's bound to know about my indiscretion by now, so it's a surprise when she reaches over and gently brushes some mud from my shoulder. I gawk at her silently, my shock rendering me unable to even form the words 'thank you' for picking me up off the ground.

Up close, I notice for the first time how large her dark eyes are.

'Careful then,' she says mildly, and that's it. She smiles and turns, her long limbs taking her around the next corner before I can reply. I'm left standing alone, absent-mindedly rubbing my shoulder where her hand brushed against me in such a casual but almost affectionate way. It feels alien after being starved of such friendly gestures for so long. Alien, but nice.

My brain finally comes back to my body and it occurs to me that if she's lapped me, then there will be others catching up soon. I've got a lap and a half of the circuit to go before I can crawl back to the changing rooms, and I'd much rather not run into anyone else. Not all of them are going to be feeling quite as kind as Neha was.

I stretch out my leg, roll my shoulders, and start up my slow jog down the track again.

I'm coated in a film of sweat by the time I finish. My hair, too short to be in a ponytail and too long to be kept off my face, is plastered to my scalp and all I can think about is a shower. The changing rooms have pretty much emptied out, except for a few girls murmuring together in the corner and Neha carefully brushing her hair in front of the broken mirrors.

Katie West is amongst the huddle, who are determinedly not looking at me. I'm instantly suspicious. It doesn't take much nowadays. They've already changed back into their uniforms, gym bags by their feet.

I stop in front of the bench where I left my things. It's empty.

My heart sinks. For a second I consider just walking out, leaving in my borrowed and grimy running kit. It's not as if my social status could fall any lower. But something inside me snaps when I hear a stifled giggle from behind me, and I turn and stomp over to the group of girls.

'Give them back.'

Katie turns to me, a butter-wouldn't-melt expression on her face. 'Give what back?'

'I'm not playing games with you,' I say, folding my arms. 'I'm tired. I smell. I want to get changed and go home. Can we all just be grown-ups for, like, five minutes? Give me my uniform back.'

'I don't know what you're talking about,' Katie replies airily, turning her back to me. The others smirk, saying nothing. I make a mental note of who's present: Abby Lenton, Emily Parker and Kayleigh Green, not surprisingly the same group who were there on our 'girls' night out'. I remember them all giggling as they handed me more drinks, Katie telling me how much more *fun* I was all of a sudden. I finally felt like I was a part of the group.

I know now that I wasn't in on the joke.

I feel my face grow hot, knowing that I'll be looking more like a beetroot with every passing second. Anger bubbles up inside me, and any kind of release I got from the run is gone. Without really planning to I reach out and grab Katie by the arm, forcing her to face me again.

'Give me my fucking clothes!'

Katie rips her arm from my grip and takes a step back, her angelic smile slowly fading into a cruel scowl. 'I don't know why you're so bothered about clothes,' she spits. 'You act like a skank, you can dress like a skank too.'

'Very original. Just stop being babies and give me back my things.'

'We're not being babies, we're sticking up for Dan!' Katie draws herself up to her full height, a good three inches above me.

'Somehow I doubt he'd be doing petty shit like stealing my clothes,' I scoff. 'Grow up, Katie.'

She stares down at me, eyes narrowed. 'I can't believe you would do something like that to him, in his condition.'

'He wasn't in a coma when I did it!' I shout, barely thinking, hysteria in my voice. There's a sharp collective intake of breath and even *I* want to hit me – I really am a monster. Who tries to justify something that way? Katie's eyes glint and I just know that's going straight online.

'You know he would be *devastated* to know what you did to him?' snipes Emily. 'You know he's going to hate you for this when he wakes up?'

'If he doesn't already,' adds Kayleigh.

I desperately fight the urge to roll my eyes. Dan was popular, sure, but aside from me, Katie is the only one here who truly knew him. What do Emily and Kayleigh know about how Dan would feel? Just because I happen to agree with them doesn't mean they've free rein to speculate.

I take a step forward and just for a second my guilt is replaced by a wicked thrill at seeing the alarm in Katie's eyes. But then she slams her hands into my chest to push me backwards, and the other girls are shifting slowly until they're circling me.

'Why don't just you fuck off, you stupid whore,' shouts someone from behind me. One of them shoves me and I lash out, striking nothing. They surge forward and I'm knocked down, cold tile hitting my back and pain vibrating up my spine.

'Slut!'

'Bitch!'

'Tart!'

The words hit me just as hard as their punches. Someone kicks me in the shoulder and I hear a laugh. Then Katie swoops down so her perfectly lined lips are right next to my ear and she whispers softly, almost lovingly, so that just the two of us can hear, *'You were never good enough for him.'*

The words echo round my skull. I scramble to my feet and throw my arms up but they're already leaving, the changing-room door banging closed behind them.

I stand on shaky legs and rub my shoulder, pain blossoming as the inevitable angry bruises form under my shirt.

I spot Neha still standing by the mirror, watching me with those wide eyes.

'What're you looking at?' I snap. 'Enjoy the show? Got anything to add?'

Neha stares for a second, and then silently points towards the showers. She picks up her bag and scurries out.

I find my clothes, sopping wet, in a ball behind an ancient shower curtain. I stuff them in a plastic bag and head out the door.

I don't bother with the bus. The way I'm feeling, if a single person comments on my appearance I'll probably shove my sodden clothes down their throat. The pale grey clouds have darkened and it starts to rain, cold droplets running down the back of my neck. I shiver in my thin borrowed polo and baggy shorts.

The last few leaves are clinging to the otherwise bare branches of the trees overhead, most of them lying in drifts on the pavement. The wet weather has taken all the delicious crunch out of them so it's like walking over soggy cornflakes, their previously vibrant colours muted and fading in the damp.

I thought I'd got used to the verbal abuse. When word first spread about what I'd done, stares of disgust and stifled whispers rippled through groups of people as I passed, kids I didn't even know looking at me with barely veiled disdain. The names started at school: slut, whore, slapper. Someone has combined a years-old joke about my red hair with that of my new status as the school pariah. If I'm completely honest, '*jammy tart*' is actually a pretty creative insult. It almost takes the sting out of it. Almost.

I never thought it would actually get physical. I figured at school I'd at least be safe from an outright assault. Most of the kids are smart enough to keep their insults to a whisper when staff members are around, but I hope that if any had been present in the changing rooms this afternoon they would have intervened.

But the only onlooker was Neha Gill, one of the few people in school that I haven't known since we were in nappies – she moved here some time ago, I'm not sure how long. I don't know if I'm angry that she stood by and watched, or relieved that she didn't join in. She could have been just as nasty to me out on the track though; why wasn't she?

I pass through the centre of the village and cross the green, keeping my eyes on the rain-slicked pavement, not wanting to see the cosy tea room where Dan and I went for our first official 'date'. Or Mr Bloom's tiny music shop, where I spent endless summer afternoons watching Dan drool over guitars he couldn't afford. There's not much to our hometown, so no matter where I look I see the ghosts of the summer taunting me with what used to be.

The village church watches over it all like a sentinel in the rain. I wonder if Dan's mother is in there now, maybe even accompanied by Katie's mother. I've heard that Mrs King alternates her praying time between the hospital and the pews of St Hilda's. Despite having attended that church nearly every Sunday since I was christened, I personally have found no comfort from talking to an entity I've never been completely sure exists.

In the distance I can just make out the rough shape of the castle ruins through the rain. Another unwanted memory of summer snakes its way into my brain: Dan spread out on a picnic blanket falling asleep as the sun dipped behind the ruin walls. Daylight seeping away, me watching his face twitch and his lips curve up as he drifted off – a world away from his terrible stillness in the hospital.

I drop my eyes again, quickening my pace. I've walked this route countless times in my life and nothing has ever changed, but today everything seems to press in on me, memories and people and places, and all I want is to get back to my bedroom so I can scream in peace.

The drizzle has turned into a downpour and my numb hands shake as I struggle to get my key in the door, hunched over and swearing under my breath.

The house seems empty when I finally get the door open. Mum must still be at work; her hours are so sporadic it's hard to predict. Sometimes I do feel a little resentful of it – she's out there taking care of other people when I need her the most here, at home. A heavy stone drops in my stomach, knowing that's completely unfair of me.

I stand in the kitchen and wriggle out of my wet clothes, stuffing them straight into the washing machine and walking upstairs in my underwear. I find myself in front of the bathroom mirror, inspecting the souvenirs of Katie and the other girls' handiwork over the pale skin of my exposed arms and shoulders. Clever girls, they avoided my face.

I twist the ends of my red hair between my fingers. Despite the predictable teasing when I was younger, I've always been fond of the colour – as the only redhead in our year it made me stand out a little, but standing out is the last thing I want to do right now. I tilt my head to one side, trying to picture myself as a brunette. I can't decide if dyeing it would be a sensible decision or a cowardly one.

I shuffle into my room and flop on to the bed, wincing as pain shoots through my side. I stare at the wall opposite, my collection of summer Polaroids staring back at me. I haven't had the energy to cull them since the incident, so I find one of me and Katie in the mix. She's smiling widely, but it doesn't meet her eyes. I could say the same for me – I just look plain uncomfortable.

I cocoon myself in my duvet, reaching out to grab my earphones from their usual spot on my bedside table before I remember I've left them with Dan, a decision I'm only slightly starting to regret. The need to scream along to some angry girl music is almost overwhelming, but I don't think my phone speakers will be able to blast it as loud as I need right now. Nor do I think the neighbours will appreciate it. I'll pick the earphones up tomorrow after school. Or the next day, or whenever. The days have all started to merge into one miserable blob.

I open up my phone. If I can't listen to music I may as well watch something on YouTube, but a sadistic part of my brain forces me to click on the apps with angry red bubbles above them. I know what they'll be and I read them anyway, giving in to the social-media storm that has quietly raged against me over the last couple of weeks.

I must have watched the video a thousand times at this point. I keep trying to tell myself that I need to know what everyone else is seeing, need to keep track of how many times it's been reposted and commented on. But really, I think I just want to punish myself.

I load it up but turn the volume down low – it's only noise anyway, the thump of the bass and the occasional outraged whisper from whoever is filming. On the small screen I see myself, easily identifiable by my stupid red hair, entwined with a dark figure amongst a sea of people.

I feel his phantom fingers on my body as I watch, my mind creating a memory where there isn't one. The rough of his hands gripping my hips, his tongue forcing its way into my mouth. I feel as though something slimy has just slipped down the back of my shirt.

What haunts me the most is that I think at first I was enjoying the attention – the only moment I can pull into true focus is me leaning heavily against the bar and a voice I didn't recognise telling me he liked my dress, and was my hair naturally that colour.

I think I even flirted back a little. In the moment, with the dry ice and strobe lights making my brain pulse, I told myself it was innocent. It didn't mean anything, so it was fine.

And then he was suddenly much too close, and everything was blurrier than it had been half an hour ago, and there were grabby hands and the stench of cigarettes and beer in my face.

Dan doesn't smoke.

Dan doesn't drink beer.

I stood in front of a group of poisonous teenage girls and kissed a boy that wasn't my boyfriend. They filmed it from at least three different angles, so I get to relive the memory I don't fully possess every time I open a social-media app.

At the end of the video someone has slapped on a lewd hashtag and my own social handles, directing anyone that feels like it to add to the avalanche of comments calling me a slut.

I drop my phone on the floor as if it's burned my fingers, rolling back against the pillow to stare at the ceiling.

I want to scream, just for something to do.

Six Weeks Before It Happened

August bank holiday weekend always means one thing in Chipping Hollow: the St Hilda's Church fete. And for the King household that means all systems go.

'Daniel, run over to Taylor's and ask if they've any more paper straws, will you, love?'

Mum doesn't wait for an answer before bustling on to check the bric-a-brac stall is suitably full of tat. Dad winks at me, busy with his own task of dropping tea bags into a giant metal urn of hot water. I glance over at the three boxes of paper straws we already have on the refreshments table, knowing it would be useless to point them out.

Still, I can make this task take a little longer than necessary as it involves leaving Mum's eyeline for a while. I swerve around the trestle table laden with jugs of orange squash and head across the village green towards the tea room. It's barely ten in the morning but the sun is already making my scalp prickle in the heat, and I push my sunglasses up the bridge of my nose where they've slipped down with the steady trickle of sweat.

Along with the refreshments stand, we've already set up the tables and brightly coloured gazebos for about eight other stalls – the Kings are always first on the scene on fete day, even ahead of the reverend. Red, white and blue bunting is strung between each gazebo and looped around the street lamps dotted around the green, hanging still in the non-existent breeze of what's likely to be a scorching Saturday.

I pluck my already-dampened T-shirt from my chest, wrinkling my nose as the mix of sweat and body spray hits my senses. God, I hope I can slip away from Mum long enough to change before things get going properly.

The door to Taylor's is propped open with a potted plant, I assume to try and tempt in a meagre waft of air. Mr Taylor himself is leaning against the counter, fanning his ruddy face with a laminated menu. He spots me and his eyes grow a little wider.

'Daniel, my boy, please don't tell me your mother wants another urn out there. Carrying the first one out has done me in.'

'Just more paper straws, Mr Taylor,' I laugh as the elderly tea-room owner feigns a swoon of relief. I swipe a couple of boxes of straws from behind the counter while Mr Taylor takes out a handkerchief and wipes his forehead.

'You're a good lad,' he says mildly, lowering himself into a chair. 'You can tell your mother I said so.'

I smile proudly, swelling a little at the compliment. I can't help it – my craving for external validation is insatiable.

There's a few more people milling around as I head back out on to the green, mostly people who have volunteered to run the various stalls. Most are moving about with purpose, probably one assigned to them by my mother – but my eye is caught by a still and lonely figure hanging around at the edge of the green. I raise a hand to shield my eyes from the sun a little and realise it's Neha Gill from school, tightly clutching what looks like a plastic cake box.

Eager to avoid another task from Mum, I head over.

'Hot enough for you?' I ask as I approach. Neha jumps a little, turning to face me.

'Oh, hi, Dan!' Her worried expression softens slightly as she holds up her cake box. 'I'm not sure how these things work, we never had church fetes where I used to live, but I baked something. I hope that's OK.'

'Of course! Is it for the bake-off?'

'Bake-off?' Her eyes widen, the worry seeping back in. 'I didn't know there was one, it's just honey cake. It's not really competition standard.'

'I'm sure it's great,' I say, though she knows as well as I do that I've no idea how good her baking is. 'But if you don't want to enter it, you could always stick it on the refreshment stand?'

'Yeah, I'll do that,' Neha says, nodding in relief. 'Which way … ?'

'Oh, I'm going back over there now. I could take it for you?'

'Sure.' Neha smiles, and I take the box from her. The smell

of warm honey lifts from the box and I make a mental note to make sure I get a piece later. Left with nothing in her hands, Neha swings her arms awkwardly by her sides, once again looking lost.

'Daniel? Daniel! I need you over here, sweetheart!'

Mum's voice carries across all the others, and I let out a world-weary sigh. Neha stifles a giggle.

'I've got to go. But thanks for this – I'll see you later. Enjoy the fete!'

'Thanks, Dan,' she says with another smile. 'It was nice to see you!'

I wave over my shoulder as I move away. I feel guilty leaving her by herself, but I'm sure her mates will turn up at some point. I hurry back over to Mum for my next assignment.

It turns out I was right thinking today was going to be a scorcher, and wrong to think we had enough paper straws. So many people have been by the refreshments stand that we've torn through all five boxes by early afternoon – from now on people will have to drink directly from the cups, like peasants. Mum will be horrified.

I'm just handing Mrs Bramley her third blackcurrant squash in half an hour when there's a tap on my shoulder. I turn to see Libby, her face glossy with the sheen of factor-fifty sun cream and peeking out from under the biggest sun hat I've ever seen.

'Are you part vampire?' I laugh, and she bats me gently on the arm.

'No, but I'm *all* ginger. You remember how frazzled I was that time at the lake.' She tugs at the hem of her shorts in an attempt to protect another inch of skin, then glances back over her shoulder. Seemingly satisfied, she turns back to me and says in a stage whisper, 'Katie tried to make me wear a dress. It was *tiny*. She kept saying how much she knew you'd like it.'

I splutter, wishing I hadn't been so busy this morning as to miss that particular conversation. I guess as Katie couldn't successfully set me up with one of her own friends, she's decided remaking Libby in her own image is the solution.

'It's not funny!' insists Libby, but the corners of her mouth are twitching upwards. 'She's furious at me, thinks it's a comment on her fashion choices. She brought it round this morning, like I'm a toddler that needs dressing!'

'Well, she does love a project.' I look Libby up and down – she's in a stripy T-shirt that's a few sizes too big and denim dungaree shorts. 'And I mean, you are looking pretty toddler chic, it must be said.'

'Yeah, but I picked this out myself. It's my most summery outfit.' She gives me a mock twirl to emphasise her point, kicking out a leg theatrically. 'How could Katie not simply *love* this look?'

'She does *mean* well,' I say with a laugh. 'She used to dress me up all the time when we were kids.'

'Now *that* I wish I'd seen.'

'I'm certain Mum has photos somewhere. We used to put on "plays" for our parents after Sunday school – she was always supposed to be a princess being rescued, but halfway through she'd decide to just rescue herself.' I smile fondly at the memory. 'You know, I think you'd have really got on with seven-year-old Katie.'

'Yeah, well, seventeen-year-old Katie is a bit of a different beast,' Libby mutters, before her eyes snap up to mine. 'Not that—'

'Don't worry, I know what she's like,' I interrupt, although even as I do, I'm not sure how much that's true any more. 'Look on the bright side – you might not have to talk to her today if she's pissed at you.'

Libby snatches a cup of lukewarm squash and holds it up. 'Well, cheers to that!'

I tap my own cup against hers and take a drink, wincing at the temperature. We joke, but with Mona away for the whole summer with her family, Libby has had to contend with the full force of Katie without any backup.

We stand and people-watch for a while, hiding in the shade of the refreshments tent. We alternate between bright, polite smiles as we serve up squash, and betting which of the village's over-70s are going to mention the weather and which are going to tell me what a 'good boy' I am for helping out.

'Mrs Fielding is absolutely going to talk about the weather,' says Libby as we spot her approaching. 'I can't remember hearing her talk about anything else.'

'You're so wrong, Dixon,' I counter under my breath, smiling and waving as Mrs Fielding ever so slowly makes her way over. 'She's wearing her *coat*. I don't think she can *feel* the weather. I'm definitely getting a "good boy" from her.'

'Loser buys ice creams?'

'You're on.'

Mrs Fielding finally reaches us, and we both fix beaming smiles on our faces.

'Hello, dears!' she says in her whispery voice. She glances up at the crystal-blue sky. 'My, what beautiful weather we're having!'

'We *are* having beautiful weather, aren't we?' says Libby, triumph in her voice. I fight the urge to groan. 'Such a *lovely* day!'

We serve her a lukewarm drink and she shuffles off again, and Libby does a little jig.

'I'll have a whippy with a flake, Daniel,' she grins, poking me in the arm.

'Double whippy or nothing on Ms Henson,' I say, spotting our school PE teacher beelining for the stall.

'Deal,' says Libby.

Ms Henson reaches us, her cheeks ruddy with sunburn and a gleam of sweat on her brow, and I fear I may have lost again. Even out of school, she's wearing her signature tracksuit, with a whistle round her neck and everything.

'Daniel!' she booms. 'Not seen your mother recently, have you? I need to talk to her about the egg-and-spoon race.'

'Not in a while, Ms Henson,' I reply. I see an opportunity to sway the game in my favour, and smile widely as I lift up a cup. 'Would you like a drink?'

'Ahh, thank you, lad,' she says. She downs the whole thing in one as Libby and I hold our breath, waiting.

'Such *wonderful* weather we're having this year!'

Libby lets out a little squeak of triumph as Ms Henson bustles off to find Mum. I turn to her and dip into a theatrical bow. I've been bested.

'A double whippy for the lady then,' I say. 'Although thanks a lot, Ms Henson. She's a family friend, I was sure I had that one in the bag—'

'LIBBY!'

Libby turns and is immediately ambushed by a blur of dark curls. She squeaks and wraps her arms around the much-taller girl, letting herself be lifted off her feet as they spin around in unison.

'*Mona!* Oh my god! When did you get back?!'

Now she's said her name I finally recognise Libby's best friend. Her skin is several shades darker than when I last saw her, tanned after nearly a whole summer in the south of France, but as she pulls away from Libby I see that even though she's grinning, there are prominent dark circles under her eyes.

'Last night at, like, four in the morning, or I'd have come straight round,' says Mona, still holding on to Libby's hands. 'I only woke up an hour ago!'

'God, it's *so* good to see you,' says Libby, and I hear a slight crack of emotion in her voice as she pulls Mona back in for another hug. I stand by the refreshments table, feeling very much like a spare lemon. I'm about to step away when Mona catches my eye over Libby's shoulder and smiles.

'And of course the famous Mr King! I hope you've taken good care of my girl this summer.' She waggles her eyebrows at me and Libby breaks out of the hug to bat her on the arm.

'Like the gentleman that I am,' I laugh, handing her a cup of squash.

'Of course, of course.' She smiles again and takes the cup from me. Libby links arms with her, and without meaning to I feel a slight pang – it's something she's done countless times to me over the summer. But she looks so pleased she seems about ready to burst, and I know how much she's missed her best friend. I've often wondered if the two of us would have become so close if it wasn't for Mona's absence, but now I feel weird for ever having been grateful for the fact that she was gone, especially given the reason why.

Before I have chance to accidentally say something awkward, Mum appears by my side, materialising out of thin air.

'Hello, Olivia!' Mum says brightly, insisting on full Christian names as always. 'Lovely to see you helping out!' She glances towards Mona. 'And this is … ?'

'Mona. You must be Mrs King, it's lovely to meet you,' says Mona, instantly switching into the same Polite Young Person mode that Libby and I have been doing all afternoon; it's something all kids in the village have had drilled into us since we could talk.

'Lovely, lovely,' says Mum distractedly, before grabbing my arm. 'Daniel, the reverend is about to announce the raffle winners, we should go over to the front.'

Libby catches my gaze and I suppress rolling my eyes. Mum has no interest in the raffle, she just knows he'll praise her for another fete organised with military precision.

Even though the scoffing is just in my head, I remind myself to try to be a bit kinder – she has worked bloody hard after all. This afternoon has been weeks in the making. And wasn't I just basking in the praise of the elderly population of Chipping Hollow?

I pull a smile on to my face. 'Sure, Mum. Let's go.'

'We'll guard the squash,' says Libby, glancing out at the crowd gathering. It's not her first fete, but it's her first as part of the King family entourage, and I know that comes with a certain level of visibility she's still not used to. Plus, she's clearly dying to talk to Mona alone. I give her hand a squeeze, and her cheeks flush pink.

We move over to the small raised platform in the middle of the green, where an ancient wooden raffle barrel has been placed. Reverend Wallace is slowly climbing the three steps up to the platform. He reaches the microphone, taps it, and a screech of feedback rips through the speakers set up on either side of the platform.

'Sorry, sorry!' He gestures to Mr Bloom, standing by the amp and frantically fiddling with the buttons.

I look back over to the refreshments stall and see Libby and Mona with their heads close together, their lips moving frantically as they catch up. I wish I knew what they were talking about.

I glance around and spot Neha, again hanging around

near the edge of the green. She's still alone. I briefly consider going over to ask how she's enjoying the fete, but just as I take a step there's another loud crackling noise and the reverend is booming 'Testing, testing' through the microphone. Mum's eyes catch on mine, eyebrows slightly raised, and I stay put.

'Yes, thank you, Arthur. Well. Welcome, everybody!'

Reverend Wallace launches into his speech, a rehash of every summer-fete speech he's made since I was in a pushchair. I tune back in at the right beat, knowing my family's mention is coming up.

'... and of course, a special thank-you to the King family for their wonderful work once again in making this day run beautifully!'

I can practically feel Mum glowing next to me as a smattering of polite applause washes over the crowd – truly, I am my mother's son. Somewhere in the back I hear Libby's enthusiastic *whoop* and I hide my laugh with a grin. This day always feels a bit like being under a microscope for the whole village to analyse, but this year at least I've got backup.

Neha

I don't walk straight home. I leave school and hurry across the village green, heading down a wide path lined with bare trees and littered with red and orange leaves. I'm tracing the footsteps of another me, two steps behind the ghost of last year. The stiff October breeze creeps up the sleeves of my coat and I shiver but keep going.

I run my fingertips over the wall that runs along the edge of the small park, counting the bricks as I've done before – each time finishing on a slightly different number. I don't mind not knowing the true answer. It's one of those little mysteries that I like to let hover on the edge of my knowledge.

I reach the rusty iron gate and push it open, the hinges squeaking in protest. Down the stone path, past the sprawling oak tree and the tiny duck pond, currently empty of ducks. I sit down gently on the bench engraved with my parents' names, sighing as I lean back to look up at the twisting canopy of branches above me. It's just starting to rain.

'Hi, Mum. Hi, Dad.' My voice is lost on the breeze, but I know it doesn't really matter. 'Sorry I haven't been by this week.'

I reach out my hand to my side, running my fingers along the smooth wood. As always, silent tears leak from my eyes and on to my cheeks, and I brush them away with the back of my hand. When their absence was still fresh and raw the tears flowed faster, more painfully. Nowadays they mostly just come quietly and I barely notice until I'm done and I feel as though I've let out a long-held breath.

It was Jas's suggestion to have the bench engraved. I know it can't have been cheap, even in a tiny nowhere village like Chipping Hollow, but she insisted on me having a place to come and talk to my parents when I needed to. I know she visits herself too, so she can talk to her big brother. The small, semi-fresh bundle of carnations tied to one arm of the bench confirms she's been recently.

'I don't think you'd have been very proud of me today,' I say to the air. 'There's this girl at school ... I don't know the full story, but she's going through a really rough time. And today I stood by and let her get assaulted.'

The words are stark in the silence of the small park, and the guilt that's been threatening to overwhelm me since the scene in the changing rooms hits me square in the chest.

'I could have helped. I *wanted* to help. But I didn't. I was too scared. No one really talks to me at school, nobody even knows I exist. I ... I see how they've been treating her and I was scared they might finally see me, just to do the same.'

I hang my head, shame wrapping around me like the arms of a predator. I think about the video of Libby and feel even more suffocated. How many times have I watched it myself? How much had I already contributed to her misery, helping those view counts grow even higher?

'I think she needs a friend.' I pause. 'I know I do.'

I sniff and stroke the bench beside me again. I close my eyes and make a wish.

When I open them again I'm still staring up at the empty tree branches. Silence, except for the whistle of the wind and the sound of raindrops hitting the leaves scattered across the ground.

I rise to my feet, lifting my bag and shrugging it on to my shoulder. I look back at the empty bench.

'I love you guys.'

I turn and quickly leave the park.

I cut around the church on the way home, drifting between the crumbling headstones scattered throughout the graveyard. I find myself wishing that we had been religious – even if not Christian. At least then I'd have something in common with the other people at school and in the village.

I tried going to a Sunday service a while after I'd moved, figuring I might be able to slip into it given the fact that we did already celebrate a lot of Christian holidays like Christmas and Easter. Culturally at least, I thought we'd be aligned. But I felt even more out of place there than I did at school. One or two of the older churchgoers had smiled at me, but there were others who stared at me with critical eyes until my skin itched. I never went back.

I spent a lot of time after my parents died thinking about different afterlives and if I believed in any of them. Religion would have made that a bit clearer, one way or another. I'd like to be able to comfort myself thinking of them being reborn, their good karma paving the way for their next life. Or maybe in some version of heaven, lounging around on fluffy white clouds. I'd be happy to believe that they're hanging around me as ghosts, looking out for me even when I can't see them.

But the truth is, I don't know what I believe about what happens to us after we die. I talk to them both at their bench in the park, but not because I think they can hear me. I started going just to get Jas to stop asking me to, and I kept going because it was therapeutic to air all my grievances to a tree every now and then. My heart hopes that they're listening, but my head isn't so sure.

I tuck my earphones into my ears and put on a playlist of my favourite musical-theatre big hitters, turning my head up towards the clouds and letting the rain hit my face to the swelling sound of 'Defying Gravity'. Pretending I'm in some kind of film montage is something I do a lot when I'm by myself, which tends to be most of the time nowadays.

A single leaf, the exact shade of red as Libby's hair, flutters down from a nearby tree and my thoughts turn back to her. If I'd ever entertained the idea of approaching her and offering some sort of support, this afternoon has ripped that possibility away from me. I don't know if the intention was ever pure to begin with, or if I was just so starved for attention that I was trying to worm my way in on the pretence of giving a shit when really I just wanted someone to talk to.

My friends would tell me I'm not like that, but even Sam isn't privy to all the treacherous corners of my mind. The tiny part of me that whispers to look directly at the train wreck I'm supposed to politely avert my gaze from. Is that just human nature? Who knows? I've only ever been inside my own brain after all.

I do know that I believe she doesn't deserve to be treated the way everyone at school is treating her right now. The video that's being used as ammo should really be her defence, but no one seems to want to see the way she's completely out of her depth, control and the ability to consent both long gone. I wish I'd taken the chance to talk to her about it, but I can't see that happening now.

The rain turns heavier and drips down the back of my coat, making me shiver. I quicken my pace.

I step through the front door to the sound of the fire alarm screaming down the narrow hall. Anywhere else I'd be concerned, but all this means is that Jas is home and she's attempted to cook something.

'Welcome home!' Jas shouts from the kitchen. I walk in to find her waving a tea towel at the smoke detector as grey smog drifts from the oven.

'What was it meant to be?' I ask, wafting the acrid smell away from my face.

'Garlic bread,' she coughs. The alarm finally seems satisfied that the house isn't about to burn down and ceases its shrieking. 'To go with the Bolognese.'

I walk over to the hob and lift a spoon from the pan, wrinkling my nose. 'Ahh, well, we can't have Bolognese without garlic bread, so … beans on toast?'

'Serves me right for attempting a nice home-cooked meal, eh?' Jas sighs, but takes the pan and dumps the contents in the bin.

I open up the cupboards to rummage for a can of beans while Jas throws the kitchen windows open, letting the cold air in but the smoky evidence of her cooking out. No matter how many times she burns something, I'll never complain. I honestly don't know where I'd be right now if it wasn't for her.

Jas is my dad's baby sister, born at the tail end of the 80s and a constant presence when I was growing up. She was endlessly fascinated by me, always wanting to dress me up and play with me and teach me to love musicals. When I got a bit older, she'd sneak me into the cinema to see films I was too young for and always cut the biggest slice of cake for me after dinner.

She always made time for me, even when she started her training to become a nurse, a pursuit that eventually brought her to Chipping Hollow after she got a job at the hospital. When Mum and Dad went, she made the absolute darkest time of my life seem not quite so never-ending. I owe her more than I think she'll ever know.

If we have to live off slightly burned canned food most of the time, that's absolutely fine with me.

'How was school?' Jas asks when we finally sit down to eat, having managed to only singe the edges of the toast.

I shrug, as if to rid myself of the arms of shame again. Jas narrows her eyes at me.

'Come on, Ne. I usually get at least a verbal answer out of you. Something happen?'

I'd curse her intuitiveness, but it's actually one of my favourite things about her. I heave a sigh.

'Yeah, actually. Some girls in my year attacked Libby Dixon in the changing rooms after PE today.' I keep my eyes down, refusing to meet Jas's eyes. 'I was right there and I didn't do anything. I just watched. I was scared and I didn't help her.'

'Oh, sweetie,' says Jas, her expression melting into sympathy. 'That's so shitty, but you can't be expected to get in front of something like that.'

'I didn't even help her up afterwards,' I admit. I push my plate away in frustration, not hungry any more. 'I could have at least said something to her.'

An awkward silence hangs over us as Jas figures out how to respond to that.

'Libby is Dan King's girlfriend,' I blurt.

'The boy in the ICU?' Jas asks, eyebrows rising. Working in Chipping Hollow Hospital, she of course knows exactly who I'm on about. 'Why on earth would your classmates be beating up a grieving girl?'

'Something ... happened.' I grapple with how to explain something I don't understand myself. 'They all think she cheated on him. It was the same night he had the accident, but no one knew he was in the hospital yet.'

'They *think* she cheated on him?'

'Well, loads of people videoed it. And everyone has seen it,' I say. Jas shakes her head.

'That poor girl. I can't imagine having your worst moment broadcast like that. Whatever she did, it's no reason to be assaulting her. But it's also not your responsibility to protect her, Neha.'

I make an indecipherable noise. I haven't even got into the video itself, and how I'm not entirely sure that 'cheating' is the best way to describe what's going on.

After a few minutes of me silently pushing the contents of my plate around, Jas sighs. 'Don't stew on it too long, OK? I'm going to go get a shower, it's been a long day.'

She heads up the stairs, and after she's gone I cross over to the cupboards and pull out sugar, eggs and flour. Neither of us may know how to knock an edible meal together, but I couldn't watch my mother work her magic in the kitchen for so many years without at least picking up on how to bake.

I throw together the ingredients, working mostly on muscle memory and letting my head clear of anything but the next step in the recipe I know by heart. The process carries me back to two years ago, five years ago, ten years ago ... standing beside Mum as her hands went through the same motions mine do now, watching her quick but careful work as she combined sugar, butter, flour, eggs and milk. As I melt down the honey syrup mixture, the smell tugs at my heart – I can never smell honey without thinking of her. Without missing her. I often find myself baking after coming home from visiting my parents' bench, desperate to do something that will help me feel closer to her.

The last time I made this was back in the summer, an attempt to get involved in a fete the church was hosting on the village green. I remember Dan taking the time to talk to me in between rushing around. If I'd have been braver, I think I might have tried to take the opportunity to hang out with him more.

Just as I'm sliding the cake into the oven, Jas pads back into the kitchen, rubbing her hair dry with a towel.

'You little angel,' she breathes, before dropping the towel on the back of a chair and snatching up the empty mixing bowl. 'Dibs.'

'You can't dibs the bowl – I made the cake!' I make a half-hearted grab for it but she holds it out of my reach, before settling back against the counter and swiping a finger through the batter.

'I wish you'd bake more when you *weren't* upset,' she sighs. 'I always feel guilty enjoying it.'

'You can feel guilty about stealing my bowl, but not about eating cake.'

'Fair enough,' says Jas. She smiles down into the bowl for a second. 'Your dad always said he fell in love with your mum because of this cake.'

'I remember,' I say softly, sitting down next to her.

'Maybe you should try taking some into school.' Jas gestures at the oven.

'What, bribe people to be my friend with cake?'

'That's not what I said,' she laughs, but then looks at me, concerned again. 'Is it still that rough?'

'I mean, today a bunch of them beat up someone in front of me as if I wasn't even there,' I sigh. 'Sometimes I wish they'd just go all in and bully me properly, but it's like I don't exist. I'm the amazing invisible girl most of the time.'

'Yeah, teenagers are vile.' Jas nods. 'Sorry, kid. They'll grow out of it eventually.'

'Could they hurry up?' I groan. 'If nothing else, it's *boring*.'

Jas swirls a finger through the bowl thoughtfully. 'You could try talking to Libby? Sounds like she might need a friend even more than you do.'

'After today?' I give Jas a look. 'I doubt she'd want anything to do with me.'

'It's just a thought,' she says, shrugging. 'In the meantime, let's do something this weekend. You've still got me, more's the pity.' She pulls a face at me, and I have to laugh.

Before long the smell of honey cake fills the kitchen, and I slide it carefully from the oven and sprinkle coconut over the top. We eat the cake with our fingers while it's still warm, silent until we're both licking scraps off our hands like little kids.

LIBBY

Lunchtime has become my least favourite part of the day. After the egg-locker debacle I've taken to carrying lunch around with me all day, for fear of it being stolen or poisoned, and my guard is up even more after the changing-room incident.

I step into the canteen, and something smacks into the back of my head, jerking me forward.

'*OW!*'

I rub the base of my skull and look around for the offending flying object. A small orange is rolling away from me. A sodding orange.

Muttering under my breath, I don't look for the thrower. I can already hear sniggers rippling around me. Instead, I look around for a spot at the edge of the room where I can jam my back against the wall and cover myself from all angles.

I feel a short-lived sense of relief when I think I see a free table, then notice a solitary figure sat there scrolling on her phone – I recognise it's Neha Gill, and for a brief moment

I wonder why she's alone. I consider going over to sit with her, maybe ask why she told me where my clothes were after the others threw them in the shower.

I decide that it's not worth the risk, and even if she was trying to help, I don't want to put her in the spotlight by sitting with her. No one else needs dragging into centre stage of the bullshit production that is St Hilda's sixth form, especially someone who might still be inclined to talk to me. Instead, I find a lone table in the middle of the canteen and dig into my tuna pasta.

Across the hall is the table where I'd normally sit. I spot Mona picking apart her lunch, seeming isolated from the conversation around her. I see Aaron put a hand on her arm and she jumps, dropping her sandwich. She turns her head and for a split second is looking right at me. I drop my eyes to the table, pushing pasta around with my fork.

I used to be able to tell just by looking at her what she was thinking, but nowadays I'm lost. Katie graciously took Mona under her wing when I decided to upend my life, and while something genuine seems to be forming between Mona and Aaron, she's been looking unhappier in Katie's presence by the day. Sometimes I wonder if I just talked to her…

Mona is rising to her feet. They usually all leave as a group, but she appears to be excusing herself and starts weaving her way through the tables towards the door.

I jump up, tossing my half-finished lunch in the nearest bin as I snake after her. By the time I burst through the doors, Mona is already disappearing around a corner. I hitch my bag into a more comfortable position on my shoulder and follow her, quickening my steps.

I catch a glimpse of her slipping through the library doors and without really thinking, follow her in. She's wandering aimlessly through the shelves, and I realise that she's doing exactly what I've been doing the last few weeks while skipping classes.

I head down the row next to hers and push apart the books to look through, making her jump.

'Hey, Mona.'

She looks everywhere but at me.

'Hi, Libby,' she says to her fingernails.

'You OK?'

'Yeah, not bad.'

I lean my chin against my arms on the shelf. 'I was wondering if you maybe wanted to go for a walk after school? Chat a bit? I've not seen you in a while.' I talk as if we've just been mixing with different circles, trying to make things as normal as possible despite the tense atmosphere that hangs over us like a fog. Her discomfort is excruciating to watch.

'I don't think that's a good idea' she says stiffly. She starts moving further down the row, and I follow parallel to her.

'Please?' I say, with a little force. I know I'm begging and I don't care. 'I'm … I'm so scared for Dan, and I don't have anyone to talk to …'

She finally looks me in the face and I flinch – the look in her eyes is one I never wanted to be on the receiving end of. I can feel the anger coming off her in waves. It's heartbreaking watching her try to maintain her cool, the tightness of her lips holding back the torrent of abuse I'm sure she'd subject anyone else to. Maybe I should be relieved. It's a testament to our friendship that she didn't chew me out the moment I approached her.

'You know how I feel about cheating.' Her words are like steel. 'I just can't believe you'd do something like that, let alone expect me to forgive you afterwards.' To my horror I see tears are welling up in her eyes, though her expression remains like thunder. 'How could you do that? To Dan, to *me*?'

'I'm … I'm sorry,' I splutter, all the words I really want to stay sticking in my throat, everything I might say but can't. 'I don't—'

'Just leave me alone,' she chokes out, cutting me off. She turns on her heel and heads back towards the doors, leaving me to desperately count my breaths as my chest constricts and I finally allow the tears to fall.

Eight Weeks Before It Happened

'Oh, don't be boring Libby, what's the worst that could happen?'

I glance over from where I'm sitting on an amp tuning my guitar at the sound of Katie's wheedling. I've been hearing that voice all my life – no one is truly safe from Katie's will when she's decided she wants something. From the uncomfortable look on Libby's face, I sense she does indeed need saving.

'What's that, Katie?' I call over, gently setting my guitar down and moving across the garage. Aaron disappeared off somewhere when we decided to take a break, and Lewis is retuning his guitar for the umpteenth time, so I've got time to run interference before we start practising again.

Katie turns her megawatt smile towards me from where she sits squashed up next to Libby in an old armchair. Libby has a paperback in her hands, closed but with her fingers casually marking her place to she can jump right back in when – if – Katie decides to leave her alone.

'I'm planning a girls' night out!' says Katie. 'And I need *all* my girls to come. But Libby is being mean.' She pouts dramatically, really pushing her bottom lip out. I don't miss her use of *my girls* – everyone in Katie's sphere belongs to her, whether they want to or not. I've got comfortably complacent in my status as 'Katie's'.

'I can't, Katie, I'll never get past a bouncer,' says Libby, squirming. 'I've got the face of an eleven-year-old.'

I wouldn't put it that way myself – we are together after all – but there is something about Libby's face that's vaguely cherubic. Round and pale with a scattering of freckles over her nose, framed by bright red hair that falls just to her shoulders.

'We can fix that,' Katie says breezily, waving a hand dismissively but not actually bothering to disagree. 'And we can get you ID as well so it won't really matter. Emily's older sister looks a bit like you.'

'Emily's older sister is blonde,' I point out, and Katie turns her steely eyes on me.

'Whose side are you on?' she laughs coolly. 'Don't you want your favourite girls to bond? People dye their hair all the time. And I *always* get in, and she'll be with me, so it won't be an issue.'

The sheer force of her confidence makes it hard to argue, but I know being underage is only half of Libby's worry about a night out with Katie.

I feel bad, and not for the first time in our relationship, that Libby is only having to deal with Katie because of me. I really like having Libby here, but I also know a stuffy garage filled with too much sound isn't the dream Saturday evening.

Katie has been coming alone since we first started practising as a band with any kind of regularity – at first in her capacity as my friend, and later as Lewis's girlfriend. She sees it as her duty to be at every practice, and she's made it clear that Libby should adopt the same attitude.

Libby says she doesn't mind, but I don't believe her. If I'm really honest with myself (which I spend a lot of the time trying not to be), it's not the only thing I know she secretly minds. But I really, truly want the two of them to get on – Katie is my oldest friend, and the closer I get to Libby, the more I want them to find some common ground despite the fact that they're wildly different people.

Before I can try and come up with an ecuse to get Libby out of Katie's plan, Aaron walks back into the garage with a tray of luminous green drinks. Katie squeals in delight.

'Refreshments, anyone?' Aaron says with a grin as he carefully balances the tray on a stack of storage boxes.

'Nice, man!' says Lewis, setting his guitar down and heading over.

'What's even *in* those? And where did you get it?' I ask, attempting to divert from my building panic as I watch Katie take a glass and immediately knock back half. She licks her lips.

'Something minty.'

'There was a bottle of crème de menthe in the back of my parents' alcohol cabinet, looked like it had been there since before I was born,' says Aaron. 'They'll never notice.' He takes a sip himself and screws up his face. 'Might've made them a bit strong.'

'Don't be a little bitch about it,' laughs Lewis, though I

notice he suppresses a wince himself after he takes an over-confident gulp. He turns to me – shit.

'Come on, Dan, drink up.' His tone is casual but his gaze is challenging. He knows I don't like to drink and isn't shy about what kind of man he thinks that makes me. 'Don't be such a poof.'

Libby's eyes flash and I worry for a second she's going to challenge him – but then she quickly swipes two glasses, pushes one into my hands and makes a big show of clinking them together. 'Cheers!' she says brightly, and throws her head back to take several large gulps.

The lads and Katie cheer her on. I keep hold of the drink, lifting it to my lips occasionally but never taking a sip – the attention is off me, exactly as Libby intended.

I catch her eye when the others are talking amongst themselves, mouthing a *thank you*. She smiles at me and mouths back – *any time*.

Eventually we make it back to our instruments, the other two playing a little more wildly than before. I keep glancing over at Libby, back in the same armchair as Katie but looking a little bit less like a trapped animal about it. I hear her laugh, and wonder if the alcohol has made her more agreeable to Katie's 'girls' night out' plan.

I try not to question if that's a good thing or not.

It's still light when we finally break up practice, the other lads having got a little too sloppy to continue. Before we left, Aaron made a comment that I was the only one to play the same drunk as I do sober. He sounded impressed but I made a mental note to mess up a bit more if I 'drink' during rehearsals again.

Libby, having been drinking from both her cup and mine when no one else was looking, is a bit unsteady on her feet as we leave Aaron's. Seeing as it's still fairly early for a Saturday night – and the fact that I don't really want to deliver her home drunk and have her mother worry about what kind of boyfriend I am – I suggest we go for a walk around the village to get her some fresh air.

'Sounds good,' says Libby, smiling up at me as she casually links her arm through the crook of mine as we make our way down the driveway and out on to the country lane. She's gripping me pretty hard; I assume it's just because she's a little wobbly. I lead us around the village and in the direction of the ruins, knowing that anyone lingering there at this time will be our age and much less likely to judge than the prying eyes of the village elderly.

It turns out to be almost empty, so we get a good spot on the small hill with a great view of the summer sky, turning a brilliant orange as the sun sinks below the horizon. Libby leans her head against my shoulder and sighs contentedly.

'Isn't it lovely?' she says dreamily. She turns her head to look up at me, our faces very close. 'Are you having a good summer?'

'I'm having a great summer,' I say, shifting a little under Libby's gentle weight against me. 'Thanks to you.'

She grins, unfiltered joy breaking out across her face. I notice how pronounced her freckles have got over the long sunny days we've been having. 'Really?'

'Really.' I move so I can put an arm around her and squeeze, feeling a rush of affection for the girl beside me. 'Best summer in a long time.'

She sighs again, closing her eyes but keeping her face angled towards mine. 'Me too.'

And then she shoots her head forwards and her lips clash against mine.

It's so sudden that for a moment I'm shocked into immobility – until my brain kicks in, tasting the minty liquor, and I gently ease her away.

'Hey,' I say softly, watching the rejection bloom in Libby's eyes. 'I don't think ... You had quite a bit to drink ... I don't—'

'No, you're right,' she says, sitting up and wrapping her arms around her legs. All the dreaminess is gone. 'I'm sorry. That was stupid.'

'It wasn't *stupid*,' I say, and she looks back at me with sheepish eyes. 'I just—'

'You don't have to explain,' she cuts in. Ironically, the kiss seems to have broken through her drunken stupor and she's now alarmingly sober. She stands, brushing grass from the seat of her shorts. 'I should probably go home.'

'I'll walk you,' I say, jumping up. She starts to protest but I grab her hand. 'Libby, you're my girlfriend. I'm walking you home.'

I raise my eyebrows at her pointedly and she finally smiles again, though more reserved than before, and allows me to take her arm and lead her back down the hill. When we finally reach her doorstep, I pull her in and hold her tight, trying to convey everything I'm feeling for her in a hug.

She grips me back, and I hope to god she understands.

Neha

The moment any perpetual 'new kid' dreads has rolled around again: our Chemistry teacher announcing that for this lesson you're going to need to work in pairs. I square my shoulders and before anyone has a chance to move, I turn to the person sitting next to me and blurt out, 'Shall we work together?'

The girl turns and blinks at me, clearly surprised. I know her name is Jennifer Fowler but the jury's still out on if she knows mine, despite us having sat next to each other four times a week since term started.

'Oh ...' She hesitates, caught between not wanting to be rude and not wanting to be lumped with me. She looks round at her friends, who are all silently pairing off together, leaving her to her fate. 'Sure, why not.'

'Great!' I feel stupid for being so thrilled that she agreed, but I don't let it dampen my enthusiasm. I rush over to the equipment cupboard to pull out the stuff we need, carefully carrying them back to Jennifer before she reconsiders.

'I'm Neha, by the way,' I say brightly, starting to arrange everything on the worktop in front of us. 'Are you looking to do sciences at uni as well?'

'I think so,' says Jennifer with a shrug. She asks nothing in return, but I plough on anyway.

'I'm applying to do Paramedic Science. I ... well, I just know how vital they are, I guess. And my aunt is a nurse so healthcare runs in the family. Where are you applying?'

My questions come thick and fast as I attempt to form a bond as we work, and while Jennifer's answers are polite enough, I can tell she's not really engaging with me.

Just as I'm about to make a last-ditch attempt before the end of the lesson, a voice cuts through from behind us:

'Watch out, Jen, I think she *fancies* you.'

Sniggers erupt from the bench behind us, and my blood freezes in my veins.

'Shh!' hisses Jennifer over her shoulder, but out of the corner of my eye I can see that she's smirking a little. My hands shake as I lift a glass vial, pretending I haven't heard, but it slips from my fingers and clatters across the worktop – thankfully not shattering.

'She's nervous around you, bless!' comes another voice, and a fresh wave of giggles.

'Stop being rude!' says Jennifer in a stage whisper, but I don't know if she means towards me or towards her. I drop my head, wishing I'd worn my hair down so I could hide behind a curtain of it and close myself off. I don't know how

I'm supposed to react; this never happened at my old school. I don't have a clue what to do.

As I'm floundering for an answer, the bell rings out and everyone is grabbing their bags and moving for the door. Before I can even gain the courage to lift my head, I'm left by myself, struggling to process what just happened. Do they know? Is it bad if they do? What the hell do I do now?!

I snatch my books from the table and stuff them into my bag, feeling hot angry tears well up in my eyes. I swipe furiously at my face and make my way quickly down the halls and towards the exit, desperate to not let anyone see how much that little encounter has got to me.

Stepping out the doors, I immediately spot the girls from Chemistry, huddled with more of their friends. I realise the girls from the changing rooms are amongst them, including Katie West, and feel as though someone has just dropped an ice cube down my back. I really, really don't like the curve of her lips and the look in her eyes as Jennifer and the others presumably report what just happened.

I'm frozen. I suppose I'm lucky not to have encountered anything like this before now, but that doesn't make dealing with it any easier. Just as I'm about to turn away, I spot a boy – Lewis Peck – break away from the group and jog straight over to me.

I panic and start walking, but I've dawdled for too long and he catches up quickly.

'Hey, Neha,' he says smoothly, falling into step beside me.

I stop. Lewis Peck knows my name? It's a small school, but

that crowd always seemed to exist on another plane of existence to the rest of us.

'Oh. Hello.' I blink. He's smiling – no, not smiling. It's more of a smirk.

'Chilly, isn't it?' He takes a small step closer to me. My eyes dart back over to the cluster of his friends, watching intently. He spots me look and laughs gently.

'Don't mind those idiots. They've never been outside the village except to Center Parcs.'

The quip making fun of his friends catches me off guard and I let out a bark of laughter before I can stop myself. In the shock of someone talking to me like they actually know me, I've forgotten the normal etiquette of talking to the popular kids. He grins wolfishly.

'Listen, I'm having a Halloween party tonight,' he says. 'It's a whole thing. You should come. It's fancy dress, we all get pretty into it.'

'A party?'

'Yeah – you know what a party is, right?' He laughs, but there's a glint in his eye that makes me question if he's being cruel.

My heart is thumping in my chest. Is he trying to make up for his friends being shitty to me? I've heard about Lewis's parties, they're the kind that 'everyone' goes to – and yet I've never had the privilege of a second-hand invite, let alone one from Lewis himself. But I've heard wild stories about the things that happen whenever I'm blessed to be welcome at someone's table for lunch the following week.

'I don't think I have a costume,' I blurt out, and he laughs again.

'I'm sure you'll find something. You'll come then?'

'Oh … yes, of course!' I curse my overexcitement and make an attempt to rein it back in, remembering what my eagerness with Jennifer got me. 'I mean, yeah. Yeah, that sounds cool.'

'Cool. I'll see you then.' He starts to walk backwards away from me, towards his friends. 'I live on Sycamore Drive, you'll see it when you get there, it's the only one with Halloween decorations. Starts at nine. Bring something to drink, it might help you to loosen up a little.'

And with that he spins around and strides off, leaving his parting comment hanging in the air. I'm left standing alone, attempting to figure out what he meant. But my face breaks out into a grin, and determined not to ruin the moment by overthinking it, I hurry away from the school – I have a costume to throw together.

I push the thought of Katie West and her gang from my mind.

'It's not going to be too wild, is it?'

Jas leans against the door frame of my room, arms folded and looking worried. She's dressed in her work scrubs and is playing with her keys – she's going to be late, but she won't leave me be.

'It's a *party*, Jas,' I say. 'If it wasn't at least a little wild it would be boring. You can't tell me you didn't go to a few wild parties when you were my age.'

I sit cross-legged in front of the mirror in my room, the contents of my make-up bag splayed out in front of me and my phone propped up against the chest of drawers. I'm hoping to somehow master an impressive enough make-up look that my 'costume' doesn't look so boring – it amounts to a black dress and a pair of cat ears that I think I got when I was ten. It was too late for me to venture out of Chipping Hollow to buy anything, and the village shops were severely lacking in anything that could be made into something resembling fancy dress.

It's ages before I need to be at Lewis's, but I'm already so nervous I feel as though I might burst. The possibility of finally breaking through into a social group tingles in my brain, and I can't suppress the excitement at the simple thought of having people to talk to in between lessons. All I originally had planned for tonight was watching bootleg versions of *Beetlejuice the Musical* on Broadway, but now it feels like it could be the start of something. I'm desperate not to mess it up.

The incident in Chemistry prickles at my brain, and I push it away. So some teenage girls teased the new weird kid in class, that's totally normal – even if actually I'm not that new, and I might be being too harsh on myself with the 'weird' bit. I bet they wouldn't have even done it if they knew I was actually gay. The level-headed part of me nags that this doesn't make it any better, but the level-headed part of me can shut up for the night. And besides, they won't be the only people at this party.

'I just worry about these kids at your school,' Jas says, watching me carefully apply eyeshadow. 'Especially after what happened to that girl Libby. They don't sound like the nicest bunch.'

I don't know if she's referring to videoing and broadcasting Libby's indiscretion, or them beating her up in the changing rooms. The fact that there's a choice sends a pang of guilt through me.

'They're fine,' I say with a wave of my make-up brush, pushing the guilt down. I try not to think about the fact that all the girls present in the changing rooms will undoubtedly be there tonight, and that their ringleader, Katie West, is Lewis's girlfriend. My hand wobbles and I curse as I smudge black under my eye.

'Are you going there with anyone?'

'Literally everyone else in my year,' I scoff.

'I mean, are you arriving with anyone?'

'Jas, we're not eleven. I can turn up to a party by myself.'

'I just—'

'*God!*' I've done my eyeliner completely wrong now, distracted by trying to defend myself. 'I just want to go to a party and make some friends! I thought you'd be pleased!'

Jas narrows her eyes. 'No need to talk to me like that. I'm trying to look out for you.'

'You're not my *mum*.'

The sharp words hang in the air between us. I want to take them back straight away, but don't know how. We never fight. I keep my eyes on the mirror, feeling the words settle on my skin and start to burn.

'OK,' says Jas quietly, after a long pause. 'Text me when you're home.'

She turns and heads down the stairs, and I hear the front door shut with more force than was probably necessary. The guilt wells up again, but I can't deal with that right now. Tonight has to go just right.

I turn back to the mirror, swiping the mistakes from my face. I stare down the nervous girl looking back at me and try to psych myself up. I kneel up and tug at the hem of my dress – it's shorter than what I usually go for, and while we won't have the faculty of St Hilda's to snap at us for being inappropriate, I don't want to look like I'm trying too hard. I do a quick mental scan of my wardrobe and realise I don't really have much of a choice.

Maybe Lewis was right and I need to loosen up. His instruction flashes across my mind: *Bring something to drink.* I wasn't able to get anything on the way home – no ID and a school uniform shockingly isn't a winner for convincing someone to sell you alcohol.

I know Jas has an old bottle of vodka left over from her birthday that she keeps in the cupboard over the fridge. I pad gently downstairs, trying to be quiet even though the house is now empty. I feel like I'm sneaking around from my own conscience.

I reach up on my tiptoes and stretch my hand to the back of the cupboard, catching the bottle with my fingers and manoeuvring it to the edge before carefully taking it down. It's fuller than I expected, and despite never having had a drop in my life I decide there's no harm in having a drink now. It might even help calm my nerves.

I slosh some into a glass and top it up with lemonade, starting to leave the kitchen and then turning back to grab the vodka bottle and bring it upstairs with me.

Settled in front of the mirror again, I take a sip and immediately start spluttering as my throat fills with fire. Maybe I made it too strong? I force down a few gulps, unsure what it's supposed to taste like but knowing that I'll look like a baby if I can't handle my drinks later.

I finish off my make-up and attempt to curl my hair, arranging it carefully around the cat ears. The headband is digging into my skull already but I daren't take it off – it's doing the heavy lifting for this 'costume'.

I take another swig of my drink as I think about how still Jas was when I snapped at her, and another when my treacherous brain gives me a play-by-play of Libby on the changing room floor, a flurry of arms and legs enveloping her. I keep topping the cup up, but as I've left the lemonade downstairs I've inadvertently made it even stronger. Luckily I'm a bit more used to it now.

By the time I'm ready, I'm feeling pretty good about the night ahead. I just know this is my chance to actually make some friends, away from the confines of school. I grab my handbag and the half-bottle of vodka and head downstairs, stumbling only a little on the bottom step.

This is it. Here we go.

LIBBY

We're out of milk.

I shut the fridge and groan. All I wanted was a bloody cup of tea.

I consider slouching back upstairs and doing some homework like I promised Mum over dinner last night, but another day of school has zapped me of any motivation. I look up at the clock on the wall, showing half past six. The minimart in the village will close in just over an hour, so it probably isn't that busy.

I square my shoulders, grab my coat and swipe my house keys off the side.

I can do this.

I can go out and buy milk like a regular person.

The wind is biting, and the closer I get to the minimart the heavier the weight in the pit of my stomach gets. It would be impossible to hope that I don't bump into someone I know, given that I've known everyone in Chipping Hollow since I was born.

My eyes catch on a flicker of light from someone's porch, and my heart jolts when I see that it's a glowing orange pumpkin with a crudely carved smile leering out at me. Shit. Tonight is Halloween. It's usually one of my most anticipated holidays, but this year I've been distracted. I curse under my breath, knowing the younger parents will be in the minimart buying last-minute sweets for the handful of trick-or-treaters. I still remember elderly Mrs McNamara slamming the door in my face when Mona and I attempted to trick or treat at her house years ago, screaming through the letterbox that we were celebrating 'the devil's holiday'.

For a split second I smile and reach for my phone to text Mona, but my last unanswered texts in the thread stare back at me and stop my fingers before they can do anything stupid. I approach the automatic doors of the supermarket and lower my head, wishing I'd worn a hat.

I can do this.

Get in, get milk, get out.

I start to wonder if I'm overthinking it as I head down the cool aisles to the fridges at the back. I begin to relax. It's actually not that busy, just the odd last-minute shopper roaming the shelves, passing under the seasonal streamers and crêpe-paper spiders. No one pays me any attention, and it's marvellous. I make it to the back of the shop.

Milk secured.

A little bubble of confidence is blossoming inside my chest as I turn back towards the front of the shop, just in time to see Dan's mother coming in through the sliding glass doors.

I drop the milk.

My feet hop away from the carton as it explodes against the hard tile, splattering liquid across the floor.

'*Shit!*' I hiss, eyes darting back and forth to check if anyone has spotted me. There's nobody around, but the sound will have someone in an apron over any second now. I skid over the sopping floor and dart down one of the aisles. *No point crying over spilt milk*, I think deliriously, suppressing a bubble of hysterical laughter.

My brain is screaming as I hurry past shelves of KitKats and Hobnobs. If I can make it to the front doors I can escape without coming face to face with her. I haven't seen either of Dan's parents since the incident, and I can confidently assume they have no idea about what went down – I know Mrs King is vehemently against social media, and of course, they'll have been preoccupied. But that doesn't mean I want to stand in front of her, knowing what I did even if she doesn't.

I'm sneaking past the fresh produce when Mrs King surfaces from behind a display of organic apples. Not knowing what else to do, I duck down and crawl underneath a vegetable rack. I kneel, hunched over, marvelling at the farce that has become my life.

'Olivia?'

Bollocks.

Reluctantly, I raise my head. Dan's mother is standing right by my poor hiding place, holding a shopping basket and staring down at me with her head on one side.

'Oh, h-hi, Mrs King!' My voice is several octaves higher than normal, and way too cheery. 'I didn't see you!'

'What are you doing?' Her face is a perfect mix of confused and alarmed.

'I ... I dropped my ...' I scan the floor for something I might have plausibly dropped, praying for the ground to open up and swallow me. 'This!'

'A parsnip?'

'Ahh.' I stare down at the object in my hand. It is indeed a parsnip. 'Yes?'

'Oh.' Mrs King blinks at me. 'Are you going to stand up?'

'Umm, sure.' I struggle to my feet and bang my head on the veg rack on the way up. I straighten, rubbing at the lump forming beneath my hair.

We stand opposite each other silently. This is not a woman I've known to allow a silence – this is a woman that fills the spaces between people with conversation and observation, whether you want her to or not. The tacky decorations above her head only act as a reminder that she should be lecturing me on the inherent anti-Christian nature of Halloween.

The awkwardness is so potent my skin itches with it.

'How have you been?'

I cringe the instant the question leaves my lips. *How have you been?* Her son is in a coma.

'Oh, coping,' she replies. Her grey face and the dark hollows under her eyes tell a different story. The subject of Dan hovers like a ghost between us.

I'm still holding the parsnip.

'I haven't seen you at the hospital?' she says, more of a question than a statement.

'I've been a few times,' I reply, shuffling my feet. 'How … how is he?'

She looks me in the eye for the first time.

'Stable,' she whispers. The way she says it, I know she's quoting the doctors. I know that it doesn't even begin to cover the severity of his situation, and the accompanying fear and grief. I wish I could hug her.

'I'm sorry,' she blurts out, and my chest aches when she gasps back a sob. 'I have … I have to go.'

She practically runs from me, her head bowed and her shoulders shaking. She abandons the basket in the aisle. It contains two packets of ibuprofen and a box of tissues.

When I arrive home, I drink my tea black. Milk is overrated.

Every year in the run-up to Halloween, I'd spend weeks trawling Pinterest with Mona, searching for costumes we could pull off together.

This year my activities are a little different.

After my miserable black tea, I set up camp on the living-room sofa with a giant fleece blanket and the remote control. I plan on ploughing through every cheesy, campy horror film I can find until the early hours. Mum has gone to bed early, exhausted from work, so I keep the volume low so as not to wake her with a cacophony of elaborate screams.

I feel a pang of loneliness. Most of my classmates will no doubt be attending Lewis's party, an event his parents pretend not to know about year after year so they don't have to excuse it to the rest of the congregation. Earlier this week in English I overheard Mona talking about her costume, a standard zombie cheerleader. Just a pleated skirt and a bit of fake blood; after all the planning and perfect execution of our previous costumes it's a weird extra layer of loss. Last year we went as Chucky and Tiffany from the *Child's Play* films, the year before the Grady twins from *The Shining*.

My sour thoughts feel wrong, and despite her recent attitude towards me I find myself wishing desperately that I was drinking punch and eating cheese puffs with her at Lewis's party.

Last year Mona and I toyed with the idea of Cannibal Barbies, and I smile at the idea of Dan joining in as our half-eaten Ken doll – that is, if he could have convinced his mother to let him attend something as sacrilegious as a Halloween party.

I look down at my *Hello Kitty* pyjama bottoms and old band T-shirt, and decide that even Mona's unimaginative cheerleader is better than this.

I hit play on one of the films and pick up my phone to order enough Chinese food to feed me for a week. When the doorbell rings just under an hour later, I've been so immersed in a make-believe horror world that I've almost forgotten about the one that I'm living in.

But when I throw open the front door, it's not a steaming bag of prawn toast, satay chicken and fried rice that greets me. It's two under-sixes in chintzy Halloween costumes, chaperoned by a bored-looking teenager in a hoodie emblazoned with our school logo across the front.

Crap.

'*Trick or treat!*' the children chime in unison, holding up pumpkin-shaped sweet bags. I stand frozen in the doorway, realising far too late that we never got anything in for trick-or-treaters – between the milk and Mrs King it didn't even cross my mind at the minimart.

I can see the boy squinting at me over the kids' heads, trying to place me. He's struggling and I'm not about to prompt him.

'Just one second!'

I run to the kitchen, pulling open cupboard doors and rooting around for something more appropriate than tomato soup to give the kids. I stumble on a packet of boxed raisins and decide I'm just going to have to be 'that house'.

I head back to the door and drop the boxes of raisins into the bags, ignoring the nose wrinkles I get in place of thanks. They're about to step off my doorstep and I reach to close the door, but the chaperone takes a step forward. I hold my breath.

'Aren't you the girl who cheated on Dan King? The guy that's dying?'

I flush to my roots, half in embarrassment and half in anger.

'He's not *dying*!' I grip the door handle and feel my fingers tingle with the pressure. 'He's just … he's ill.'

'He's in a *coma*,' the guy practically spits, his face twisted in disgust. 'You're a right piece of work.'

I open my mouth to reply but nothing comes out, and I

gape at him like a fish with concussion. He shakes his head and takes the arms of the children he's with, who are staring at me in undisguised awe. He pulls them down my driveway and they disappear around the corner.

I'm still standing there when the delivery driver arrives a few minutes later, walking hesitantly up the driveway towards me.

I take the food and close the door, making my way back into the living room. On the TV my film is still on pause, a darkened hallway with a shadowy figure at one end.

Aren't you the girl who cheated on Dan King?

The words echo around my head.

The guy that's dying?

Dan isn't dying.

He's in a coma.

He can't die.

You're a right piece of work. He's in a coma.

If he dies it's over. Everything is over.

I look down at the bag of food, feeling the least hungry I've ever been in my life. The smell of sweet-and-sour sauce is making me want to gag and I nudge the bag away with my foot, the familiar sting of tears prickling at my eyes.

It was sick of me to think that I could forget about my broken boyfriend by watching American teenagers get ripped to shreds by various killers, stuffing my face with grease and batter. I hit the remote to turn off the TV and pick up the bag of food, rushing to the kitchen to dump it on the side. Throwing open the back door, I gulp down a lungful of cold air. My skin prickles with goosebumps as the late-October cold washes over me, seeping right through my thin cotton pyjamas.

I shiver and pull back, closing the door. The rich aroma of the takeaway food is still turning my stomach, so I leave the kitchen and run upstairs. After ransacking my bedroom I find a thick jumper, a pair of leggings and my rubber-soled boots. I drag them on and head back downstairs, shrugging into my coat, and I'm out the front door before realising I made the decision to leave.

My boots slide over the soggy leaves underfoot. I walk blindly down my road and beyond, paying no attention to the direction I'm going in. The flickering smiles of the sporadic jack-o'-lanterns outside Halloween-friendly households seem to mock my non-participation in the festivities this year.

Keeping my eyes on the ground, I ignore the sugar-frenzied shouts of a small group of children, their young parents trudging along behind them. As they approach I cross the road, wishing I'd been able to make it back to the hospital to pick up my iPod before now to soundtrack this dismal walk through the cold, dark streets.

I hope Mum doesn't wake up and wonder where I am. I should have written a note.

When I finally look up at my surroundings, I suck in a sharp, cold breath. My feet have taken me to Lewis's neighbourhood. I can hear the noise of the party just a few houses away, Lewis's insane sound system blasting Michael Jackson's

Thriller at a volume that has to be generating at least three noise complaints from the elderly neighbours.

I consider turning around and going back the way I came, but I know that by walking the length of this road I can be home in another ten minutes, and my toes are starting to go numb.

As I approach the house the music gets louder, and I tug my hood up to conceal my face. I force myself not to look, knowing that with my recent bout of luck someone would be bound to spot me skulking past. There's a burst of sound, voices and music and shrieking, as a window is thrown open and the party pours out into the night air.

I walk faster. I don't look back.

By the time I'm around the corner and the sound of the chaos is fading behind me, my heart is thumping hard against my chest and blood is pounding in my ears. I curse myself for walking so idly, letting my distracted thoughts drive me right towards a congregation of people that hate me. I'm so dizzy with relief at not being spotted that it takes a moment for me to notice I'm approaching two people, walking just ahead of me.

There's a guy helping a girl along the road, supporting her as she wobbles on sky-high heels. She sways wildly to the right and he drags her back against his body, one arm wrapping around her waist. As they pass under a street lamp I spot a pair of cat ears perched crookedly on the girl's head, and a silky tail swinging from the back of her dress. Her friend doesn't appear to be wearing a costume, but I know instinctively that they've come from Lewis's party.

'Wherr'ee goin'?' The girl slurs her words, her voice thick with alcohol. I guess it's not just the heels making it difficult for her to stay upright. I dig my hands deeper into my coat pockets and keep my head down. I'm about to cross the road and get out of their way when I hear the jangle of keys and see that they've stopped beside a small car.

This guy is planning on driving. Either he's a complete idiot, or he's sober.

The hairs on the back of my neck start to prickle and my feet are refusing to move, but I mentally scold myself; it's none of my business.

'I'm helping you home, remember?' the guy insists, letting go of her momentarily to open the car door. His voice is clear and steady; sober it is. 'Let's get you home.'

My heart clenches. The words echo around my head in a hauntingly familiar way, the ghost of something I only half remember. My mouth opens and I'm calling out like it's a reflex.

'Hey, are you OK?'

The guy looks up straight away. The girl takes a second to locate where the sound came from. They both stare at me with differing degrees of focus for several long seconds. Something seems familiar about the girl, and as she sways to the right her face catches under the street lamp and I finally place her: it's Neha Gill, the girl from cross-country.

I clear my throat a little. 'Are you OK?' I ask again, directing the question solely towards Neha now. She squints at me. She doesn't recognise who I am, I can tell, but that doesn't matter.

'We're fine, thanks,' the guy says. His grip on Neha's waist tightens.

'He'ss helpin' me home?' burbles Neha. She looks up at the guy holding her, frowning. 'I thhink?'

I study this guy's face, which is scowling at my interference. He doesn't look like a monster. He just looks like a guy. He could be anyone.

I think that's what makes him all the more terrifying.

'No, love, *I'm* helping you home.'

I don't know what I'm doing. I definitely don't need any more drama right now. But here I am reaching out and pulling on Neha's arm, dragging her away from this stranger. She totters into me, grabbing my shoulders for support.

'Don't be such a cow!' He tries to snatch Neha's arm back, but she's clutching me and looking over her shoulder at him like she's never seen him before. Fear dawns in her eyes as the threat breaks through her drunken stupor. I swing her round so my body is between hers and his.

'Frigid bitch!' he shouts after me as I pull Neha away. I loop her arm over my shoulder and try to hurry her along the street. It's not an easy task but I don't care one bit.

By the time we've made it back to my house, Neha is half asleep and, despite her gangly frame, my shoulders are killing me from bearing most of her weight. Unlocking the front door with another person leaning against me proves to be a difficult task, even if that person is as petite as Neha.

We stumble through my front door and I glance up at the ceiling, praying we haven't woken Mum. I don't know how to explain that I've essentially just kidnapped a girl. There's no sound of her stirring, so I sit Neha down on the bottom stair while I lock up, wondering just what in the hell I'm doing. God knows what she'll say about this when she's sober. We hardly even know each other.

But I have no idea where she lives and given that she can barely string a sentence together, right now she might not either. There's absolutely no way I'm leaving her out there alone.

We struggle up the stairs together as quietly as possible, and make it into my bedroom. I lower her gently on to my bed, then pause.

'Hey, Neha, is there someone I can call to come and pick you up? Your parents?'

Neha screws up her face and doesn't say anything, but grabs for her handbag and pulls out her phone. After she jabs at it fruitlessly for several seconds, I gently take it from her hands and see the words '*Security Locked – Try Again in 8 Hours*'. I guess she'd been unsuccessfully attempting to unlock it before I found her.

I have no idea who she hangs around with at school so I can't even text someone to get a message to her parents. I resign myself to just sorting it all out in the morning. Neha yawns widely, murmurs something unintelligible, then lies down. She's asleep so quickly I wonder if she actually sleep-walked up the stairs with me. I lean down and pull the duvet up over her dress, plucking the cat ears from her head and placing them carefully on my bedside table.

I stand over her, lying unconscious amongst my soft toys and covered by my cartoon bedsheets. My chest starts to tighten and before my eyes she's changing, her tangled dark curls turning red, her face shifting and rounding into the one I see every day in the mirror. Before I can stop my brain from forming the picture I'm staring down at myself, passed out drunk and vulnerable to anyone around waiting to take advantage.

I carefully roll her on to her side, just in case, then curl up on the floor under a spare blanket. Listening to the sound of Neha's soft snoring, I fall asleep with images I thought I'd forgotten snaking their way into my mind.

Ten Weeks Before It Happened

'Are you sure I look OK?'

I want her to believe me, so I take a second to look Libby up and down as she stands on my front porch. She's wearing a belted floral dress and tights, her baggy denim jacket draped over the top despite the hot July weather. There's a small ladder in the tights by the ankle just above the Doc Martens she lives in, but I don't point it out. I look back up at her and smile.

'You look great! You don't have to worry so much, they're just my parents. You've met them before.'

'Yeah, but not as your *girlfriend*,' she says, a touch of panic in her voice. 'This is entirely different.'

'I promise you, it will be fine,' I say, as much to myself as to her. I know what Mum can be like when she gets going, but I'm not about to say as much when Libby is already twisting strands of hair between her fingers in worry.

I push the thought from my brain and reach out to take

her hand, squeezing gently in encouragement. She smiles at me, and I take it as a sign that she's ready to come in.

'Mum, Dad, Libby's here!' I call as she steps through the door. Libby goes to walk down the corridor, but I pull her back and nod pointedly at her feet. She flushes red and hastily kicks her boots off. The ladder in her tights gets a tiny bit bigger, and I pray that Mum at least doesn't comment – there's no god in heaven that could stop her noticing.

For a moment, Libby stands in the hallway and her eyes roam over the sideboard filled with photographs. There's several of me, Mum and Dad on various holidays over the years, and more than a few of me and Katie as kids. Libby's eyes linger on one of the two of us on a beach, grinning up at the camera as we kneel proudly beside a very lopsided sandcastle.

I gently take her hand again and we head through into the kitchen, where Dad stands sweating in front of the Aga. Only my parents would fire that thing up in the middle of summer.

He turns and grins warmly at us both, and I feel Libby relax a little at his open expression.

'Hello there!' he booms, throwing a tea towel over his shoulder and striding over to clasp Libby's hand in a vigorous shake. They must have crossed paths hundreds of times in this tiny village, but I suppose he's feeling the first-time-as-a-girlfriend vibes as much as she is. 'Lovely to meet you properly, Olivia.'

'You can call me Libby, Mr King,' she says, the corners of her mouth twitching up into a smile as Dad continues to pump her hand up and down in his.

'Libby, of course,' he says, finally letting go and moving back over to the stove. 'And please, you can call me Stuart. Welcome to our humble abode. Dinner will be ready soon, why don't you kids grab a drink?'

'Good idea,' I say, reaching over to the fridge to swipe a couple of cans of Diet Coke. I nod towards the dining room, and Libby follows me through.

Mum is hovering around the dining table, adjusting the forks so they're perfectly perpendicular to the spoons and straightening the salad bowl. She looks up as we enter and, before saying anything to greet Libby, tuts at the cans in my hand.

'Daniel, please, glasses,' she scolds gently, brushing past me to a large cabinet full of glassware. 'What will Olivia think of us?'

'It's Libby – and I don't mind, really,' Libby replies quickly. Mum turns to fix her with an assessing look and Libby shrinks back into herself a little. Mum's eyes flick down at her tights.

I clear my throat. 'Sorry, Mum, I'll sort them,' I say, reaching past her to take two heavy glasses from the cabinet and pouring the Coke into them. They fizz over a little on to the tablecloth, and Mum tuts again.

'Your house is lovely, Mrs King,' says Libby, smiling nervously and trying to fill the silence. Mum glows with pride, as she always does when someone compliments her home. She does not tell Libby to 'call me Mandy' though.

'Thank you, Olivia,' she says primly. 'It's nice to finally meet you properly. I can't tell you how long we've been waiting for

Daniel to bring a girlfriend home! We did maybe think he and Katie would make a lovely couple one day, but—'

'Mu-um!' I groan, dropping down into a chair. Libby stays standing, hovering until Mum lowers herself into the chair next to me as though waiting for the Queen to be seated first.

Thankfully, we're saved from any more of Mum's comments on my dating life by Dad entering the dining room, holding a casserole dish in his oven-gloved hands.

'Dinner is served!' he says, placing the dish in the centre of the table with a flourish. He picks up the salad tongs and starts dishing up on to Mum's plate before offering them to Libby.

Once we all have food on our plates, Libby goes to take a bite – I give her a quick nudge under the table. She looks up at me, and then at my parents, who are watching her expectantly. The three of us have taken each other's hands, and I hold mine out to Libby with a nod.

She goes bright red and drops her fork, hastily grabbing my hand and my dad's on her other side. 'Oh, sorry. I didn't, umm, realise.'

'Do you not say grace at home?' Mum asks pointedly.

'Well, it's just me and Mum at home, so ...' Libby trails off with an apologetic shrug. Mum purses her lips a little, but launches into the Lord's Prayer, thankfully without another comment.

We all murmur an *amen* and, finally, can start to eat.

'So, Olivia,' says Mum, spearing a cherry tomato precisely

on the end of her fork. 'What A levels are you taking?'

Libby fumbles with her cutlery. 'English Literature, Psychology and Photography,' she reels off with the air of someone who's been practising her answers.

'Hmm.' Mum pops the tomato in her mouth, chewing thoughtfully. She finally swallows. 'So, will you be pursuing Psychology at university?'

'Umm, I'm more into the photography really,' Libby admits. 'I've actually been thinking about looking into an apprenticeship instead of a degree.'

'I see,' says Mum. 'Well, that's nice.'

I want to die. It looks like Libby shares the sentiment.

Mum, oblivious to how her words are coming across, turns to me and smiles. 'Daniel is going to Cambridge.'

'Mum, I've not even applied yet,' I say, rolling my eyes. 'I've no idea if I'll get good enough grades to get in.'

'Of course you will,' says Mum airily, as if that settles the matter.

'For music?' asks Libby innocently, and I wince.

'Maths,' Mum replies, before I have a chance to say anything. 'Music is a hobby.'

'Well, for now,' I say. 'You never know.'

'Daniel, we've had this discussion,' Mum cuts in. Libby's eyes flick back and forth between us, and I feel my skin crawl with embarrassment. 'We're happy for you to have your little band –'

I shrivel up at the phrase *little band*.

'– but you can't make a career out of it.'

'Lots of people make careers out of music,' says Libby. I widen my eyes at her pointedly, but she's not really looking. Her and Mum's gazes are locked together. 'Not just the people you hear on the radio. You could go into sound engineering, writing scores for film, songwriting for other people. There's loads of stuff.'

'"Stuff",' Mum repeats, and I shoot a desperate glance over at Dad. He is resolutely eating his dinner as though this conversation isn't happening. Maybe he has the right idea.

'Dan's really talented,' Libby continues. 'He's got as good a chance as anyone else at being successful in music.'

'Oh, I know he's talented, dear,' Mum says coolly. Her gaze turns to me again, warming a few degrees. 'I still remember his first solo in the church choir. But it's not the same as a *real*, stable career.'

'It's not just—' Libby starts, but Dad finally looks up.

'Mandy, this salad is exquisite. Libby, did you know Dan's mother grows most of our vegetables herself in our garden? You can really taste the difference.'

'I … yes, it's lovely,' says Libby, her eyes dropping back down to her plate. I feel bad, but also a surge of relief. At some point, either one of them would have expected me to weigh in on my own future, and I've no idea what I would have said.

The rest of the meal passes without any further incident, if a little stilted. After Dad has cleared away the dessert plates, I quickly excuse Libby and myself from the table and lead her out into the garden.

We sit down on the bench on the patio, looking out over Mum's perfectly manicured flower beds. There's a lengthy pause.

'So, that went well,' I say.

Libby groans and drops her head into her hands. 'I was so terrified about saying the wrong thing, I didn't consider I should also not get into an argument with your mother about a uni degree you've not even applied for yet.'

'That was pretty special,' I admit. I place an awkward hand on her shoulder in an attempt at comfort. 'I love how you couldn't defend your own future choices, but you were very ready to go to bat for mine.'

'Well, obviously,' she says, sitting up again. 'I can stand up for everyone but myself. It's one of my defining features.'

'Maybe we should work on that,' I laugh. 'It'll get you into proper trouble one day.'

'Probably,' she sighs. 'If it hasn't already. Your mum hates me.'

'She definitely doesn't.' I say it with such conviction that Libby frowns at me, confused.

'You cannot think that went well.'

'Well, it might not have been ideal,' I laugh. 'But trust me, she might disagree with your opinions on my future career path, but she'll like that you had something to say.'

'Are you sure?' Libby is twisting her hair in her fingers again. 'I really wanted this to go well. I want them to like me. At least half as much as they like Katie.'

'They both like you,' I say firmly, sidestepping the Katie

comment. 'Mum just won't be as open about it as Dad. Promise.'

Libby sighs again and leans back against the bench, still looking unconvinced.

I feel a light prickle on the back of my neck – I turn my head slightly and see the living-room curtain fall into place.

'We're being watched.'

Libby's back straightens. 'Oh. Should we be sitting further apart?'

'I have no idea. Like Mum said, I've never had a girlfriend round before. I don't know the protocol.'

Libby laughs, then her brow crinkles a little in thought. After a second, she leans in to settle herself against my shoulder. 'I think this is safe.'

It feels weird, but kind of nice. I shift a little to put my arm around her carefully, making sure my hand stays respectfully and visibly on her shoulder. I pretend not to notice, but I see goosebumps break out over Libby's arms. I'm not sure how to feel about that.

We sit in comfortable silence for a while, the evening still pleasantly warm as we look out over the garden. Despite the speed bumps over dinner, I feel like this might actually work out.

NOVEMBER

Neha

Even before I open my eyes I know that something is wrong: the feel of the sheets beneath me, the heavy dryness of my tongue, the not unpleasant but entirely unfamiliar smell of the room.

I'm not at home. I don't know where I am.

I open my eyes.

Weak sunlight is filtering through a gap in the curtains, falling across my face and making me squint. My brain feels as though it's been coated in lead and I struggle to sit up. I stare round the room that isn't mine, trying to pick out something that I recognise and failing. My hands brush against something soft and furry; I'm surrounded by stuffed animals. They seem to have a calming effect on me, and my heart rate slows just a little.

It jumps again when what I thought was a pile of blankets on the floor starts moving. My body jerks, and I bang my head on a low shelf above the bed that of course I didn't know was there. A mop of brilliant red curls emerges from the top of the blankets, and a face I know but can't immediately place turns towards me.

'Hello,' I say blearily. 'Why are you on the floor?'

The girl blinks at me with unfocused eyes. 'Because you were in my bed?'

'Oh.' I look down, pushing back the covers to reveal my rumpled dress, bunched up around my waist. I hastily cover myself again. 'Why am I in your bed?'

'I ... uhh ...' The girl seems momentarily thrown, and before she answers it hits me like a truck: the girls' changing rooms, Katie West and her gang throwing a pile of clothes on to the dirty shower floor, me standing by while they kicked her to the floor ...

My face grows hot with embarrassment and I pull the sheets that aren't mine further up over my body. Oh god. Was she at the party?

I want the ground to open up and swallow me as I think about how embarrassing I must have been last night to need to be taken home. *What if I made a pass at her in my drunken state? Did she put me in her bed, or did I just get into it?!*

After what feels like an age of my hungover mind running away with me, Libby finally speaks again.

'I don't know if you knew him, but this guy was trying to get you into his car last night. You seemed pretty drunk.'

Fingers of shame poke at me, and my brain works frantically to pull back something, anything from last night. 'Was I really that drunk?' I croak.

Libby looks embarrassed herself, probably on my behalf. I

steel myself to ask my next question. 'What happened?'

Libby looks sheepish. 'It didn't seem like you were really with it so I interrupted and brought you here. I tried to call someone for you, but I couldn't unlock your phone.' She gestures to her bedside table. I pick up my phone and see that it's security locked for thirty more minutes, but it must have been way longer if Libby couldn't unlock it before we went to sleep. The shame pokes harder.

'I thought it would be best for you to just stay the night,' Libby finishes. 'I'm sorry if that's weird.'

There's a silence. My heart is thumping, the belated panic rushing through my body making me squirm. I run a hand through my tangled hair, fingers catching on the knots. 'I had no idea where I was when I woke up, I was starting to freak out to be honest, and then I saw you.'

Libby is staring into her lap. 'I was worried I might have interrupted something.'

'God, no!' I sit up straighter, and when Libby looks up I force myself to look her in the eye. 'I don't know where I'd have ended up if you hadn't … Were you at the party? I don't remember seeing you at Lewis's. But then, I don't remember much.'

Now I've stopped babbling, she's looking at me like I've just grown a second head. *Shit*. Of course she wasn't at the party. My cheeks start burning again.

'I wasn't exactly invited,' she says slowly, and I wince. 'I was just out walking. I heard you and it didn't look right. I didn't like it.'

My head swims as my imagination runs through a

thousand scenarios in a split second. The possibilities of where I could have been waking up this morning send a wave of nausea over me.

'I don't remember leaving,' I whisper. 'I don't even remember talking to anyone I don't know. I didn't think I'd had that much to drink, but then I've not much experience, so …'

Libby is nodding, but her expression is one of someone listening to something happening very far away. She's difficult to read, but in my gut I feel that she believes me.

'That could have been *so* bad,' I say, more to myself than to her.

'It could have.' Her face has gone pale, light brown freckles standing out sharper across her cheeks. 'Yeah, it could have.'

We sit in silence for a moment. I give myself a mental shake and swing my legs over the side of the bed, trying to ignore the throbbing in my head at the sudden movement.

'I have to call my aunt,' I say decidedly. I glance at my still-locked phone, guilt swirling in my already delicate stomach. 'She'll be going mental that I haven't told her where I am.'

'Do you know her number? You can borrow my phone if yours is still locked.'

'Nah, it'll have to wait another half an hour,' I sigh. 'Hey, are you hungry? Let me take you for breakfast. I owe you for last night.'

'Oh, you don't have to do that,' says Libby, eyebrows furrowed in an almost comical picture of bemusement. 'Anyone would have done it.'

'No, they wouldn't.' The serious note in my voice makes

her look up at me again. 'And you know they wouldn't. Most people would have walked past and thought it was none of their business. So it's the least I can do, unless you have other plans?'

She snorts, a sound that seems ludicrous after the heavy conversation we've just had. The corners of my mouth twitch up into a smile.

'No, no plans,' she says, wriggling out from under the blankets.

'Breakfast it is then.' I look down and tug at my dress. 'Umm, I hate to ask, but have you got anything … ?' I trail off, eyes drifting over to the wardrobe in the corner.

'Oh, sure!' Libby jumps over to the wardrobe with an energy I am envious of (my head is still pounding) and finds me a jumper and a pair of leggings that should fit. I start to change and then halfway through it strikes me that I'm now half-naked in front of Libby, and I nearly topple over trying to drag everything on more quickly. Not that I need to – Libby has become entirely engrossed in the opposite wall.

Once I'm fully clothed again, I stuff last night's dress into my handbag. From the bedside table I pick up my cat ears and wrinkle my nose.

'God, I was boring. I mean, a cat? That's original,' I snort. 'I only got invited yesterday afternoon. I didn't have time to think of anything good.' I push the ears into my handbag alongside the dress. The urge to throw the lot in the bin is overwhelming and my skin crawls at the thought of the stranger last night with his hands on me.

I swallow my disgust and hitch a smile I'm not really behind on to my face. 'Come on. I know a great place.'

'Where on *earth* have you been?!'

Jas's voice through my phone is like needles on my skin, and it must show on my face because Libby very politely peers down the road for the bus that's not due for at least another five minutes.

'I'm sorry,' I half whisper, taking a couple of shuffling steps away from the bus stop to have this conversation. 'I'm so, so sorry. I just lost track of time, and then I was invited to stay at a friend's house—'

'Which friend? You don't have any friends.'

God, she must be mad if she's throwing the truth at me so freely. I rub my temples with my free hand.

'It's Libby Dixon. The girl I told you about. She was … We bumped into each other last night.' I don't specify that we bumped into each other in the street, with me completely out of it in the arms of a total stranger.

There's a shocked pause, and then a sigh that's so loaded it nearly knocks me back on my heels. 'Neha. I was so worried. I even drove back to work to check in A & E for you. Why didn't you *call* me?'

'My phone ran out of battery,' I say weakly, the lie sticking in my throat and making my eyes burn. 'I really am sorry. I just completely forgot.'

'How much did you have to drink?'

I squirm. 'Not that much.'

I can almost hear her roll her eyes through the phone. 'Sure. Don't think I didn't check the cupboard for that vodka. This is a conversation we'll be having as soon as you get home.'

'About that.' I glance back at Libby, who's still pretending not to be hearing my side of our conversation. 'I'll be home at lunchtime? Me and Libby are going out for breakfast. I'm just trying to make a friend?' I say this all in a rush, as if that will somehow make her less mad.

'I thought she was already your friend,' Jas says sceptically, but I can sense her relenting. I hold my breath.

'Fine. But don't think you're off the hook. I want a full explanation as soon as I see you, a true one, please. You owe me that.'

I knew it would be fruitless to try and lie to her, but at least she's not demanding I come home right this second. 'Thanks, Jas. I really am sorry.'

'I know,' she sighs again. 'Keep me updated. I've got to get back to the hospital so let me know when you're home. Don't be too long.'

We hang up just as the bus pulls around the corner. Libby smiles at me as we hop on, but the bus is crowded with Saturday-morning shoppers so we don't talk much. I lean my head against the steamy window and try not to think about last night, or the furious relief in Jas's voice on the phone. I was so close to giving her something worse to worry about.

'Bit of a trek for breakfast,' says Libby, interrupting my thoughts.

I lift my head from the window to turn to her. 'It will be worth it, I promise.'

Twenty minutes later the bus trundles into the small station at Market Stepton, and I usher us off. We're crossing the town square when Libby grabs my arm to stop me.

'Neha? Do you mind if we pop in here for a minute?' She nods towards a Boots on our left.

'Sure.' I figure I could probably use a few more minutes to let my stomach settle before I start shovelling food into it anyhow.

We step inside and I trail after Libby, who moves with determination towards the aisle marked 'Haircare'. I gaze round at the shampoos, wondering if I need to pick anything up myself. When I turn around Libby is frowning at the shelf of hair dyes, chewing on her lip.

'Oh! You're not dyeing it, are you?'

Libby jumps and looks at me as though she'd forgotten I was still there.

'Your hair is lovely,' I say. 'I'm so jealous of your red.' I reach out absent-mindedly as if to touch it, realise at the last second how bizarre and rude that is, and swerve my hand to grab a bottle of shampoo on the shelf opposite instead.

'Just trying not to stand out so much,' Libby mutters, grabbing a box of brunette dye. 'Hoping not to get so many names shouted at me at school, y'know?'

'Oh,' I say quietly, and follow her as she heads towards the tills.

Libby turns, a slight frown wrinkling her forehead. 'What?'

'I just don't think you should have to change yourself for other people,' I blurt, the words out before I can properly organise them into something less presumptuous.

She stops. 'I'm not *changing* myself,' she says, more than a little forcefully. 'It's just like a disguise. I only want to be less visible.'

'OK,' I say. I turn to stare at a display of Maybelline. Behind me I can feel Libby's eyes on the back of my head, and after a moment I hear her move away towards the tills. My chest tightens as the air between us shifts, and I curse myself for ruining the easy-if-awkward vibe we've been cultivating since I woke up in her bed.

She buys the hair dye, and we leave the shop without saying any more.

I lead us over to the centre of the square, towards a Tudor-style building with whitewashed walls and wooden beams stretching up over a rolled-out canopy bearing the sign *Beanz Cafe*.

When I push open the door, a familiar breath of warm coffee-scented air washes over us, the bell above the door tinkling to announce our arrival. I make a beeline for my regular table by the window and drop into a seat, shrugging off Libby's mother's coat and draping it over the back of my chair.

Libby sits down opposite me and immediately starts fiddling with the packets of sugar from a jar on the table. She keeps glancing around the room, eyes darting over each face, and I realise she's checking for anyone we might know, despite having travelled beyond the confines of Chipping Hollow.

I push the laminated menu across to her, breaking her concentration on the people around us.

'You take a look, I could recite that from memory.'

Libby picks up the menu and looks over it with glazed eyes, and I wonder if I'm going to have to order for her. I'm staring idly out of the window, thinking about buttered toast, when she slaps the menu back down and blurts, 'Doesn't this bother you?!'

I blink in confusion. 'What, breakfast?'

'Being here with *me*,' she says emphatically, snatching up the crumpled sugar packets again.

'What's wrong with being here with you?' I say with a soft laugh, but her face is twisted with tension and I know that this isn't going to be a laughing along sort of conversation.

'You know what I did.' She won't meet my eyes, and one of the packets splits open under her fingers and sugar spills out on to the table.

'Actually, no, I don't,' I say. 'I know what Katie West has been telling people, but I'm inclined not to take anything she says as gospel, even if she is Dan's *bestie*.'

At the mention of Katie, Libby finally looks up. I think of the scene in the changing rooms again, and a haze of shame descends over me.

'Don't tell me you haven't seen the video,' she says miserably. 'It's everywhere. People on TikTok who don't even have a clue where Chipping Hollow *is* are stitching it to judge me. I can't open Instagram without it popping up every other post. And people keep bloody tagging me in it just to troll me.'

I consider lying about having seen it but ultimately know it's useless; of course I've seen the video. She sees my expression and winces.

'So, yeah, it's all true. From what I can remember.'

'You don't actually remember it happening?' I lean in a little closer, frowning. 'You mean like you blanked it out?'

'I suppose,' she says, eyes cast down once more. 'But I was pretty drunk so I don't know.'

'Like, lowered-inhibitions drunk or …' I shift uncomfortably, trying to push away the feeling of phantom hands on my waist, 'or like I was last night?'

She looks conflicted for a moment, but finally admits, 'Yeah. Like you.'

My insides squirm as everything I'd wondered about that video comes into focus. I'm not feeling very hungry any more.

Libby goes on. 'It was "girls' night out". I was trying to get involved, I always felt like I was hovering on the outside of that group, and that night I thought … well, I thought wrong. They were taking the piss by getting me drunk and stupid, and I was too far gone to realise.'

With a pang I remember the look in Lewis's eyes when he invited me to his party. They were doing the exact same thing to me, and I was so desperate I fell for it. I swallow hard.

'So where were the others when … ?'

'They were about, I guess.' She pushes the spilt sugar around with a finger. 'They must have been because they all saw everything and filmed it.'

'And no one tried to help you?'

Libby looks up again, scrunching her nose in confusion. I try not to think about how cute it is. 'Help me what?' she asks.

'They see you, blind drunk, being manhandled by some creep in the middle of a club and no one thought, hey, maybe she could use a hand?'

'You said it yourself earlier.' She shrugs. 'They'd have thought it was none of their business.'

'Except it *was* their business!' I say. 'They got you into that state, and even if they hadn't, they weren't some strangers on the street. They were your friends!' A horrible thought strikes me and I reach across the table to grab her arm. 'Libby, you got home OK, right? You went home alone?'

'I woke up at home, yeah,' she says. She doesn't pull her arm away, even as I relax my grip in relief. 'My mum says I turned up in a taxi by myself.'

'Well, that's something,' I sigh, sitting back in my seat. 'And that's what everyone is blaming you for? That's what you're blaming *yourself* for?'

'Of course they blame me for that.' She shakes her head, seemingly in disbelief. 'I *cheated* on Dan. It's there on video for everyone to see. And the same night that he became a *coma patient*. That's … that's low. That's really low.'

'They plied you with alcohol and then left you vulnerable. And when you were in trouble they just stood by and then made you into a *meme*.'

'I still did it.' Libby wriggles in her seat. 'I think I was flirting with him. It was my fault.'

'It doesn't matter if you were flirting. That doesn't give anyone the right to touch you without consent, *especially* when you were in the state you were.' I lean forward, desperate for her to understand. 'Was I responsible for myself last night? If something had happened –' I suppress a shudder at the thought – 'would that have been my responsibility?'

'That's different,' Libby insists. 'You don't have a boyfriend, let alone—'

'Girlfriend,' I correct without thinking. 'I don't have a *girl*friend.'

Libby's eyebrows rise just a fraction. I scoot all the way back in my seat, heat rising to my cheeks, worrying I've revealed the wrong thing.

'Which is another reason I know for a fact I wouldn't have consciously been leaving with some guy,' I say, with a nervous laugh. Whatever she might think of what I just said, I need to make this point. 'But either way, even if I was in a relationship, that doesn't change the state I was in. Right?'

'Right,' she says slowly. I sense it's not that she disagrees, but she's having a hard time applying the same logic to herself. 'So, you don't think I'm a dirty slut for kissing some other guy?'

'I don't think of anyone as a slut, dirty or otherwise,' I say firmly. 'But no, to answer the real question, I don't think you're responsible for anything that happened to you when you were barely able to stand, let alone consent.'

We sit in silence for a second, the weight of the conversation settling over us.

'Everyone still hates me for it,' Libby finally whispers. 'No one will even talk to me.'

'I'm talking to you.'

She looks up and for the first time she smiles. It's weak, but it's something. The sight of it does something funny to my insides. *Careful, Neha*.

'Are you two going to order, or do I need to kick you out?'

Libby jumps and drops the sugar packets she's been fiddling with, but I recognise the voice instantly and look up to see the blondest boy I know, bouncing on the balls of his feet, wearing a *Beanz Cafe* apron and a wide grin.

'Sam!' I jump from my seat and pull him into a hug. I hold him for longer than usual, dark thoughts about last night still swirling in my head. When I pull away, his eyes narrow a little at the expression I can't keep off my face.

'I didn't know you were working today,' I say in a rush, mentally begging him not to saying anything now. I'm emotionally exhausted from the talk with Libby and not ready to go over everything again.

'Overtime,' he replies, as always seeming to read my thoughts. He turns to Libby with an easy smile. 'Who's this?'

'Hey, I'm Libby.' She looks a little more relaxed, having figured out we're not actually being booted out.

'Nice to meet you,' he says. I see a flicker of recognition in his eyes as he takes in her red hair, her freckles; that video went further than just our school. But I know I don't have to worry about him saying something about that.

'We need breakfast,' I say, sitting back down and picking up the menu. Sam grins, and takes his notepad from his apron pocket with a flourish.

'That I can help you with.'

On the bus home, I share my headphones with Libby (she mumbled something about lending hers to someone) and make her listen to the *SIX* soundtrack with me. Libby's stop is before mine, and as she stands to leave and starts saying goodbye I feel a flash of urgency.

'See you at school?' I say in a rush.

'I guess so,' Libby says, as if she'd forgotten that we even went to school together. 'See you. Thanks again for breakfast.'

The bus has already pulled to a standstill and Libby steps off with a parting wave in my direction.

When I reach home and see Jas's car isn't parked up on the road in front of our row of terraces, I say a silent thanks to the universe that I don't have to talk about last night yet. I feel like the further away I get from it, the more likely I am to not cry.

I step inside and wrap my arms around my body, shivering even though the house isn't cold. It's a bit of a tip, but that's nothing new. With Jas on an awkward shift pattern and me being, well, a teenager, it's never a palace of domestic order.

I slowly walk up the stairs, pausing to kiss the tips of my fingers and press them to Mum and Dad's photograph on the way up. I squeeze into my tiny bedroom, plug my phone into its charging cable and open up Instagram. I tap Libby's name into the search bar to bring up her profile, hesitate for a moment, and then click Follow. I've been too shy to up until now.

Her latest post, from back in September, is of her and another girl from school, Mona Emmanuel. She's giving Mona a piggyback in the photo, both laughing at each other and ignoring the camera. It's a nice photo, and I wonder who took it. I try to remember if I've seen Libby and Mona together at school recently, and draw a blank.

I close the app and stretch out on the bed. The jumper I've borrowed still smells of Libby's perfume.

LIBBY

It's strange going back to being an outcast after spending time with Neha at the weekend, but Monday rolls around as it always does and feels almost worse from having a taste of socialisation.

Before the cross-country incident, I was barely aware of Neha Gill. Now that she's on my radar, all day I find myself spotting her around school – bending to retie her shoelaces at the gates in the morning, stopping to take a drink from a water fountain in the corridor, emerging from one of the science classrooms as I pass them on my way to English Lit. I feel creepy, like I'm somehow seeking her out, and I wonder if that is actually true.

I still have no idea what to make of our breakfast trip. All signs point to her having just been tolerating me because I did her a favour, but then she did seem genuinely worried for me after I told her what I remember of the terrible thing I did.

As I move through school, head down and eyes laser focused on a spot in the distance, I think again about how she looked lying on my bed, completely out of it. The sight of her morphing into me, my subconscious trying to tell me what Neha seemed to be telling me in the cafe, it feels like I've just swallowed something large and spiky.

I shake the thought away – I can't handle that right now.

Just as I'm telling myself to stop obsessing over Neha, I turn a corner and of course, there she is coming straight towards me.

She locks eyes with me and for a moment I freeze. But then she smiles, and her whole face lights up and I can't help it, I'm smiling back. For a bizarre second I'm reminded of Dan, and the way his smile just invited you in as if the two of you were sharing a secret. Neha's smile feels like that.

A bump on my shoulder reminds me that even though this corridor is packed with people moving between lessons, I'm the one under scrutiny and I probably shouldn't be standing here grinning like an idiot. I rearrange my face into a more demure smile, nod at Neha down the corridor, then turn and hurry away.

What the hell was that?

I'm still seeing Neha everywhere around school, but now it seems that she's seeing me too. I haven't actually approached her – what would I even say? – but I find myself lifting my head a little more as I move around the building to make sure she spots me when I spot her.

We seem to be dancing around each other and I'm beginning to wonder if this strange, distant friendship is all we'll ever have, when I'm heading for the Photography classrooms and a hand lands on my arm. I jump, snapping out of my reverie to see Neha herself in front of me. I stumble to a halt, causing a blockage in the flow of students around us heading for their next subject.

'Hey!' she says. 'How're you?'

'Uhh.' My eyes flick around the corridor – the longer I stand here, the longer I'm a target, but I don't want to just cut off the first person to speak to me properly in weeks. 'Fine.'

'I was wondering if you wanted to—'

'Hey, can we chat in here?'

I grab her hand and pull her through a nearby door and out of the way of the jostling students before she can answer. I shut the door and the din becomes muffled as we're enveloped by a claustrophobic quiet – Neha looks round in surprise, taking in the fact that we're in a storage cupboard. The smell of bleach and floor cleaner is sharp in my nostrils, but underneath it is something sweeter. I think it's Neha's perfume.

'Sorry,' I say hastily. 'I just, I can't really stop in the corridors. It doesn't end well.'

'Oh, I see,' she says, blinking at me in the gloom. The corner of her mouth twitches upwards. 'I always did feel like I'd gone back into the closet at this school.'

I let out the most undignified snort, which takes me by surprise – I can't remember the last time I laughed properly.

Then I think about Mr Harper, and the threat of further consequences if I keep missing lessons, and the mirth in me dies as quickly as it arrived.

'Did you want something?'

'Oh, yeah!' She smiles, her cheeks dimpling as she does. 'I wanted to invite you to this Bonfire Night thing I'm going to on Thursday. You probably know it better than me, it's the one they have at the ruins every year? I'm going with some friends and thought you might want to come.'

For a moment I don't answer, completely taken aback that someone wants to hang out with me by actual choice. Then a smile breaks out over my face.

'That would be great! But …' I shuffle my feet. 'They're not from St Hilda's, are they?'

'No, they're from my old school in Market Stepton. The same as Sam, you met him on Sunday,' she replies.

'OK,' I say, considering. 'Then, yeah. I'd really like that.'

The sound of students outside the door is subsiding, and I know we're both definitely going to be late for our next classes. Despite this knowledge, I find that I don't really want to leave the cupboard.

'I should probably go,' I say reluctantly. 'I'm already in trouble for skipping classes, so …'

'Yeah, of course.' Neha pushes open the cupboard door and we step out, blinking in the harsh artificial ceiling lights. 'I'll talk to you soon?'

'OK. And thank you!' I hurry off down the corridor, unable

to keep the smile off my face. I'm late for Photography, but it was worth it.

I'm tugging on my wellies when the doorbell rings, and I almost fall over in my haste to answer it. I open the door to reveal Neha, smiling nervously in a thick coat and a humongous rainbow scarf.

'Happy Bonfire Night!' she squeaks, handing me something wrapped in tinfoil. 'Jas sent me with some of her homemade treacle toffee. But I'd warm it up a bit to soften it before you try it, unless you don't enjoy your teeth fully intact.'

I laugh and stuff it in the pocket of my coat, grabbing a beanie from the hook by the door and shouting a hurried goodbye to Mum over my shoulder.

'Have fun!' she calls back, lifting her head briefly from the stack of paperwork she has spread out over the coffee table to beam at me and Neha. I know how excited she was for me to be leaving the house for something other than school, to have someone to actually hang out with.

Apart from that brief conversation in the store cupboard, it's the first time we've actually hung out properly since the morning after Halloween. We head across the village in the direction of the ruins in silence; the only sound is that of our boots on the ground and the slight whistle of the wind.

As we walk, I find myself watching Neha. Despite the awkwardness I feel, she seems to be bouncing slightly with every step, a small smile on her lips. There's an energy about her that makes me marvel at how I'd never really noticed her at school before. Her long dark hair billows around her in the wind, making her look like some sort of siren.

'We're meeting everyone at the gate,' Neha says, snapping me out of my thoughts. 'I think you guys are going to really get on.'

I'm unconvinced but don't say anything, silently praying for her to be right. I desperately need a break, and I hope tonight can be it.

As we approach the ruins I can already smell the bonfire, breathing in the heady scent. Leaves crunch underfoot as we make our way towards the entrance, a gap worn away in the outer ruin walls. Mr Bloom appears to be this year's volunteer to sell tickets. I shrink down further into my coat, hoping not to be recognised.

'Two, please!' Neha hands over a note. Mr Bloom smiles at her before his eyes drift over and land on me. The smile falters, and even in the dark I see his eyes change.

'Ah, hello, Libby,' he says gently. 'How's our Daniel?'

'The same,' I mumble, although a rumble of shame washes over me as I realise I haven't been back to the hospital in over a week. 'I think.'

'Well, at least he's no worse.' Mr Bloom nods and hands Neha a pair of ticket stubs. 'Have a nice time, girls.'

We move away, and Neha ignores my attempt to offer her change. 'My treat,' she insists, swatting at my gloved hand. I stuff the coins back into my pocket, inexplicably feeling even more guilty.

We head through and stand off to one side, bopping up and

down on our heels to keep warm. I stare round at the crumbled remains of the walls that circle the modest park area and am thankful for the anonymity the dark brings me, knowing that most of our classmates will be around here somewhere.

The silence has settled back over us, and I'm relieved when I finally hear a cry of 'Neha!'

We both turn at the sound of her name, and see three people huddled just outside a patch of grass illuminated by the lights of a doughnut truck. I spot Sam with his shock of blond hair, waving at us, and we hurry over.

'Can I interest either of you wonderful people in a doughnut?' he asks by way of greeting, offering up a paper bag that smells of hot batter and sugar. I lean forward and inhale, the corners of my mouth twitching up.

'I think I'll need my own bag,' I say, and Sam laughs.

'You've not met my entourage, have you?' he asks. The question earns him a shove from one of the others. 'The violent one is Zoe, and this is Robyn.'

'Nice to meet you,' says Robyn. My eyes pause on the '*they/them*' pronouns badge they have pinned to the front of their coat, and I feel a lot more optimistic about the openness of Neha's friends.

'You too!' I say brightly, and beside me I sense Neha let go of a tiny bit of tension. That's fair. This is Chipping Hollow after all.

'And I'm only violent around this one,' says Zoe, giving Sam another playful push. 'You go to school with Neha, right?'

'What time are the fireworks meant to start?' Neha

interrupts as I start to nod awkwardly, and I'm grateful for the tactical change in subject – I don't want to think about school.

'Not for another twenty minutes, I reckon,' says Zoe. She pulls out her phone to check, and the light it casts illuminates her vivid blue hair, which had looked brown in the dark.

'Oh!' I gasp. 'I love your hair!'

'Thanks,' Zoe grins. 'It takes one hell of a lot of bleach.'

'I wish I had the nerve to do something like that,' I say wistfully.

'Oh, not to your hair, yours is gorgeous!' says Robyn, stepping closer to examine my curls. 'Is it natural?'

'Grew it myself,' I say mock-proudly, and Neha laughs. It's a nice sound. I catch her eye and feel embarrassed, remembering the box of brunette hair dye currently sitting on the bathroom windowsill at home.

I quietly resolve to throw it in the bin.

'Shall we go and check out the bonfire?' asks Robyn.

'Doughnuts first!' Neha grabs my arm and we get into the queue, and soon I'm sinking my teeth into the steaming fried batter, burning my tongue. I watch as Neha does the same, closing her eyes and licking sugar from her lips. When she opens them I look away quickly, but not before I see her start to blush. I can feel my own cheeks heating up from being caught looking.

We trudge across the field to join the others in front of the fire, flames licking the sky and sending sparks flying as the wood pops and crackles. There's a warmth spreading through me that has nothing to do with the proximity of the bonfire. With a mouthful of hot doughnut and enveloped by the smoky darkness, it's the best I've felt in weeks.

I jump at the shriek of the first firework, screaming up into the sky and exploding in a cloud of green sparks. Neha seems to notice, and quietly links her arm with mine. I stiffen at the unexpected and recently unfamiliar gesture of friendship, but then relax against her, my arm tingling pleasantly with the warmth. We stand there, watching the fireworks overhead and oohing and aahing along with the crowd until the last spark fizzles away, leaving a fog of smoke drifting over the ruins to the sound of applause.

After the final firework has exploded (and Sam has procured another bag of doughnuts), we pile into Zoe's beat-up Mini; Robyn and me side by side in the tiny back seats, Neha squashed on Robyn's lap with her long legs draped over mine. Sam, who had the presence of mind to call shotgun, turns to grin at us all sardined in the back.

'Cosy?' he asks brightly, and Robyn throws their screwed-up doughnut bag at him. The car splutters, Zoe gives it a thump on the dashboard, and it lurches to life. Neha is thrown sideways almost immediately and sprawls across us.

'Just how far is this pub?' I ask, my voice muffled by Neha's rainbow scarf which has somehow ended up in my face.

'Not far!' Sam calls back. I hear him slot a tape into place and the car is filled with the sound of Guns N' Roses.

'Not far at all!' shouts Zoe over the music, revving the engine and swerving wildly around a corner. Neha shoots to the other side of the car again, a soft '*oof!*' from Robyn confirming her landing.

We pull into a small pub car park several minutes later – it's just far enough out from Chipping Hollow that I feel as though I can relax, and I cringe at the thought that that was the point. All of us in the back are thoroughly squashed and Neha appears a little dizzy. I grab hold of her arm to steady her as we head inside, and she shoots me a grateful smile.

Stepping in, we're blasted with central heating, and my face flushes from the sudden warmth. I struggle out of my layers as we make our way over to a small table in the corner. Robyn heads to the bar to buy hot chocolates, and the rest of us pull our chairs up around the table, shoulder to shoulder with our knees all bumping against each other. I sit across from Neha, wedged between Sam and Zoe.

After Robyn returns with a tray of mugs piled high with whipped cream, Neha's friends begin introducing themselves properly to me. Zoe wants to be a comic artist and tells the story of revealing this snippet of information to her barrister father. Her laughter is booming and infectious, causing several other patrons to glance around as she finishes her story. Robyn says when they were five years old they wanted to become a Ghostbuster, and this dream has never quite gone away since then. Sam claims that he's already found his dream career at Beanz because he can help himself to all the tiny biscuits and mini marshmallows he wants.

'What about you?' Zoe asks, turning to me. 'Any big plans for the future?'

I haven't said much so far, content to sit and let everyone else's words wash over me. It's been so lovely to be around people again without wanting the ground to open up and tip me into a fiery abyss.

'Right now, I'm more concerned about the immediate future,' I admit, taking a sip of my drink. I hope they'll take this generally, but then they all look serious and I catch Zoe shooting Neha a look across the table.

'Oh. I guess you *do* all know then,' I say, feeling the heat rising in my cheeks. 'I sort of hoped—'

'We know that a bunch of pricks are giving you a hard time for something that wasn't your fault,' says Zoe forcefully, interrupting my pity spiral. 'Anyone watching that video can see that you're not in any state to make a conscious decision.'

Oh god. They've even seen the video. Here I was thinking I was spending the night with people that would just meet me as *me*, not the notorious slut, and they all knew.

'We know what happened at Halloween too,' says Robyn gently. 'How you looked after Neha when she was in the same situation. That must have been pretty scary. We wanted to say thank you.'

'And let you know that we're on your side,' says Neha, reaching out to take my hand.

I feel hot tears of shame brimming in my eyes at the knowledge that they all know what I did, except, Neha's right. They didn't judge me, even though they knew. They knew and they treated me like a person anyway. I look around the table, all eyes expectantly on mine.

'We don't have to talk about it any more tonight,' Neha says gently, pulling her hand away. 'We just wanted you to know.'

And just like that, Sam starts telling a story about an entitled customer at the cafe and the others are laughing again. The heat starts to ebb from my face, and I look up to see most of them are no longer watching me – except Neha, whose eyes keep drifting over to land on mine, and each time she gives me a small, reassuring smile.

Slowly I start joining in the conversation again, and soon I'm laughing along with these people like I've known them for years.

Most of the group are going back to Market Stepton, so Zoe drops Neha and me off first at the end of my road. We struggle out from the tangle of bodies in the back and spill on to the street, giggling. Zoe steps out of the car and pulls me into a bear hug.

'Don't let the bastards get you down!' she says as we break apart. The affection is still startling after so long, but I'm smiling so hard my cheeks ache.

Zoe climbs back into the car and speeds away, Robyn bouncing around in the back seat and waving through the fogged-up window.

'I'm the other way,' Neha says, gesturing up the street. 'I'm really glad you came out with us tonight.'

'I'm really glad you invited me.'

I'm unsure whether I should strike up one last conversation or say goodnight. I'm saved from the decision when Neha steps forward and hugs me. Her hair smells like bonfire smoke and the lingering scent of mango shampoo.

'Why are you being so nice to me?' I blurt into her hair. Neha pulls back and frowns.

'Why wouldn't I be?'

'We've never really spoken before,' I say, pulling at the fingers of my gloves. 'I mean. I know I helped you out and everything but—'

'You *really* helped me out.' Neha takes hold of my arm, as if willing me to understand. For a second she looks embarrassed, hesitates, and then apparently decides something. 'Remember the other week, after cross-country?'

I cringe. Of course I remember.

'Those girls really laid into you and I didn't do anything. I figured it was none of my business. But then you got between something even more intimidating to help *me*.' She takes a breath. 'I guess I realised I should have spoken up or something. And I wanted to make it up to you. And besides that ...' She gives my shoulder a squeeze. 'You really don't deserve the shit you're getting at the minute. Dan would be horrified, if everything I know about him is true.'

At the mention of Dan my eyes widen and my heart starts thumping in my chest. For the past few hours I've barely thought about him. It's almost a relief, having the weight lifted momentarily ... and then I feel awful for even thinking that, and the guilt comes crashing back down.

I must be making a face, because Neha drops my arm and casts her eyes to the ground. She starts slowly walking backwards.

'Meet me at the gates tomorrow after school,' she says, lifting her head again. 'We can go and get a coffee, talk if you want to.'

I nod vaguely, my mind already firmly back at the hospital, hovering over Dan's lifeless form. I watch Neha walk all the way to the end of the street, where she stops and turns to wave.

I wave back, managing what I hope is a grateful smile.

She disappears around the corner and I turn to head towards home. Just as I'm stepping through the front door my phone lights up with a notification, and I so nearly don't look – tonight has been such a relief I don't want to ruin it with another troll post about me. But curiosity gets the better of me and I look down to see that I've been added to a group chat.

For a second I wonder if someone is trying a fun new way to harass me more directly, but the notification reads '*Zoe Ward has added you to the group BONFIRE SQUAD*', with three fire emojis. My heart flips as I click into it and see that Sam has already posted a string of random memes.

For the first time since that awful night out, I feel like I'm a part of something good.

Twelve Weeks Before It Happened

My ears ring as the song we're playing crashes to a halt. From up on the cramped stage, I look over at Libby standing next to Katie and wink over the microphone. She waves, then immediately looks embarrassed. I suppress a laugh as we launch into the next song.

We've been a couple for about a month now, and this is the first gig we've had where I've officially had a girlfriend in the crowd. I'd always thought that might add more pressure, but over the last few weeks I've found myself playing songs to Libby that I wouldn't dare share with even the rest of the band. I know she's feeling nervous about being a member of the 'entourage', but having her out there feels like a good-luck charm.

Especially as the crowd feels particularly into it tonight. People are actually bothering to *look* at us up onstage, a couple of them even bobbing their heads in time with Aaron's drumbeat. It's just a social club in the next town over, but it might as well be Wembley for how exciting it feels to have people interested in what we're doing.

The relief I usually feel at the end of each performance is tinged with a hint of disappointment as we finish out our short set. We trundle offstage, all grinning as the small crowd gives us the most enthusiastic applause we've ever had. It's such a rush – all I want to do is get back up there.

Unfortunately, we need to start packing up. For now and the foreseeable future, we're our own roadies, so the next half an hour has us shoving our equipment into the back of Aaron's dad's transit van. Although it's mostly me doing all the packing – Lewis has baited Aaron into another argument over the third song in our set. At one point Aaron catches my eye over the drum kit and cocks his head with a *what's he like, eh?* grin, but I find myself irritated – this isn't the first time Lewis has managed to get out of loading duty. If it's not me doing the heavy lifting, it's Aaron or occasionally his dad.

After what feels like a lifetime I finish packing up (just in time for Lewis to concede on their argument, I notice) and we head back into the club for the girls. Libby has her back to me, but even from behind I can see the tension in her shoulders as she nods along to whatever Katie is chattering to her about.

'Hey, you.'

She turns and beams at me, and my stomach clenches lightly with guilt. Katie squeals and throws her arms around Lewis, proceeding to eat his face. Libby scrunches her nose.

'Now, why don't I get that kind of welcome?' I tease. She quirks an eyebrow at me and for a second I worry she might actually attempt it, so I quickly lean forward and brush my lips against her cheek. She flushes red.

For a beat we just stand there, unsure of what to do next, trying to ignore the slurping sounds coming from Katie and Lewis. It strikes me that we can just leave, and I reach out to grab her hand.

'Shall we get going?' I ask, starting to pull her towards the exit. Libby glances back over her shoulder at the thoroughly entwined couple.

'We're not waiting for the others?'

'Nah, Katie's mum is picking those two up and Aaron is going back in the van. You get me all to yourself.' My stomach flips through the potential interpretations of that statement. I drop her hand and clear my throat. 'I thought we could get something to eat and then grab a taxi – you hungry?'

As if it heard me, Libby's stomach answers with a loud grumble and she blushes all the way up to her roots, blurring her freckles. I can't help it – I burst out laughing, all the tension vanishing.

'So, chips then?' I say when I've regained my composure, as we head for the exit.

'Bye, Dan!' we hear Katie call from somewhere back in the darkness of the hall. 'And Libby!' she adds, a carefully calculated afterthought. She's still not quite adjusted to the fact she's not the only girl in our little group now. I roll my eyes at Libby and grin as I push open the heavy doors.

The cool evening air is a relief after the heavy sweatiness of the hall. It's one of those rare British summer nights that actually feels like summer. We walk slowly, chatting a little about the show as we meander down the deserted high street. Now that there isn't a guitar to occupy my hands, I pull idly at the loose thread inside the pocket of my jeans.

Libby stumbles a little and I catch her arm, laughing.

'How much did you drink?' I joke, but she looks up at me sheepishly.

'Katie kept buying more,' she admits, and we sit down on a low wall so she can collect herself. 'Her bar face is better than mine and Mona's ever was – if we wanted to drink we had to do it all before going out and nick it from Mum's alcohol cupboard.' She sways a little on the wall. 'Katie said she was wearing her best "distraction" top",' she adds, looking down at her chest. 'I don't think I've enough cleavage to try that trick.'

I don't know if I'm supposed to laugh, and I *really* don't know what I should say. My body settles for a weird, high-pitched giggle, and Libby snorts.

'It's still so strange to be hanging out with her,' she admits, mercifully moving on. 'She seems to have decided that because we're both "band girlfriends" we should be besties by natural law. I think I'd had about three conversations with her before we started going out.'

'Is it a bad thing? Hanging out with her?' I ask lightly. I know Katie takes a while to warm to people, and vice versa, but Libby and I have been spending so much time together lately I'm hoping that process will fast-track a little. 'I know she can be ...'

'... a lot?' Libby finishes, and from the glint in her eye I know she's being *extremely* tactful.

'Well, that's one word for it,' I laugh.

'She also talks about you like she owns you,' she says carefully, glancing at me sideways. 'It's a bit weird. Does she do that with everyone, or just to me about you?'

'Oh, everyone belongs to Katie,' I say, waving a hand. 'We've all got used to it.'

'It feels a bit like she's marking her territory. You guys were never ... ?' Libby double pumps her eyebrows.

'Me and Katie? God no,' I laugh. 'I don't mean to be a cliché but she's genuinely like my sister. Our parents made it clear they wanted us to grow up to be childhood sweethearts, but it was never like that.'

'Hmm,' Libby hums. I think she believes me, but is still overall sceptical about Katie. I decide to change the subject.

'Is Mona still away?'

'Still in France, yeah.' A shadow of worry passes over Libby's face. 'We call each other every day but I just wish I could be there for her properly. It's horrible not being able to give her a hug.'

I nod, unsure of what I could possibly say to help the situation.

'She'll be back before school starts again, right?'

'Yeah, her mum won't make her miss any school time,' Libby says. 'But I think they'll be there for another few weeks at least.'

We stand up and start making our way down the street again.

'Did you guys talk about playing some more acoustic stuff?' Libby asks, catching me off guard with the change of topic. I screw my face up in annoyance, but not at her.

'Lewis doesn't think it will go with our "sound",' I huff. 'Like we're so established that people will freak out if we changed tempo on one or two songs.'

'Have you even played them any of your new stuff?'

I know she's being supportive. I know it. But my teeth grit themselves anyway.

'They don't want to hear it. They wouldn't like it anyway.'

'You don't know that!' Libby insists, but I do. When I very casually broached the idea of adding in some slower songs at our last practice, bolstered by Libby's reaction to what I'd played for her, I was firmly shut down. Lewis had vetoed it before I'd even got a chance to play a single chord.

I don't mention that he'd said that acoustic guitars are for f-words, or the fact that he didn't say 'f-word', and that I just let that slide.

Libby links arms with me. 'Your songs are really, really good, you know. You're wasted singing other people's music.'

'You're the only person that seems to think so,' I sigh, kicking at the pavement. I feel like a petulant toddler.

'Only because I'm the only person you play them for,' she points out.

'That's different.' I look up at her and smile, despite the disappointment swirling in my gut. I look back down at my scuffed Converse. 'You get it.'

Libby nods. 'I know. They'll regret not being part of your backing band when you're winning all your Grammys though.'

I scoff, but find myself grinning at the thought. We discuss what would be on my rider for my sell-out shows, choosing more and more ridiculous things. By the time we walk into the chippy, my gloomy mood has vanished.

Neha

If I ever needed a reminder of how awesome my friends are, the way they welcomed Libby with opens arms last night is it. When Zoe made a new chat specifically to include her and we spent all night sending each other the stupidest stuff we could find, I felt a swell of love for my little group of idiots.

Libby had joined in immediately, but today her contributions have slowly tailed off. I haven't spotted her around at school to check in, but I assume the weight of the judgement she's been getting has made it harder to get involved.

Thank god we prearranged to meet up after school, so I can actually see how she's doing. I'm standing bouncing on my heels by the school gates, and most of the other students are long gone. I've been waiting for at least twenty minutes and am just wondering if I've missed her or if she's decided not to come, when she slopes out of the building with her head down. As she approaches I decide not to say anything and smile widely. I should have known that she'd want to avoid the rush.

'God, it took me three washes to get the smell of smoke out of my hair last night,' I say breezily, and we fall into step beside each other as we head towards the centre of the village.

Libby grunts something in response, twisting the ends of her own hair in her fingers.

'Slut!'

Some kid in a uniform barges past, knocking Libby into me. I glare after him.

'You know, I *really* hate that word,' I huff.

'It's not a favourite of mine either,' she says, digging a hat out of her pocket and jamming it over her head, pushing red curls under the woollen edges.

We keep going down the road, reaching the edges of the shops before long. There are no more insults thrown our way, but Libby walks with hunched shoulders and throws furtive glances over her shoulder every few steps.

'How was today?' I ask.

'Well, there was the box of pencil shavings in my bag during first period,' she starts, lifting a hand to count off on her fingers. 'The word "tart" in red marker on my locker over lunch. Oh, and Ethan Porter has started a rumour that I've been shagging him on the side,' she finishes bitterly. 'I mean, I assume he started it. I don't know anyone else that would think he was getting laid.'

I wince. 'Yeah, I heard that one actually. I felt bad for you, even if you did only sleep with him in his imagination.'

She groans. 'How am I supposed to claw back any semblance of dignity if I'm being judged for things I *haven't* done?'

'You didn't actually do the first thing, remember?'

She doesn't answer. We approach Taylor's tea room on the edge of the green, but Libby grabs my arm and steers me away – there's a group inside that I recognise from school. She darts into the second-hand shop next door and heads right to the back.

I trail after her, feeling helpless. 'How long are you going to keep hiding from people?'

'Until it all goes away,' she says stubbornly, plucking a CD from the shelf in an attempt to browse. I raise my eyebrows at her choice.

'*Barney's Greatest Hits?*'

Libby blinks down at the cover, the giant purple dinosaur leering up at her.

'Not really appropriate moping music, is it?' I say in an attempt to lighten the mood. When I see that isn't going to work, I gently take the CD from her hands and put it back. 'I won't pretend to know what you're going through right now, but this can't be a particularly healthy coping mechanism.'

'I never said it was healthy.'

'I just don't think Dan would have wanted you to hide like this—'

'Don't talk about him like he's dead!' Libby snaps.

We stand in silence. I know I probably crossed a line, but frustration is welling up in me and I can't push it all the way down.

'I'm sorry,' I say carefully, fighting not to add a *that you feel that way*, knowing how much of a non-apology that would be. 'I just meant that you can't keep skirting around life like this—'

'It's been working fine so far.' Libby is glaring down at her boots. 'Whatever. I'm just going to go home. I'll see you later.'

She stomps off towards the front of the shop. I take a step forward, opening my mouth to tell her to stop. But instead, I just watch her leave in silence and wonder if I've just blown up the first real friendship I was starting to have in this sodding village.

'So what's the deal with you and Libby?'

Direct as ever, Sam grins over his eggs and bacon at me from across the table. Since I moved, we've maintained a Sunday-morning ritual of breakfast at Beanz Cafe nearly every week – it's how he ended up with a job here.

I pretend to look thrown by his question while pushing hash browns around my plate.

'What d'you mean? We're friends. Or I think we are. She kind of snapped at me the other day. And she's gone completely quiet in the group chat.'

'That'll be over by Monday,' Sam says, waving it away. He picks up the ketchup bottle and pours a sticky blob out in the corner of his plate. 'You haven't introduced us to anyone from your school in the whole time you've been there, so she's obviously someone to make the effort with, right?'

'There's never been anyone I wanted to hang out with

outside of school,' I say with a shrug, hoping that's the end of it. Of course it is not.

'So then what's special about Libby?'

'You met her – you tell me.' It's a cheap tactic, but Sam chews thoughtfully and it seems to have worked. He swallows and points his fork at me.

'All right then. She's obviously got half a brain in her because she kept up with Zoe and Robyn the other night in the pub, and in the group chat. She's a little bit of a loner, which you find interesting, but she's friendly and witty so not in a boring way. And she's a redhead.' He shrugs, as if that settles something. 'You've got a thing for redheads.'

'Says who?'

He starts listing them off. 'Sadie Sink, Chappell Roan, Nicole Kidman specifically in *Moulin Rouge* …'

'Oh, all right,' I mutter, shovelling eggs into my mouth as my cheeks heat up. Sam laughs. He loves to win.

'And what's happening with this Dan guy? That really sucks for her that he's in the hospital.'

'It does,' I murmur in agreement. 'He was nice. One of those people that's friends with everyone but not many people really *know* him, y'know? Except for Katie, I guess. And Libby, when they started seeing each other.'

Sam nods, thinking. 'So are they still together then? With everything that happened?'

'It all happened at once. I don't think Dan ever found out, but who knows?' I shake my head. 'I think Libby is a bit in limbo about it all. They're together but he's not really "here", and everyone at school seems to think she deserves burning as a witch or something.'

The word *slut* echoes in my head from the other day. My hand curls into a fist without me telling it to.

'They're just being so shit to her. It wasn't even her fault. They all got her roaring drunk and then just *left* her to fend for herself.'

I think about waking up in Libby's bed the morning after Halloween, no idea where I was or what had happened the night before, and give an involuntary shiver.

'What's up?' asks Sam, noticing my switch from fury to fear.

'Halloween,' I say quietly, staring down at the table. 'When Libby found me … it was bad, Sam. Or rather, it could have been bad. And from the video, it seems like Libby was in the same state. Maybe even worse. Only no one was there to help her like she was with me.'

'That's why you need to invite her out again,' Sam urges. 'She's clearly someone worth being friends with. We like her. Show her we want to be her friends. She probably only snapped because she's wound like a yo-yo right now.'

I regard him ruefully. I don't want to let him win again, but it's hard when he's right all the damn time.

'I'll see what happens Monday,' I say.

'Attagirl,' Sam grins, and goes back to his bacon.

As it turns out, I don't have to be the one to extend a hand. Libby is waiting at the gates to school when I walk up on Monday morning.

'Morning,' she says sheepishly, offering out a steaming takeaway cup. 'I got you a hot chocolate. To say sorry for being an arse the other afternoon.'

'Apology accepted,' I smile, taking the cup. The warmth seeps through the cardboard and warms my hands. I take a sip prematurely and burn my tongue. *Argh!*

'Well, it does say "CAUTION HOT" on the side,' Libby chides, relief evident on her face at the fact that I took the apology. It's not what she's used to lately. I have to admire the way she holds herself as we walk towards the building, her shoulders back and her chin held high. I remember how she kept her head low the last time I saw her and wonder if that's the effect the day has.

'I didn't get a chance to say before I turned into Bitch Libby,' she says, glancing at me sideways. 'Your friends are all really lovely.'

'I only pick the best,' I say, a bubble of pride swelling in my chest. 'I'm just relieved we've all stayed so close after I moved away from Market Stepton.'

'Why did you move? It was, what, six months or so ago?'

'Well … more like eleven.'

Libby's eyes widen and her face flushes pink. 'Oh. Shit.'

'Don't worry about it,' I say, waving vaguely. 'I get that a lot, to be honest.'

'That doesn't make it better! God, our school is rubbish.' She looks down. 'Something I've learned quite quickly the last few weeks.'

We sit down on a low wall to drink our hot chocolate

before lessons start. Libby is quiet, waiting for me to answer her first question. I appreciate the patience. Even now it's still no easier to say.

'My parents died in a car crash. I had to move in with my Aunt Jas, so needed to change schools.'

'Wow.' I look round and Libby is staring at her hands, frowning. 'That ... that's shit.'

I laugh without meaning to. 'That's the best anyone has ever put it so far. Yes, it's total shit.'

Libby is still frowning at me. 'And here I am moaning about people calling me names.'

'It's a bit more than that,' I say, and give her a nudge. 'Anyway, my problems don't make your problems any smaller. That's not how it works. You're still grieving.'

Libby sighs. 'I don't even know if it's grief I'm supposed to be feeling. He's still technically here. How do you grieve for someone who's alive?'

I don't know how to answer that, but I'm no stranger to sudden complicated emotions. 'You feel whatever you need to feel, and you deal with it however you can. That's all you can do when something happens so out of the blue.'

Libby nods, and looks over at me. 'Do you mind me asking, how did you deal with your grief?'

I angle my head up to the pale grey sky. 'I sort of didn't? For weeks I refused to talk to anyone about it, not even Sam or Jas. It was so sudden, and from something so preventable, that all I felt for a long time was just anger.'

'At them?' Libby asks. It's not judgemental, just curious.

'I guess so.' I shrug. 'At them, at the driver of the other car, at the universe. At everything really.'

'That's understandable. I can't even imagine.'

'After a while I finally started to open up about it, process it a bit. I spoke to a grief counsellor for a while. They helped me to work out what I was feeling, and then what to do with those feelings – that was when I decided I wanted to be a paramedic. I want to help people the way they tried to help my parents, to give people that fighting chance. I'd been partway through driving lessons when it happened and at first I thought I'd never get behind the wheel again, but I knew I'd need it to qualify and the counselling helped me push through it and pass my test. It helped me to take control of it all.' I shrug. 'Maybe counselling is something to look into?'

'Maybe.' Libby sighs again and shakes her head. 'The situation feels so unfinished. The hope is the worst. It's crushing. A tiny, horrible part of me just wants it to end one way or another so I can start to process whatever happens, but I'm just stuck.' Her head snaps up as if she wasn't really concentrating on what she was saying. 'Oh god, that's awful, isn't it? Especially when you actually *have* lost someone. I'm so sorry.'

'You don't need to be sorry! What did I just say about feeling whatever you need to feel?'

Libby smiles sadly. 'I think after the accident I just felt numb,' she says. 'I couldn't work out what to feel then either. And with what I'd done on top of all that, it was just easier to get angry at myself.'

'You know you're really not what people are saying you are, Libby,' I say quietly. I stare down at my hot chocolate but I can feel her eyes on me. I clear my throat. 'I hate that you can't see how unfair they're being. It scares me to think what could have happened.'

Libby shivers and shrugs down a little deeper into her coat.

'Remember how I was, on Halloween?' I push. 'I was surrounded by people I knew, in someone's house. Some creep still managed to take advantage and separate me from everyone. I feel stupid for drinking so much when I wasn't used to it, but I don't blame myself for what happened. And I'm so grateful you came along.' I nudge her shoulder with mine. She leans into me.

'Halloween ...' she begins, and now it's my turn to stay quiet to give her the space to talk. 'How you were, it made me think of that night. It felt so uncomfortable. I didn't want to think of it that way.'

'I know,' I say gently. 'But you can't stay mad at yourself. You're safe, that's all that matters now. And so am I. Thanks to you.'

Libby looks up at me, our faces inches apart. 'I wish we had some subjects together,' she says. 'I'd like to have met you under better circumstances.'

'Hey, call it a silver lining,' I joke, and then feel stupid. But she smiles, and my insides do something funny. I swear her eyes flick down to my lips, just for a split second.

The school bell's shrill ring screams from inside the building. Libby and I jolt back from each other, and I look around quickly as though we've been caught doing something we shouldn't. With a feeling like I've swallowed cotton wool, I spot Katie West and her posse over by the school gates. Her head is turned in this direction but we're too far away for me to tell if she's looking at us.

I don't mention it to Libby.

We hurriedly stand and start walking towards the building.

'I've got Psychology now,' says Libby, gesturing as we reach the foyer. 'Can I meet you at lunch?'

'Sure,' I reply, and find myself looking forward to lunchtime for the first time since joining this place. She smiles and turns to walk away, and I speak before I have the chance to check myself.

'Libby?'

'Yeah?' She turns back to face me and I notice what a pale grey her eyes are.

'Oh.' I realise I don't have anything to say – I just wanted her to stay. 'Nothing. I forgot.'

She grins. 'Must have been a lie. My nan always used to say if you forget what you were about to say, it was a lie.' She heads down the corridor and I watch her go.

'I don't think it was,' I say to no one.

Over the next week I relax a little around Libby. We hang out after school, avoiding the places the rest of our classmates tend to frequent in the evenings. Mostly we sit on the swings in the small park by the ruins, talking until the sky grows dark and the air gets freezing.

We laugh at each other's childhood stories, and talk about what we want to do in the future. I tell her about my parents, how much I miss them, all the little things that remind me of them every day. We talk about almost everything. Everything except Dan.

It feels as though his ghost follows us around wherever we go. A phantom that, whenever Libby starts to relax, taps her on the shoulder and reminds her that she should be feeling terrible. I see it in her eyes; one second they're lit up, creased in laughter, and then she goes quiet and stares at the floor. Despite our conversation outside school, I know she can't shake the guilt away.

And no matter how much I try and ignore it, I'm starting to feel it too.

I relish the moments she spots me across the corridor, and being the reason her face changes from tight and anxious to open and smiling. I hold her gaze for longer than I know I should. When I hug her goodbye, I inhale her perfume in a way I can't deny is different from when I hug any of my other friends.

I find myself resenting a person that still might not recover, who's far from OK. And I feel terrible about it.

LIBBY

Every time I ask Neha to hang out with me outside of school, I'm terrified she's going to pull a face, sigh and tell me that she's getting a bit sick of being my social babysitter. But that never happens. She always agrees to whatever I've suggested with an enthusiasm that can only be genuine, and I feel a little bit giddy. It must be the novelty of having someone not horrified to be near me.

'So, my mum is working late tonight,' I say, as casually as I can muster. We're heading out of school, at what has become our scheduled lateness to avoid the crowds of people that might throw things at my head. Neha turns to me and smiles, eyebrows raised in anticipation.

'I was thinking maybe you could teach me how to bake?' I ask, as though it's a thought that's only just occurred to me. But I've noticed how animated Neha gets when she talks about either baking or her favourite musicals, those huge eyes of hers lighting up in excitement. I can't afford expensive theatre tickets, so baking it is.

'Oh, I'd love to!' Neha bounces on her heels a little and I laugh. 'Are you OK to walk through the village to pick up supplies?'

I hesitate, not having considered that would need to be part of the plan. I usually walk home the long way to avoid as many people as possible. But Neha looks so hopeful, and one look at her face makes the idea of other people feel far, far away. I smile. 'Of course. Let's go.'

We make it through the village without incident, and I let Neha take the lead in picking out ingredients from the minimart. As we breeze past the fresh produce, the ghost of the horrific conversation with Dan's mum on Halloween sends a shiver through me. I resolve to leave it in my rear-view, focusing instead on Neha as she plucks flour, eggs and chocolate chips from the shelves.

When we get back to mine, Neha sets to work straight away, nattering as she starts throwing ingredients together as though it's muscle memory. I just sit at our small kitchen island, resting my chin in my hand and occasionally adding in a '*mhmm*' or '*OK*' to show that I'm paying attention. And I *am* paying attention. Just not to the process of baking cookies. At some point Neha gets a smudge of flour on the side of her nose and it's so cute I can't bring myself to tell her.

'… and then they bake for about fifteen minutes!' Neha says with a flourish that snaps me out of my reverie. 'Well, a little under, if you want them gooey, which any sane person does.' She neatly slides the tray of dough blobs into the oven, closing the door and spinning back round to face me, beaming. The flour is still on her nose and I almost reach out to brush it from her face, before balling my hands into fists to squash the weird impulse to do something so embarrassingly intimate.

My expression must change because Neha's smile falters for a second. 'You OK?'

'Ah ... yeah,' I say, flustered. 'Erm. You've got flour on your nose.'

She swipes at it with her hand, getting most of it. 'Occupational hazard – oh!' As she moves her head, her ponytail suddenly unravels and dark hair cascades over her shoulders in waves. It's almost like a cheesy movie scene, and I blink at her in surprise as my cheeks start to burn.

'Hairband snapped,' she says, scooping her hair back over her shoulders. 'Um, do you have a spare? I hate having it loose when I'm baking.'

'Sure!' I spin on my heel and half flee from the room, then have to stop myself because I don't know why I'm being so ridiculous. 'Uh, I've got some upstairs.'

'Cool,' she says, seemingly not noticing my bizarre behaviour. I hear footsteps behind me and realise that she's following me upstairs. Which is fine. Of course that's fine. It's not like she's not been in my room before.

But this time feels different – for one thing, she's entirely conscious as she steps into my bedroom and looks around, smiling a little. I cross over to my dresser and start rummaging around for a hairband.

'I love your photos,' Neha says from somewhere behind

me. I finally find a band that doesn't have strands of red hair wound around it from being yanked off my own head and straighten up. Neha is standing over by my bed, staring up at my wall of Polaroids.

'Oh, thanks.' I move over to stand next to her. 'These aren't my good ones though.'

'They're not?' Neha turns and raises an eyebrow at me. 'Are you being self-deprecating, or are there other good ones you have in mind?'

I snort, in an entirely unattractive way, backing up towards the dresser. I'm worried my brain might have fallen out. I attempt to pull myself together, reaching down to grab my heavy scrapbook from the bottom drawer.

'*These* are my good ones.'

Neha takes it from me very carefully, and I feel a rush of affection at how much respect she has for it. She sits down on the edge of my bed and opens up the scrapbook.

As excited as I was to show her, I now feel extremely self-conscious. I'm also not sure where to sit. After dithering for a minute, awkwardly standing over her, I perch on the bed about a foot away and watch as she turns the pages slowly, taking her time to study each and every Polaroid.

While the ones up on my wall all feature people, the ones in the book are a bit less personal – and yet, they somehow feel even more personal to me. Like little pieces of my soul, reflected back at us on glossy photo paper.

I haven't shown this to anyone else before now. Not Dan, not even Mona.

'Libby, these are amazing,' Neha breathes, and I swell with pride. 'You're so good!'

'Odds were I'd be good at something,' I joke, and she jogs me with her shoulder. We're sitting much closer than we first were, but I don't move away again. She keeps flipping through the scrapbook and I simply watch her, the sound of the pages turning almost hypnotic. My eyes drift over her, down the length of glossy black hair as it runs down her back …

The smell of something like burned toast catches my senses. I wrinkle my nose. 'Can you smell—?'

'Oh my god, the cookies.' Neha jumps up, panic on her face. 'I forgot about the cookies!' She takes a second to carefully place the scrapbook back down on the bed, then dashes out of the room and down the stairs. I scramble up to follow her. When I reach the kitchen she's already yanking the oven door open, coughing and waving her other arm as a cloud of dark smog billows out. She snatches up the oven gloves and slides the tray out, carefully balancing what look like shrivelled discs of charcoal sitting on it.

I open the back door to let some of the smoke out as Neha gingerly places the tray on a wire cooling rack, staring dismally down at what were once cookies. I step towards her, looking down at the tray.

'Are they not supposed to look like that?'

Neha lifts her head to stare at me incredulous for a second, and I can't keep a straight face. I start to twitch, unable to hold in the mirth, and Neha's face relaxes into a reluctant smile as she shakes her head.

'Oh my god, don't. I'm mortified. I *never* burn stuff. That's Jas's trick!'

'Maybe they're salvageable,' I choke out, poking one of the cookies with a finger. Black dust crumbles away from it, and I'm off again.

'This isn't funny!' Neha insists, but her own voice is trembling and then we're both in hysterics. She grabs my shoulder to steady herself as we double over, howling, in a cloud of smoke, and I truly can't remember the last time anything was this funny.

After the cookie debacle, I resolve to leave it awhile before suggesting hanging out with Neha again. Despite no evidence, I'm still convinced that she feels obliged to look after me, so when I wake up on Saturday I'm steeling myself for a long, lonely weekend of staring at the ceiling. So it's a relief and a delight when my phone lights up with a notification from the Bonfire Night group chat.

NEHA
Bored. Anyone up for seeing the sights of Chipping Hollow today?

ROBYN
As enticing as that sounds I'm booked today! Gutted tho

NEHA
Har har

ZOE
I'm free! Sam, want a lift? I know you're not working today and you've no other friends

SAM
Excuse you, I am very popular and important

SAM
I'll take that lift tho

I laugh, but I don't chip in yet. Maybe Neha didn't mean to make plans in this chat and I'm not actually invited. I hold my breath as three dots appear besides the words *'Neha is typing'* ...

NEHA
Fabulous. Meet at the village green at 11? Libby, you up for it?

An hour later I'm heading across the village green towards Taylor's tea room, still unsure I like the outfit I picked out despite changing my jumper three times. Neha is already there, wearing the giant rainbow scarf again. For a moment I get to watch her before she's spotted me, swinging her arms by her sides as if she's nervous. When her eyes do catch mine, I feel the tension that seizes me whenever I leave the house melt from my shoulders.

'Hey!' she calls as I approach. I grin and wave a gloved hand, before feeling silly and stuffing it deep into my coat pocket instead.

'Heya,' I say, my breath coming out in clouds in the cold November air. 'Been here long?'

'Nah,' she replies. 'You're right on time. The others should be here in a sec—'

The sound of a car spluttering around the corner cuts her off. We turn to see Zoe's ancient Mini turning into the square, Sam waving at us like a maniac in the front seat.

They park up and tumble out of the car. Zoe, with no hesitation, immediately sweeps me into a hug and squeezes me against her chest. I feel a perfect blend of delight and alarm.

Sam bounces on the balls of his feet, grinning. 'Love this. A day out with my bitches!'

'Your what now?' Zoe releases me and turns to Sam, staring him down. Over her shoulder, Neha giggles.

'Uhh. A day out with my strong intelligent female friends?'

'Marginally better,' Zoe sighs, rolling her eyes.

We step inside Taylor's, the little bell above the door tinkling as we swing it open. For some reason this sends Sam into hysterics as we shuffle up to the counter.

'That's so *quaint*!'

Mr Taylor turns and beams at us. 'Good morning! How can I help …' His eyes land on me and he trails off, his jolly Father Christmas smile faltering.

'Hello, Libby. How're you getting on?' His voice is laced with pity. It feels somehow worse than any of the outright hostility, cloying and undeserved.

I shrink behind Neha, managing to squeak out 'Fine!' in a

voice a couple of octaves higher than normal. Mr Taylor just nods, then gruffly clears his throat before asking again, 'What can I get you all?'

Neha, Sam and Zoe all glance at each other, the frizzle of tension clearly detected. Then Neha steps forward and confidently says, 'Three coffees and an English breakfast tea to go, please.'

I smile at Neha for remembering my exact tea preference, feeling seen in a way that reminds me of Dan. But a noise from the back of the tea room catches my attention, and I turn to see a cluster of girls from school all staring daggers at me. One of them coughs something that might have been the word *slut*.

To my absolute horror, the others hear it too. Their heads snap round and Zoe looks like she might be about to say something, but I catch Neha shaking her head at her just slightly. I stare at the floor, my face on fire.

'There you go, m'loves,' says Mr Taylor, setting the drinks down gently on the counter in front of us. Zoe hands him some money and we leave in silence, Sam finding the little bell above the door much less amusing this time round.

We stand on the pavement outside the tea room, no one really knowing what to say. I want to bolt, and strongly consider opting out of the afternoon as I stare at the lid of my takeaway cup, unable to meet anyone's eye.

But then Zoe turns decisively and marches down the street, calling cheerily over her shoulder, 'Come on, let's see these ruins in the daylight.'

I raise my head and look at Neha, who's smiling encouragingly at me. I squash down the desire to run and hide, and start following Zoe.

We make our way across the village and up towards the ruins, the four of us squishing on to a bench by the edge of the park to get a good view over the whole of Chipping Hollow. Neha clears her throat.

'So, what do you think of our bustling village in the daytime?'

Sam and Zoe glance around at the 'bustling' scene. A bird takes flight across the ruins. In the distance, Mrs Bramley is ever so slowly making her way down the path towards the village green.

'Charming,' says Sam. 'It's giving *there must be more than this provincial life*, but I like it.'

I splutter into my tea and Zoe gives him a shove. 'Be fair!'

'No, no, he's being entirely fair,' I say. 'I semi-regularly run through the fields, searching for a greater purpose.'

We laugh, shaking as one with our shoulders bumping up against each other. I'm wedged between Zoe and Neha with Sam on her other side, and I feel a glow of warmth as the tension from Taylor's seeps away from us. With every passing moment the need to flee fades, and for the rest of the afternoon it's like I'm a whole person again.

Neha

I'm lying on my bed staring at the ceiling, the voice of Idina Menzel singing at the highest volume my puny laptop speakers will allow. Held loosely in my hand is my phone, which burns with anticipation of the call I'm about to make.

It should be simple – calling a friend I hung out with at school yesterday to invite them to a casual group event. We've been hanging out all week, for god's sake, but that guilt is nagging at me, reminding me that my feelings for Libby are a little less than casual and I need to get a grip. She has a boyfriend. A boyfriend who is in a coma.

I lift the phone in front of my face, still lying on my back. I scroll through my contacts until I get to her. Newly added: Libby Dixon. I hit call. I hang up. I wonder if that will show up as a missed call for her.

Seconds later the phone buzzes, answering my question. My fingers flinch as her name flashes on the screen and I promptly drop the phone on my face. Pain vibrates through my nose and I hiss, scrambling to pick it up again. I consider not accepting the call, but I can't think up a single reason why I shouldn't. I hit answer.

'Hello?' I squeak. Damn it.

'Neha?' Libby's voice is distant and curious. 'You just rang me?'

'Oh, did I?' I laugh unnaturally. 'Oh, I must have … I must have leaned on my phone or something.' I pray I sound casual, and not like I've forgotten how to be a human being.

'Ah, the victim of a butt dial,' Libby says knowingly. 'I was going to say, I can't remember the last time I got an actual phone call, even before my social estrangement.'

I laugh, cursing myself for not just sending a message like a normal person.

'Well, I guess I'll see you Monday then?'

'Wait!' It's half a yelp. What is wrong with me? 'Uhh, while I've got you on the phone, we're having a thing. Tonight.'

'OK … who is "we" and what is a "thing"?' she replies. 'Because this sounds like it might be illegal and you know I'm not that kind of girl, most of the time.' I hear her chuckle to herself on the other end of the line – the sound makes me want to spend all day just making her laugh.

'It's Sam, Zoe and Robyn. And me. I'll be there. Obviously.' Again, I laugh, but not my normal laugh.

Shut. Up. Neha.

'Sounds fun. What are you guys doing?'

'Just hanging out, watching some films. We're sleeping over at Zoe's.' I take a deep breath. 'You want to join us?'

'Oh!' There's a silence on the phone, and I can't decide if she feels awkward saying no or if she's still not used to people asking her to hang out with them. 'Yeah, will they not mind?'

'Of course not! They like you,' I say, probably a bit too eagerly. 'Do you want me to walk past yours? We can go together. About six o'clock?'

'Perfect. I'll be the one carrying my mother's awful green rucksack.'

I grin. 'Thank god you said – I'd never have spotted you otherwise. See you in a bit!'

'Bye!'

I drop the phone at my side and sigh. I look up at my poster of *Wicked*, pinned in prime position above my headboard.

'Don't look at me like that,' I tell Elphaba, and pull myself off the bed to get ready.

When I reach the corner where we'd agreed to meet, Libby is already standing on the kerb as promised with a lime-green rucksack over her shoulder and a pillow tucked under her arm. She smiles as I approach and hoists the bag a little higher on her shoulder.

'It's been a while since I've done this,' she says. 'The last sleepover I went to I must have been maybe thirteen?' She looks lost in a happy memory of something I wasn't part of, and not for the first time, I wish we'd met sooner. 'Unless you count Halloween.'

'Let's not.' I grimace, more than happy to forget about that night.

We reach the stop just as the bus is pulling up and climb on, wedging ourselves and our bags into two seats near the back. The windows have fogged over with the breath of a dozen other passengers, and the sun is saying its final farewell to the day, sinking away to nothing behind the skyline.

'So what's the plan?' Libby asks, her arms wrapped tight around her pillow.

'Oh, the usual,' I say. 'Pizza. Bad horror films. Sam will probably want to dig out the karaoke machine we gave Zoe for her birthday two years ago.'

Libby laughs, and seems to savour it. I'm gripped by the urge to hug her but swallow it.

We turn a corner and I reach across Libby to press the stop bell. As I bring my hand back it brushes against her shoulder, and I blush.

Stop it, stop it.

We hop off the bus and I lead us down a street of tightly packed terraced houses, towards one with a bright blue door. Libby grins.

'Matches Zoe's hair,' she says.

'Maybe not,' I laugh, lifting the door knocker.

Sure enough, the door swings open and Zoe stands before us with freshly dyed bubblegum-pink hair spilling over her face.

'Libby, you came!' She pulls Libby into another of her signature bear hugs.

'Nice to know *I'm* welcome too,' I say, stepping over the threshold. Zoe releases Libby and throws an arm over my shoulder, pressing her cheek against mine.

'You too, pudding,' she says, kissing the air next to my head. 'Shoes off, we're all in the front room.' She vanishes through a door, leaving us alone in the cramped hallway.

'She really is brilliant,' Libby laughs softly, bending to unlace her boots. I do the same, and we bump heads in the tiny space.

We go into the living room, both of us peeling off jackets and jumpers as it becomes evident that Zoe has the heating cranked right up. Sam is lounging across the whole sofa, with Robyn sitting cross-legged on the faux-fur rug. I just sit down on top of Sam's legs, causing him to yelp and mutter darkly at me.

I notice Libby's head turning slowly, taking in the whole room. It's small but bright and definitely, definitively Zoe. The wall adjacent to the fireplace is covered in paint swatches and doodles in thick black pen.

'Your house is amazing.' Libby breathes, eyes roaming the illustrations on the wall as she perches on the arm of the sofa. 'Did you paint all that?'

'I did,' says Zoe, chest puffing out in pride.

'Your parents let you?'

'They didn't have much choice, this isn't their house,' Zoe replies airily. 'I live with my nan and she lets me decorate how I want. She's also happy for me to have friends over whenever – she's upstairs right now with her hearing aid out and a Mills & Boon, so she's happy as long as I take some pizza up to her later.'

'Pizza?' Sam leans forward.

'Yeah, there's about eight in the freezer.'

'Dibs!' Sam leaps up and rushes from the room.

'You can't eat that much pizza!' shouts Robyn.

'Challenge accepted!' Sam calls from the kitchen. Robyn just shakes their head wearily, accepting that Sam will probably attempt to eat his weight in dough and mozzarella no matter what we do.

Zoe turns back to Libby. 'So, my lovely. How're things?'

'Thing-y,' replies Libby, twirling the ends of her hair. 'The last couple of weeks have been better, since I met Neha and you guys. I don't feel quite so much like burying my head in the garden.'

Zoe nods. 'That's progress.'

'How's Dan doing?' asks Robyn.

'More of the same,' Libby replies heavily. I reach over and squeeze her hand, and she smiles at me.

'That sucks,' Zoe murmurs. 'What are the doctors saying?'

'Just that he's stable but non-responsive. That's the last I heard. I haven't actually been in a while.'

Zoe opens her mouth to reply, but is interrupted by a call from Sam in the kitchen.

'Zoe, how the hell do you work this oven again? It's from the stone age!'

'It's just a regular oven! You've used it a million times!' Zoe shouts, pulling herself up from her chair. She gestures at Robyn. 'Help me with that idiot?'

'Why do you need my – oh!' Robyn grins, jumping up as I groan internally. 'Yeah, course!'

The two of them leave the room, Zoe shooting me a look on her way out of the door. Libby pretends not to have noticed and leans back into the sofa. Despite the heavy conversation, she's smiling a little.

'This is so nice. It feels as though I've got friends again,' she sighs. 'It's all still a bin fire, but at least I can talk about it with people now.'

'You *do* have friends,' I say. 'We're your friends. You don't have a choice once this lot latch on. Tonight is your official absorption.'

She laughs. 'I think I can handle that. It's been so weird going from all to nothing. When I was with Dan …' She trails off, looking wistful, and I feel another guilty pang that I can't pretend isn't jealousy. 'It was weird, suddenly being quote-unquote popular.'

'Nice weird?' I ask, curious. At my old school I had Sam, Zoe and Robyn, but I never felt that mysterious glow of school popularity.

'I suppose,' she muses. 'I dunno. It was all a bit "squad goals", I never felt like I actually belonged there.'

I groan. 'Relatable. Since I moved I feel like there's "squads" everywhere that I'm not a part of.'

'The thing is, part of me feels like that was sometimes the point?' says Libby.

'How do you mean?'

'Well, Katie, for example,' she says. 'She was forever posting photos of the two of us with captions like "sister from day one", which is kind of hilarious. We've definitely *known* each other since we were tiny, but she never had time for me before I got together with Dan. It just felt like she wasn't doing it to make me feel included, but make other people feel *ex*cluded. Does that make sense?'

'It does,' I say, thinking about all the times I've scrolled through the profiles of my classmates, feeling like I'm on the other side of the glass at an exhibit, looking in.

'I'm sure that's not the case for everyone.' Libby continues. 'But it's so hard not to take it that way sometimes. Especially now, when I see posts of people that used to be my friends talking about how great it is for them all to be together.'

'I bet.'

Libby looks over at me and smiles again, making my chest squiggle. 'It's a lot easier when I've got other people to focus on though.'

I try desperately not to read into that. We're sitting close on the sofa despite being the only ones now on it. I can smell the mint of her toothpaste; she must have brushed her teeth just before leaving the house.

'Pizza!' Sam calls, bursting back into the living room with a plate held high above his head. 'Not burned or anything!'

Sam, despite his assumptions about my feelings for Libby, seems oblivious as he takes a huge bite of pepperoni pizza. Zoe and Robyn come back into the room bearing bags of crisps and pretzels.

Zoe puts on the first film and turns out the lights. Next to me I can feel Libby's arm, pressed against mine, burning through my jumper. I laugh when the others laugh, paying no attention to what's happening on screen. My brain is buzzing. I don't know what's wrong with me. Or I do, but I don't actually want to know.

When the film finishes, we separate off and change into whatever it is we're sleeping in. Libby emerges from the bathroom in sweatpants and a Fall Out Boy T-shirt. I feel silly in my Hello Kitty pyjama set, but she grins at me and says she has some similar ones at home.

We pile back into the living room, wriggling into sleeping bags and kicking at each other for more floor space. Sam has commandeered the sofa. He grins at us all from his snuggly position amongst the cushions.

Zoe puts the next film on and again I find myself in the dark next to Libby. This time, separated by two layers of quilted sleeping bag, I relax a little more and actually take in the film. Or maybe it's more to do with Sadie Sink gracing the screen, attempting to break a witch's curse. I remember what Sam said about redheads and blush in the dark.

I notice the others have started to drop off. Zoe starts snoring softly in her armchair, pink hair fluttering in front of her face. Robyn has gone quiet and Sam is still, a sure sign that he's no longer conscious. I sneak a peek at Libby. Her eyes are still open, the TV screen reflected in them. She's smiling ever so slightly.

The film ends, the credit music starting up as names roll across the screen. Libby stretches a little and looks around. Realising we're the only ones left awake, she tips her head towards the door.

'Cold pizza?' she whispers, slowly unzipping her sleeping bag. I nod, and we make it out of the living room into the hall without kicking Robyn on the floor in the dark.

The remnants of our pizza feast are left on the kitchen counter, and we both take a piece and lean up against the worktop in the dark. Libby's face is thoughtful as she chews. I wait for her to speak.

'Thank you so much for inviting me tonight. It's great to do something normal.'

'You call that lot normal?' I laugh, but she's looking at me with serious eyes.

'I mean it,' she says. 'I love that they're just so themselves. I don't think I noticed how cookie cutter everyone in Chipping Hollow tries to be, even after …'

She trails off, staring into the distance for a moment before coming back to herself, blushing at something. But she breezes past it without comment.

'But with these guys, I feel like I'm not seconds away from tripping myself up. I always felt so on edge, as if I was going to say the wrong thing and ruin everything.' Libby laughs bitterly. 'And then I went and did something way worse than saying something a bit silly in front of Katie West.'

She looks over at me again. 'I never said thank you for what you said the other day as well. About grief and alcohol. I think I'd have beat myself up about it for the rest of my life if it wasn't for you. I sort of still am. But not quite as much.'

'You're smart, you'd have figured it out eventually,' I say. 'I'd just rather you figured it out sooner, that's all.' I push her gently. She shoves me back. We're standing very close together in the tiny kitchen, lit softly by the moonlight streaming in through the window behind us. I'm seized by the wild notion that I should kiss her.

Just as I feel like I might do something really stupid, Robyn walks in and I jump back a little.

'Why are you in the dark?' they ask, flicking on the big light and then blinking at the glare. They swipe a piece of pizza and hoist themselves up on to the counter. 'Midnight feast without us? How very rude.'

'We're having a side party,' says Libby, and I must be imagining it but she sounds almost flustered. 'Care to join?'

'Don't mind if I do.' Robyn grins and takes a large bite of pizza. 'I'm sure I can elevate this party.'

I raise my eyebrows at them. They throw a tea towel at me.

The three of us return to the living room, stifling giggles. We climb back into our bags, Libby and me squashed up together by the sofa.

Libby falls asleep quickly, breathing deeply and murmuring a little. I trace the curves of her face with my eyes, mapping out every last freckle from memory as her face is bathed in darkness. I start to feel creepy and stare at the ceiling instead.

We wake up the next morning, groggy and uncomfortable with elbows and knees all in each other's backs. With nothing but pizza crumbs in the house, we pile into Zoe's car and drive to McDonald's for breakfast.

Over McMuffins and steaming cups of coffee we perk up

a little, and it isn't long before Sam is throwing balled-up napkins around the table. We leave giggling, lukewarm paper cups in hand. Zoe makes us finish them before we get back in her car.

She drops us all off home, one at a time. I notice she deliberately takes the long way around to make sure Libby and I are the last two left in the back seat. We pull up to Libby's house and she struggles out.

'Thanks so much!' she calls, waving as she heads down her driveway. I wave as we pull away, falling back against the headrest when we round the corner. Zoe eyes me in the rear-view mirror.

'What?'

'Nothing,' Zoe says, eyes flicking back to the road. 'Just thinking.'

She drops me outside my front door. The house is quiet, Jas probably passed out in her room after a long night shift. I head up to my room and collapse on my bed, abandoning my sleeping bag in a heap on the floor. I'll pick it up later.

I think about what Sam said, what Zoe insinuated. The way Libby looked, so incredibly peaceful, when she was fast asleep …

No. She's got a *boyfriend*. She doesn't need any more complications right now. I resolve to put aside any weird feelings when she's around. I decide to pretend it's indigestion.

Having made this decision, I feel a little safer. It's fine. It's platonic. All good.

I hit play on the *Beetlejuice* soundtrack and crank up the

volume on my headphones to distract myself from thinking any more on this.

November rolls along without anyone really noticing. One evening I come home to find Jas up a ladder, rummaging around in the loft disturbing the dust.

'What are you doing?' I ask, taking hold of the ladder to steady it. 'Also, what's the rule about potentially dangerous activities while alone in the house?'

'Christmas decorations aren't dangerous!' Jas shouts down through the trapdoor.

'You could electrocute yourself on fairy lights,' I call back. 'Or what about falling down the ladder?'

'Grinch!' she shouts back. Her feet appear at the top of the ladder and she wobbles down, balancing a box bursting with fake pine branches on her arms.

'It's not December yet, you know,' I say when she's safely back on the landing. 'People will talk.'

'Let them.' Jas dumps the box and heads back up the ladder. 'I like them up as early as possible! It's December next week anyway.'

We get the rest of the decorations down without incident and pile the boxes up in our tiny living room. There's the annual festive battle to get the tree up, and at least twenty minutes spent detangling lights. Jas removes herself to the kitchen after a particularly violent fight with the cords, and I call her back in when they're all neatly arranged on the tree so we can start tinsel duty.

'So, what's going in your letter to Santa this year?' Jas asks as we're hanging baubles.

'I was thinking maybe a Porsche,' I say lightly. 'Or a Ferrari. I haven't quite decided.'

'What's wrong with my Nissan?'

'You mean besides all the McDonald's packaging in the back seat?' I laugh.

'Rude!' Jas throws a plastic candy cane at me. 'So does that mean you don't want to share … ?'

'What?' I stop and stare. Jas is grinning.

'I've put you on the insurance. Call it an early Christmas present.'

I drop the string of silver beads I'm holding and throw myself at Jas.

'Oh my god, are you sure?' I squeal into her ear. 'I mean, with Mum and Dad …'

Jas squeezes me tight. 'I'm so proud of you for carrying on with your lessons when you did. I nearly burst when you told me you wanted to train to be a paramedic. And I figure you'll need to keep up with driving for that! No point you having your licence and not being able to use it. Besides –' she pulls away and grins at me – 'I'm only *really* doing this so I don't have to give you a lift any time you want to go beyond the village. Calm down.'

'Shan't.' I pull her back in for another hug and she laughs.

We go back to decorating. I can't wait to tell Libby. It takes me a few minutes to consider that I should be excited to tell everyone, not just Libby. I sigh out loud without meaning to.

'What's up?' Jas frowns. 'You were buzzing a second ago. Decided against it?'

'Definitely not.' I look down at the carpet. 'I was just thinking about something.'

'Libby?'

I look up in surprise. 'How did you know?'

'Because I know you,' Jas replies simply. 'Come on. Spill. Tell me all.'

I drop down on the arm of the sofa. 'She's still kicking herself about "cheating" on Dan. She's not going to even *start* to forgive herself properly until he wakes up.'

'If he wakes up,' Jas says softly. 'Have you two talked about the fact he might not? She's going to need a lot of support if worse comes to worst.'

'I know,' I say miserably. 'But she doesn't like to talk about it. I think she tries to forget, but then feels guilty so just dwells on it.'

'Poor kid.' Jas nods. 'I'm glad you two became friends. I think she needs you.'

I don't reply, twirling a loop of ribbon between my fingers. I wonder if I'm starting to need her a little bit too.

As if she's reading my mind, Jas gives me a nudge. 'Anything else about Libby you want to talk about?'

I give her a look, but she just carries on hanging tinsel. 'Like what?'

'Come on, give me some credit,' she replies breezily. 'I know you well enough to know when you've got a crush on someone.'

'I do *not* have a crush on Libby!' I protest, but too forcefully.

Now it's Jas's turn to give me a look. I crumble. 'OK, fine, I have a teeny-tiny-completely-unreciprocated crush on the only friend I've made since I moved here. So what?'

'Teeny-tiny, huh?' says Jas, raising an eyebrow.

'She has a *boyfriend*,' I groan. 'A boyfriend *in a coma*.'

'I'm aware of the particulars,' says Jas. 'That doesn't invalidate your feelings though.'

'It's not like I can act on them.'

'Maybe not,' Jas muses, and for some reason I feel a little bit disappointed, as if she might have been about to give me some sort of permission. 'But that doesn't mean they're not there. I figured you'd probably need to talk about it at some point or you'd explode.'

I feel a rush of love for my aunt, and, despite how annoying it is sometimes, relief that she can read me so well. I glance up at the photograph of my parents on the mantelpiece and the familiar nostalgic sadness settles over me.

'I wish Mum and Dad were here,' I say wistfully.

Jas smiles. 'Because they'd know what to do?'

I laugh, surprising myself. 'Oh, definitely not. Wouldn't have a clue. Would still be tripping over themselves to reassure me that it was totally OK I liked a girl.' I smile fondly at the memory of Mum shouting at the TV whenever an Asian family was depicted as homophobic as default. 'I just wish I could get a hug, that's all.'

'Well, it's a poor substitute, but I can help with that a bit,' says Jas, opening her arms. I hug her again, and this time I don't let go for a long time.

LIBBY

I'm only half paying attention when I hear my name called at the front of the class, rousing me from a daydream. Having arrived early to hide myself in the back corner of the room, I'm now forced to watch everyone take turns twisting around to stare at me.

'Libby Dixon?' Mr Grahams calls again, reading from a running order printed on a sheet of paper. I rise slowly and drag myself to the front, twirling a memory stick between my fingers. There are a few murmurs but nothing audible in the vicinity of a teacher.

I stuff the memory stick into a USB on the computer at the front, searching for the hastily thrown-together presentation on character tropes I finished last night. We were supposed to work in pairs, but there's an odd number of people in this class, and guess who drew the short straw of working alone.

'When you're ready, Libby,' says Mr Grahams. The room

falls silent and all eyes are on me. It feels strange to think that they're supposed to be.

I clear my throat and boot up the presentation. The first slide pops up.

'*Slut.*'

It's quiet, barely a whisper. But I hear it. I'm supposed to. My eyes dart around the room but every face is straight.

'*Whore.*'

Again, but a little louder. I look desperately to Mr Grahams, who's frowning out at the room – he heard that one too. 'I'd like to think you're all more mature than this,' he says in a warning tone. 'I won't have that kind of language in my classroom.'

'*Tart.*'

My hands fumble and I drop my cue cards. Someone sniggers as I scrabble on the floor to pick them all up.

'*Skank.*'

'All right, come on, at least stand up and say it to my face,' I snap, jumping up and glaring around the room. There's a ripple of laughter and I know I must look ridiculous, shouting at no one. Mr Grahams stands and walks over to me, turning his back to the class and bending over me to speak in a lower voice.

'Libby, do you need to step out for a moment?'

'I'm not doing anything wrong!' I say, struggling to keep my voice level as my chest tightens. I feel almost hysterical. Someone is still giggling, though Mr Grahams is blocking my view of who.

'I know, I know,' he says, in a tone that I think is meant to be soothing but just feels patronising. 'But maybe it would be less disruptive for you to do your presentation at another time?'

I feel as though I'm shrinking, or maybe that's just my lungs. I take a step backwards and bump into the computer table, sending the mouse clattering to the floor.

'Libby!'

I turn and run from the room, but not before I hear another muttered '*slut*' called out behind me.

I stagger down the corridor, desperately trying to drag air into my lungs. I reach the main doors and burst through them, and run straight into Neha.

'Whoa, Libby!' she laughs, stumbling to one side but staying upright. 'I'm so glad I literally ran into you!' She digs her hand into her pocket and pulls out a cluster of jangling key rings, a single car key hanging next to a miniature fluffy dice. 'Jas put me on the insurance, I can finally use my – hey, what's wrong?'

I shake my head and try and sniff back the tears, resulting in the most ridiculous snort I've ever heard. Neha grabs my shoulders and angles me towards her, bending her knees to look directly into my downcast face. My chest heaves as the air seems to become thinner and the world spins wildly in front of me. I lurch into Neha for the second time in thirty seconds, but she catches me and manoeuvres me quickly to the stone steps leading down from the school doors. She sits me down, crouching in front of me so she's looking up into my face.

'OK, Libby? We're going to sort you out, yeah?' She puts

her hands lightly on my knees as if steadying me, but without making me feel claustrophobic. 'I know it feels like there's not enough air, but I promise you there is. We're going to breathe together, OK?'

I nod breathlessly, my knuckles going white as they grip the edge of the step and I stare without seeing over the top of Neha's head. Somewhere in the back of my mind, I remember gratefully that we're still technically in the middle of morning lessons so the likelihood of anyone coming across me freaking out is slim.

Neha gives my knees a squeeze and draws a deep, deliberate breath in.

'Come on, Libby. In ... out ... in ... out ... in ...'

I struggle to match Neha's rhythm, but she keeps it up and soon my shuddering breaths are in time with her soothing voice. Even once I've steadied she keeps going, waiting for me to nod that she can stop. She rises to her feet and perches next to me on the step, leaving me a little space.

'Bit better?'

'Thank you,' I whisper. I rub my head as the oxygen rushes back into my brain.

'Any time,' she replies softly, placing a hand on my arm and squeezing gently. I turn and bury my head into her shoulder, dampening her jumper with my tear-streaked face. She wraps her arms around me and draws me in, saying nothing.

Eventually I pull back and rub my face with my sleeve. I feel weightless, enveloped in that weird floaty feeling you get after having a good cry that you really needed. It makes me a little light-headed as I close my eyes and concentrate on the distant sounds of the occasional car passing by, the feel of the breeze on my tear-stained cheeks, the warmth of Neha's body beside mine.

As the world returns to me, I finally think to ask, 'What are you even doing out here?'

'I overslept,' Neha replies simply. 'Probably going to get called up on for being late, but to be honest, now I'm pleased that I was.'

I smile weakly and go to rest my head back on her shoulder, but Neha jumps off the step and grabs me by the hand, pulling me away from the building.

'What're you doing?'

'We're going on a trip,' Neha replies, still moving swiftly towards the small car park at the side of the school. 'We're already both going to be in trouble for missing lessons. You need some head space from all this. And I've got the car now, so this can be our first road trip!'

'Can we really do that?' My protest is weak, backed by nothing as I allow myself to be pulled across the tarmac. I cast a look back over my shoulder, struck by the paranoid thought that someone will be watching us from the windows. Even as sixth-formers, we're not supposed to leave the grounds in the middle of the school day.

But no one is watching, and although Mr Harper's terse warning about me missing more lessons is in the back of my mind, it somehow doesn't feel so important with Neha's hand in mine. Her conviction is infectious.

We approach a small, pale blue car parked on the far side and Neha unlocks it with a pip of her new car keys. She swings open the door and places me firmly in the passenger seat, before moving around to the driver's seat, dropping into the car and starting the ignition.

'Where are we going?' I ask.

'Far enough away for it to matter.' Neha smiles sideways at me and pulls on to the main road out of the village, heading towards the motorway. She taps on her phone a few times to connect to the car's Bluetooth and the soundtrack to one of the more obscure musicals she's tried to introduce me to over the past few weeks fills the car.

My eyes begin to flutter closed, my body feeling entirely worn out. Bundled up in the passenger seat of Neha's car, with her singing show tunes under her breath beside me, I feel my body slowly, finally start to relax. I sink back into the seat, allowing the exhaustion to overtake me without having to really think about it. I'm safe.

I must doze off because when I sit up straight to stretch, we're pulling into a car park in front of a wide expanse of beach. 'Where are we?' I ask blearily, squinting at the pale white sunlight that streams through the clouds.

'Oh, you're awake,' says Neha. She pulls into a space and shuts off the engine, turning to smile at me. 'Portness. I thought we could do with a couple of hours on the slot machines.' She nods across the car park to a row of tourist shops and arcades, the few open ones looking a little over-eager in bright neon colours on this overcast day. An elderly couple in matching anoraks are shuffling along the front, soon disappearing behind a row of claw machines stuffed with Care Bears.

We step out of the car into the late November chill, pulling our coat collars up. The air feels damp on my skin, and I inhale the tang of the sea salt deep into my lungs. Neha takes my hand and we rush over to an arcade with 'Freddie's Funhouse' in half-popped light bulbs above the entrance, bowing our heads against the wind.

We stumble to a halt just inside the entrance, laughing at nothing and ignoring the looks we're getting from the arcade's few patrons. I realise that we're still in our school uniforms, but before I have time to feel self-conscious about it everyone has already gone back to their machines. I look round at Neha, and as she smiles at me, any worry about being caught truanting fades away completely.

Neha pulls her purse from her bag and makes a beeline for a change machine. She begins feeding in pound coins, and I struggle to catch the two-pence pieces the machine spits out.

By the time we emerge an hour later, giggling with our fingertips reeking of copper, we've won three lollies, two more key rings for Neha's new car keys, a plastic yo-yo and a rubber bouncy ball that we immediately lose down the seafront.

'Good haul.' Neha nods appreciatively as we head back to the car to dump our slot-machine treasures. She digs around in the boot for a while before unearthing a slightly musty woollen blanket, and I look at her questioningly.

'You can't have a picnic without a picnic blanket,' she says, tucking it under her arm.

'You can't have a picnic without a picnic either,' I laugh, but she's already leading us to one of the many fish and chip shops lining the front.

A short time later we're making our way down to the beach with a steaming bag of hot chips. Neha unrolls the blanket and spreads it out over the firm sand, sitting down quickly to stop the wind from snatching it away.

I drop down next to her and accept the greasy parcel she passes me. 'Isn't it a bit late in the year for a beach picnic?'

'This way we get the whole place to ourselves!' she says, gesturing to the empty beach. Over to the left a pier stretches out across the flat sand, the end stopping well before it reaches the sea. Nestled against the coastline is a fairground, a pop of colour and noise against an otherwise grey scene. In the distance by the sea are two figures walking close together, but other than that we're completely alone.

Neha's head is turned, taking in the view, her long dark hair billowing around her in the wind. I remember Bonfire Night and smile, quietly taking my camera from my rucksack. There's a *click* and *whirr* as I snap a shot, and Neha turns in surprise.

'Sorry,' I say, taking the yet-undeveloped Polaroid from the front of the camera and placing it face down on the blanket. 'I haven't really felt like taking many photos lately, and I never usually warn people when I'm about to take one. You get better shots that way.'

'That remains to be seen!' she protests, but seems pleased. I know it will be a great photo.

We dig through the chips, burning our mouths and fingers. When I look up at Neha, she starts laughing.

'You've got ketchup on your mouth,' she says, gesturing.

I rub my face and she laughs again.

'Wrong side! Bloody hell, come here.'

She leans across the blanket towards me. Her breath flutters across my face, and I'm close enough to count every eyelash. She gently swipes at my lips with a napkin, hovers for a moment, and then quickly draws away.

I clear my throat. 'Gone?'

'All sorted,' she says, eyes cast down. She lies back against the blanket, stretching out and staring up at the deep grey sky. I lie down next to her, watching the shifting clouds above us. The dampness from the sand starts seeping through into my back, but I don't care. When I move my arms to my sides, I find my hand brushing against Neha's. She doesn't move it away, and we lie there silently for a few minutes just watching the sky.

A heavy raindrop splashes against my nose, making me jump, jerking upright as Neha laughs. More droplets follow the first and in seconds we're sitting on a soggy blanket in a downpour.

We shriek and laugh, scrabbling to collect the rubbish and stuff it into the now-empty chips bag. I snatch up the Polaroid and tuck it away in my pocket as Neha whips up the blanket, and we take off across the sand. I look over at her as we run, her hair streaming and soaked, blanket flying behind her like a tartan cape, eyes screwed up against the rain but her face lit up in laughter. The sky may be getting darker but she's glowing from the inside out.

We stumble back up the beach and over to the car park, throwing everything in the boot in one sodden mess. We dive into the car, panting, still laughing and shivering from the icy rain.

'Well, that's one way to b-break up a p-party,' I gasp, grinning.

Neha fishes a hair scrunchie from the glove compartment and pulls back her wet hair. 'I was going to suggest an i-ice cream, but it might be a bit too c-cold.'

'Well, a day at the beach in N-November was a bit of a long shot,' I chatter, running my hands through my own dripping hair. Neha pulls off her school jumper, heavy with rainwater, and tosses it in the back seat. I divert my eyes away from the way her damp shirt clings to her, my cheeks warming despite the chill throughout my body.

I wriggle out of my own jumper to distract myself. 'I know we're fecking f-freezing and the chips got wet b-but that's probably the best afternoon I've had in a-ages.' I grin, teeth clacking together, audible even over the sound of the rain drumming against the car bonnet.

'G-good!' Neha reaches over and hugs me, and something warm blooms in my chest. 'You needed it.' She pulls away and reaches for the ignition as I suppress a giddy shiver.

'R-right, well, the beach portion of the adventure has been cut sh-short,' Neha stutters. 'What n-now?'

I don't want the day to end, but I also don't want her to feel like she has to babysit me. I delay having to answer by fiddling with the car's heat settings, feeling a blast of hot air against my feet that gives me pins and needles. We sit for a moment just waiting to stop shivering.

'Jas is working tonight?' says Neha tentatively. 'We could go back to mine and watch cheesy Hallmark Christmas films?'

'Oh, sounds bliss,' I sigh, dropping back into the seat.

We pull up alongside a row of terraced houses, Neha managing to squeeze her car into an absolutely tiny space. I find myself breathing in as she parks up.

'Can you believe that's the first time I've done that?' Neha laughs as I breathe out theatrically. We climb out of the car and head towards the house with a bright red front door, a Christmas wreath hanging from the door knocker. Neha unlocks it and steps inside.

'Welcome to our humble abode!' She gestures around the hall, small but decorated with bright Christmas ornaments and tinsel. She kicks off her boots and catches me staring at the decorations.

'Yeah, Jas likes to put stuff up early,' she says by way of explanation. 'And we're strong believers in crêpe paper and gaudiness.'

We head into the living room, which is dominated by a tall

fake pine tree glistening with baubles and silver streamers. An open fireplace is across from a large, squashy-looking sofa. The mantelpiece is adorned with more tinsel and figurines of gingerbread men and chubby angels with tiny wings.

Neha is lighting Christmas candles on the coffee table, and the smell of apple and cinnamon wafts into the air. I wander over to the tree and examine what appears to be a piece of a cardboard egg box, daubed with red paint and glitter. I lift it gently and see 'NEHA G' written in Sharpie on the underside. I smile and imagine a tiny Neha in playgroup, hacking away at an egg box to make a Christmas ornament for her tree.

'Do you need a fresh jumper?' Neha asks. 'Mine's still wet and I'm freezing.'

I nod and she disappears from the room, returning with a bundle of wool. She tosses it to me and I unfold it to reveal a bright green jumper with a giant Rudolf face knitted on to the front. I raise my eyebrows at her.

'I did tell you we like tacky,' she giggles, yanking her own blue jumper over her body. Hers is adorned with a snowman in a bobble hat. 'These are my and Jas's Christmas Eve jumpers.'

I pull mine on and stand up, wriggling around trying to find the armholes. I get all my limbs in the right place and look down at the monstrosity. 'Well,' I say, deadpan. 'Aren't we attractive?'

Neha laughs. 'They're festive! Just what we need after a day at the beach.'

I snort, then reach for my bag to grab my camera again.

'Whoaa, I didn't say I wanted to document this,' Neha says, waving her hands. 'You could use it as blackmail.'

'Trust me, this is just for us.' I drop down on the sofa next to her, turning the camera around so it's pointing at us. 'Say cheese!'

I pull my tongue out at the lens and the bulb flashes. I take the square of developing paper from the front as we blink away the lights dancing in front of our eyes.

We choose something awful-sounding from the True Christmas channel, and by the time little Jimmy has discovered the true meaning of Christmas we're both nodding off. As the credits begin to roll, Neha's head drops on to my shoulder and she snores softly. I reach carefully for the remote and switch the TV off.

As the music cuts off and the screen goes black, I become very aware of Neha's body, warm against mine and shifting slightly as she dreams. I lower my head against hers, smelling that her shampoo has changed from mango to strawberry.

I slowly realise it's been hours and hours since I thought about Dan – at the arcade, on the beach, even on the drive back home as we sang along to the radio. Even watching an emotional Christmas film didn't stir up any feelings, any longing to be sitting with Dan instead.

I look down at Neha, oblivious and asleep.

I think I might be in trouble.

Fourteen Weeks Before It Happened

A trickle of sweat slips down the back of my neck, making me shiver for a second despite the late June heat. We're sat on a picnic blanket on the grassy banks of a sprawling lake, the midday sun bouncing off the water and making any of us who forgot sunglasses (me) squint any time they turn in that direction. There's only so many times you can hang out at the ruins in the village before you're ready to tear down every remaining brick out of boredom, so we piled into Aaron's dad's van and drove out to our nearest beauty spot to make the most of the sunshine.

Lewis and Aaron are mucking about down by the water, but I'm waiting up on dry land because I know Libby will be here soon. Stretched out beside me across the blanket is Katie, wearing a frilly pink bikini top and the shortest pair of denim cut-offs I think I've ever seen. I can hear the thump of the bass from her earbuds so I can't imagine she's asleep, but a pair of thick-rimmed white sunglasses are obscuring her eyes so I can't be sure.

Just as I'm having this thought, she lifts her head and props herself up on her elbows, looking round and realising that we're alone. She smiles.

'Still no Libby?' she asks, an innocent lilt in her voice. 'Not stood you up, has she?'

'She'll be here,' I say mildly, knowing better than to give her a rise. I glance down at my phone to confirm to myself that yes, she did text to say she was on her way. I repress a sigh of relief – it would be hell to have to tell Katie if I had, in fact, been stood up.

'Mmm,' Katie hums, turning her head to survey the expanse of lake. 'Such a funny couple, you two.'

'How so?' I try to keep my voice level, bored even, because I can tell Katie's gearing up for a challenge – we've done this dance together so many times.

'Oh, you know,' she says vaguely, waving her hand. 'I just wouldn't have put you two together. And you *know* I tried to pair you up with one of my girls. You could have picked anyone.'

'I don't think that's accurate,' I say. 'Even if it is, I picked her.'

Katie laughs, but there's no humour in it. 'Don't pretend like you don't know you're hot shit, Dan. Every girl in our year has had their eye on you since Year 9. I'm surprised it's taken you this long, to be honest.'

As much as it makes me feel arrogant, I can't really argue

with her. You notice when people notice you. I've just never totally eased into being that guy.

'You sound like my mother,' I say instead, and she laughs again.

'Don't change the subject – what's so special about Libby? Come on, it's me. You can tell *me*.'

I glance down at her, wondering on the implications of a secret. My stomach twists.

'She's funny. She makes me laugh. I like hanging out with her,' I say simply. I hope it's enough, but of course it isn't. Katie's smile grows more wolf-like.

'Just "hanging out"? How very PG of you,' she says, raising an eyebrow.

'If you're looking for sordid details, you're asking the wrong guy.' I meet her eyes, the challenge still glinting in them. 'You know I'm not one to kiss and tell.'

'I haven't known you to be one to kiss at all, babe,' she says delicately, and I feel heat rush to my cheeks. She finally breaks eye contact with me, stretching back out over the blanket and arching her back. 'Whatever. I just don't see it, is all. I think she's a bit ... not in your league.'

I know what she really means is *our* league – despite our friendship never having moved anywhere beyond platonic, I know she's always seen us as a pair. In another time, we'd have probably been a marriage of convenience, arranged by our parents and dutifully followed. As it is, she's spent our teenage years trying to set me up with someone she can control.

Before I can argue back though, the lads turn up at the blanket. Katie shoots up, squealing as Lewis leans over her, dripping lake water on to her tanned skin.

'Lewis, you're getting water all over me!' she shrieks, batting the droplets off herself. Lewis grins and shakes his head, sending more water flying from his damp hair.

'You're in a bikini, they're supposed to get wet,' he says, falling down on to the blanket besides her.

Aaron sits down on the grass beside us. 'No Libby yet?' he asks, in an entirely different tone to Katie. 'Did she say Mona was coming as well?'

'She did.' I raise my eyebrows at him, smirking. 'Which you already know, seeing as you've asked me that twice already this morning.'

Aaron grins shamelessly, and I have to laugh. I glance back down at my phone to make sure Libby hasn't messaged since I last looked, just as we hear the sound of a car pulling up at the top of the bank.

'That's her!' I say, relief flooding over me. This is our first time properly hanging out with all my friends (if you don't count the party), and I can't say I've been super chill about the prospect – Lewis and Katie can be a lot when they're together. I really want it to go well.

'Did her *mum* drop her off?' asks Katie, watching Libby climb out of her mum's car over the rims of her sunglasses. Despite the bite in her tone, she swats Lewis on the arm when he sniggers.

'Don't be *rude* about it!' But the corners of her mouth are turning upwards, and I know her better than to believe that wasn't fully her intention. As if us arriving squashed up in the back of a battered transit that smells of sawdust is any more glamorous.

I say nothing, because of course I don't, and instead jump up off the blanket and head over to where Libby is standing looking a little lost.

When she turns and sees me her face lights up, and I grin awkwardly.

'Hey!' I jog up to her and then stand, swinging my arms by my sides. It strikes me that I should hug her, so I reach out and wrap one arm around her shoulders before dropping it just as quickly. I look round, registering for the first time that she's alone. 'No Mona?'

'No ...' Libby casts her eyes down at the ground. 'She, uh, a family thing came up. Her mum is taking her and her sister to France to their grandparents' for the summer.'

'The whole summer?'

'I don't really know.' She twists a strand of hair between her fingers. 'It was a bit of a last-minute plan.'

She doesn't elaborate, even though I sense there's something more going on. But I don't want to pry, and it feels like even if she did want to tell me, it's probably a conversation for somewhere more private than a lakeside beach heaving with our classmates.

I look back at our picnic blanket, where Katie is still openly watching us both. She smiles coolly and lifts her hand in a loose wave. Libby spots her and waves back awkwardly.

'Shall we?' I gesture towards the others, and Libby nods wordlessly. We head back over to the blanket, and just as we reach it I realise I probably should have tried to hold her hand.

'Hey, Libby,' coos Katie. 'Glad you made it.'

'Hey, guys,' she says, sitting down on the blanket.

I watch as Katie gives Libby a full examination. 'I like your T-shirt.'

'Oh.' Libby looks down – she's in a faded grey band T-shirt, the Rolling Stones logo emblazoned across the front in cracked vinyl transfer. 'Thanks. It was my mum's.'

'Cute,' says Katie, in a tone that implies she thinks the exact opposite.

'Is Mona still coming?' cuts in Aaron, looking back towards the car park as if we might have left Mona standing there by herself.

'Something came up,' says Libby, and then quickly so she doesn't have to explain further, 'I can't believe I forgot sun cream. Does anyone have any I can steal?'

'Nah, I want to get a tan,' says Katie, stretching her arms above her head. She fixes her eyes on Libby again. 'So, have you met Mandy and Stuart yet?'

'Who?' asks Libby, blinking in confusion. Katie laughs, a mirthless tinkling sound.

'Oh god, sorry, babe,' she giggles. 'I'm just so used to calling them that. Dan's parents?'

'Oh,' says Libby. 'I just know them as Mr and Mrs King. I've *met* them before, but not since we ...' She trails off and shoots me a nervous glance. I smile in what I hope is a reassuring way.

'Shame,' says Katie airily. 'They're *so* lovely.' She slips her sunglasses back over her nose and lies back on the blanket. 'Although, I think they always thought that me and Dan would get together! Bless them,' she laughs, before falling silent with a smile playing across her lips.

I was just having the exact same thought a minute ago, but Katie saying this out loud in front of Libby makes me bristle at her in a way I don't think I ever have before. But I've spent so many years allowing Katie to say whatever she wants that I can't come up with any kind of retort, and just give Libby an apologetic smile.

The rest of the afternoon passes without too much incident, besides Libby's skin slowly growing pinker and pinker in the sun. At one point she suggests moving under the shade of some nearby trees, but Katie quickly vetoes it for the sake of her tan.

It only occurs to me later that I should have fought harder against her.

Neha

I must have fallen asleep, because when I open my eyes there's sunlight streaming through the partially closed curtains and I'm curled up under a fleecy blanket on the sofa. I'm alone. But the smell of the Christmas candles, which have been extinguished, has been replaced with the enticing smell of cooking bacon.

I yawn, swinging my feet down on to the carpet. A square of colour on the coffee table catches my eye, and I gently pick up the Polaroid Libby took last night. My lips lift into a smile I can't control. We're leaning in together in our equally tasteless Christmas jumpers, our hair still a little damp from the rain. Libby's eyes are scrunched up, tongue out at the camera. My cheeks are puffed out, eyes comically wide.

I remember my toes being cold, and the warmth of Libby's body against mine.

I put the photo back on the table, shrug the blanket over my shoulders and shuffle from the living room, following the scent. I head down the hallway to the kitchen, where Libby is standing over the stove, spatula in hand, over a pan of sizzling bacon. She looks up and smiles as I enter.

'Morning,' she says. Something moves inside my chest and I smile back nervously, hoisting myself up to perch on the edge of the counter opposite the stove.

'I ran out while you were still asleep to get this, by the way,' Libby says hastily, gesturing to the bacon and a packet of rolls on the side. 'I didn't just help myself. I wanted to say thank you, for yesterday.' She pauses, eyes flicking over to me. 'I hope that's OK?'

'That's absolutely OK,' I laugh. 'We rarely have anything decent in anyway. You can come and cook me breakfast any time.'

I blush at the potential implications of what just came out of my mouth, but Libby seems oblivious to my discomfort. She bustles around our tiny kitchen space, buttering rolls and searching the cupboards for condiments. I'm so lost inside my own head that I jump a little when she pushes a plate with a bacon butty under my nose.

'Still asleep?' she laughs, sitting down at the small kitchen table and pulling her own plate in front of her.

The sound of the lock in the front door makes us both start, and then Jas is stepping into the kitchen in her scrubs.

'Well, good morning, early birds!' she chirps, her cheeriness edged by the tiredness of her eyes. 'Has someone managed to cook something in this kitchen that didn't turn to charcoal?'

'Speak for yourself!' I laugh. 'Jas, this is Libby. Libby,

this is my Aunt Jas.'

Jas smiles at Libby. 'Nice to meet you. Any chance I could get involved in the bacon I smell?'

'Of course!' Libby leaps up, bangs her knee on the kitchen table, and moves back to the stove. 'Ketchup or brown sauce?'

I know from experience that all Jas wants to do after a shift is collapse into bed, but she chats away with Libby for an admirable amount of time before excusing herself to go and get some sleep. As she bids us 'good morning' and heads up the stairs, I resolve to give her an extra big squeeze later on.

Once she's gone Libby turns back to me. 'Any plans for today?'

'Nothing exciting,' I say. 'You?'

'You're my entire social calendar nowadays,' Libby laughs, the colour in her face rising as it so often does. Once again, I fight not to read too much into it. She clears her throat. 'They show old films at the cinema on Saturdays sometimes, we could … ?'

My whole body tingles with the fact that she wants to keep hanging out with me today. 'Sounds fun!'

We step into the foyer, breathing in the smell of fresh popcorn and old carpet. The tiny cinema is ancient and boasts a total of two screens, but it's bright and welcoming. Faded posters for films that have long since had their run peer out from behind glass panes along the walls, and possibly the oldest woman I've ever seen sits behind the ticket counter.

'What—?'

'Do you—?'

We both start speaking at the same time and collapse into giggles, even though it isn't that funny. I feel giddy.

We approach the ticket counter and the old woman smiles at us. I see recognition light up in her milky eyes. 'Eleanor Dixon, is that you?' she asks in a wavering voice. My brow creases in confusion, but Libby is smiling gently.

'No, Mrs Bramley, Ellie is my mum. I'm Libby.'

'Oh goodness, dear, you do look like your mother!' Mrs Bramley exclaims with a tinkling laugh.

Libby hands over some money and Mrs Bramley tears two ticket stubs from a roll.

'Isn't she a bit old to still be working?' I whisper to Libby after we've collected our tickets and moved away from the counter.

'Oh, by decades, I'd say. But what else is there to do around here?' Libby says, shrugging. 'Bless her, every time I come in she thinks I'm—'

'I fucking *knew* it.'

The sharp voice snaps us out of our little bubble, and as I watch Libby's face closes up, taut and guarded. We turn to see Katie West stomping across the foyer, eyes laser-focused on Libby. Behind her a cluster of other girls from school watch with wide eyes and raised phones.

'You really are a disgusting skank, aren't you?' Katie spits, coming to a halt in front of us.

'What? I'm not doing anything!' says Libby, but her voice is high and she sounds like a kid who's been caught sneaking sweets before dinnertime. It doesn't help.

'*I'm not doing anything!*' Katie mocks, her voice even more shrill. 'Don't play innocent, it doesn't suit you. I've seen the two of you sneaking round together.'

She turns her icy stare to me and for the first time I understand what Libby has been feeling for weeks – the blast of hate and disgust is nearly physical.

'Trying to be edgy, Neha? Finally realised how bloody boring you are?'

I stare at her, my jaw actually dropping a little. I don't think I've spoken more than five words to this girl in my life. 'Excuse me?'

'If you think hanging out with this cheating scum is going to make you interesting, you—'

'Leave her alone.' As high as Libby's voice was a second ago, it's now low and dangerous, a voice I haven't heard her use before. It's Katie's turn to look shocked, blinking rapidly at Libby for a moment, and then she throws her head back in ugly laughter.

'Listen to her now!' she barks, with a glance back over her shoulder to make sure her friends are still filming us. 'Finally grown a backbone for your new girlfriend?'

I flinch, but Libby's eyes don't even flicker. Katie isn't finished.

'First you cheat on Dan with some rando, and now you're flaunting yourself around with this –' her eyes land on me – '*dyke.*'

There's a collective intake of breath, and the line of raised phones wavers. Even Katie looks like she knows she's taken a step too far.

'I … I mean …'

'We know what you mean.' Libby's voice is still low and calm but her face is turning an alarming shade of red, and her fists are clenched by her sides. I can practically feel the rage radiating off her. 'Just leave us alone.'

Katie finds her voice again. 'Or else what?'

For a moment I really think Libby is going to hit Katie. Her whole body seems to swell with anger, and then slowly deflates. She lets out a long breath.

'Or nothing, Katie. You're not worth it. You never were.'

Libby turns to leave, grabbing my hand to pull me away. I let myself be pulled, my hand in Libby's, with Katie glowering after us. She's clearly furious she's not getting her sequel video to Libby's original humiliation, but I can't help but notice the other girls looking decidedly more uncomfortable, all of them with their eyes cast down as we leave.

As soon as we get into the car, all of Libby's dark calm explodes.

'I am so *sick* of Katie West,' she half shouts, slamming the door shut with such force that I wince. 'Who the hell does she think she is, bigoted piece of—'

'It's fine,' I say hastily, turning on the ignition and pulling out of the car park in case Katie decides to emerge for round two.

'It's *not* fine!' bursts Libby. 'What year does she think this is? I can't stand it, it's just wilful ignorance.'

'It's not uncommon.' My hands are gripping the steering wheel so tightly I feel like my knuckles are about to pop. 'It's why I'm not out at school.'

'That doesn't make it better!'

Libby is vibrating in the seat beside me and I wish she'd calm down. It starts to rain as I pull on to the main road and I flick the switch for the windscreen wipers. My nerves are already jangling, and I'm not concentrating on the road as much as I know I should be.

'How are you not more bothered?'

'Because I *can't* be,' I snap, and Libby goes still. 'I'd be exhausted if I got worked up over every homophobic slip of the tongue, every microaggression. Do you think I don't want to call it out? Of course I do. But I don't have the *energy*.'

I think about all the times I sat by myself in school, debating if I should use my sexuality as some kind of cheap social bargaining chip. Katie's jibe at me 'trying to be edgy' prickles my skin, the implication that who I am is just a publicity stunt. I think about how I had to go from an open, accepting environment at my old school to an archaic model of queer misery, never knowing if I was safe to be myself.

From the corner of my eye I can see Libby breathing heavily, staring hard at the dashboard in front of her. She shakes her head, as if trying to control what she says next.

'I don't—'

But I never find out what Libby doesn't. Through the blur of rain there's suddenly no longer road in front of me, but the headlights of an oncoming van.

I slam on the brakes but the wet road means I don't stop, just skid into a turn with a hideous shriek of rubber on tarmac. My head shoots forward, and everything goes dark.

LIBBY

I sit on the edge of a plastic seat, nervously jigging my legs up and down as I wait for the nurse to come back in and tell me I can leave. I need to know that Neha's OK. Shame stabs sharply in my chest – if I hadn't been so obliviously gung-ho in my outrage at Katie, Neha wouldn't have been distracted from the road. Dan is in a coma from a car crash. Her parents *died* in a car crash. What the hell was I thinking?

I've not prayed in years, but I send up a small thanks that we both walked away from the car. Neha blacked out for a moment, which was terrifying, but she came to quickly and the paramedics assured me it wasn't serious after they bundled me off into a separate ambulance. She'd need a few stitches from where her head hit the steering wheel and would be checked for concussion, but she'd be all right – physically, at least.

The car has a serious dent in its side and I've no idea if there's any internal damage. I cringe when I think of the expense, and start desperately thinking of ways I might be able to repay Neha and her Aunt Jas. I called Mum a little while ago to let her know where I was, and after a very panicked conversation she's on her way. Maybe I can ask her to dip into the modest amount of money she's saved up for my university years.

My senses are overwhelmed with the sounds and smells of the hospital, things that have become so background to me over the last couple of months. But now that I'm here for a different reason, not just to visit, everything is so much more pronounced. The sting of the disinfectant in my nostrils, the incessant beeping of machinery, even the chatter from the nurses' station – it's all too much.

Unable to bear sitting here alone any longer, I rip aside the privacy curtain and go in search of Neha.

I can't stop thinking about the way she looked at me when I picked up that box of hair dye the first time we hung out, when she thought I was about to change something about myself. About how her hair smelt when she hugged me after Bonfire Night. Those huge, beautiful eyes of hers and how they light up when she smiles. I'm thinking about the sound of her breathing when she sleeps, with her head on my shoulder and her hair tickling the underside of my chin. I'm thinking about how much I love the way her laughter sounds. How much I love just hanging out on the sofa watching terrible films with her. How much I love …

… her. I love her.

And in one fell swoop I have taken the tangled mess that is my life and thrown it into a blender.

Maybe I should have seen this coming. At first, I was so caught up with Dan and the job of being Chipping Hollow's Biggest Social Outcast that when someone came along who made me feel better, I figured it was just because everyone else was being so lousy.

But I can't deny that my feelings towards Neha are entirely different to how I feel about Mona. Different in a way I didn't understand, or maybe I was just too scared to examine it any closer.

Growing up in a place like Chipping Hollow, I'd never even thought to consider if I was attracted to girls as well as guys. But thinking about it, I'm always unusually pleased to see Billie Lourd pop up in anything, and felt strangely drawn to both Steve *and* Robin in *Stranger Things* season two ... oh, god damn it.

Despite the signs all being there – large, flashing neon signs, now that I actually think about it – I feel as though someone has just hit me with a truck. A big truck. Full of bricks. And fireworks.

I try and imagine what people would say if I tried to explain I was breaking up with my coma-bound boyfriend. Not that I'm breaking up with him. I think. Would it even count? A strangled groan escapes my throat and a nurse pushing a trolley of medicine shoots me an alarmed look.

I stop pounding down the corridor for a second and lean against the wall, closing my eyes against the world and trying to pretend, just for a second, that I'm not Libby Dixon. I'm not the girl whose boyfriend lies motionless in an indefinite coma. I'm not the girl whose 'friends' allowed her to become so drunk she didn't know what she was doing, and then passed her off into the arms of a stranger. I'm not the girl going crazy about her only friend, the only person she has any kind of decent relationship with any more. I'm not that girl.

What am I going to do?

I loved Dan the way a girlfriend is supposed to love her boyfriend. I still love him, I just don't know *how* to love him any more. I don't think I've known how to love him since the accident.

I steel my nerves and push myself off the wall. This can all wait. Right now, I need to make sure Neha is OK.

I head back the way I came, retracing my panicked steps. About halfway down the corridor, I finally spot Neha perched on the edge of a bed in an open ward area. My heart leaps.

'Neha?'

She looks up, her eyes dazed, and for a moment I wonder if I should have just left her alone.

'Libby!'

She jumps from the bed and wobbles a little. I rush over and she throws her arms around my shoulders. 'Oh my god, are you all right?! I'm so sorry, I can't believe that happened, I wasn't concentrating and—'

'Shit, Neha, *I'm* sorry!' I'm sobbing, all the emotion bursting from me in a wave. 'I was the one distracting you, it's all my fault, it could have been so much worse and I'd never forgive myself.'

'If you take on much more to not forgive yourself you'll burst,' she says with a half laugh, squeezing me tighter.

'I'm so sorry,' I whisper into her hair, sniffling. 'I was just so mad, but you were right, it's not up to me to tell you what to get upset about.'

'It's not that it doesn't upset me,' she says gently. 'I just—'

'I know.' I pull my head away but keep my arms around her shoulders. 'I … I know.'

Neha sways in my arms a little, and I move her gently back towards the bed and sit her down. My eyes trace over the bandage on her forehead and I wince.

'Are you OK?' I half whisper. We still have our arms around each other, and despite the tempest in my head, this feels completely right. She leans into me and I rest my chin on top of her head.

'I'm OK now,' she whispers back, but there's a tremor in her voice. She shifts slightly under my arm but doesn't pull away. 'It was scary. I blacked out for a minute and when I woke up you were gone, and I thought …'

'You were scared because of *me*?' My chest aches. She pulls away from me slightly so she can look into my face. She's so close.

'We both know what can happen in an accident like that. I thought maybe I'd lost you. I thought I'd lost someone else and that this time it was my fault. I told myself that I'd always be such a careful driver, but then—'

'It was *my* fault,' I insist. 'I distracted you.'

To my surprise, Neha laughs softly. 'Yeah, you do that a lot actually.'

My heart starts hammering inside my chest. I think about all the things swirling around inside my mind. I think about letting them spill out. Neha's eyes are wide and there's something like anticipation in them, as if she knows that there's something I'm holding back.

She leans her head forward gently, resting against mine, closing her eyes. I don't know how to be closer to her without doing something irreversible, but I can't stop myself from reaching out to brush a strand of hair from her face.

'Libby?'

We jump apart as though a current has sparked through us. We turn to see Jas standing by the bed, and the look on her face makes my stomach drop. 'What's wrong?'

'Libby, I just heard. It's Dan …'

The silence following his name stretches out in front of us for an eternity. The sounds of the ward fade away and it's just the three of us, frozen.

And then I'm running, sprinting down the corridor towards the stairwell. I'm vaguely aware that Jas and Neha are following me, Jas calling something out, but the pounding in my ears overwhelms it as I burst through the doors and take the stairs up two at a time.

We reach Dan's floor and I fly down the hallway towards his room, towards a ripple of noise that is so out of place in the intensive-care unit. I round the corner to see a crowd of people outside the door to Dan's room, a few wearing scrubs and another in a white coat holding a clipboard. I skid to a halt. My heart turns to ice in my chest and every single thought I've had in the past half-hour vanishes and is replaced by one: Dan. Something has happened to Dan.

I take a step forward, then stumble back two. Forward. Backwards. I feel like an idiot and I can't help it. Somebody spots me from the crowd around Dan's room and I recognise a handful of faces – Aaron, Lewis and Katie are all here. They all stare at me, blank-faced. It's the first time Katie has looked at me with anything but contempt for weeks.

Oh god. Oh my god.

I rush forward, try to push my way through into the room.

'I don't think you should go in there, Libby,' Aaron blurts, reaching out and catching my arm. 'I don't think—'

'Let me go!' I wrench my arm from his grasp and burst through the doors.

The room is crowded, and I can't see the bed. More doctors are in here muttering. I see Dan's parents. They grip each other with shaking arms over by the window, their faces streaked with tears. I feel as though someone has just kicked me in the gut, and a cold sweat has broken out over my entire body.

'What's going on?'

Faces turn towards me and I realise I've spoken out loud, the weird croaking sound unidentifiable as my own voice. Or so I think.

'Libby?'

I freeze.

I know that voice.

I know that voice.

People part and I can finally see. The sheets, usually so stiff and unwrinkled, are rumpled and look as though they've been disturbed by a sudden burst of activity. My eyes move up the bed. Around the top there aren't half as many machines as there were, just a simple heart monitor and IV drip.

And propped upright in the middle of it all, his face an alarming shade of grey, is Dan. His eyes are sunken and circled with purple bruises, but they're lit up and they're open and they're looking right at me.

He's awake.

He's woken up.

He's alive.

The room spins wildly in front of me, and I reach out instinctively for something to grab hold of. Behind me, I hear Neha gasp.

The last thing I see before my eyes roll back into my head is Dan's face, twisting in horror as I collapse on to the hospital-room floor.

Sixteen Weeks Before It Happened

The sour sting of the apple-flavoured shot hits the back of my throat hard, and I barely suppress a cough. Aaron grins at me over the rim of his shot glass as I run my tongue over my teeth, trying to get rid of the sticky taste.

'Another?' Aaron shouts over the music, leaning against the massive island in Craig Shaw's kitchen.

'Let me take a breath,' I laugh, pushing the shot glass away. It's immediately lost in the collection of plastic cups, half-drunk bottles of beer and other assorted alcohol vessels that are scattered across the marble worktop. 'We're walking home, remember?'

'You make an excellent point, but I'm choosing to ignore it,' says Aaron, already pouring another shot. 'Besides, you know what Lewis is like. If we go home any less than wankered we'll be "pussies".'

I wince, knowing he's right. I don't know where Lewis gets

his ideologies on life and manhood from, but I'm glad they're not the same as mine.

I lean back against the cool marble island, casting a glance over the party. Music pours from the speakers set up across the open space that runs the length of the ground floor, all polished wood flooring and plush sofas. Bottles of spirits and empty cans are scattered across every coffee table and sideboard, nestled amongst expensive-looking pottery and vases of flowers, but so far no one has shouted at anyone to 'be careful, for god's sake!' A part of me wants to shout it on behalf of Craig's absent parents, but I've been to enough of his parties to know they don't seem to care.

Through the expanse of glass at the other end of the long room, the party shimmers and throbs. Girls walk awkwardly across the lawn on heels that keep sinking into the grass, and I lift a plastic cup to my lips to hide the smile on my face.

'Oi oi!' shouts a voice, and I turn to see Lewis wandering over with his cup held high. 'Are you lads drunk yet or do I need to go get a funnel?'

I smile again, but this time it's forced. I glance around the room for Katie.

'Getting there,' I lie, lifting my cup and knocking it against his. I don't mention that this particular drink is just water – my head is fuzzy from the shots and I'd rather keep it clear tonight. I'm not particularly in the mood.

'Good man, good man,' Lewis slurs, nodding. Before he can ask me what I'm drinking I say something about needing the loo and slip away into the party.

I weave my way through bodies in various stages of dress and decorum. I'm accosted several times by friends and classmates, wanting a selfie or to chat about how mad it is that in a few months we'll go into our final year of sixth form. Abby Lenton keeps me chatting for a good few minutes, standing so close I can smell the fruity cider on her breath. At one point she puts a hand on my arm and laughs, but doesn't take it away afterwards. Across the room, Lewis catches my eye and winks, mouthing, *You're in there*.

My chest constricts and now it's much too hot in here, too many people. I excuse myself from Abby, trying to ignore the hurt pout on her lips as I pull away.

I stumble through the house, wishing I didn't respect Craig's parents enough to follow the one rule for their son's parties: nobody goes upstairs. Craving cold air, I go in search of the garage instead, stumbling along an oppressively white hallway before I find the right door. I dip through to discover that, mercifully, it's empty.

I cross the weirdly neat space and flop down on a bag of compost, dropping my head into my hands and reminding myself to breathe. My chest squeezes as I think of Abby's hand on my arm, Lewis's leer from the kitchen. Everything I've tried to push down for as long as I can remember wells up and without much warning there are silent tears dripping down my face.

There's a bang as the garage door opens and my head jerks up to see Libby Dixon, standing in the doorway looking first lost, then surprised and then concerned as she takes me in. I quickly drop my head again and rub my face with the sleeve of my shirt.

'What d'you want?'

It comes out harsher than I mean it to.

'I … uhhh …' Libby stumbles over herself. 'I just needed somewhere to cool down a bit. Kind of hot in there.'

'Oh, yeah.' I sniff and try to inconspicuously shift my body so it's facing away from her slightly. She stays stranded in the doorway, seemingly debating whether to come in or go.

'Are you OK?' she finally asks, with an air of someone having just made a decision. She takes a small step forward. 'I know I'm probably supposed to ignore this, but you've obviously been crying.'

'No, I'm fine, it's fine,' I say quickly, rubbing my face again. 'I'm fine.'

'Well, you're not.' Libby gently closes the garage door behind her and I properly look round at her for the first time. 'You're definitely not. You don't have to tell me what's up or anything, but I don't want to just leave you in here by yourself.'

'It's nothing you can help with,' I mutter.

Libby strides across the garage and drops down on to the compost bags beside me. I stare at her in confusion.

'Budge up,' she says, looking me squarely in the eye. 'Try me.'

I look at her carefully, weighing her up. We're not exactly close, but we've known each other since we were five. I like her. She makes me laugh. I catch the smell of her perfume and remember hugging her when she first arrived.

I roll my neck and sigh, leaning my arms across my knees and staring at the concrete floor. I can't look at her when I say this.

'I'm gay.'

There's a long pause while alarm bells go off in my head and I fight the urge to take it back, tell her I'm just kidding and hurriedly make up some other viable reason I'm upset.

'Oh.'

It's not the reaction I'm expecting, but then I'm not sure exactly what reaction I *was* expecting. I risk a glance at her sideways, and she smiles.

'Well, that's nothing to cry about.' She leans back against the garage wall, holding eye contact with me. There's a tension in her, but it doesn't feel unsafe. I allow myself a deep breath.

'Does anyone else know?'

'No.' I run a hand through my hair, heart still hammering against my chest. 'You're the first.'

'And that's why you're hiding in Craig's garage?'

I groan and drop my head back into my hands. She's judging me, one way or another she's judging me. But then I feel her arm around my shoulder and I lean into her instinctively, just a little.

'I know it's not a big deal,' I say. 'I know what year this is. This shouldn't be an issue. But I ... I don't know how my parents will react.'

I think of my mum, dressing the church with flowers every Sunday morning before service. My dad, his kind eyes and how devastating it would be to see disappointment in them. 'They raised me to be a Good Little Christian Boy and I have no idea how being gay will fit into that for them. And then there's everyone else. I'm not ready to find out how old-fashioned Chipping Hollow really is. I'm not ready.'

Libby nods along, keeping her arm around my shoulder. I take a deep breath and sit up, staring over at a long workbench filled with tools. Now that I've started talking, letting out everything I've held in for so long, it's hard to stop.

'Katie is always trying to set me up with her mates, and I'm just not interested. She's been obsessed with micromanaging my romantic life lately. I think she's trying to be nice, but it's getting harder to say no without looking like something is up.'

Libby stays quiet, and I wish I knew what she was thinking. I'd always thought the first time I said it out loud I'd feel the weight lift off my shoulders. It stays hunched over me, pressing down and making it hard to breathe.

'You must think I'm a right wuss,' I say miserably.

Libby's head snaps round. 'No! Why on earth would I think that?'

'Because I should just get over myself and get on with it!' It comes out as a near shout, and Libby flinches. I twist my hands together. 'I should just tell people and not care what they think. I wish I didn't, but I do. It might be different in a couple of years, when I can get out of this bloody village and into the real world where people won't have known me since I was a baby. Hopefully by that point I won't be living with my parents, because if they react badly – I mean, it will hurt like hell – but at least we won't be under the same roof.'

We sit together in silence in the dim light. The noise of the party seeps under the door, overloud music and drunken calling reminding me that at some point soon I'm going to be missed. Libby turns to me again.

'If you don't mind me asking, why don't you go out with one of the girls Katie tries to set you up with, if you don't want anyone to suspect?'

'It just seems cruel.' I sigh. 'I couldn't do that to them, knowing it wouldn't mean anything.'

There's a pause, and then …

'Go out with me then.'

'What?'

'Go out with me,' Libby repeats, sitting up a little straighter. 'I know it doesn't mean anything, that way. You'd have someone to talk to about it and you won't have to kiss me or anything in public. Or in private, for that matter,' she adds with a soft laugh. 'We'll be one of those couples that isn't into PDA.'

I blink at her. 'That's insane, you can't do that.'

'Why not?' She shrugs. 'It's not like I'm rejecting a line of disappointed suitors for you.'

I frown as she slips in this bit of self-deprecation, but she moves on quickly before I can say anything about it.

'Look, I know we've never been besties or anything, but we've known each other since forever. I hope you know you can trust me with this. You can relax and not be badgered to go out with someone you don't want to …' She trails off, tilting her head to one side. '*Is* there someone you want to go out with?'

I let out a kind of strangled laugh. 'You know, I've been so busy angsting about keeping this a secret, I've never looked twice at anyone that's not on TV.'

Libby smiles, and for the first time in a while I feel a little bubble of hope bloom in my chest.

'Why would you do this for me?'

'Because I like you.' Libby says it so simply I can't help but believe her. 'I think you're a good guy. You don't deserve to be going through this, let alone by yourself.' She links her arm through mine. 'What do you say? Want to be my boyfriend, Daniel King?'

I stare at her for a moment, and then a grin breaks out across my face.

'Libby Dixon, I'd love to.'

DECEMBER

Neha

'*Is she oh ... OK?*'

I don't know the answer to Dan's question, because while I can still hear his voice croaking with disuse (oh my god, he's *awake*), I can no longer see what's going on in his room. Jas has a grip on my upper arm and is steering me away from the crowd of people. We're back in the emergency ward before I even think to protest.

'Wait, no, we need to go back,' I stammer, turning around, but Jas still has hold of me and keeps me rooted to the spot. 'I need to make sure she's ...'

'She's on a hospital ward surrounded by brain specialists, she'll be fine,' says Jas firmly. She manoeuvres me back over to the gurney where Libby and I ... what?

'What just happened?'

'You tell me,' says Jas. Her tone is gentle but her expression is stern. 'What did I walk in on?'

My mind is spinning. Everything happened so fast: the van

hurtling towards us. The car skidding out of control despite my death grip on the wheel. Waking up blinking blood from my eye, wondering if I was dead. Panicking at where Libby was. Holding her in my hospital room. Dan's face, like a ghost, lighting up when Libby walked into the room …

I lunge up from the gurney and throw up all over the floor.

'Oh god, Neha,' says Jas, taking my arm again but much more softly this time. She rubs my back as I heave again, and when nothing else comes up, I burst into tears.

Jas shushes me as she sits me back down, poking her head out of the curtain just long enough to call for someone to get a mop before she's back by my side, holding me while I blubber.

'It's all right,' she murmurs, but it's not all right. Now that it's finally hit me, delayed terror at the car crash sweeps over me and I sob harder into her shoulder. My heart races so fast and the air feels unusually thin – the panic so intense I think I might be sick again.

After a few minutes, the tidal wave recedes a little and I concentrate on drawing air into my lungs. Jas waits patiently while I calm myself down, one arm wrapped around me, stroking my shoulder rhythmically.

'Better?' she asks, peering into my face.

'Not really,' I say hoarsely. I feel like a husk. 'I can't believe I crashed the car. Jas, I'm so sorry.'

'You can be sorry later,' she says. 'Right now, I'm just glad you're OK.'

I reach up and touch the bandage covering my stitches. My face crumples again. 'I could have killed us. I'm no better than the person that … that hit …'

I'm transported to another time, another hospital. News that couldn't possibly be true. Instinctively turning to look to my parents for comfort and realising that they'd never be able to offer it again.

I'm crying again, and Jas is rocking me back and forth. I think she might be crying too.

Someone in scrubs comes in with a mop bucket and quietly sorts the floor out while Jas and I get ourselves under control and apologise. When they've gone, I sniff and look up at Jas.

'Can we go and check on Libby?'

'I don't think that's the best idea,' she says, not unkindly. 'I think they all just need some space right now and so do you. I'm sure she's fine. You can call her later.'

I want to protest but I've no energy left, so I just nod and drop my head back against her shoulder. Later. I'll call Libby later.

Dan

Mum is crying. I recognise her now. A couple of hours ago, I remembered absolutely nothing, not even my parents' faces. It was terrifying, but with every minute that passes it feels blurrier, more like a bizarre and horrible dream.

There are a lot of people in here. I still don't know them all, but I don't think I'm supposed to. Some of them are doctors, or other miscellaneous medical staff. I'm in the hospital. I think I've been here for a while.

It hurts.

'Where'sss Libby?'

I can't quite recall how many times I've asked that now, but it's the one thing I'm sure of. Libby was here, and now she's not, and I think something was wrong. It feels important, and I hang on to it as though it's the only thing tethering me to reality.

But Mum just clutches my hand, and Dad stands over her with tears in his eyes. I think I can hear Lewis and Aaron somewhere but I can't focus enough to decipher what they're saying. My whole body feels very heavy and I let go of everything and slip back into the comforting darkness.

When I wake up again, the room is quieter and the sun has gone down. Everything seems just a little bit sharper than before, and I want to sit up to look around. But as I try to move, fire shoots through my body and I hiss between my teeth. My brain and my limbs won't coordinate with each other, and I realise that my right leg is in a cast.

'Whoa, son.' A gentle hand lands on my shoulder, calming my stammering heartbeat. I twist my head to see my dad, smiling down at me. 'Take it easy.'

'What happened?' I say groggily. Dad fiddles with something by the side of my bed and slowly raises me up into a sitting position. The fire flares again, then fades to a dull throb as the bed stops moving.

'You were in an accident,' Dad says softly, resting his hand on mine. His eyes well up. 'But you're back with us now. That's the main thing.'

I flick my eyes around the room again, empty apart from the two of us. 'Where's Mum?'

'She'll be here soon. You can go back to sleep if you want to.'

I do, but something tells me that I've done a lot of sleeping recently. I fight the exhaustion overwhelming me, straining to keep my eyes open.

'Katie and Lewis are still here,' Dad says. 'They'd love to see you, if you're up for it?'

There's something else, something I was supposed to remember. But I can't. 'Yeah, sure.'

Dad leaves the room and a second later Katie bursts in, tears running down her face. She looks almost dishevelled, or as close to it as Katie can get.

'Oh my god, oh my god,' she sobs, rushing over and throwing her arms around me. 'I can't believe you're awake.'

Pain explodes across my body at the sudden pressure, wiping all other thoughts away for a moment. I must make some sort of noise though, because Katie jerks back with wide eyes.

'Sorry, sorry! I didn't ... I just ...'

She dissolves into tears and drops into the seat by my bed, slumped forward with her head in her hands.

It takes me a second to properly react while I wait for my heart rate to return to normal and the pain to subside. I haven't seen Katie cry like this since we were kids, when she came flying off her bike as we were racing down the hill our parents had told us never to ride down. Even Lewis looks taken aback.

Bikes. Collisions. A pair of bright white lights hurtling towards me, my heart jumping out of my throat, the sound of screaming ...

That's why I'm here.

'Hey,' I say weakly, finally reacting. Lewis sits down on the opposite side of the bed, staring at me as though he can't really believe I'm here.

'Hey, man,' he says in a tone something like awe. 'Are you OK?'

It seems like a silly question, but I suppose I wouldn't know what to say in his position either. I just nod, wanting to reach out to Katie in comfort but still unable to get my limbs to cooperate. It takes several minutes for her to compose herself, finally sitting back and sniffling.

'So are *you* guys going to tell me what happened?' I eventually ask. 'Dad just said I was in an "accident".'

'You got hit on your bike,' says Lewis, seemingly pleased to have something concrete to say. 'It was a hit-and-run, someone just passing through the village, they think. Here …' He digs into his pocket and pulls out his phone. He scrolls for a second, then turns the screen towards me.

It takes me a moment to understand what I'm looking at. It's a photo of my bike, if you could still call it a bike – all twisted metal and shredded rubber. It dawns on me fully for the first time that I nearly died.

I look away from the phone and already know – when I close my eyes, it's not those lights I'm going to see. It's that bike.

'What were you *doing* out there in the middle of the night?' asks Katie, and again I see that flash of headlights. But this time, it brings another memory with it.

'Hey, where's Libby? Is she OK? I think she fainted …'

To my shock, Katie scoffs at the questions. 'You wouldn't be asking that if you knew what she did,' she says cryptically, still sniffling.

'What? Why?' I'm desperate to sit up, everything becoming slightly more focused the longer I'm awake. But my body and my brain still don't seem to be talking to each other properly, and the harder I try the more everything screams at me to stop. My eyelids droop with the effort of just thinking about moving, until Lewis speaks again and I snap back to attention.

'She cheated on you, mate,' he blurts. Katie's head jerks round, glaring at him, clearly angry she didn't get to be the one to announce it. Lewis visibly shrinks inwards.

'It was the same night as your accident,' Katie says, turning back to me. 'On our girls' night. She just started necking on this random guy right in front of us, like we weren't even there! It was gross.' She stops to shake her head. 'I'm so sorry, Dan. She never deserved you. She's such a tart.'

I stare at them, my mouth hanging open as I try to process this information with a brain that only feels half in gear. Something in the back of my mind is telling me I should be careful, think about how a straight guy would react to his girlfriend cheating on him. But all I can think of is Libby, the girl I got so close to over the summer, and how that doesn't sound like her at all.

'Are you … sure?' I ask hesitantly. 'I mean, that doesn't seem like her.'

'You never really know people though, do you, mate?' says Lewis. 'We were all shocked.'

'You were out in town?' I press at Katie, still in disbelief. 'Was she drinking?'

The two of them exchange a look. 'I guess a little …' Katie suddenly looks uncharacteristically sheepish.

'So she was wasted then?' I ask. A bubble of anger forms in my chest. 'And you let a stranger … what? Did he take her home? Did you check?'

'Someone put her in a taxi,' mumbles Katie, avoiding my eyes. 'I don't think she went anywhere with him.'

'You don't *think*.'

We sit in silence for a few moments while I seethe. I want to jump up, run and find Libby and check that she's OK. But once again it feels as though my bones have turned to lead, and my head sinks further into the pillows.

'That's not important now though,' Katie shushes me, reaching out to put her hand on my arm. 'What's important is that you're awake.'

I don't know what to say, and am worried about what might come out if I try. When my parents eventually return, my mum bursting into tears again, Katie and Lewis both slip quietly from the room without saying goodbye.

Mum is fussing over my blankets, again. I swear to god, she must think that I'll drop back into a coma if my feet aren't tucked in just so.

I let her faff; I can't imagine what it must have been like for her the past couple of months. I had the blissful ignorance of unconsciousness; she had the forceful slap of reality. She hasn't talked about how it was for her and Dad, but I can see it in her eyes when I catch her looking at me, just before she looks away. She was terrified. Absolutely terrified. She thought I might not wake up. Nearly two weeks later, I still don't think she quite believes that I did.

It's something I'm trying not to dwell on too much myself.

'Can I bring you anything, love?' Mum asks, folding down a corner with absolute care.

'I'm OK, Mum,' I reply. She looks up at me, tears brimming in her eyes.

'Yes, yes, you are,' she manages, before she's crying again and hugging me with quite a bit of force. I suck in a breath, not wanting to tell her that she's hurting me. 'You're OK, you're OK, you're OK …'

I pat her awkwardly on the back with a shaking arm. Thankfully, Dad walks in with two steaming paper cups of coffee. I give him my best 'save me' look over Mum's shoulder, and he sets down the coffees on my bedside table. He gently prises Mum from my chest, hushing her and letting her turn and sob all over his cardigan. I smile gratefully, and he winks at me.

Mum appears to have finished crying, turning away from Dad with red puffy eyes. There's a damp patch on Dad's shoulder, which he doesn't mention. Mum turns back to me and grasps my hands. 'Will you pray with me?'

She's been doing this a lot, although I imagine still less than when I was out. I stopped actively partaking in my parents' faith a few years ago, joining in as a matter of routine rather than actual belief. I never fully decided what I believed myself, but since waking up I've felt like I probably owe someone somewhere a great big thank-you.

I smile at Mum. 'Of course.'

She sits down beside my bed, Dad moving to stand behind her with his hands on her shoulder. Her hands stay clasped in mine. She takes a deep, shaky breath, and launches into a prayer of gushing thanks for my recovery.

'In Jesus's name, amen,' she finishes, Dad and me

murmuring *'amen'* with her.

'You guys should go and get some lunch,' I suggest. 'Something proper, not one of those crappy sandwiches from the vending machines.'

'Language, Daniel,' Mum says softly. Apparently near-death experiences don't excuse you from cursing in your parents' presence.

'Are you sure?' Dad asks.

'Yeah, course,' I say. 'I'm all set.' I shakily pat the metal pole that holds up my drip, and Mum finally smiles.

They pull on their coats and leave, but not before Mum hugs me again and I assure her, really, it's OK, I'm all right, I think a hospital full of medical staff will be enough to take care of me while they're gone.

After they leave I doze a little, drifting in and out of sleep as doctors and nurses wander in and out to check my vitals or whatever. They've been telling me all week how my progress is nothing short of miraculous, considering how long I was out for and the damage they thought I'd done to my brain. The fact that I can still talk makes me a walking advertisement for the importance of wearing a helmet, apparently.

But my intense need to overachieve won't let me be satisfied with how quickly I'm recovering. I started physio a few days ago and have been moved to a new home on the ward, which is a great step that my parents were thrilled at, but I want to go home.

My physiotherapist ('Call me Richie!') was irritatingly cheery this morning. I had to grit my teeth to keep from snapping at his encouragements as I shuffled forward, leaning hard on the metal support frame, ignoring the lightning shooting through my entire right side. Even when I can get my legs to move roughly the way I want them to, doing it consistently enough to walk – and doing so with one leg in a cast – is bloody difficult. My tiny, excruciatingly slow 'walk' across the room has left me exhausted and aching.

In between check-ins with the doctors and physio sessions, I've had a pretty steady stream of visitors. It's tiring but it keeps me out of my own head, even if I do have to keep brushing off questions about Libby.

She's still not been by.

Katie and Lewis are on a campaign to convince me she's the devil, and every time they try it makes my blood boil. In frustration I try to kick out at the blankets Mum so carefully arranged, but they barely move, and I only succeed in sending waves of pain through my broken leg.

I close my eyes to try and calm down but it's killing me not knowing if she is, and was, OK. From what I've been able to gather, everyone has been making her life hell. No one seems to want to tell me the full story. But it does explain why she was so shocked to find me awake – no one had even bothered to tell her I'd started to show signs of coming out of the coma weeks ago.

The most I was able to get out of anyone came from Mona, who came by with Aaron a few days after I'd woken up. I figured she'd be able to iron things out, at least let me know how Libby was doing – but from the sounds of it, they're not even talking. You get hit by *one* car and everyone around you loses their damn minds.

The more I'd pressed Mona, the more uncomfortable she looked, which I can't say made me feel particularly guilty given the circumstances. Before she left, I made her promise she'd try and talk to Libby. From my hospital bed, it's the most I can do to help her right now.

Libby was doing me a favour, and a big one at that. I keep rolling it over in my mind, what it must have been like for her. And still, she didn't out me to anyone. She could have made it easier on herself by admitting our relationship was completely fake, at least to Mona, but she didn't. She just took it.

I don't know how I'm even going to begin to make it up to her. She must hate me.

I hope it's not too late.

It's another couple of days before I can bring myself to start opening up social-media apps, avoiding them mostly because I don't want to see what people have been saying about Libby, but also because the glare hurts my head and I can't look at the screen for too long. I sift through a seemingly endless stream of notifications – people tagging me in sad statuses or recovered photos from primary school and beyond. At least once a day for the last few months someone has posted on my wall, wishes that I 'get well' that I would either not see or not need.

I consider posting a status myself, something along the lines of 'still alive!'

I consider again. Maybe not.

A few people, for reasons known only to themselves, have

tagged me in the video. Katie tried to show it to me on her last visit, seemingly as proof that everything they'd put Libby through was justified. I'd feigned exhaustion (not a hard task, if I'm honest) and made her leave me alone.

She assumed, and I let her, that I'm putting off the visual because it's too painful. In a way, she's right. I can't bear the thought of Libby being pawed at by a stranger and no one stepping in to help her. But I also have no idea what I'm going to say to the people who were there doing the not-stepping-in when confronted with the visceral reality of it on film.

And honestly, I don't want to see it before I've had a chance to clear things up with Libby. During the long night hours, trying to sleep in a building where something is always bleeping or whirring or someone is shouting, I overthink until my brain practically vibrates. Over the summer I got so used to being able to call up Libby whenever I needed to air out the tangled feelings I had about my sexuality, and she'd carefully lay them out until it all made sense and I could sleep again. I don't know if I can call her now, and I doubt that she'd even pick up.

I can't remember a time when she didn't pick up, even the countless times I called her after she'd already gone to bed.

Without her calm, measured voice on the other end of the phone my thoughts are like spiders, scrambling around in my head and tripping over each other.

I fall into a rough sleep plagued with dreams of bright lights speeding towards me, soundtracked by the endless sound of a phone ringing out.

LIBBY

I honestly didn't know it was possible to feel so many things at once before now. I'm happy to the point of giddiness at the knowledge that Dan is awake, guilty at the fact I still haven't been to see him properly, and confused beyond all reason over what to do about Neha.

The last week at school before we break up for Christmas has been interesting. With Dan awake, everyone (or at least nearly everyone) seems to have forgotten about me, and I've enjoyed a blissful week of being mostly ignored. A couple of the Year 9s still call names out at me in the corridors, and Katie stares daggers at me in assembly – but other than that, people seem to have backed off. I haven't felt the urge to hide in the library for a whole week.

I've even been able to start paying attention in lessons again, and have realised how woefully behind I am. Come January I'll have to really buckle down to get myself back up to speed, but that's next-year-Libby's problem.

This year's Libby is still dealing with a few things.

By now, it's inevitable that Dan will know what happened, what I did. But the fact that the onslaught against me has let up rather than got ten times worse makes me think he, at the very least, hasn't jumped on the Libby Must Die train. Which makes sense, seeing as he's the only one that knows the truth of our 'relationship'.

But still. I put all that in jeopardy, everything we worked all summer to build up. I keep telling myself that today will be the day that I go back to the hospital to see him and talk to him, but then the day passes and I'm still too much of a coward to do it.

It feels like forever since that impromptu visit to the hospital, which was also the last time I saw Neha.

She hasn't said a word to me since, and vice versa. I don't know what I would say even if I was brave enough to try. The longer I leave it the worse it gets.

Today is likely my last chance to say something – as of this afternoon, school will officially be over for the term and I'll have to go from hoping to see Neha in the halls and then avoiding her, to hoping I'll see Neha around the village and then avoiding her. There's been a few times I think we've locked eyes, and I've had a moment of feeling like maybe I am brave enough to talk to her and then I've chickened out, scurrying away and praying she hasn't actually seen me, even though I know deep down that she has.

I remember how it used to feel, spotting her coming down the corridor towards me, how the lead balloon in my chest would feel a little bit lighter. How her whole face would break into a smile, just for me.

I feel like I can't have an honest conversation with her until I've spoken to Dan, but I can't bring myself to do that either. So instead I carry around the Polaroid from the last time we hung out, tucked into my pocket where I can slip my hand in and reassure myself it really happened. The captured moment where it felt like no one else in the world even existed. Just the two of us, damp from the downpour and giddy from the high of simply being together.

I slip into the English classroom, skirting around the edge of the room to avoid walking directly past Katie. She's chattering away to the people around her, holding court, and ignores me completely. I sit down at my now-usual place at the back.

'Libby?'

I freeze at the sound of someone using my actual name. That makes a change. I turn slowly and am shocked to be looking up at Mona, hovering by my lone desk. She's holding a packet of sweets.

'Tangfastic?' She offers the bag to me, looking nervous.

'Uhh.' My overactive imagination has me picturing her dropping rat poison into the bag seconds earlier. I shake the image from my mind and reach out to take a sweet. 'Thanks. You, um, want me to scootch?'

She nods, shy in a way that's so out of character it's unnerving. I shuffle my bag over and she sits down next to me. We both stare at the front of the class, watching others file in and take their seats. Mr Grahams is late again. Then Mona grasps my arm.

'I'm so, so sorry, Libs,' she blurts, still not looking at me. 'I should have just spoken to you about it. I know you tried, but I was just so *mad*.' She runs a hand over her curls, looking frazzled. 'After what happened with my dad I could only see it in black and white. I watched the video again and I can't believe I didn't see it before. You weren't in control. I should have been there, that night and afterwards …'

She draws in a deep breath after the rush of words. 'I just, I feel like an idiot. I'm supposed to be your best friend and I dropped you. If I could go back in time and give myself a shake I would. I miss you so much.'

I stare at her. I remember the weeks of sitting by myself in the canteen at lunch. Sitting here at the back of every class, every day, trying to cobble together two people's worth of work whenever we were asked to do things in a pair I couldn't make. Running alone during cross-country. Walking through the corridors with my headphones clamped over my ears so I could pretend I didn't even *want* anyone to talk to.

I want to be able to let it all go.

'I miss you too,' I say, and Mona's eyes light up. 'But I can't pretend that none of this happened. It *hurt*. It still does.'

Mona bows her head, crestfallen. Everything in me screams to reach out and hug her, tell her everything is all fine, but it isn't, not yet, and I'm trying to get better at not putting my own feelings dead last.

'Do you think you can ever forgive me?' Mona asks in a small voice.

I take a deep breath. 'I do. I want to. It's just still very fresh.'

Mona nods. 'I understand. Of course I understand. Take all the time you need. But I'm here for you, if you want me to be. Whenever that might be.'

We sit in silence for a moment. Katie still has her back firmly to us.

'What made you change your mind?' I ask.

'It was Dan,' she says, and I'm stunned into silence for a moment. *Did he tell her?!*

'Dan ... ?'

'I went to see him at the hospital and he made me see sense. That you never would have cheated on him in your right mind,' Mona explains. 'And then when I watched the video again ... I think I'd already made up my mind before I saw it the first time, and it made me sick to look at. It still does, but for different reasons.'

I nod slowly, staring down at the desk. 'And what did Dan say, exactly?' I'd been aiming for casual but of course it comes out desperate.

'You haven't been to see him yet, have you?' she asks. It used to be a bit annoying how clearly she could read me, but my god I've missed it.

'No, I haven't,' I admit. 'I'm just terrified. What if he hates me?'

'I can tell you he doesn't,' says Mona firmly. 'Honestly, if he had his strength back I'd have been in trouble. I think he tried to hide it but he was – rightly – furious with me. With everyone, for how they've treated you.' She pauses, and casts her eyes down again. 'How *we* treated you.'

I can't help it – I take her hand and squeeze it, and she smiles back up at me. I'm not convinced, but it's enough to make me decide. I'll go and see Dan. Soon.

For the rest of the day, I feel like I float through the corridors. I'm in such a daze about making up with Mona that I almost don't hear Emily Parker calling my name as I head towards the lunch hall.

I turn in confusion, still not used to people using 'Libby' instead of some variation of 'slut'. Emily stands off to one side, her eyes darting up and down the corridor.

'Can I talk to you a minute?' she asks, gripping the strap of her satchel and looking like talking to me is actually the last thing she wants to do. I nod silently, and she grabs my arm and drags me away from the hall and off into the girls' toilets.

We stand on the damp tiles, and she looks everywhere but at me.

'What?' I ask, feeling a spike of irritation. This is someone who's contributed to making my life hell for the past months after all.

'I needed to talk to you,' she says in a rush. 'About the other day. At the cinema.'

I blink, having almost forgotten the whole interaction with Katie and the others at the tiny village cinema. It feels like it happened a million years ago, and to someone else.

'What about it?'

Emily stares resolutely at her shoes. 'I … I wanted to say I was sorry.'

I am, not for the first time today, shocked into silence. First Mona, now Emily Parker?

Emily takes a big breath. 'It was so out of order. I don't think I ever really realised how far she'd go.'

'Even after the changing rooms?' I ask, surprising myself this time. I seem to have found a boldness I didn't know I had.

Emily flinches. 'That too. I want to say sorry for everything. We went too far.'

I stare at the top of her head, incredulous. I want to put in the work to forgive Mona, but Mona never kicked me in the kidneys. I don't feel the same willingness towards Emily, or any of them.

'I can't really do much with an apology, Emily,' I say. It's ballsy – people have only just started to forget I exist in a way I've been longing for, for weeks.

'I know,' Emily says, digging around in her bag and pulling out her phone. 'That's why I wanted to give you this.'

For a moment I'm baffled, until I see that she's not giving me the phone but showing me something that's on it. It's a video.

On the small screen I recognise the foyer of the Showcase cinema with me, Katie and Neha in the frame. I remember the row of phones filming our interaction and cringe a little at the guilty look on my face.

That is, until the on-screen Katie turns on Neha and I change almost instantly. I hear the foul word again reverberate around my brain and the icy fury I felt in that moment floods back through me. The video wobbles and goes black.

I look back up at Emily, confused. Why is she showing me this? I was there. I know what happened.

She's tapping away now, and I hear a quiet *whoosh* of a message sending. She looks back up at me, in the eye for the first time.

'I've sent it to you,' she says. 'I thought you should decide what to do with it.'

It takes a second for the penny to drop. Katie destroyed my life with a video. Emily is giving me the power to do the same to her.

Seeing the realisation dawn on my face, Emily gives a shrug. 'I know this village isn't exactly progressive. But I don't think she'll get away with that.'

I don't know what to say, so I just nod. Emily hitches her bag back on to her shoulder and leaves me in the girls' toilets, feeling my phone burning in my blazer pocket with what it now contains.

Neha

Mrs Clark is saying something about A-level mocks and UCAS points, but I'm hardly listening. I'm thinking about Libby, something I've been doing almost constantly as of late.

I've still not heard from her since that day at the hospital. I haven't reached out either, having wanted to give her some space after the shock of everything that happened. Except that turned into a lot of space, and then it seemed too late to try and get in touch, and now I have no idea what's going on or where I stand.

I know she felt something. The way she held me when we saw each other for the first time after the crash – tight. Comforting. And the way she spoke ... I can't have imagined any of that. I can't. I came so close to just telling her how I felt. How I *feel*. Why didn't I take the chance when I had it?

But then Dan was awake, and I'm so pleased he's OK, but a not-insignificant part of me won't let go of wondering what that means for me and Libby. It's the most mixed up I think I've ever felt about anything, and I can't deny that there's also a tiny bit of hurt – maybe I was just seeing what I wanted to see, willing her to like me the way I liked her, but we were definitely at least friends. And now she's undeniably avoiding me.

I'd suspected it for a while. Our school is so tiny we'd been running into each other every day since we first started hanging out, so it was impossible we were simply just not crossing paths. I'd occasionally catch a flash of red hair disappearing around a corner, and convince myself that maybe it wasn't her.

But yesterday, on my way to Biology, I can't deny that she saw me. We made eye contact and froze, mirror images of anxiety and uncertainty. The moment felt like it dragged on forever, even though it must have been seconds at most. A tiny hope bloomed in my chest, and I almost smiled, but then she ripped her eyes away from mine and half ran back the way she'd just come.

It stung. A lot. And I can't shake the fear that maybe everything we went through together was just a placeholder for her. The thought of it digs into my skin like a splinter I can't shift.

I'm snapped out of my worry spiral when the bell rings, signalling the end of not just the school day but the whole term. A small cheer goes up around the lab as everyone throws their stuff haphazardly into their bags and heads for the door, Mrs Rawlinson shouting a hurried 'Merry Christmas!' at their retreating backs.

I stay sat on my stool. After I leave today, that could be it until next term. I know I might see Libby around the village, but the reality is I'll probably just hide away at home. At least with school I was forced to come out.

Mrs Clark looks up at me from where she's gathering some papers together on her desk, getting ready to leave herself. 'Is everything OK, Neha?'

'I'm fine,' I lie, forcing myself to finally stand up.

She shuffles her papers again. 'Well, merry Christmas!' she says with a forced brightness, clearly ready for the term to finally end. A confused look crosses her face. 'Oh, do you celebrate Christmas?'

I fight the urge to roll my eyes. I'm asked this every year, and it never gets less annoying. 'I do,' I say simply, shrugging my bag on to my shoulder and leaving before she can say anything else.

The corridors have mostly emptied out, everyone keen to get away and start their Christmas holidays. But as I'm rounding a corner I still manage to run straight into someone.

'Ooof!' I stagger a little, righting myself. 'Shit, I'm sorry …'

I look up and see a tangle of dark curls. I've run into Mona.

'Oh!' Mona stares back at me, and for a moment we're just standing there looking at each other like we've never seen another human being before.

I'm the first to break eye contact, looking down at the floor as I back away.

'Sorry. Uhh … have a good Christmas.'

I turn, about ready to start running as soon as I'm out of her eyeline, but she grabs my arm.

'Neha, wait!'

I stop. Mona lets me go and takes a big breath, as if steeling herself.

'Listen, I just wanted to say thank you. For looking out for Libby these past few weeks.'

I blink, not knowing exactly what I had expected, but it wasn't this.

'I don't know if I'll ever forgive myself for leaving her like I did in the middle of all this,' Mona continues, 'but I know I feel a lot better knowing that she had someone with her. And I wanted you to know how much that means to me. And her.'

'Oh.' I honestly don't know what to say. 'You're welcome?'

Mona laughs, and it's the kind of warm sound that makes you want to join in, so I do. 'I know that's probably weird,' she says, shaking her head. 'But I had to say something.'

'It's all right,' I say. 'How is Libby? If it's OK to ask.'

Mona cocks her head at me, confused. 'Are you two not hanging out any more?'

I cast my eyes down and mumble something incoherent.

'How come?' She asks it so openly I almost feel compelled to answer – because I think I'm falling in love with her and she has a boyfriend who's fresh out of a coma. Because I don't even know if our friendship was real. Because, because, because.

'I don't know,' is what I go for instead.

'Hmm.' She regards me carefully. 'Well, whatever you guys

fell out about, one of you needs to talk to the other. I've known Libby for years, and besides Dan, I'm the only close friend she's had, so you two must have had something special.'

I can't respond to that without giving myself away, so I just nod.

Mona smiles and starts to back away. 'Anyway. I wanted to let you know. Hopefully see you soon?'

'Sure,' I say, feeling dazed. I watch Mona walk away and through the double doors. When I look round, I see that I'm now completely alone in the school corridor.

Feeling an oppressive sense of eeriness, I hurry out.

I can't even bring myself to soundtrack my slow walk home. I think about Mona, wonder what it would be like to make up with Libby and have the three of us become our own little group. But then, if Dan and Libby are still together he'd probably be there too, and I'd have to act like I wasn't burning up inside every time they so much as looked at each other.

I arrive home and immediately stomp to the kitchen, throwing down my bag and banging around the cupboards for the baking tins. I've got almost everything together before I spot the flour lurking on the top shelf, just slightly out of reach. I'm too aggravated to drag over a chair so just claw at the bag while on my tiptoes, but when I finally grasp it the bag slips through my fingers and lands with a thud on the floor, sending a bitter, musty cloud right into my face.

I'm spluttering over the sink when Jas walks in.

'Are you angry-baking?' she asks mildly, picking the offending bag up off the floor and setting it gently on the side.

'No.' I run myself a glass of water and take a big glug. 'Maybe. Sorry. Did I wake you up?'

'I couldn't sleep anyway,' she lies, sitting down at the kitchen table. 'What's up?'

I flop down at the table. 'Everything?'

'Ooh, that's rough.' Jas nods thoughtfully. 'Care to get specific?'

'You probably already know,' I sigh.

'Well, I am very perceptive.' She reaches over and brushes a streak of flour off my cheek. 'Especially when it comes to you.'

I drop my head into my arms and make a kind of strangled cry.

'That's it, get it all out,' Jas says, patting me on the back. 'But seriously. I think it's probably time we had an extremely open conversation about everything that's going on?'

I raise my head again to look at her. I thought I'd got away with this after our chat at the hospital, but I should have known that she'd push eventually – she always knows what's going on when it comes to me, but I suppose I've never actually said the words out loud.

'I have a massive crush on Libby.' I drop my chin back on to my folded arms. 'Libby who's the first person to treat me like I even exist since I moved here, Libby who has a boyfriend, Libby whose boyfriend has been in a coma up until very recently, and who hasn't spoken to me since he woke up.'

'There we go,' says Jas softly. She reaches out and squeezes my arm. 'Have you tried reaching out yet? I think you've both had plenty of time to stew on it now.'

'And say what?' I moan. 'If I tell her how I feel, she might think I was trying to take advantage of her while she was grieving. And what use is there telling her now Dan's awake? Oh god.' I sigh dramatically. 'I'm a monster for seeing him coming out of a coma as a *bad* thing.'

'You're not a monster,' Jas says firmly. 'And I know you're not actually wishing Dan didn't wake up – despite everything else you're feeling.'

The rational side of me knows she's right – but I can't stop my lizard brain from picturing what might have happened if we'd been left alone in that hospital room for a little bit longer.

'I just think that there's a chance they might patch up their relationship,' I say quietly. 'And I don't want to get in the way of that.'

'Do you think Libby felt the same way about you?'

The question that's haunted me every moment since the hospital sounds ridiculous when spoken out loud.

'No,' I say, though without conviction and I think Jas knows it. 'But that's not the point, really. I want my friend back. It's horrible being invisible again. I guess I feel like … I was a placeholder for the people Libby actually wanted to be with.' I think again about Mona, and how it probably won't be long before she's Libby's best friend again. I lower my head back down to the table. 'She doesn't need me any more.'

'I don't think that's true,' says Jas. 'You two had a real connection, whether that was as friends or something else. And I *definitely* walked in on something at the hospital.'

She raises her eyebrows at me and I squirm. But I can't say it doesn't help a little to know that it wasn't all in my head.

'I think you're going to feel a bit unmoored until you talk to her properly,' she continues. 'I know it's easier said than done, but that's the only thing for it.'

I mumble into the tabletop. Jas stifles a yawn.

'OK, well, you actually did wake me up so I'm going to try and get another couple of hours.' She stands up and stoops to kiss me on the head. 'I love you, even when you're a screaming mess. Do something nice for yourself tonight, yeah?'

'Fine, I'll be nice to me,' I say into my arms. 'Love you too.'

I hear her move away and up the stairs. I stay sitting at the kitchen table, staring off into the distance and turning it over and over in my mind.

Despite having sat here for over an hour, I still don't know what I want or what to do.

Dan

With every day that passes, I get more and more frustrated with myself.

Although my physio sessions are going well, and the cast on my leg has been replaced with a hefty orthopaedic boot, I've also had to start practising getting around with a wheelchair. It's taking a while to get used to – not least because after a couple minutes of practice I need to pause for long enough to let my body stop shrieking at me. I'm already pushing it further than I probably should.

The sense of not being fully in control is infuriating, especially when I was getting to grips with the simple process of moving myself around. I've never felt that lack of physical control over my body before and it's jarring. Being occasionally moved out of the way slightly by a passing hospital porter or visitor if I'm in their way certainly doesn't help.

I'm trying very much to remind myself that the chair is a tool that means I can do things other than sit in bed, and repeating that to myself is helping. A little.

'You just need more rest,' Mum says, as if one more nap will repair all the wonky neurons in my brain, the deterioration of my muscles from lying in bed for months and the bones that are still knitting themselves back together.

'I wish I could rest *faster*,' I huff. I am, as usual, propped up in my hospital bed while Mum bustles around me, making up tasks so she has an excuse not to go home and leave me to it.

There's a tentative knock at the door. I pray it's not Katie – she comes by a lot. She asks how I'm doing, I reply that I'm fine, and then we mostly sit in awkward silence for a while before she leaves. A couple of times she's tried to press me again on why I was out on the road that night, but I don't think I'd tell her even if I could remember. It feels like something has soured between us, and I'm still trying to figure out if what's broken can be repaired.

But it's not Katie that appears at the doorway.

'Libby!'

She smiles at the tiled floor, bright red curls poking out from under a woollen hat dusted with snow.

I go to shoot up, hiss in pain, and Mum gently rubs my back. I resolve to lie back against the pillows again.

'Not too fast,' she instructs, unnecessarily in my opinion, before turning her head back towards the doorway. 'Hello, Olivia. We were wondering when you might come by.'

Libby flinches, and it looks like it's taking everything in her not to turn and run.

'Come in!' I say quickly before she breaks. 'Mum, do you

want to … ?' I lean my head towards the door. She purses her lips but doesn't object.

'I'll go and get a coffee in the canteen,' she says lightly. As she passes Libby in the doorway she pauses as if considering, then gives her a squeeze on the shoulder. 'It's nice to see you.'

Libby visibly relaxes, if just a tiny amount.

I pat the space beside me on the bed, still grinning like an idiot. Libby slowly crosses the room and lowers herself down beside me, pulling off her hat and scarf but not her coat. There's a stilted silence.

'Oh! I have something for you!' I say, struck with inspiration. I carefully lean over to the bedside table, gritting my teeth as my side protests, and pick up the iPod I found a couple of days ago. It had been hiding at the bottom of the table drawer, under some 'Get Well Soon' cards. I hold it out to her. 'This is yours, right?'

Libby stares at it for a second, her lower lip trembling. Then her arms jerk out as if she wants to hug me, sees me wince in anticipation, and settles for an eerie mirror of exactly what Katie did the first time she saw me – collapsing into the bedside chair and throwing her head into her arms as she sobs.

'Whoa!' I laugh, but I lift a heavy arm to lay across her shoulders. 'Steady on, people will talk.'

'I just c-can't believe …' she manages between gasps for breath. 'I thought … I thought that …'

'Yeah, everyone "thought that",' I reply. 'But you all thought wrong. I'm here. It's OK.'

'It's not OK,' Libby sniffs, sitting up and swiping roughly

at her eyes. 'It's not OK at all. Dan, I really messed up.'

'I kinda heard,' I say. She inhales sharply and I reach out to squeeze her hand. 'Except it's not you that messed up, it's everyone else. Are you all right?'

'Am I … ?' Libby stares at me in disbelief. 'Am *I* all right?! Dan, I cheated on you!'

'Look, even if we were, y'know, a proper couple, you were drunk. Even Katie admits you were drunk, and she's trying to sanitise it to save her own skin, so I know it must have been bad. It wasn't your fault. Seriously, what went down? I've only heard Lewis and Katie's sordid version.'

Libby casts her eyes down. 'You know what happened. I'm sure you've seen the video.'

'I haven't actually.'

'What?' Her head snaps up. 'Why?!'

'I didn't think you'd be comfortable with it,' I say with a small shrug, like it's obvious. But her eyes are filling up again.

'God, I don't even deserve you as a fake boyfriend,' she says miserably. 'But I think you should see it. I'd rather you knew. I don't want you thinking it wasn't as bad as it was.'

She pulls out her phone and starts tapping, then turns it towards me. I hesitate, then take the phone and look down at the video that's already started playing.

It's a crowded dance floor, and I quickly spot Libby's red hair amongst the throngs of people. She's swaying hard, and not in time to the music blaring tinnily through the phone speakers. Fear spikes in my gut, seeing just how out of it she really was.

As I watch, a figure moves out of the crowd and grabs her waist, and she clings to him like he's a lifeboat and not the current about to carry her away. Then his face is on hers and she's half-limp in his arms, her head trying to move away, but he's stronger and more sober and she can't get away.

I throw the phone down on the bed in disgust.

'I told you it was bad,' says Libby, misery heavy on every syllable. 'I can go if you—'

'*No one* helped you?' I half shout, making her jump. 'Libby, how can you look at that and see yourself as the one in the wrong? How can anyone blame you for that? Please tell me you got home OK.'

Something passes behind Libby's eyes, like an echo.

'You're really ... you're really not mad at me?'

'Of *course* I'm not mad at you! I'm absolutely *furious* at everyone else though, how could they—'

'My mum says I came home alone,' Libby interrupts, seemingly sensing the rage building up inside me. 'I was OK.'

'Were you though?' I shake my head. 'That happened to you, and then everyone was on your case for it? All this time?'

'They thought I deserved it.'

'And they made you believe that too. I can't imagine what it's been like for you.'

We sit in silence for a while, but this time it's more comfortable, familiar. Libby's brow is creased as she stares down at the bed, and I give her the space to work through whatever it is she's thinking.

'We need to break up,' Libby blurts out, shattering the quiet.

'What?!' I yelp, my voice rising as I feel the walls of our heteronormative community closing in on me again. My head pounds. 'No, we shouldn't! It was working, I can't go back to having to pretend.'

'You *were* pretending,' she replies. 'And as far as everyone else is concerned, I *did* cheat on you. In case you forgot.'

'But you *didn't*,' I say. 'That's not what happened, and I'm going to make damn sure everyone understands that.'

Libby smiles at me. 'And maybe some of them will. But the rest will think I need to be punished, and whether they're right or wrong –'

'They're wrong.'

'– I still have to deal with them. And if you fight it too hard, it might look weird. You don't want people to clock that it was never real. And besides, what about … me?'

I blink at her. 'What?'

'I mean, what if I don't want to do this any more?' She sighs. 'Dan, this was never just pretending for me. You have to know that.'

I squirm, avoiding her eyes. She pushes on.

'It was real for me, without it being real. I got to be with you but at the same time I wasn't. And it was hell.' She takes a deep breath. 'And now, I think I've maybe found someone else.'

I look up, eyebrows raised. 'Do I know him?'

'Not exactly.' Libby shifts a little on the bed. 'No, it's Neha. Neha Gill. From school.'

'Neha Gill?' I remember a nervous-looking girl with big eyes and dark hair, and sitting next to her in assembly so she wouldn't be alone. Speaking to her at the summer fete and how amazing the cake she made was. 'She's, well, a she.'

'Yeah,' says Libby, smiling softly.

'So you're … ?'

'Not straight, I guess.' She shrugs. 'I haven't really had a chance to overanalyse it yet. She might not feel the same way about me, or if she did I might have already ruined it, but I can't not find out because of something that's not real.'

I stay quiet for a moment, absorbing. Then I look up and into her eyes, and she's looking at me so openly I can't bear it. I'm struck by everything she's done for me, everything she's been through, and I feel like the biggest arse in the world.

'I'm sorry,' I whisper. 'I was so selfish.'

'You were scared,' she says, reaching out and taking my hand. 'And I made my own decisions. I just can't keep it up any more.'

'I understand.'

She raises her arms again, asking permission with a look, and I nod. She leans over and hugs me, *very* gently. 'I still love you. But now I love you in the way you're supposed to love your best friend.'

'I love you too,' I say into her hair. 'So we're still friends then?'

'We'd better be, I need all the friends I can get at the minute.' She leans back and smiles. 'But maybe in secret at first? Seeing as you've got to dump me.'

'Why do I have to do the dumping?'

'Because then people might think I've got what's coming to me, and stop torturing me so much. While you were gone it was as if I hadn't been punished so they took it upon themselves to do it for you.'

'Right,' I say grimly. 'Does it have to be a big public drama-fest?'

'Please, no drama,' Libby laughs. 'We can just say it happened tonight. Start telling people you ended it, and it will spread quickly enough. I assume you're getting enough visitor traffic through here to spread the word pretty fast.'

'I guess.' I sigh, twisting the edge of the bedsheet between my fingers. 'I really kind of enjoyed being your not-boyfriend.'

'And I enjoyed being your not-girlfriend, most of the time,' Libby says with a smile. 'But right now I kind of want to be someone else's.'

'Did you know?' I ask, glancing over at the door to make sure a nurse isn't about to walk in or something. Excitement is building up in me as I realise this is the first time I've had an open conversation about sexuality with a fellow queer person, but I'm not so excited that the idea of being overheard doesn't worry me. I lower my voice. 'Before now, that you liked girls? Do you *only* like girls?'

'Dan, I haven't had chance to ask *myself* those questions,' Libby says, but she's still smiling. 'Honestly? I think I did know, a bit. But I think I like both, or all, I guess. And given where we live …' She waves her hand and I nod. 'It was just easier to put myself in the straight box and not think about it too much.'

'That makes sense,' I say. She looks at me with her head on one side.

'When did you know you were fully gay?' she asks in a half whisper. She laughs a little. 'Did I *ever* have a shot?'

I grin at her. 'Libby, if I couldn't fall for you, no girl ever had a shot.'

'Give over,' she says, blushing, but she's laughing properly and it's such a good sound. 'But seriously. I feel like I've just discovered something about myself, I don't even know what label to put on it yet. Did you always know?'

I sigh, and lean back against my pillows. 'I think so. I can't really say how. I never had a light-bulb moment, I just knew. All I can really remember is stressing over keeping it a secret.'

'That sucks,' says Libby.

'It really does,' I say slowly. 'I never even had a chance to, like, have a crush on anyone. There was no room for anything else except desperately keeping it under wraps.'

'Maybe you can give yourself some room now?' she says, and I screw my face up. It seems I can only talk about it openly for a limited amount of time in one go, even with Libby. I decide to swerve the subject.

'Yeah, maybe. But in the meantime, Neha Gill, huh? How'd that happen?'

'Her being the only person in school that would still talk to me was a big factor,' she replies, and I laugh.

'Fair enough. That puts her a head above everyone else in our year, in my eyes. But why do you think you've ruined it?'

Her shoulders slump. 'I've done the incredibly mature thing of ignoring her ever since you woke up.'

'You what?' I sit up straighter. 'Why on earth have you done that?'

'Well, what was I supposed to say!' she says defensively. '"Hey, Neha, you know that high-profile relationship of mine with a coma patient? It's all a cover-up for the fact that he's actually gay. Also, I appear to have fallen a little bit in love with you. What do you say?"'

'Well, I wouldn't put it like that,' I huff. 'Sugar-coat it a bit more – don't scare the girl.'

'I can't believe I'm getting romantic advice from my gay boyfriend.'

'Gay *ex*-boyfriend,' I remind her quietly, shooting another look at the door.

She tuts at me, but she's grinning and I'm filled with sheer relief that she's OK, and still my friend.

But then she sighs, heavier than I've ever heard anyone sigh. 'We also got into a fight, right before you woke up.'

'What about?'

'How to appropriately handle blatant homophobia, funnily enough,' she says. My confusion must be evident on my face, and she tells me about their argument in the car. And then the crash.

'Neither of you were hurt, right?' I say hastily, and she shakes her head.

'Neha needed some stitches. We were OK for the most part, physically at least. It was pretty rattling. But I just got so *mad*, thinking about how often people casually say that shit.' She looks up at me. 'I couldn't stop thinking about how it must make you feel. And how I'd never really spoken up against anyone before.'

'Oh, Libs,' I say, feeling another rush of love towards her. 'But you said you guys made up in the hospital?'

'Barely,' she says, shaking her head. 'We found out that you were awake and I've been too scared to speak to her ever since.'

She sighs again and rises to her feet. 'Listen, I should go and let you rest. I've heard what's probably your mum walk past the door three times already.'

'Come back soon, yeah?' I say. 'You might need to text ahead in case someone else is here. But definitely visit. We'll get this sorted out, I promise.'

'I definitely will.' She bends quickly and gives me a feather-light kiss on the cheek, then smiles. 'I'm so glad you're OK, Dan. No matter what was going on, I don't know what I'd have done without you.'

'It'll take more than a silly coma to get rid of me,' I quip, and she snorts as she heads towards the door. She pauses and turns back, a quizzical look on her face.

'Dan, your accident, it was on the road to mine; I figured you'd found out about what happened and were coming to confront me. But you said you didn't know before you woke up, so why were you coming over so late?'

I stare at her for a moment, my brain working backwards. And then I gasp.

'Oh my god! I can't believe I forgot.'

'What? What is it?'

Grinning, I lean forward as much as my body will let me.

'I kissed someone! A boy!'

Libby's eyes widen. 'You what?!'

'That night, I'd just got back from a gig in the city? After our set, I got chatting to this guy backstage and I dunno, I never even got his name, and I was terrified that one of the guys might come back and see us. And it was only for a minute, but I got off with a boy!'

'THAT'S BRILLIANT!' Libby squeaks, then claps a hand to her mouth and shoots a look at the door, lowering her voice to an excited hush. 'Why didn't you tell me?!'

'Um, I was in a coma, remember, ,' I say, tutting dramatically. Slowly, her face turns incredulous.

'Do you mean to tell me that after everything that went down, *you* cheated on *me* first?'

We stare at each other for a moment, and then her shoulders are shaking and we're both howling with laughter. At the sound, Mum bursts in from lurking just behind the door, demanding to be told what's so funny.

We can't answer of course, and not just because neither of us can breathe for laughing. Eventually she just shakes her head and leaves us laughing harder than I can ever remember. I'll pay for it later – god, will I pay for it later – but right now, it absolutely feels worth it.

'Come on, come on, home time!' I say with gusto. I know I shouldn't get myself worked up, and I should really stop moving so much, but the excitement of leaving these four sterile white walls behind is taking over. My parents are faffing around with my bag, checking we've got all my medication, prescriptions and socks packed.

'I still think it's too soon,' Mum huffs, slowly counting all my pill bottles again. 'Just a while longer, to make sure—'

'Mu-uuum!' It took me long enough to talk the doctors round – scheduling in months' worth of check-ups and physio visits, arranging for a hospital bed to be set up at home, promising to be a good boy and take it easy. I can't go through it all again with Mum.

'Mandy, he's ready,' says Dad. He smiles at me and again I wonder how on earth I'd have ever made it out if he wasn't here to back me up. Without his influence I get the feeling Mum would have chained me to the radiator. I'd have never left.

'I'm just going to speak to Dr Phillips before we go,' Mum says, bustling out the room. I sigh, but don't call her back. She's only looking out for me, I guess.

'So,' says Dad, folding up a jumper and placing it carefully in my duffel, 'excited to be leaving?'

'*Yes*.' I grin and throw in a crumpled T-shirt on top of the jumper. 'I just want to get back to normal.'

'Normal might look a bit different for a while,' Dad says pointedly, and I grumble in agreement. He sits down on the end of the bed and looks at me thoughtfully. 'And how are things with Libby?'

'They're good,' I say, a little bubble of happiness inflating in my chest as I say it. Dad nods.

'Oh good. I was a bit worried. She seemed so distressed when you came around.'

I make a non-committal noise in the back of my throat, and become intent on refolding everything in the bag. But he won't be dismissed.

'We didn't see her for so long after you woke up. She's a lovely girl. It just doesn't seem like the kind of thing a girl like that would do, not visit her boyfriend while he's in hospital.' He pauses and gives me a very pointed look. 'Do you have any idea what might have been the matter?'

His voice is even, and without judgement. He knows something is up, had perceived that Libby wasn't plain ignoring me. He's got more insight than the entire student population of St Hilda's, it seems. I'm sure they dismissed her absence here after I woke up as just further proof of her status as devil spawn.

'I might have an idea,' I mumble.

'You want to talk about it?'

I look up at him. I wonder what he would say if he knew. Or maybe he's already guessed?

'Dad, I—'

'Right, well, we'd best be making a move then.' Mum breezes back into the room and Dad and I jump a little at the interruption. Dad stands quickly and zips up my bag, and the moment is lost.

It's a very short drive, but all the way I watch the back of Dad's head as he drives us down the winding country roads towards home. Maybe it's just me, but it looks as though there's a bit more silver laced through his dark hair.

We pull up in front of the house and I let out a small sigh of relief at the familiar sight. The hanging baskets that are usually so carefully preened are looking a little dead, and the front lawn hasn't been mowed in a while. It looks a bit scruffy around the edges, but then so do I. I'm still me. It's still home.

Mum helps me from the car while Dad unloads my bag and a hospital-loaned wheelchair from the boot. He unfolds the chair and I lower myself into it, annoyed that it's needed for the short distance between the car and the house. I suppress a groan at the thought of more frequent appointments with Call Me Richie in my foreseeable future. But I can't deny the fact that I've not even made it through the front door yet and the stabbing sensations in my leg are making me a little woozy.

As we cross the threshold I inhale deeply, the smell of lemon-scented furniture polish and potpourri filling my senses. For a second the three of us pause in the hallway, smiling like dorks at one another.

'The spare room is all set up for you,' says Mum, taking the handles of the wheelchair to push me down the hall. 'We know you want to be back in your own room, but a room downstairs makes more sense for now.'

I eye the stairs as we pass, remembering how I would usually bound up them two at a time to my bedroom. My leg twinges again and I have to concede that it's for the best.

We reach the spare room, which is clean, neat and nothing

at all like my bedroom upstairs. But they've brought down some of my posters and photos from the walls to make it feel more familiar, and have even propped my acoustic guitar up in the corner of the room.

It feels like my fingers have been itching to pick up a guitar since the moment I opened my eyes, but seeing it now I don't feel the usual urge to grab it and start strumming. I blame it on being knackered after the journey from the hospital. My bones feel like lead.

'I was going to do a roast for dinner,' Mum says. 'Something home-made will be nice after all that hospital food, mmm?'

'Thanks, Mum,' I say. I look down at my scrawny arms. I wasn't exactly bulky before the accident, but I could probably use three roast dinners right about now. 'That'd be great.'

She beams, and heads into the kitchen. Dad clasps a hand on my shoulder, before following her from the room. I'm left alone, and I run a hand over the soft, flowery-scented sheets that feel a million miles away from the stiff, starchy hospital bedding.

Despite the chaos in my head, it's so good to be home.

LIBBY

'So what d'you reckon? Do we want the snowman that might steal your soul, or the Christmas tree that looks like it's on drugs?'

Dan lifts up two equally scary Christmas decorations from the basket at our feet, one of which is destined for my front door. After I complained about the carollers, he suggested we should find something hideous to hang from the porch in an attempt to scare them away.

'Whichever,' I mumble, staring blankly across the over-crowded garden-centre coffee shop.

Dan called me this morning sounding desperate, proclaiming that the walls of the spare room were already threatening to eat him and he'd convinced his mum to let him venture out further than the village. On the condition that she could drop him off and pick him up again, and of course he'd need to use his chair so as not to overexert himself (and because he can't walk more than ten steps unaided yet).

I didn't admit it to Dan, but I agree with her. He's not one to take things slowly, and I know how eager he's been to throw himself back into 'normality'. I'd suggested the garden centre in a town just far enough away from Chipping Hollow that we'd be less likely to run into anyone we knew.

I feel like a complete Grinch but my mood is so low it's scraping the ground, and I can't buoy myself up even with the help of tinny Christmas music and tacky decorations, everything from classic to gaudy and back again. I know I should be floating – not only have I got Dan back, but I'm finding my way back to Mona too, one shy DM at a time.

But I can't stop thinking about Neha.

I drop my head into my arms on the tabletop, resolutely ignoring the cooling mug of hot chocolate by my side. Dan finished his five minutes ago and I keep seeing him looking at mine – I'll put him out of his misery soon and offer to share.

'I take it you haven't spoken to Neha yet then?'

Damn him. 'Of course I haven't, I'm a coward,' I mumble into my arms.

'*Why* didn't you talk to her at school?' he asks, barely able to hide his exasperation at me.

'We don't share any classes,' I say. It's a rubbish excuse but it's all I've got. 'Whenever I saw her in the halls I ran the other way. I didn't want to get in her face.'

'You know there's a good chance she's doing the same thing, right?' he says. 'It sounds like the two of you had quite the moment before I rudely went and woke up in the middle of it. She might not have even heard that we "broke up" and doesn't know where she stands.'

'Or she's finally realised she should be mad at me for making her crash her aunt's car. And that she *definitely* should be for ignoring her for so long after the hospital.'

'You need to talk to her,' he says. 'That's it! Just talk to her! It will be fine!'

'What if it's not?' I moan. 'What if she shuts the door in my face, or puts the phone down on me or something?'

'You won't know unless you *try*,' he insists. 'And besides, from the sound of it she wants to speak to you too. But maybe she wants you to make the first move.'

'But what if she's avoiding me because she just plain doesn't want to see me?'

'Libby, I love you, but I am going to scream at you in a minute. She clearly *does* want to see you!'

'How do you know that though?'

'Because I know everything!' he splutters indignantly. 'My near-death experience has left me with incredible perception and the ability to see the future.'

I finally look up at him, eyebrows cocked, and he grabs my now-cold mug of chocolate and waves his hands over the melting foam. 'I see a lot of bitterness and regret in your future, with seventeen cats and self-knitted cardigans. *Unless* you go and talk to Neha!'

I crack a smile. 'What else do you see in your crystal ball, Mystic Marge?'

'I see a tall dark stranger, who will sweep me off my feet so we can ride off into the sunset together,' he says, but not before casting a quick glance around the coffee shop. I raise an eyebrow at him.

'No one here cares that you're gay. Except maybe the waiter. He was checking you out.'

'Really?' He looks back at the counter so eagerly I can't help but laugh, and he reaches across the table to swat at me with the menu card. 'Mean.'

He settles back in his seat, and I watch how his brow knits together just slightly and he fights against a wince at the wave of pain after his burst of movement. He's desperate for us all to believe he's totally fine, but I can see right through him. I'm about to say something when a mischievous grin grows across his face and his eyes start to widen – I can almost hear the cogs turning in his head as he forms a new idea.

'I'll tell you what,' he says. 'We'll make a deal. If you talk to Neha and tell her you like her – I'll tell someone else that I'm gay.'

'What?' I look up from stirring my cold drink. 'You'd come out?'

'Just to one other person,' he adds quickly, already looking like he regrets the suggestion. 'I mean, I'm going to need to at some point, right?'

'Well, yeah, when you're ready,' I say, putting a hand on his arm. He twists his wrist so he can take hold of my arm too, looking me solidly in the eye.

'I think I am ready.'

There's a beat, and then I jump out of my seat to throw

my arms around him. 'Dan, that's huge! That's brilliant! I'm so proud of you!'

'I've not done it yet,' he mumbles into my hair, but when we pull apart he's smiling. Then his face turns serious. 'But you've got to talk to Neha.'

I go still, and for a moment I think about refusing. But I know how hard it's been for him, how badly he wanted to be himself but how scared he was to do so. I can't not do it.

'All right. Deal.'

'Sorted.' He grins, raising his hand to wave down a waiter. 'We need more drinks. We can toast hot chocolates to seal the deal.'

'Fine by me,' I smile, pulling my purse out. 'These ones are on me though.'

I actually drink the next one, but find myself lost in thought again. This time, it's about Katie.

I've still not told Dan the full extent of everything she did. He knows about the name-calling and the shutting me out, but I don't think anyone has told him about what happened in the school changing rooms, and definitely not the incident at the cinema. The one that I have on video, sitting quietly in my photos app like a bomb I haven't decided to light yet. I can't deny that a part of me really, really wants me to.

While I never fully understood Dan and Katie's friendship, I got it enough to know that there was a bond there that was very difficult to break, no matter how different they may have grown to be.

I run my hands over my arms, remembering the feel of the

changing-room tile as it slammed into my back, the bruises that bloomed over my skin for the weeks afterwards, the sting of the word that Katie used against Neha.

'I need to tell you something,' I blurt, the secret bursting out of me the second I've decided that he would want to know.

'OK?' Dan looks up at me, one eyebrow raised.

'It's about Katie.'

'Ah.' Dan sighs. 'What's she done now?'

'It's what she did,' I say, and quickly give him the short version of that day after cross-country.

'She *attacked* you?' Dan's voice is incredulous, and for a moment I worry if he'll even believe me. A cloud of rage descends over his face. 'Who else was there? Did any of the teachers know? I don't believe this. I mean, I *do*,' he reassures me, and I breathe a sigh of relief. 'Of course I *believe* you. I just—'

'I know.' I stare down at the table. 'I won't lie, I knew she could be catty. Maybe even a little bit cruel sometimes. But I didn't see that coming. It was like, after your accident, her mask slipped right off.'

'She's always liked to play with people,' Dan says quietly, staring off into space. 'But I just thought it was always harmless, you know? Maybe I was just used to it. Or I didn't want to have to deal with it, I guess.'

He looks so crestfallen I almost don't want to tell him the rest, but I know I have to.

I take a deep breath. 'There's something else.'

I swipe through my phone and push it across the table to him.

'Keep the volume low.'

Dan frowns down at the video, watching the brief argument between Katie, Neha and me on screen. When Katie shouts, he visibly recoils.

'What the fuck.'

'Yeah.' I fiddle with the sugar packets on the table. 'What the fuck.'

'You didn't film this,' Dan says slowly. 'How do you have it?'

'Emily gave it to me,' I say.

'What?'

'Yeah, I know. It was bizarre. She said she thought I should get to decide what to do with it.'

Realisation dawns on Dan's face, and he looks back down at the phone. 'Oh.'

'Which doesn't mean I *am* going to do anything with it,' I say hurriedly.

'But you want to.' Dan sighs. 'Which makes sense. She was so awful to you.'

'That doesn't mean it's right to do the same to her,' I counter, relieved to finally be able to vocalise the debate I've been having in my head for days. 'And, well, she is your friend.'

'Is she?' Dan shakes his head. 'I feel like I don't even know the person you've been dealing with the past few months. She took it to another level. *Beyond* another level.

I don't really know how to get over that, or if I should even try. I dunno.' He sighs. 'Sometimes I just wish we never grew up.'

I try to push away my own feelings for Katie and just nod. I know Dan is trying to reconcile the Katie he grew up with, with the Katie she's shown herself to be. We sit in silence for a few moments, sipping our hot chocolates.

'Whatever you decide, I support it,' Dan says finally. 'It's you that had to go through all that. Emily was right. You should decide.'

I groan. 'I was afraid you'd say that.'

Dan laughs but lets me drop it. We spend the rest of the time before his mum comes to pick us up discussing the merits of the horrible Christmas decorations in our basket, and I try to put it all to the back of my mind.

For now.

Neha

Ever since Year 7, Zoe, Sam, Robyn and I have organised a group Secret Santa for Christmas. Every year we set a price limit, which we all flagrantly disregard and buy each other whatever we want.

I sense that this year will be no different – I pulled Robyn, who is exceptionally easy to buy for as their taste matches a lot of mine, so I can just buy silly things I know I'd love and be certain I've hit the jackpot for them. The assortment of brightly coloured packages bumps up against my legs in the footwell of the courtesy car the repair place loaned us while they determine if ours can be fixed.

Jas pulls up in front of Zoe's nan's house, where we're holding our pre-Christmas gathering again this year. I'm wearing my cheesy Christmas snowman jumper, which only serves as another reminder of Libby, and I'm regretting it already. Jas looks over at me as I unbuckle my seat belt, lifting Robyn's gifts into my lap ready to carry them inside.

'Try and have fun tonight, OK?' she says, reaching over to give my knee a squeeze. I arrange my face into a smile and nod wordlessly, before climbing out of the car and hurrying to Zoe's front door, hunching up my shoulders in the cold.

'Hey, pudding,' says Zoe, swinging open the door and enveloping me in one of her signature bear hugs. 'How're you getting on?'

'Good,' I lie, badly. Zoe gives me a look. 'Oh, all right, kind of rubbish. But I don't want to talk about that tonight, it's Christmas.'

'If you say so,' she replies, watching me carefully as I struggle out of my boots, balancing the gifts in my arms. We head into the living room, where Sam has already commandeered the entire sofa as usual. I drop my present under the tree and arrange myself in the armchair by the window, just as there's a knock on the front door.

Zoe goes to open it, and then from the hallway we hear:

'Robyn, what in the name of the tiny baby Jesus is that?'

'It's my Secret Santa present!' Robyn exclaims. 'I sort of ran out of wrapping paper though.'

Robyn emerges in the doorway, followed by Zoe, who is slowly shaking her head. We can instantly see why. Whatever the present is that Robyn has brought, it's 'wrapped' in a combination of Christmas paper, corrugated card and wallpaper. It is massive. It overwhelms Robyn's skinny frame as they carry it across the living room and place it by the tree, smiling proudly.

Sam is the first to go, clapping a hand to his mouth to try

and stifle the splutter of laughter he can no longer contain. As soon as the sound escapes him we all fall about, hooting and clutching our sides. Robyn looks disgruntled.

'It's a good present!'

'We know,' I gasp, reaching over to pull them into a hug. 'God, I love you. Never change.'

Robyn smiles, seemingly placated as they settle down on the fluffy rug in front of the fire and the rest of us finish giggling.

Sam, who has self-appointed himself as Santa, begins the process of dishing out the presents from under the tree by finding the one with his own name on it and tearing it open. Robyn opens my collection of ridiculous gifts. They exclaim their delight over every one, despite most of it being complete nonsense, but assure me they love everything.

I'm so preoccupied with everyone else's gifts that I don't notice they're all looking at me expectantly, and then I turn to see the only present left is the giant bundle of assorted paper that Robyn brought.

'Oh my god, it's for me!' I laugh, shooting up to start pulling off the paper.

'Seriously, Robyn, is there a person in there,' asks Zoe, and for one wild second mid-tear I wonder if maybe she's wrapped Libby. Then I pull away the final piece of cardboard to reveal …

'IT'S A SPACE HOPPER!' Robyn cries, completely unable to contain their excitement at their own gift-giving skills. 'Do you like it?!'

'I love it! I can't believe you inflated it to wrap it!' I'm laughing as I jump on the giant rubber ball and start bouncing right there in Zoe's living room.

'Christ, watch the tree,' says Zoe, but she's laughing too. Robyn is beaming and Sam is already asking for a turn, and for a few wonderful moments this is all that matters: these wonderful weirdos that are my friends, Christmas, and bouncing on a space hopper.

At around eleven Sam and Robyn say their goodbyes. I stay cocooned in a fuzzy blanket on the sofa as I've arranged to stay the night, waving as they head out the door with final calls of 'Merry Christmas!'

Zoe swings the door shut, a gust of cold air making me scrunch my toes under the blanket, and immediately comes straight back to me with a serious look on her face.

'Right. Christmas on pause for a second. Tell me what's happening with Libby.'

I let out a long breath, feeling the tension from the last couple of weeks settle back over my shoulders after a blissful few hours off.

'Honestly, I don't know. After I crashed the car we only had a minute to talk before we found out that Dan was awake, and after that, well, she's been avoiding me, and I didn't want to get in their way.'

Zoe nods thoughtfully. 'I get that, given the fact that you're clearly smitten with her.'

'Says who?' I mumble, knowing full well my friends can read me like a book.

'Neha, how long have we been friends?' Zoe says, giving me a pointed look. 'If you weren't all tied up in feeling weird and guilty about your feelings for her, she'd have been here tonight. You'd be treating her like any one of us, but you're scared because you like her and she has a boyfriend.'

'How dare you judge me so accurately.' I rest my head on her shoulder and sigh. 'What if it all meant nothing to her? What if we weren't even friends?'

'You forget that I met her. I know we only hung out a few times, but I'm a solid judge of character and none of that seemed fake to me. Have you at least tried messaging her?'

'I've *tried*. But I just don't know what I'm supposed to *say*.' I dig my phone from my pocket and bring up a series of long, rambling messages drafted in my Notes app. 'Look at all this rubbish.'

Zoe takes my phone and gives the messages a cursory glance. 'Mmm. Needs some workshopping.'

'You're telling me.' I shuffle a little. 'I think she's made up with her friend Mona.'

'That's good,' says Zoe neutrally, handing my phone back. I turn to her.

'Is it? I don't know if she really deserves it.'

'Mona might not,' says Zoe, 'but Libby does. And it's up to Libby to decide.'

I grumble, but I can't really argue with that. We sit quietly for a moment, watching the lights from passing cars send rainbows of light across the room as they bounce off the baubles hanging on the tree.

'If you're not going to talk to Libby, maybe you should talk to Dan.'

'What?' I jump up and look at her in surprise, wondering if I've heard her right. 'I barely know him, he probably doesn't even remember who I am. What good would that do?'

'He's a classmate that's just come out of a coma, it makes total sense for you to go and see how he's doing,' says Zoe, matter-of-factly. 'I know you – if Libby wasn't in the picture you would've already gone.'

I groan. 'What would I even say to him?'

'What would you say to him if you weren't crushing on his girlfriend?'

I stare at the ceiling. I remember my first day at St Hilda's, how terrified I was of this new place where everyone around me had known each other since their mothers had taken them to baby classes in the church hall. I remember Dan sitting down next to me before assembly started, the sincerity of his smile, the warmth I felt from him. How he came to talk to me at the village fete when I was floundering on my own. How he smiled at me in the corridors and made me feel a tiny bit seen.

I realise that I've been so messed up thinking about Libby, I forgot that I do care if Dan's OK.

'God, I am really self-absorbed at the minute,' I say. 'You're right. I should go and say hi. Maybe it's weird that I haven't already.'

'Trust you to immediately find a new thing to worry

about,' Zoe laughs, but she puts an arm round me and hugs my body to hers. 'If nothing else, he'll stop being this mythical figure in your brain and turn back into a real person. Real people are way easier to handle.'

'In theory,' I mutter, but I know that she's right. Talking to Dan, relating to him as just another human, might make it all a bit less scary. The decision feels good, and for the first time in weeks I have a plan.

I can figure out what, if anything, to do with everything else later.

Dan

KATIE
Are you finished sulking yet?

KATIE
You know you can't ignore me forever

KATIE
Please Dan. It's me. Just talk to me

The unanswered messages stare up at me from my screen, the final plea already a day old. I don't remember the last time I left any of Katie's messages on read – it's probably never. Katie isn't the kind of friend you do that to.

But then I don't really know what kind of friend she *is* any more.

I think of the video again, the ease with which Katie used that word. I knew what Lewis was like of course, but his homophobia always manifested so casually I tried to write it off as small-town ignorance and not take it to heart.

Outright calling Neha the d-word I can't ignore. Maybe it's because it's against someone who isn't me, or maybe it's because I know that anyone ready to roll a word like that off their tongue has some deep-seated bigotry in them. I never saw it coming, and now I don't know what to do about it.

When Mum pops her head round the door to say there's someone here to see me, I barely look up from the words burning on my screen. The steady stream of visitors hasn't slowed down since I got back, so it's no surprise that yet another person is coming to say hi.

Still, I'm a little shocked when Neha Gill walks through the spare-room door, smiling and politely declining my mother's offer of a hot drink. I quickly toss my phone on to the bedside table as Mum goes off to the kitchen, presumably to make her one anyway, and we're left alone.

'Hi, Dan,' Neha says tentatively, hovering in the doorway.

'Hey.' We stare at each other for a second. 'You, uh, want to sit down?'

I gingerly push a tangle of console wires and empty crisp packets no one has cleared away yet off the edge of the hospital bed, and gesture to the armchair that's pulled up beside it. She perches on the edge of the cushion. I've never really looked at her that closely before. She's pretty – big smile and dark hair falling in waves over her shoulders. There's a mark on her forehead that looks fresh.

'How are you feeling?' she offers. I try not to roll my

eyes – that's all anyone ever asks me any more, but that's not her fault. Besides, she actually looks like she wants to know, and isn't just making awkward small talk.

'I'm good.' I nod. 'I've been home about a week. Finally on solid food.' I gesture sheepishly at the empty packets now littering the floor. 'Which is good.'

Neha smiles, her eyes dropping to her lap. 'That's good. That's really good. I'm so glad you woke up. You had everyone going for a minute there.'

I find myself grinning. Bar Libby and the doctors, she's the only person to acknowledge out loud how bad the situation was. Everyone else seems to be pretending I just had a really long nap.

'Are you here about Libby?'

Neha's eyebrows shoot up, startled at my bluntness, but I can't help it. She looks worried. 'I mean, I wanted to see how you were doing …'

'I know.' I smile in what I hope is a reassuring way. 'But you also wanted to ask about Libby?'

Her hands start twisting in her lap, long fingers twining and untwining. Her eyes are shiny, and I watch with alarm as a tear escapes her eye and she hastily brushes it away. I glance at the open bedroom door and wonder if Mum will come back in any time soon.

Neha lowers her head and tears fall on to her clasped hands. 'I mean, I thought we were friends, but maybe that was just while you were ill. Maybe that was just while everyone else was being so horrible to her. On one hand I feel like she was using me, but on the other …' She trails off, looking worried again. 'It didn't seem like that at the time. I thought—'

'You thought she liked you?' I ask. Again, her eyes widen at how direct my questions are.

'It's OK,' I say, leaning forward a little. 'Really, it's OK. Neha, I'm gay.'

We both stare at each other in shock; her at my revelation, me at the fact I revealed it with such ease. Telling Libby that night in Craig's garage was like clawing something spiked from deep inside my chest. This just slipped out.

'Sorry, what?' Neha is no longer crying, which is something at least.

'I'm gay,' I say, again surprised at how easy it is to say. Two little words.

Huh.

'B-but, but you …' Neha splutters. 'You're Libby's boyfriend!'

'*Was* Libby's boyfriend, and not really.'

I try and explain the agreement we made, an agreement I now can see was incredibly selfish on my part. I tell her how we were close, but only ever as friends. That she was helping me hide from a world I was scared of coming out to.

'So, Libby *did* like you,' Neha says slowly, her face twisted in confusion as she tries to line it all out. 'But you didn't like her, not like that, because you like guys. And you were together but not really, all this time. And, what, she doesn't like you any more?'

'No,' I say firmly. 'She doesn't. Not in that way.'

'And you're not together now. At all, even pretending?'

'No.'

'Right.' Neha nods, brow still furrowed a little. 'Wow. Why didn't she *tell* me?'

'Honestly, I kind of wish she had,' I say, surprising myself again with the truth of it. 'But I think we both know she never would've outed me without my say-so.'

Neha nods, and we sit silently for a minute.

'So, I don't like Libby, and Libby doesn't like me,' I say, raising my eyebrows to emphasise that I'm making a point. 'Which means, if someone *else* were to like her …'

Neha shoots me a glance but doesn't say anything. I sense the time isn't right, and don't want to screw up Libby's life more than I already have. I just shrug and hold up my hands. 'Just saying. Field is open.'

'Mhmm,' Neha hums. She rises to her feet, buttoning up her coat. 'I should probably get going.'

'Sure,' I say, sitting up a little straighter. 'Hey, Neha?'

'I won't tell anyone,' she says with a smile, turning back to me. 'Don't worry.'

'Thanks,' I sigh. 'And about Libby—'

'We'll see.' With that, she leaves the room. I hear her exchanging pleasantries with Mum in the hallway before the front door opens and she's gone.

At least I can't complain life isn't interesting.

Mum usually has the Christmas shopping bought, wrapped and hidden away well before the beginning of December, but I had to go and throw a spanner in the works this year. She's been rushing in and out of the house for the last few days, flustered and complaining that there's nothing good left in the shops. She's determined that we have a regular Christmas after the horror of the last few months. Bless her.

Dad comes in to check on me during another one of Mum's last-minute shopping sprees ('I can't *believe* the butcher doesn't have any turkeys left! I'll have to go all the way into the city three days before Christmas!') and finds me sitting in my chair by the guitar that's still propped up in the corner, slowly strumming my fingers over the strings and brooding. Every time I look at it I feel flat. I haven't said it out loud because it feels so silly, but it's as if whatever musical drive I had was knocked out of me when the car hit.

'I did wonder when you'd pick that up,' he says conversationally, skimming over the fact that I haven't actually had the strength to 'pick it up' in the traditional sense.

'I don't think I've wanted to.' I stare it down like it's betrayed me.

'How d'you mean?'

'I just don't feel that spark any more, I guess,' I say, grasping at a way to describe what I'm feeling. 'I can't ever remember going so long without playing before. It always came so naturally and I always loved it. I can't even remember learning.'

'Oh, I can,' Dad chuckles, sitting down in the armchair. 'Trust me, you never forget the sound of your beloved only child learning an instrument for the first time. I was just grateful you didn't take a shine to the drums.'

I let out a reluctant bark of laughter.

'It's just, this was my thing. This was what I'm good at.

What if I can't do it any more?'

'What you're good at is making music, and the guitar isn't the only way to do that,' he says. 'The fact that you're so upset about this tells me it's not the music you've fallen out of love with. Maybe you could try something else?'

'Like what, the triangle?' I huff.

'It's an option.' Dad smiles, and his eyes flash with an idea. 'Come on, I'll get your coat. We're going out.'

Dad drives us the short distance into the village, pulling up by the green and opposite our modest row of small shops that constitutes a high street. He takes my chair out of the boot while I sit and watch as snow starts to fall from the iron-grey sky above, settling briefly over the pavement before melting away to nothing.

Dad brings the chair around for me and I climb in, grateful again that my reduced mobility isn't a barrier to getting out of the house. He pushes me across the road, waving through the window of the coffee shop to some blurry shapes inside, and over to the music shop.

The ancient bell above the door tinkles as Dad reaches over me to push it open, and the familiar sound sends a pleasant shiver down my spine. I can't remember ever really registering it before, despite having heard it a thousand times, but now I relish it so much I almost want to go back outside just to have the joy of entering again.

Before I can act on this impulse, Dad manoeuvres me fully into the shop. Behind the deep mahogany counter, the owner, Mr Bloom, looks up from examining a stack of receipts.

'Daniel!' he cries, swinging out from behind the counter with the grace of a much younger man. 'Absolutely marvellous to see you out and about!'

'Hello, Mr Bloom,' I say with a grin, allowing him to grasp my hands in his and shake vigorously. 'Marvellous to be out and about.'

Mr Bloom laughs, still pumping my hands up and down. I bite back how much the movement is aggravating my whole body. I gaze round the shop, drinking in the sight of jumbled instruments and the heady smell of furniture polish. I remember all the Saturdays I've spent in here over the years, poring over new sheet music or plucking the strings of every single guitar in the place. As I look round I try to capture that excitement again, but the flat feeling remains and my chest deflates.

'What can I get for you today, my favourite customer?' says Mr Bloom, oblivious to my change in demeanour, though thankfully, finally letting go of my hands. 'I have a stack of new guitar sheet music I've been keeping by.'

'We just thought it would be nice to have a browse today, Archie,' my dad cuts in, firmly but without being rude.

'Of course, of course!' Mr Bloom gestures to the shop. 'Take all the time you need. It really is *wonderful* to have you back, Daniel.'

I manage a half-smile before Dad takes hold of my chair and moves me gently away. He navigates around the various shelves bursting with songbooks and stacks of instrument cases over to an upright piano sitting in the window. With the powdery snow drifting down on the other side of the glass, and the string of fairy lights lining the window frame, it looks like a scene from a John Lewis advert.

'I thought you might like to try picking up piano again,' Dad says.

'Dad, I haven't played piano since I was eight.'

'I know, I know,' he says, running a hand along the top of the upright. 'But you're very talented, I'm sure you'd pick it up again pretty quickly. And besides, it's strange having you back in the house and not making music.'

I look down at the keys, trying to remember why I stopped in the first place. I liked it, both the sounds it made and the cosy front room of my piano tutor's house where I took lessons. Most of the other boys at school didn't think it was particularly cool.

Ah. Now I remember. I stopped because Lewis said it was 'gay'.

I have no idea if, at the age of eight, I even really understood what being 'gay' meant. But I had come to understand that, at least in Chipping Hollow, it was something to be avoided, something you didn't want to be and certainly didn't want anyone to know if you were.

I look back up at Dad, but he's turned away to talk to Mr Bloom some more.

I pull off my gloves slowly, finger by finger, and rest my hands gently on the keys.

Dad was right – I definitely hadn't fallen out of love with music, and all the emptiness I felt for the guitar is quickly filled with renewed motivation to get back up to scratch on the piano. For the next couple of days in the lead-up to Christmas, whenever I'm not at a physio appointment, I insist on visiting the music shop to sit in the window and play.

I can't deny it has something to do with the fact that I can, for the most part, just sit still in peace for a while. Instead of twitching about, desperate to be doing something and regretting it when the pain flares through my limbs, I can let the music soothe my brain and allow me to gently pass my fingers over the keys.

Mum and Dad have been taking it in turns to drop me off, sometimes sitting with me for a while but mostly leaving me to it for a couple of hours. Anywhere else would have banned me by now, but Mr Bloom is just as delighted to see me each afternoon as he was the first time I came in. He insists having me tinkling away in the window is great for business, and brings me steaming mugs of tea and fresh sheets of music to try.

I wake one morning with an idea half-formed in my mind, the ghost of something Libby once said to me whispering from my dreams. The house is quiet, Mum and Dad both still fast asleep upstairs. Filled with fresh determination, I manage to lift myself into my wheelchair and wheel down the hall towards the stairs, my mind fixed on the drawer where I keep my half-used notebooks. This alone takes longer than I expected and I'm already exhausted and aching as I stare up in the direction of my bedroom. Maybe not.

Undeterred, I wheel myself back to the spare room and find a small flip pad and pen by the corded landline phone Mum insists we still need, even if it is banished to a previously unused room. I pause for a second, the nib hovering above the paper in anticipation. I bite my lip. And then I start writing.

I finish nearly an hour later, just as I hear the creak of the stairs. One or both of my parents are probably about to come in to check on me. I slip the notepad, now fat with scribbled chords and lyrics, into the bag that I've been taking to Mr Bloom's shop.

Dad and I are in the living room, hanging baubles and candy canes on the tree. Mum finally decided it wouldn't be too much of a 'strain' on me to do something as taxing as decorate the living room with fake foliage.

She's currently upstairs, pretending not to be hurriedly wrapping presents.

'You got anything for Libby then?' Dad asks as he arranges the plaster nativity scene around the base of the tree. I look down at him. For two weeks he's been asking regularly about Libby, trying to re-create the moment we almost had in the hospital when I was coming home. As happened then, we've somehow been interrupted by Mum every time. But now she's safely occupied upstairs, there's no chance of that happening.

'Yeah, I got her something.' I occupy myself with detangling a string of lights we probably won't need. I've already filled up the middle of the tree, which is all I can reach from my chair.

'So, does that mean the two of you are still a couple?'

Maybe it's remembering the weird rush I got from coming out to someone and not feeling as though I was presenting my raw beating heart to them in my bare hands. Maybe it's my penchant for overachieving. But something in me wants to double up on my promise to Libby.

I take a deep breath. 'Actually, Dad, we're just friends. We, umm ... always were just friends.'

He looks up at me, setting down the pile of tinsel. My fingers twitch against the corded lights.

'Oh?' he says lightly. 'How do you mean?'

'I mean, we were only pretending to be a couple.' I roll myself back a little to better look in him in the face. Dad sits back on his legs, keeping eye contact with me.

'Why were you pretending to be a couple?' He says it so neutrally, as if he's asking me if I'd like cranberry sauce on my turkey, not why did I fake a relationship with someone for a whole summer.

I look down at the lights in my lap, pulling idly at the cords in a poor attempt to untangle them. 'Because I didn't want people to figure out that I'm ... I'm gay.'

At first he doesn't say anything, and there is only silence. I continue to pick at the string of lights. When I can't take it any longer I look up, and see he is smiling at me.

'You shouldn't be afraid of being yourself, Dan,' he says. I stare at him.

'You don't seem very surprised?'

'No,' he replies matter-of-factly. 'I thought you might be.'

'What?!' I yelp, dropping the lights. 'You – Why didn't you say anything?!'

'Well, I'd never presume to *know*. And if it was the case, I wanted you to feel like you could come to me yourself.'

I stare down at the carpet, barely able to believe how this is going after dreading it for so long. 'I just didn't know how you'd react. Or if you'd think there was something wrong with me. The church, it hasn't always been super accepting of queer people, on the whole. We've never talked about it so I didn't know what side of that argument you came down on.'

Dad leans forward a little. 'Dan, I want you to know that your mother and I love you very much. Nearly losing you ... I can't think of a time in my life that I was more scared. All my prayers turned into stupid bargains with God, like if I could get to the hospital in under twenty minutes you'd be awake when I got there. I'd fall asleep on the sofa, not wanting to go to bed in case something happened to you in the night and we didn't hear the phone.'

He pauses, rubbing his face with a hand. When he takes his hand away his eyes are shining. He looks back up at me. 'I don't care who you fall in love with. Hell, you could bring home an alien to Sunday dinner if you wanted. I just care that you're here, and you're happy, and you're OK. God made you this way and I will never stop thanking him for giving me you, and for bringing you back to me.'

I don't know what to say, so I just open up my arms. He

stands and embraces me tightly, gripping my shoulders. We stay there by the Christmas tree holding each other until we hear Mum moving about upstairs. When he straightens up, both of our faces are wet with tears. I do a big fake man cough, and Dad laughs.

'I don't think your mother suspects,' he says. 'It might be best to get Christmas out of the way before you say anything. We've had enough drama this month,' he adds with a gentle laugh.

I smile, but a spike of worry stabs at my chest. 'Do you think she'll be mad?'

'No,' he says firmly, quickly. 'Your mother loves you as unconditionally as I do. And once she's over the surprise of it, she'll be your biggest advocate. I just think it might take her a little while to get used to the idea, and both of you need a bit of breathing space before you have to deal with that.'

I nod silently, still a little overwhelmed. Dad claps his hands together and climbs back to his feet, picking up the box of baubles. 'Come on then,' he says briskly. 'Your mother will be down soon and she'll throw a fit if the tree isn't finished.'

I dig the star topper from another box and hold it out to Dad, who smiles but doesn't take it.

'I think you can just about manage that,' he says.

I take a deep breath and slowly pull myself to my feet, gritting my teeth with the effort. I stand teetering on my tiptoes, Dad hovering behind me just in case, and push the star on to the top branch of the tree. We both step back to admire it, Dad with one hand on my shoulder as my chest puffs out in quiet, knackered pride.

LIBBY

The first time Mona spent Christmas Eve at my house we were eight, and still believed in Father Christmas. We'd spend the evening fervently promising each other that we would make the effort to stay awake all night once we got home, to catch him in action. Neither of us actually managed it, so we vowed to do it again the year after.

This quickly turned into a tradition that went on long after we'd stopped believing in a magic man in a red suit. I'd assumed that tradition would be broken this year. But here I am, bouncing my knees up and down as I sit perched on the edge of the sofa cushion, waiting for the doorbell to ring.

I'm so tightly wound that when there's a creak on the stairs I jump out of my skin.

'Sorry, love!' says Mum, pausing on the bottom step. She's already wrapped up in her dressing gown, heading to bed to get out of my and Mona's way. 'I just wanted to say goodnight, and good luck, and Merry Christmas.'

She smiles at me, the dark circles under her eyes more pronounced in the half glow of the Christmas tree lights. She works so damn hard.

'Merry Christmas, Mum,' I say, scrambling up from the sofa to rush and give her a hug. 'I love you.'

'Love you too, sweetheart,' she says, and stifles a yawn.

'Go get some sleep. A Christmas treat,' I laugh, giving her a gentle push back towards the stairs. She waves sleepily at me as she climbs, and I head back to the sofa.

My phone buzzes in my lap and for a second I convince myself that it's Mona calling to cancel, but then I see Dan's name lit up on my screen. I let out a small sigh of relief and hit answer.

'Hey, I'm bored. Want to come and watch *Wizard of Oz* with me before midnight mass?'

'Could you be more cliché?' I laugh, the tension seeping out of me just a little. 'I can't, sorry, I'm waiting for Mona to come round.'

'Oh, of course!' Dan sounds genuinely delighted. 'Your Christmas Eve tradition. I'm so glad you're doing that.'

'Me too,' I say, and I mean it. I'd pretty much resigned myself to the fact that it wouldn't be happening, but then Mona messaged me yesterday asking if I was up for it. I'm glad we're doing it, but I'm also glad she was the one to reach out – the hurt still hasn't completely dissipated yet, so I'm not completely sure I would have done it myself.

'Well, while we're waiting,' says Dan, 'I held up my end of our deal. I came out to my dad and—'

'Oh my god! Dan, that's amazing!' I squeak. 'How did it go, what did he say?'

'That he didn't care if I got with an alien, he's just glad I'm OK.'

I laugh. 'Amazing. I knew I always liked your dad. Although got to be honest, there would be some judgement from my end if you start going out with an extraterrestrial.'

'Noted,' he laughs. 'And what about you? How's your end going?'

There's a silence.

'Still nothing?'

'I didn't want to do it on Christmas!' I say, in a voice that's annoyingly like a whine. 'How awkward would that be?'

'Not awkward, romantic!' he says. 'What you should have done was turn up on her doorstep tonight, beautifully thoughtful gift in hand, and proclaim your undying love for her right there under the mistletoe.'

'You need to stop watching the True Christmas channel, Dan.'

'Never.'

I sigh down the receiver. 'I feel like I need an excuse to talk to her. I can't just turn up.'

'Disagree,' says Dan. 'Why don't you see what Mona thinks?'

'What? About Neha?'

'If you're up for it.'

'That might be a tricky conversation to navigate,' I say slowly. 'She's only just accepted that I didn't actually cheat on you. Falling for someone else while you were in a coma might be dancing a bit too close to that line again, even if we are broken up now.'

There's a very long silence down the phone, so long that I wonder if the call has dropped. And then Dan says, 'Well, you could tell her everything.'

'*Everything* everything?!' Now I'm wondering if I blacked out for a moment.

'If it would help.'

'Dan, I can't do that to you.'

'You can if I say you can,' he says, in a voice that's so confident I can't think of anything to say back. 'Listen, you went through hell for me, for the sake of keeping my secret. It's the absolute very least I can do so that you can talk to your best friend properly again.'

'You really don't have to, you—' I start, but Dan interrupts me.

'I know I don't. I want to. And I'm trying to get more comfortable with people knowing.'

I want to reach down the line and hug him. But before I can say anything else, there's a knock at the door and I nearly drop the phone. 'Shit, she's here.'

'Don't sound so panicked,' Dan laughs. 'Seriously, tell her. It's OK. And try and have a good night – you deserve one.'

'Debatable,' I say, almost out of habit at this point, and I hear Dan scoff. 'Thank you. I really appreciate it. I'll talk to you later?'

'You'd better, I'll need to know how it goes. And hey –' Dan's voice brightens – 'Merry Christmas!'

I smile despite the nerves swirling in the pit of my stomach. 'Merry Christmas, Dan.'

I hang up the phone and take a deep breath, before hurrying over to the door. I pull it open to reveal Mona in her winter coat, smiling sheepishly as a dusting of snow settles on to her curls.

'Hey,' she says. 'Am I a bit early?'

'No, no, you're fine,' I say, although I honestly have no idea. I feel like I've been waiting all night, but it's probably only been five minutes. 'Come in, it's freezing.'

She steps in and stamps the snow off her boots on to the rug before kicking them off, while I hover in the hallway, unsure what to do. We move into the living room and sit down, backs straight as if we're in the company of the reverend. It feels wrong that it's all so awkward.

'Tea?' I offer, leaping to my feet and not waiting for an answer before I disappear into the kitchen to flick the kettle on. As I bustle around, out of the corner of my eye I see her stand up and move to the kitchen doorway, watching me.

'I still can't believe you're talking to me.'

I pause, one hand in the box of teabags.

'Well, I don't really have a choice. I've no other friends left,' I laugh nervously, but then finally look over to her. 'And besides, you didn't do anything malicious. I suppose I'd have treated you the same if you'd done what I did.'

'No, you wouldn't,' she says, and I don't respond. 'You

wouldn't have been half as stubborn as me about seeing the truth. I'll never stop being sorry for what I put you through. I can't believe you're still not mad.'

The kettle clicks off and I carefully lift it over to the mugs, thinking hard about what I want to say. 'I'm not *not* mad, I guess,' I say slowly, focusing hard on pouring the water. 'It's different with you. You felt betrayed, and what happened with your parents must have made it seem so cut-and-dried to you. I get it. But everyone else … I guess I'm mad that not a single person gave me the benefit of the doubt. So much so that even *I* didn't. The first person to do that was Dan.'

Without having to ask, I add two sugars to Mona's tea, one to mine. I frown. 'No. Dan wasn't the first. Neha was.'

I can feel Mona's eyes boring into the back of my head. 'Did you guys fall out or something?'

I don't know how to answer that. Everything got so complicated I lost track of the whys and hows of things. I swallow. 'Well, no, we didn't fall out. I just stopped talking to her because I was scared.'

'Scared of what?'

'Nothing, probably,' I sigh. 'My decision-making these last few months has been a tad off.'

'Mood,' Mona replies with a knowing nod. I hand her a steaming mug of tea, and we go back into the living room. I take a deep breath.

'No, actually, I do know what I'm scared of …'

I let that hang in the air for a moment, staring into my tea and watching the steam coil up from the surface. This must be how it felt for Dan, hanging on to the secret out of fear that the people he loved might reveal themselves to be less than understanding. The thought alone is horrendous.

'You're scared because you're into her and you don't know if she feels the same?'

My head snaps up. 'What? What do you mean?' I attempt to cover up the palpable panic in my voice with a weird, high giggle, as if that's the most ridiculous thing I've ever heard and of *course* that's not what's going on.

Mona tries her best not to smirk at me. 'Libby, you forget I watched you moon over Dan for half our lives. I know what it looks like when you're smitten. Once I got my head out of my own arse for five minutes it was obvious.'

I must still look mildly terrified, because she quickly adds, 'Obvious to me! I don't think anyone else knows, if that's what you're worried about. But yeah. I guessed.'

'Oh my god.' I drop my head into my hands and let out a kind of strangled laugh. 'I can't believe you just *guessed*.' I raise my head a little and glance at her sideways. 'And you're OK? With that?'

'Of course I am,' she says. 'I won't say I'm not a little surprised. I mean, you were head over heels for a guy for so long.' She glances at me. 'Does Dan know?'

'He does,' I say. I take a sip of my tea to give myself a second. 'And, on the subject of Dan, there's something I need to tell you.'

When I'm finished, the look on Mona's face is more what I was expecting when I told her about Neha.

'Well,' she says, when I eventually stop babbling. 'I can't say I guessed that one.'

'He hid it pretty well.'

'You *both* did.' Mona shakes her head. 'I can't believe you've been holding on to that all this time. But you really did love Dan, didn't you? That wasn't fake.'

'No, it wasn't,' I admit.

'God, Libby. That must have been really rough.'

I stare off into the Christmas tree until it's just a blob of distorted twinkling lights. I think about all those times I was with Dan, holding his hand, walking with his arm around me. It feeling like everything while knowing it was nothing.

'It was.' I let out a sigh. 'Yeah, it was. I guess I wanted to be close to him. It's not like I thought I was going to turn him straight or anything like that. It was just worth it to be with him, even if I wasn't really. And I genuinely did want to help.'

'I believe that,' says Mona softly, resting her hand on mine.

'I don't regret it,' I say. 'But in hindsight, it probably wasn't the best thing for either of us. I'm glad I stopped it. I think I deserve a bit better than a fake relationship.'

'You definitely do.' Mona leans over, then hesitates for a second. 'Can I give you a hug? I really want to give you a hug.'

I smile and open up my arms, and she launches into them. I squeeze her shoulders, and any remaining bitterness I might have been holding on to fades away. 'I've missed you so much!'

'I've missed you too. It's been so boring without you.'

She pulls away. 'I have to ask though, does Aaron know about Dan?'

'I don't think so,' I say. 'Shit, I didn't really think about that. You and him are … ?'

'Oh my god, it's been so rubbish not having you to talk to about this stuff,' Mona gushes. 'Not officially – we didn't want to start anything while Dan was still in the hospital.'

'Well, he's out now,' I say, raising my eyebrows.

'I know, I know. But he still hasn't *asked*!' Mona flops back against the cushions. 'Do you think he might have changed his mind?'

I think about how Aaron used to ask after Mona over the summer, and the way he's been looking at her for the past few months. Even from across the room it was obvious.

'I definitely don't think he's changed his mind. You should do what everyone has been telling me to do and just talk to him about it!'

Mona looks over at me, her eyes glinting. Oops.

'Talking of which, what are you going to do about Neha?'

I pick up my tea again. 'What about Neha?'

'Libby, come on!' Mona is suddenly animated, so much more herself than I've seen her in forever. I'd be thrilled if it wasn't for the subject matter. 'Obviously you two need to make up.'

'It's not that simple,' I moan. 'I haven't spoken to her in weeks. She probably hates me. I've written out a message to her about sixteen billion times and deleted every single one of them.'

Mona gives me a look. 'Listen, I know recent history has given you good reason to think that, but Neha is different. Obviously. When I spoke to her after school the other day—'

'You spoke to her?' I sit up straighter. 'What did she say?'

Mona grins again. 'God, you two are adorable. You both have the same hopeless yearning look.'

'Mona!' I throw a cushion at her. 'What did she say!?'

'She very clearly misses you!' Mona dodges the cushion with ease. 'She asked how you were; you should go and see her.'

'You sound like Dan,' I huff, and Mona laughs.

'OK, well, maybe not right now. Besides, I've got you for tonight.' Mona budges over and loops her arm through mine. 'If you'll still have me.'

I think about all the Christmas Eves we've spent together, and am filled with gratitude that we are again tonight.

'Of course I will.'

Dan

One of my favourite Christmas traditions is our Christmas Eve walk to church for midnight mass. After I turned twelve I stopped coming to church regularly with my parents (much to Mum's dismay), but I never missed a Christmas Eve. Nothing fills me with that buzzy Christmassy feeling like walking through the village arm in arm with my parents, singing carols by candlelight in St Hilda's and then wishing the other churchgoers a merry Christmas over hot chocolate and mince pies in the church hall afterwards.

This year's 'walk' will be more of a roll for me. But that's OK. After I've settled into my chair, Mum wraps two scarves around my neck and tucks a blanket around my legs to make sure I don't catch a chill, and then the three of us set off on our traditional pilgrimage to the church.

The night sky is crisp and clear, the snow clouds having drifted off to reveal a dazzling canopy of stars. The wheels of my chair crunch over the yet-unmelted snow as we make our way down the long winding path that takes us from our house into the village, and across the green to the church.

With a light dusting of snow across the parapets and the warm glow of light falling through the stained-glass windows, St Hilda's looks like a Christmas card. Others from the village are making their own way across the green towards the church, smiling and waving as they spot us – the three Kings. I wonder how long it will take Dad to make that joke this year, and find myself almost giddy in anticipation of it.

It hits me how wonderfully, wildly happy I am to be here. To be alive.

We make our way inside, pulling off our hats and gloves but leaving on our coats in the draughty hall. Up at the front, Reverend Wallace stands by the pulpit, nodding and smiling as everyone files in and takes their seats. He spots us and waves us to the front, where Dad parks my chair in a spot at the end of a pew.

The choir launches into their rendition of 'The Holly and the Ivy', and I smile. *This* was the first time I fell in love with music – sat in the pews of the church, feeling the glow of positivity from all around me. Even when my childhood resolution in the church started to waver, the music and songs always felt warm and welcoming.

I look up at my dad, who's watching the choir with one arm around Mum. I think about his reaction to me coming out, his unquestioning acceptance, and I feel that same warmth emanating from him.

I'm not naive – I know not everyone will be as accepting, and I'm still unsure how Mum will take the news. But right now, surrounded by Christmas and music and love, I know that whatever happens I can handle it.

As we're all filing out of the church, my phone buzzes in my pocket. I slide it out and start to read the new message.

MONA
Hey Dan! Need your help. I've had an idea …

I broach the subject on Boxing Day, over a lunch of cold turkey and stuffing sandwiches.

'Mum?' I ask, dolloping cranberry sauce on to a slice of bread. 'I was wondering if I might be able to have a couple of people round on New Year's Eve?'

Mona had explained her idea to me on Christmas Eve, her messages coming in rapid succession as she tried to get me on board before Libby came back from the bathroom. Not that she needed to try too hard – I was definitely in.

Mum eyes me warily over the plate of turkey. 'How many is a couple?'

'Just a few friends from school,' I say lightly.

Mum 'hmmm's at that, buttering bread. 'I'm not sure if you're up to a party.'

'I never said party.' I put down my knife and lean against the table. 'Please? Someone else is bound to try and invite me to something, and you know I'll be begging to go – at least this way you know I'm at home.'

'I just don't think it's the best thing for you right now,' Mum says. 'You've only been home for a week.'

'It feels like an age,' I moan. 'A long, boring age, where I've stayed close and eaten my vegetables and been a good patient. I just want to see my friends again, as friends and not hospital visitors.' I turn to my dad, who has yet to speak. 'Please?'

He exchanges a glance with Mum, who still looks unconvinced.

'We'll think about it,' he says. 'Can you pass me the stuffing?'

And just like that, the conversation is over.

It's another two days of grovelling before they finally relent. I'm on the sofa skipping through the channels for something to watch when they come in together looking serious, sitting down either side of me.

'We've decided you can have a party for New Year's,' says Dad, and before he can say anything else I'm already reaching for my phone.

'Thanks, guys!' I need to call people as soon as possible. I want to make the most of my three days' notice.

'Slow down!' Dad laughs, and I drop the phone back to my lap. I try to contain my excitement, as Mum is already looking as though she regrets this decision. 'We have a few rules.'

'Sure, of course,' I say quickly, already mentally composing my triumphant message to Mona. 'What are they?'

'First off, we'll both be here,' says Mum. 'We'll stay out of the way upstairs, but we won't be going anywhere. Yes?'

'OK.' That's not too bad. I can work with that.

'Second, we don't want you drinking. We don't mind the others having a few drinks, not too much, but none for you. You're on too much medication and too fresh out of the ICU for that.'

'I don't like drinking anyway,' I say, and they both give me that *what a good son we raised* look that makes me squirm a little. But so far, so good.

'And lastly,' Dad says, reaching over me to take hold of Mum's hand, 'everyone gets a lift home from a responsible adult, or they sleep over. No one goes home alone in the middle of the night in the dark. If they're not staying or getting collected, then they're not coming.'

I stare at them for a second, initially confused by this very specific demand. And then I realise. They don't want anyone else in the situation I was in.

I smile. 'I don't think that will be a problem.'

'Then call your friends,' says Dad. 'And we'll go out tomorrow and get some balloons or something.'

They gently hug me between them, and I squeeze them back. I think Mum is crying again.

'Guess what!'

'Hello to you too,' says Libby, instead of what she was meant to say. I suppose I should have started the call with some form of greeting, but it's too late for that now.

'I'm having a party!'

'You what?'

It's a little later on and Libby is the second-to-last person I've called. I wanted to get enough guests confirmed so that I could call it an actual party (at least to anyone except my parents) before inviting her. I know that she's free – Mona told me that she'd already checked.

'A party. You know. Music, leftover Christmas chocolate, the inevitable breakage of something expensive in my parents' living room,' I say. I have the phone on loudspeaker as I hastily throw a playlist together on my laptop. 'My parents finally caved and let me host a New Year's Eve thing. They just want everyone to stay over so no one has to walk home alone in the dark. Isn't that sweet?'

'I guess,' Libby says slowly. 'Dan, you know there's no way I can come, right?'

'You have to come!' I practically shout at the phone. 'Why can't you?'

'Uhh, because everyone still hates me?' Libby says as though it's obvious.

I snort derisively. 'No, they don't. They'll be fine with you. I'll make sure. So will Mona.'

'Dan, I know you think you have magical powers now, but they tortured me for two months. I'm pretty sure they hate me.'

'You forget that half the population of our year have already been round here to visit,' I say. 'And trust me, I've been very vocal on how I feel about how they treated you. Besides, it's my party – if they see I've invited you, they'll know it's all cool anyway. Come on, Libs, have a little fun.'

There's a silence on the end of the phone, and then a barely audible, 'Will Neha be there?'

'Maybe.'

More silence.

'OK.' And the phone line goes dead.

I grin, allowing myself a second to feel accomplished. Then I scroll through my phone to find Neha on Instagram and do something I've never actually done before – hit 'Audio call'.

Several seconds pass before she picks up, with a quizzical 'Hello?'

'Hey, Neha! It's Dan. Did you know you can call people on Insta?'

'I did not.' Her surprise is evident, but she quickly recovers. 'How're you doing?'

'Not bad, not bad,' I say breezily. 'Listen, have you got plans for New Year's?'

'You mean this New Year's?'

'Course this New Year's. I'm having a kind of party. You free?'

'Well.' I can practically see her chewing her lip down the other end of the phone. 'I was going to just hang out with a friend and watch the usual rubbish on TV.'

It's not a complete no. I don't say anything, refusing to give her an easy out.

'I suppose I could make an appearance,' she draws out. 'Can I bring a friend?'

'It's not a boyfriend-slash-girlfriend, is it?'

'None of the above.'

'Perfect. Then bring them along!' I lean back into the sofa cushions and congratulate myself on my manipulation skills. Surely it's OK if I only use my powers to do good.

'Dan.' Her voice is tinged with suspicion and I know I need to wrap up the call. 'What are you up to?'

'Just getting people together to bring in the New Year!' I say brightly. 'Gotta go, loads to do, I'll see you in a couple of days!' I end the call before she can reply.

I go back to my playlist for a while, before another idea strikes me. I poke my head out of the spare-room door.

'Daa-aaad?'

NEW YEAR'S EVE

Dan

'Are you sure you're feeling up to this, Daniel?' Mum rearranges the bowls of crisps for what must be the seventh time. Dad takes her gently by the arm and starts leading her towards the hall.

'Mandy,' he says sternly, 'come on. He's fine. He can handle this. We promised we'd stay upstairs.'

'I'm OK, Mum, honestly.' I slowly hobble along behind them towards the bottom of the stairs, gripping the handle of my new cane as my ortho boot thumps along the hall. The cane was a Christmas present from my parents, a custom stick in a cool blue chrome, and over the last few days I've been practising getting about the house with it instead of the chair.

Mum looks back at me sadly.

'I just can't believe it's been a month already. When you were in the hospital, the time, it was like walking through treacle.' She lifts a hand to my face, and I don't move away. 'I feel like I've blinked and here you are at home throwing a party.'

'That's a good thing, Mum,' I say gently. 'And I'll be just downstairs all night.' I reach out for her hand and squeeze. 'And of course I'll say Happy New Year at midnight.'

Her eyes brim up again, and I quickly let go. 'I'll see you in a bit. Enjoy the crap on telly.'

'Language,' she says softly, but smiles and finally starts to climb the stairs.

The first guests arrive in the form of Aaron and Mona, arm in arm with plastic bags clinking with bottles. It feels very weird that Mona knows about me and he doesn't, but I trust her to let me tell him in my own time.

'How was Christmas?' I ask, showing them both through to the kitchen to set down their drinks.

'Great!' says Aaron, ever enthusiastic.

'Weird,' says Mona. 'It was the first without Dad so Mum *really* spoilt us. I don't think Avril even noticed he was gone, to be honest, the present pile was that big,' she laughs, shaking her head.

'Are we the first ones here?' asks Aaron, looking around at the empty kitchen.

'Yeah – I wanted you both to get here early, for Libby's sake,' I say. It feels like testing the water, and I watch Aaron carefully. He exchanges a look with Mona, and then smiles at me.

'Yeah, that makes sense. We'll keep an eye on her.'

I let out a quiet sigh of relief. He must be at least a little confused – as far as he knows, we did just break up. But he seems to trust both me and Mona enough to go with the flow.

There's another knock at the door, and I usher the two of them into the living room. My hand is already aching from holding on to the cane, and my legs are beginning to throb, but I steel myself – I want to stick with it for as long as possible this evening.

The house starts to fill up, people arriving and proclaiming how good it is to see me. Under instruction, a lot of them bring blankets and pillows and sleeping bags, which I have them drop off in the spare room until later.

When I hear Katie's and Lewis's voices at the door, I busy myself in the kitchen, still not sure how to really act around them. I honestly didn't even know if I was going to invite them, but the choice was made for me when Mum obliviously told Katie's mum about the party when she popped in this week to drop off some stuff for the church's New Year's raffle.

But to be honest, I don't know how much longer that leftover loyalty or nostalgia for those friendships is going to last.

I listen to their voices float down the hallway, try to muster up a scrap of affection for them.

I just feel empty.

Neha

The air is freezing cold, and I shiver in my dress and tights. I'm clutching a Tupperware that contains what is either a hilarious icebreaker or the worst idea I've ever had, and a bottle of red wine. Next to me, Sam bounces on the balls of his feet with his hands stuffed in his coat pockets. Just as I'm about to press the bell again the door swings open, and Dan is standing there in a navy cable-knit jumper holding a metallic blue cane, grinning ear to ear.

'You came!' he says, drawing me into a one-armed hug. When I hug him back I can feel his shoulder blades protruding under the wool of his jumper.

'I did,' I say, pulling back and smiling at the one sock not encased in a boot. It's got penguins on it. 'And I brought my friend.'

'Sam,' says Sam. The two boys smile and nod at one another.

I awkwardly offer up the bottle in my hands, trying to

keep hold of the tub. 'I brought this for your parents.'

'That's sweet, though they'll of course tell you that you shouldn't have,' Dan says, ushering us in from the cold. As we step through the door a wave of warmth and noise washes over me, and I shrug out of my coat. The last time I was here the house was deathly silent; now it's buzzing, with balloons and streamers and a *Happy New Year!* banner strung above the entrance to the living room.

There's a mess of discarded shoes by the door so I slip my feet out of my boots and add them the pile. The carpet is soft and plush under my feet and I wriggle my toes to warm them up a little. Sam starts hopping like an idiot on one foot trying to pull a shoe off, and Dan laughs and puts out a hand on instinct to steady him. But the movement makes him wobble himself, and I end up grabbing both of them by the arm to stop anyone from falling over. I worry the gesture is far too familiar for Dan, but he laughs and smiles at me gratefully. His eyes drop to the tub in my hands.

'What's that?'

'Oh, something for later. I can put it in the kitchen for now.'

Dan gives me a curious look but doesn't ask any more. He takes the tub and points us towards the living room, where a dozen or so of our classmates have already gathered. It appears we're some of the earlier ones.

We hover by a group of people I know vaguely from form period, and luckily Dan returns quickly so we're not left standing about like lost lemons. Sam, entirely on form, launches into a conversation with the others and soon has them eating out of the palm of his hand.

I notice Dan smiling at him a lot. I wonder.

Dan peels away eventually to mingle with his other guests, every now and then the doorbell going and sending my heart fluttering up to my throat. So far, no Libby. Dan catches my eye almost every time he shuffles back into the room with another guest, giving me a reassuring smile that becomes a little more strained with each one. I try to smile back, but I think my tongue has turned to cement in my mouth.

I'm halfway through my second glass of wine when the music in the room seems a little bit louder, and I realise it's because the conversation has faltered and gone quiet. I look round, frowning, and my eyes land on Libby.

She's standing in the doorway to the living room beside Dan, her face slowly turning a deep shade of magenta as her eyes dart around the room. Her arm is linked through Dan's and she's holding on as if she's the one who needs the extra support, a sight that causes a ripple of murmurs. Dan appears unfazed, but Libby is looking more uncomfortable by the second. Before I can think to hide, he's walked her slowly but solidly towards me.

We stand in front of each other for the first time in a month. When I finally lift my eyes to hers, they're wide in anticipation.

'Hello,' she whispers.

LIBBY

I'm pretty sure the only reason I'm still standing is Dan's arm linked in mine, holding me up but also holding me in place. I'd be surprised at his strength, but I should have known he'd find it for this. Curse him.

Neha's stupidly gorgeous eyes are on mine, and I feel like I'm about to burst into tears. My face is burning, the rest of the party guests still excruciatingly quiet as they keep their conversations on pause for a few beats longer. It feels like an eternity.

I want to say something. I want to say *sorry*. I want to tell her how much I've missed her, how I can't stop thinking about her, how all I want to do is run away from everything with her …

Before I'm even able to articulate any of that into a coherent human sentence, someone coughs, and it's all it takes to spook Neha. She mumbles something about going to get another drink and disappears from the room.

That's it. That was our big reunion.

'Happy?' I hiss at Dan, thankful that at least the level of chatter in the room seems to have returned to what it was. 'I told you she didn't want to speak to me.'

'She's probably just nervous!' Dan says, giving my arm a squeeze. 'Same as you are.'

I don't share his endless optimism.

Dan urges me to mingle, but I tell him to mingle on without me and find an armchair in the corner to squash myself into, sipping slowly from a bottle of cider as I contemplate this new level of social hell.

Out of the corner of my eye I see someone making their way towards me, and stare resolutely in the opposite direction. I'm not giving them an opening to ruin my night, not that it was all that great to begin with.

'Budge over, I brought bubbly,' says Mona, and I heave a sigh of relief. I shuffle over and she squashes in next to me, handing me a glass. I eye it warily.

'Champagne? Isn't this stuff pretty strong?'

'Don't worry, it's about seventy per cent lemonade,' Mona reassures me. 'And it is most definitely not champagne, it's cheap supermarket Prosecco. But we're celebrating.'

'I suppose,' I grumble.

She gently nudges my shoulder, unable to do anything else with our arms trapped in tight. 'Have you talked to Neha yet?'

'Barely,' I groan. 'I don't think she wants me to.'

Mona shifts round so she's facing me, a difficult feat in the cramped armchair. 'Libby. You know that both of you are thinking the exact same thing. One of you has to go first!'

I glare at her. 'You sound like Dan again.'

'Maybe because Dan's right?'

I try to think of a comeback, and annoyingly I can't. I huff. 'You didn't bring me enough not-champagne for this.'

Dan

So, my grand plan to reunite Libby and Neha isn't off to the best start. I probably should have known centre stage wasn't the right place to have them come face to face after so much time avoiding each other, but the night is still young. There's plenty of time left for my and Mona's meddling to start actually working.

Although I haven't actually seen Neha since the 'big reunion', and I'm a little panicked that she's fully scarpered and I've lost my chance to help fix what I inadvertently broke by waking up from a coma at the least opportune moment.

But then I turn around and spot that her cute friend Sam is still here, leaning casually against the door frame and sipping something from a plastic cup. He flicks his hair out of his eyes and I allow my eyes to linger on him for just a second longer than strictly necessary. I decide to take Libby's advice: I'm going to give myself room to have a crush.

I should really keep searching for Neha, or at the very least sit down and rest for a minute, but Sam looks up and catches me watching him. I blush, panicked that he'll think I'm creepy, but he grins and makes a beeline towards me.

'Nice party,' he says as he reaches my side. 'Haven't seen Neha, have you?'

'I was going to ask you the same,' I laugh, casting my eyes around the living room again. There's not *too* many people here, though probably still more than my parents had imagined when they agreed to it. Just enough to make it difficult to locate one specific person.

I'm about to abandon the search altogether in favour of standing next to Sam for a bit longer, when we hear raised voices coming from the hall. Sam glances sideways at me.

'I should sort that,' I say reluctantly. 'I'll talk to you later?'

'Looking forward to it,' Sam says, with a smile that makes my face feel hot. I guess this is the other side of gay panic I hadn't had chance to experience yet.

I step into the hallway, right into the middle of a heated conversation between Lewis and Aaron. Katie is nowhere to be seen, and I'm slightly relieved – I still don't think I'm ready to deal with her just yet.

'Everything all right?' I ask, looking between Aaron's frustrated expression and Lewis's near-thunderous one.

'You invited Libby tonight?' Lewis splutters, gesturing with his cup. I glance at Aaron, who grimaces and shrugs apologetically. I turn back to Lewis, fingers tightening around the handle of my cane.

'Yes. We're friends. Why?'

'What do you mean, *why*?' He looks absolutely incredulous, and I know not a single word I've said over the last few weeks on the matter has sunk in. 'After what she did?!'

'What *did* she do, Lewis?' I ask, with such force that he blinks in surprise. 'Trust completely the wrong people to look after her when she was vulnerable? Drink whatever she was told to?'

'You'd know what she did if you let me show you the video—'

'As a matter of fact, I *have* seen the video. The one of her getting assaulted while all her supposed friends watched. The one you shared around like it was this week's TikTok trend. So yeah, I know what she did. Or rather, I know what *you* did.'

He stares at me, mouth hanging slightly agape. I don't think I've ever spoken to him, challenged him like that before in our entire lives. I stare right back. Whatever old loyalty I once held for him, it's not strong enough to eclipse the anger I feel right now, which has been simmering ever since he first told me in the hospital what had happened.

I take a deep breath. 'Anything could have happened to her with that guy. If I'd have woken up and found out you'd let a stranger …' I trail off, not knowing how to finish the sentence. I don't know what I'd have done.

'You need to leave,' I say. 'I think we're done here.'

Lewis gives me the dirtiest look, and for a moment I wonder if he's going to hit me. Then he turns on his heel and stomps towards the door. 'Fine,' he spits, snatching his coat from the hook, and then he's gone in a flurry of snow.

I think of all the casually homophobic remarks he's thrown my way. How he squashed any deviation from his definition of 'manhood' that he saw in me. How, when I really think about it, I can't remember a single time I was actually pleased to see him recently. And I feel a particular lightness that I don't think I've felt in years.

Aaron exhales next to me – I'd almost forgotten he was standing there. I turn to him, shoulders tensed. 'Any of that you disagree with?'

'Nope,' he says quickly, and I relax again. The corner of his mouth twitches up a little. 'I think the band was due a bit of a switch-up anyway.'

The tension melts away completely and I allow myself to laugh, leaning my whole body weight against the wall for a second to rest. Now that my brain isn't occupied with righteous anger it finally registers how much everything hurts, and I let out a resigned sigh.

'Come on, I think I need a sit-down.'

Neha

I'm not sure if it's the music, the drink or the fact that I ran away from Libby the moment she appeared that's made my head spin, but I do know one thing – I probably can't keep hiding in the utility room forever. At some point Sam is going to notice I'm gone and send out a search party.

I'm sitting cross-legged on the washing machine, staring at the shelves neatly stacked with cleaning and laundry supplies. The sound of the party is muffled, as if it's happening very far away, and the air is cool against my burning skin. But the blissful peace is trickling away with every second that passes, and I know that the longer I stay here the weirder it will be when someone eventually finds me. I'm not sure who else will appreciate the strange sanctuary of the utility room.

I close my eyes and think about Libby's face in front of me, wide-eyed and so pale her freckles had all but disappeared. *Why did I run?* I've been waiting for that moment for weeks, but when it came down to it, I had too many feelings all at once and just bailed.

I slip down off the washing machine and gingerly push open the door, stepping away from the comforting smell of whatever fabric softener the Kings use and into the bright and, mercifully, empty kitchen. Laid out on the table are some bowls of crisps, cocktail sausages, chocolate mini rolls and an assortment of different alcohol bottles.

I hesitate, and then pick up bottle of pink fizzy wine, a cheap supermarket brand, from the very back. I figure it's not as hard as vodka and I've learned my lesson from Halloween, not to drink anything too quickly. I take a plastic cup from a cluster by the sink and pour myself a small helping, taking a delicate sip. The sting of it hits me in the back of the throat and I cough.

'Never had you pegged as a wino, Neha.'

Of all the people to walk in right now of course, it's Katie West. I inhale sharply as I turn around, remembering the last time I was face to face with her, at the cinema. It feels like a million years ago.

She saunters over to the alcohol, keeping her eyes on me. She pours herself a vodka and Coke, slopping a little over the glass, and takes a slow sip as she stares me down. I start to wonder what exactly is happening.

'Bold of you to show up, after the way you've been carrying on,' she says bluntly, narrowing her eyes. 'Why *are* you even here?'

'I was invited.' I stand very still, refusing to move backwards. 'Dan invited me.'

Katie snorts. 'Yeah, all right then. You just showed up again like you're fucking royalty, like you did at Lewis's Halloween party.'

'I was invited to that one too.'

She laughs at that, throwing her head back. 'Come on. Really? You didn't just turn up in your skimpy shitty costume and expect to be let in because you fluttered your eyelashes at someone? No wonder you got on with Libby. You're made for each other.'

I feel anger start to bubble up inside me, and clench my fists by my sides. She notices and laughs again.

'Going to hit me?' she taunts.

'No, Katie,' I say, forcing down the red that's rising in front of my eyes. 'I don't feel the need to resort to physical violence when I have a low opinion of someone.'

'And what's that meant to mean?' she snaps.

'You know what I mean.' Filled with a weird sort of confidence, I close the gap between us in one stride. I see her eyes twitch a little as she takes in my expression. 'I'd stay away from me tonight, Katie. I'm really not in the mood to deal with people like you.'

She opens her mouth to reply but I've already started walking away, striding from the kitchen and back into the living room.

LIBBY

I'm perfectly content staying secluded in my corner with Mona, but at some point my treacherous bladder betrays me and I give in to the fact that I need to use the bathroom. I slip out of the room into the hallway and run straight into Katie.

She's alone, which makes a change, leaning against the bathroom door and moodily staring at her phone. When I appear, her head shoots up and her eyes lock on to mine. There's something dangerous in them, and I almost turn and run.

But I've got something more dangerous. I feel my phone burning in my pocket, the video still sitting there. Waiting. It steels my resolve, and I take a step towards her.

'Excuse me.'

Katie narrows her eyes but doesn't budge. 'What?'

'I need the bathroom. You need to move.'

'Why don't you make me?' Katie's signature cold smile plays on her lips, her eyes still holding mine.

It's my turn to smile. 'I promise, you really don't want me to.'

'Seriously?' Katie laughs. 'What could *you* do to *me*?'

'More than you think,' I reply, and a cruel thrill shoots through me as a flicker of worry crosses her face. I pull my phone from my pocket and swipe through the camera roll until I reach the incriminating video. 'Remember this?'

Katie's eyes widen as I tap the screen and her own vitriol plays loud and clear. She glances frantically round to make sure we're still alone.

'Are you going to post that?'

Her words are tight, anxious, and it's music to my ears. I have to marvel at her audacity – no apology, no admission that what she said was vile. Just concern for her reputation.

'I haven't decided yet,' I say brightly, enjoying the terror in her eyes. 'But if I were you, I'd get out of my way.'

She shoots away from the wall and I stroll past, stepping into the bathroom and locking the door with a decisive *click*. As soon as I'm alone all my bravado evaporates, a breath whooshing out of me as I slump down on the toilet lid and have to count my breaths for a while until I regain my composure. I splash my face with some cold water before I head back into the party.

Mona is still in our armchair but Aaron has appeared and they seem to be deep in conversation. I hesitate for a moment, wanting to trust Aaron as Mona does but still feeling unsure, given the last couple of months. Then Mona spots me and waves frantically, gesturing for me to join them.

'Oh my god, guess what,' she gushes as I squeeze back into

the chair with her. She looks back at Aaron and grins. 'Lewis is gone.'

'Gone?'

'Yeah, Dan fully told him where to go. Really laid into him about everything over the past couple of months.'

I glance up at Aaron, who nods. 'Yup. It felt kind of final.'

'And you're OK with that?'

It's about as close to a confrontation as I'm comfortable getting. Aaron stares down at his feet, and Mona quietly reaches over and takes his hand. It seems to give him the strength to look me in the eye.

'Yeah, I am. He was a shit friend, especially to Dan. We let a lot slide for too long. And talking of which …' He looks even more sheepish. 'The way we treated you over the past few months – we were idiots. *I* was an idiot. Dan made us see sense but it shouldn't have needed to come to that. I'm really sorry, Libby.'

It's short, but it looks like it took mammoth effort and I have to give him credit. 'It's OK,' I say with a shrug. And it kind of is – maybe not what they did, but now? It's OK.

I look down into my drink. I remember how I felt every time someone tagged me in the video Katie took, how frequently she shared it around, how it haunted me for weeks and made me feel like a monster.

I picture the fear in her eyes when I told her I had the power to make her feel exactly the same.

And when I really think about it – I don't want to be

responsible for that kind of misery, no matter how much the person kind of deserves it.

I take out my phone, hit delete on the video, and sigh. It doesn't feel like backing out. It feels like a power move, even if no one else knows about it. A full stop on the end of a particularly nasty sentence – not as satisfying as an exclamation mark maybe, but when do people like that ever truly get what they deserve.

It's enough that she believes I could share it, even if I no longer can.

Dan

After the clash with Lewis, I knew it would only be a matter of time before Katie found me and I'd be forced to face her. I'm just heading to the kitchen to check on the snack levels when a hand lands on my arm.

'Dan?'

There's a wavering in her voice that I can't remember hearing before, and as I turn to face her my heart can't help but tug a little.

'Can we talk a minute?' She cocks her head towards the hall that leads to the spare room, and I consider not going. But I can't avoid this forever.

'Sure.'

We step quietly into the room, side-stepping the hospital bed and the pile of blankets and sleeping bags. I want to bury myself in it. But I softly close the door and finally turn to face Katie.

She stands with one arm crossed over her body to hold on

to herself. She wobbles a little, and I wonder how much she's had to drink. I can tell she wants me to speak first, but I'm not going to give her the pleasure. I let the painful silence stretch out in front of us until finally she snaps.

'You kicked Lewis out,' she blurts. 'He's your friend. Why'd you do that?'

'I don't think he is my friend,' I say. I think she's going to probe more, but her attention has already switched to herself.

'You're mad at me,' she sulks, and without meaning to I let out a bark of laughter that startles her.

'Yes, Katie. I am mad at you.'

'But *why*?' she whines. 'I didn't *do* anything!'

'You forget how well I know you,' I say calmly. 'I know you're smarter than that. You know exactly what you did.'

'I was sticking up for you when you couldn't stick up for yourself!'

'How is *beating Libby up* and making her life a living *hell* protecting me?'

The words come out louder, angrier, than I intended, the steady calm vanishing. My legs start to tremble but I refuse to sit down. Katie looks taken aback – we both know I've never spoken to her like that in our entire lives. Neither of us has spoken to each other like that. That's not how we work.

'Dan, she cheated on you,' she says, pacing around the small amount of floor space in frustration. 'I always knew she was wrong for you. I knew it as soon as you started going out. You were never yourself when she was around, she completely took you away from us and then … then she—'

'She didn't *cheat* on me.' I interrupt, and Katie's eyes snap to mine. For a tiny sliver of a second I think about coming completely clean – but then that word and the venom behind it reverberates around my skull and I accept with a sinking sadness that I will probably never be able to properly, comfortably come out to this girl I grew up with. The girl I've considered a sister half my life.

I take a deep breath. 'She didn't cheat because she wasn't in control. You got her completely wasted, Katie, and then you just left her. You videoed her getting *assaulted*. You made her believe it was her fault. And you physically attacked her for it. Do you know how messed up that is?'

A flash of uncertainty crosses Katie's face, her lower lip trembling. She looks so much smaller than I've ever seen her. I think that maybe she's going to see sense. Maybe she's going to realise what she's done, and apologise, and we can salvage some semblance of a friendship.

A memory from childhood surfaces in my brain – the two of us in this very bedroom, top-and-tailing at a sleepover while our parents drank wine and chatted down the hallway. Whispering away to each other, giggling at how naughty we were to be still awake past bedtime, making shadow puppets on the wall using the glow of the night light.

Then her face stills and her eyes grow cold and I know it's all over.

'I'm not going to tell you I'm sorry for something I'm not.'

'Then I think you need to leave too.'

Katie's shoulders sag for a moment, as though she was still

expecting me to give in. But then she draws herself up, tosses her hair over her shoulder and strides out of the room without another word. I wait until I hear the sound of the front door slamming shut before I sink down into the armchair and give myself a moment to process what just happened.

Neha

I see her, but she doesn't see me.

I'm just stepping into the hallway after weaving my way through the living room, searching for where the hell Sam's got to, when Katie emerges from a doorway with her head thrown back and her shoulders set. But as the door swings shut, her face crumples and her body slumps forward and for a second I wonder if it's actually some other blonde I've mistaken for Katie.

No, it's really her, and whatever just happened in there has clearly broken her.

I stay quiet as she stuffs her feet into her shoes and rips open the Kings' front door, slamming it behind her as she leaves.

Good riddance.

I check the downstairs bathroom for Sam but find it empty, and am just about to circulate through the party again when Dan comes out of the same room Katie came from.

'Oh, hey!' he says, more brightly than his face says he's feeling. My eyes flick down to where he's gripping his cane with white knuckles. 'I wondered where you'd got to.'

'Just looking for Sam,' I say, gesturing vaguely to the space beside me where Sam isn't. 'He makes friends so easily, I doubt he'll grace me with his presence until next New Year.'

Dan laughs. 'Yeah, he seems pretty cool. Have you … ?'

'Nope.' I hug my body and stare at the floor, not needing him to finish the question. 'I don't think she was very pleased to see me.'

'I know that's not true,' says Dan, and I look up at him. His face is serious, but his eyes seem a little red and I strongly suspect that's not to do with this conversation.

'Not to very awkwardly change the subject for a minute, but are you OK? I just saw Katie leave and she looked, well, kind of upset. And if I'm being totally honest, so do you.'

'Ah, yeah,' Dan sighs. 'I guess we friend broke up? Is that a thing?'

'I don't think there's a word for it, but yeah,' I say. 'Sounds intense.'

'I think it was overdue. And very definitely deserved. It just feels kind of weird.'

I nod, probably only half understanding. We stand in silence for a moment, and then it's broken by the sound of footsteps padding down the stairs. A tall man with dark hair and Dan's eyes, wearing a very sensible knitted waistcoat, comes into the hall and smiles at both of us before turning to Dan.

'You ready?'

Dan looks down at his phone in shock. 'Bloody hell, it's ten to already! Yeah, Dad, let me round everyone up.' He goes to head back into the living room, and then turns back towards where I'm standing, feeling confused.

'Hey, grab your coat and go get a spot outside, OK?' He pauses, and then adds, 'Make sure anyone looking for you can see you.'

LIBBY

It's getting closer to midnight and I'm starting to wonder where Dan has got to, when he bobs up next to me as I'm standing with Mona and Aaron by the fireplace.

'All good here?' he says, throwing an arm over Aaron's shoulders, huffing a little with the effort but smiling widely at the three of us. He nods at me and Mona. 'I knew you guys would be all right.'

I feel like I should resent his cocky self-assurance, but my friend count is up to three now and I can't quite muster up the bitterness. Must be giddy on the wine.

'You might want to grab your coats,' Dan says, nodding in the direction of the hall.

I exchange a glance with Mona. 'Are you asking us to leave? Sick of us already?'

Dan laughs. 'We've got a surprise in the garden. It's nippy out.'

The coats have been piled up in a walk-in cupboard under

the stairs, and we scrabble to find our own in the tangle of thick material. After a brief but futile search for Mona's left shoe, we make our way out to the patio with Mona hobbling on one heel, supported by Aaron.

Fairy lights have been strung up around the canopy that's built over the patio area. At the end of the Kings' considerably large garden, a torch beam swishes about over the ground.

Dan appears at my shoulder, gently taking hold of my arm in the dark to steady himself. 'Wouldn't be a New Year's party without fireworks!'

Standing sandwiched between the two of them, I feel a happy little bubble bloom inside my chest. It feels exactly like it did before.

Except ...

Except I don't want it to be exactly like it was before.

I need to find Neha.

'I'll be right back,' I say, detangling myself from between my two best friends.

'You'll miss midnight!' says Mona, but Dan catches my eye and wiggles his eyebrows at me just as the first firework screams up into the sky.

I scan the modest crowd of people clustered on Dan's patio, their faces lighting up at intervals as the sky booms and glitters. I weave through unnoticed, everyone's attention captured. I think about the last time I was watching fireworks, arm in arm with Neha on Bonfire Night, feeling like a human being for the first time in forever.

Just as I'm starting to think she's left and I've blown the only chance I'll have to make things right, I spot her. She's sitting alone on top of a compost bin, swaying gently, the flashes of the fireworks lighting up her hair. I don't think. I just walk over to her.

She looks surprised at my sudden appearance, and her eyes roam over my flushed cheeks and solid stance. 'Libby?'

'Neha, I mucked up royally by freaking out and ignoring you for the past few weeks. I didn't know what to say, I didn't even know if you liked me like that, or that I even liked you like that, or that I even liked *girls* like that. And then Dan was awake and everything was a mess because we're not together, we never were, and all I wanted to do was come and see you and wear stupid Christmas jumpers and have beach picnics and … and …' I stop, panting a little, having run out breath.

'Neha, I'm pretty sure I love you.'

She stares at me, eyes wide, lips slightly apart. And then her face breaks out into the most beautiful smile, sending the butterflies already fluttering in my stomach wild. She slides down from the plastic bin, dropping down in front of me.

'I love you too, you big idiot.'

I don't say anything else. I just lean forward and kiss her.

At first she doesn't respond, her body frozen. And then her arms are around me, and her hands are in my hair, and I can smell the spray of perfume on her neck as fireworks explode in the sky and in my chest.

Neha

O H MY GOD SHE'S KISSING ME WHAT DO I DO WITH MY HANDS??!!

Dan

Everyone else had been looking at the fireworks. They didn't see what I saw, and that's probably a good thing, but that doesn't mean I'm not itching to start jumping up and down about it. Or at least I would be, if the evening's various exertions weren't very much catching up with me.

I should probably stop staring and grinning or I'll draw too much attention that they don't want, so I turn back to Mona and Aaron, who are just pulling away from each other, cheeks flushed.

'Happy New Year!' says Mona, planting a huge kiss on my cheek. She lifts her head to scan the patio. 'Did Libby—'

'I'm here!' Libby appears next to us, Neha at her shoulder. Libby's cheeks are the colour of beetroot and she's smiling wider than I ever saw her smile when we were 'together'.

'Happy New Year, babe!' Mona scoops Libby into a hug, and then turns to Neha. 'And you two made up! I knew you would.' She hugs Neha as well, grinning from ear to ear. She's clearly noticed, as I have, the fact that both of them have flushed faces and ruffled hair.

'Happy New Year, guys,' says Neha, swinging her arms by her sides now that Mona has let her go. That is, until Libby reaches down and clasps Neha's hand in hers, steadying her.

Mona's eyes flick down to where their hands are locked together. She grins even wider, but doesn't say anything.

I sway a little on the spot, my knees finally buckling as my body decides enough is enough. Aaron grabs my arm.

'Whoaa, buddy. Shall we maybe go back inside?'

'Probably best,' I laugh, allowing myself to lean into him a bit for support. My shoulders tense in anticipation of a jab from Lewis, but then I remember, he isn't here. I smile.

Neha glances around as we start to make our way back inside. 'Um, has anybody seen—'

'HAPPY NEW YEAR!' A flash of blond appears from the crowd and jumps on Neha's back, sending her staggering and squealing. 'Sorry, chatting to some people, lost track of time!'

'I can't take you anywhere,' Neha laughs, finally stabilising herself and setting Sam back down on the ground. As Sam steps away she instinctively takes a small step back towards Libby, and Sam grins and wiggles his eyebrows at her. Then he catches my eye and winks, and I feel a bit wobbly again.

We get back into the house and start pulling off all our shoes and layers again, Libby and Neha shooting each other smiling glances every five seconds. They look so smitten I can barely stand it. I feel giddy.

So much so that I decide it's probably about time I did something brave myself.

As we head back into the living room, I step over to the keyboard my parents got me for Christmas. I'd aspirationally refused to let Dad move it out of the way this afternoon, but didn't think I'd be bold enough to use it. I graze my fingers over the smooth keys, a niggling part of my brain telling me I can't do this.

I think of what I've already managed tonight.

I sit down and play a few notes, testing the air. The sound lifts into the air and calms my stammering heart as I pull comfort from the familiar pressure of the keys. The chatter around me fades away as people start to notice and gather around.

'Anyone for a classic?' I ask, and launch into a few verses of 'Auld Lang Syne' while I build up my nerve. To my relief everyone joins in, although I can tell some are improvising the words. I end the song and take a deep breath.

'Would anyone mind if I played something I've been working on?'

There's a murmur of encouragement, and I glance over my shoulder to see Libby looking at me, a questioning look in her eye but a small, hopeful smile on her lips.

I pull a few crumpled pages torn from my flip pad out of my pocket and rest them on the music stand. My hands are shaking as I rest them back against the keys, and I'm fighting back the urge to bail (though I wouldn't get very far on my shaking legs). But then my hands are moving across the keyboard and I'm singing the lyrics that I wrote and playing the music that poured out of my head and on to the paper. I've never dared share this with anyone other than Libby before.

I finish playing and there's a moment of silence as the echo of the last note rings out through the room. And then there's applause, and someone claps me on the back. I turn around and lock eyes with Libby. There are tears on her cheeks but she's beaming, clapping harder than anyone else, and I grin stupidly at my best friend. I finally feel like maybe right now everything is exactly as it should be.

Neha

I can't believe my high-tension but perfectly resolved evening is actually ending in a musical number.

As Dan starts to play, Libby's grip on my hand tightens and I hear her suck in a breath. When I turn to look at her, her eyes are brimming over and she looks about ready to burst.

'That's his own song!' she whispers, squeezing my hand again in excitement. 'That's his music!'

I glance around and see that everyone in the room is smiling and nodding along to the music, but Dan has his back to them all as he plays. While the music is soft, his shoulders seem tensed and nervous. I slip my phone from my pocket and snap a few photos. I'll show him how much they're all enjoying his work later.

When he's finished, I let out a whoop and start clapping loudly, spurring everyone around me to follow suit. Dan turns around and he and Libby just beam at each other. I wait for a crush of jealousy, but seeing them look at each other like that feels nothing other than wonderful. I'm glowing.

Dan makes his way back over to us and Libby immediately pulls him into a hug.

'That was amazing!' she gushes. 'I'm so proud of you!'

'I'm a bit rusty, but I think it went OK,' Dan says with a shrug, but he's grinning from ear to ear.

'Mate, you wrote that?!' Aaron says, incredulous. 'How come you never shared that with us before?' Dan looks so pleased I think he might pop when Libby gently elbows him in the ribs.

'Dan, I didn't know you could play piano!' One of our other classmates has appeared at his shoulder, and he turns to chat with them. I marvel at the difference between how I imagined this moment would feel versus how I feel right now.

'Anyone got any cards?' asks Sam, before the silence that has settled over the five of us can turn awkward. Aaron quickly swipes a deck from the bookshelves at the back of the room and Sam proceeds to try and teach us the rules to gin rummy.

A handful of people leave over the next hour, collected as instructed by Dan's parents. Sometime after 1 a.m., there's a gentle knock on the living-room door.

'Everything good in here?' Mr King pops his head into the room, smiling at the group of us sitting cross-legged on the floor playing cards.

'We're fine, thanks, Dad,' says Dan, who has been winning every game since he joined us. 'Everyone not staying has already been picked up.'

Another head appears at the door. 'Love, are you sure you're feeling OK? It's getting quite late—'

'All good, Mum!' Dan says, his voice an octave higher. 'You can go back upstairs now!'

Mr and Mrs King wave at the remaining guests before disappearing back upstairs, and Dan groans a little while we giggle behind our cards.

'Is there any food left?' asks Mona, once we've all composed ourselves. 'I think I only got a handful of crisps earlier.'

'I'll check,' says Dan, rising to his feet with a wobble. Libby starts to jump up to help him, but he waves her off, his mouth set in a grimly determined line.

He emerges from the kitchen moments later with the Tupperware that I'd all but forgotten about. My heart leaps into my throat.

'Oh, don't mind that,' I say quickly, sitting up straight and throwing a panicked glance to Libby, who looks curious. 'I thought it might be funny and ironic, a peace offering, but it's probably not, it's probably not funny at all, in fact you can just throw the whole thing in the bin—'

'Neha, you're babbling,' says Sam, raising his eyebrows at me. I never told him what was in the tub, almost certain I'd throw it in a bush on the way over here if I said it out loud. 'And now I *need* to know what's in there.'

'It was a bad idea,' I splutter, just as Dan prises the lid off the tub and holds it out for everyone to see.

It's a strawberry tart.

The idea snaked into my brain yesterday afternoon and

before I'd really thought about it I was rolling out the pastry, crafting it more carefully than anything else I'd ever baked before in my life. It's a pretty cracking tart, if I do say so myself.

There's a tense moment that Dan doesn't get, as everyone else's eyes flick between the tart and Libby.

And then she bursts out laughing. Mona follows, and then Sam, until eventually we're all clutching our sides and howling as Dan stands there in the middle of us going, 'What? What is it?! What's wrong with the tart?' and we start all over again and don't have the breath to answer him for ages.

Libby eats two slices.

When the whole thing is demolished and there's only crumbs left in the Tupperware, Libby takes my hand and pulls me out to the kitchen.

'Are you sure that was funny and not just weird?' I ask, unable to look her in the eye. She cups my chin with her hand and angles my face towards her.

'It was adorable,' she says, smiling. And then she kisses me again.

Just like the first time she did it, for a second my brain can barely compute what's happening – a moment I'd guiltily dreamed about, convinced myself would never happen. Relief washes over me so suddenly I feel light-headed, and then I wrap my arms around Libby and lift her into a spin so that we're giggling and kissing and I didn't think there would be a more perfect moment than the fireworks, but here we are.

She tastes like strawberries.

LIBBY

It's sometime after six in the morning, and I haven't slept yet.

With most people staying over, finding a patch of living-room floor to sleep on proved to be a task I wasn't up to. I don't mind. Neha has stayed up with me.

Over the last few hours, people have slowly peeled off to go to sleep. Mona and Aaron were amongst the first to go, nabbing a prime spot by the bay window and wriggling into sleeping bags next to one another. Last I saw they were holding hands in their sleep.

Dan fell asleep around four, curled up in an armchair and snoring softly. I draped a blanket over him, and he muttered something in his sleep. I couldn't quite catch it, but he smiled very slightly afterwards, so I assume it was something happy. Sam fell asleep on the floor in front of the armchair. I noticed Neha smile at something, but I didn't ask.

At around half five in the morning, Mrs King came

downstairs in her dressing gown for a glass of milk. She poked her head into the living room, not saying anything but smiling at the few of us left awake. When her eyes fell on the sleeping Dan, they filled up a little, but she excused herself and hurried back upstairs.

With everyone else now having crawled into a sleeping bag or under a blanket on the living-room floor, Neha and I pull our coats, gloves and hats on and step back out into the garden, teeth chattering in the predawn cold. We wander across the lawn and stretch out on the frozen grass, the soft rustling of our coats breaking the silence of the still morning.

We lie comfortably together under the new sky as it turns from black, to blue, to pale grey. Our breath rises in clouds above our faces. My toes have gone numb. I don't particularly care.

As the first sunlight of the New Year peeks over the horizon, I pull off one glove and move my arm over so it's lying next to Neha's. Slowly, gently, I link my fingers with hers. When I turn my head towards her, she's already looking at me. She's smiling. It feels like home.

'Happy New Year, Neha,' I whisper.

'Happy New Year.' She leans in towards me.

I close my eyes.

Sixteen Weeks After It Happened

LiBBy

I bounce on the balls of my feet, partly in anticipation and partly just to keep warm. In my haste not to be late I am of course the first one to arrive, and paying the price by having to stand under the cinema awning in the gathering dark of the frosty January evening.

Not that I have to wait too long. And it's definitely worth it.

Across the green I spot a familiar flash of rainbow wool and raise a gloved hand to wave at my girlfriend.

My girlfriend!

My teeth ache with the cold as I smile widely, but I don't care and keep smiling anyway. Neha hurries over and throws her arms around me.

'Hey!' she says breathlessly, pulling away. 'You were early.'

'Nah, everyone else is late, or however the saying goes.' We grin stupidly at each other and I slip my gloved hand into hers. I glance around at the square, then tug her further into the shadows of the awning.

She's wearing strawberry lip balm.

'And what have you two been up to?' asks Mona several minutes later, strolling up with Aaron and wiggling her eyebrows at our mussed hair and giddy smiles.

We're saved from having to answer by the arrival of Zoe's battered Mini, which pulls up on the kerb with a splutter. Sam jumps out of the back, shouts a cheery 'hello!' in our direction, and then goes around to the boot to pull out Dan's wheelchair.

'Honestly, Zoe, I appreciate it, but I could have just wheeled myself here,' says Dan, opening the passenger-side door and taking a wobbly step out with a fist curled tightly around his cane for balance.

'Don't be daft, it was on the way,' Zoe lies breezily as she climbs out and comes around to hug me and Neha. Sam unfolds the chair and Dan lowers himself into it, smiling up at him for a second before turning to the rest of us.

'Sorry, did I make us late? Leaving the house nowadays is a nightmare.'

'Ahh, your mum not wanting you to leave on your own?' asks Aaron with a sympathetic grimace.

'No!' Dan bursts out. 'She just needs to reassure me every five minutes that it's OK I'm gay and she still loves me. It's really very sweet, but god is it time consuming.'

He says it with the same furtive glance round that I did before kissing Neha, but it still feels so wonderful to hear him talk about it so openly. We all laugh, and I go to take the handles of his chair to help him inside but Sam has beaten me to it.

Neha and I exchange a look, and now it's our turn to waggle our eyebrows, still smiling like idiots.

We step into the tiny cinema which has the heating cranked up to full, and immediately have to start shedding layers. The foyer is fairly busy, though I think we're the youngest ones here by at least twenty years. One of the framed film posters has a fresh print tacked to the glass proclaiming SPECIAL SCREENING: MOULIN ROUGE.

'What's this about again?' asks Aaron as we shuffle forward in line for the ticket booth.

'Consumption and elephants,' quips Neha. 'And bohemians!'

'And a redhead,' adds Sam, winking at Neha. She blushes, but smiles so that her dimples come out. I fight the urge to kiss them, but only because we've just reached the front of the queue.

'Two, please, Mrs Bramley,' I say, holding out a note.

'Oh, Eleanor, lovely to see you, dear!' says Mrs Bramley, reaching for the ticket roll. 'One for you and for your ... friend?'

I side-eye Neha, who's stifling a giggle. 'It's Libby, Mrs Bramley. And, sure, thank you.'

We take our tickets and move aside so the others can get theirs. It's busy enough that we can stand close, still holding hands, without it drawing too much attention. We still haven't really struck the balance we want between not broadcasting it without hiding it. But we'll get there.

'Daniel!'

We turn to see Mr Bloom crossing the foyer, waving at Dan, who takes his ticket from Mrs Bramley and manoeuvres his chair around.

'Hey, Mr Bloom. I should have guessed you'd be here for a musical.'

'Oh, I never miss a chance to see *Moulin Rouge* on the big screen,' says Mr Bloom, smiling at the poster. His eyes flick over me and Neha, then Dan, and then back to the poster. 'I love a musical, always have. And Ewan McGregor, such a talented man. And so …'

Dan tips his head to one side. 'Versatile?'

'I was going to say handsome,' says Mr Bloom airily, turning back to just Dan. '*Very* attractive man – don't you think?'

Dan gawks at him, and my heart starts thumping harder in my chest. Neha lets out a little squeak that might be excitement.

'Well, enjoy the film, kids,' says Mr Bloom, raising a hand in a lazy wave. 'Have fun!'

He moves away and we all stare after him.

'Did he just … ?' begins Dan, locking eyes with Neha. She grins and nods emphatically.

'Yeah, I think he did.'

The others step over to us, ticket stubs in hand.

'Ready?' asks Mona brightly, and then frowns. 'You all look weird. What happened?'

Dan, Neha and I all exchange a glance, and then burst into giggles. The lights in the foyer start flickering, indicating that we should really be taking our seats.

'I'll explain later,' I tell Mona as we make our way through to the screen. She raises an eyebrow at me but smiles, taking Aaron's arm.

We settle down into our seats, and I notice that Neha and Zoe have managed to quietly orchestrate it so that Sam and Dan are sitting next to each other in the cosy darkness of the room. Neha grins at me, and my stomach flutters.

As the lights go down, I reach over to take her hand again, lacing her fingers through mine. I never want to let go.

Acknowledgements

I've been writing since I learned how to hold a pencil, but *Tart* is the first full novel I ever conceived of and, crucially, finished. It started life as an unrecognisable first draft in November 2014, needing a lot of work and a whole heap of support to become the book you've just finished reading.

First, thank you to my all-round Good Egg husband, Lee, for being there for every single moment of this journey – every milestone, every breakdown, every celebratory tart. An extra thank you for being the first person I ever came out to as bi and for making it the most chill experience I could have hoped for. I love you, you're the best.

Thank you to my mum, Tracey, for always being there and believing in me even when I didn't believe in myself. Thank you to my little sister, Hannah, who I can always count on to help stretch a pair of tights and who will be genuinely furious I just referred to her as my 'little sister'.

Endless thanks to my incredible agent, Saffron Dodd, who took a chance on this book first and whose enthusiasm for the story made me feel like it wasn't destined to remain a pipe dream. Thank you also to Alice Sutherland-Hawes for all your support, and for talking to me about the Eras Tour when I was really nervous about a meeting.

Thank you to the amazing team at Bloomsbury, who have been an absolute joy to work with – my editor, Cathy Liney, who helped make this manuscript the best it could be. Danielle Rippengill for the cover of my dreams and Sarah Long for the wonderful illustrations. Thank you to Fliss Stevens, Alex Antscherl, Katie Ager, Jessica Bellman, Sara Jafari, Michael Young, Talya Baker and Jessica White. And to sensitivity readers Krish Jeyakumar and Elly Valdez, thank you for your invaluable contributions. A huge thanks to Isi Tucker and Tim Hardy in Publicity and Marketing for making me feel so at ease and for bringing me a strawberry tart at my first YALC, which saved me from passing out.

Thank you to my favourite teacher, Mrs Hardiker (it still feels weird calling you Gill!), who was the first person other than my mum to support my creative writing. I never forgot about it.

A massive thank you to Charlotte Moore, who read an embarrassingly early draft of this book and told me it was worth pursuing. I'm so serious when I say that without you this manuscript would have died in the drawer.

Thank you to my beta readers, Liz Sunter and Caroline McDonagh-Darwin, for all the encouragement, feedback and for answering my frantic questions whenever I panicked about chunks of the plot. Thank you to CJ DeBarra for all the sushi chats and book talk, and to Jack Harrison for being such a tireless cheerleader.

To the 'uni lot' – Laura, Kate, Hannah, Matt, Rachel, Chris, Dave, Reece, Igy, Luke and Sarah. Thank you for being my friends and for all your support. Daisy, Cora and Baby Tom Hanks from *Big*, you guys can't read yet but if you could I'm sure you'd be very supportive too.

Thanks to my dad, Amelia, Jack and Shelley for cheering me on. Jack and Riley, you're both too young for this book, but thanks for being so gosh darn cute. To the Crossley clan, thank you for all the support and for being so wonderfully, exceptionally weird. And to Nan and Grandad, thank you for everything, including my name, which I'm incredibly proud to have on the front of this book.

Thanks to Beth Ashley and Goblin, of my most unhinged group chat (a difficult title to maintain). Cheers for the memes and for coaxing me down from a spiral every time I convinced myself my publishing dreams were in tatters.

Eternal gratitude to the Soup Group, without whom there would simply be no book. I honestly couldn't have dreamed up a more perfect circle of author pals. Sarah Cook, Liv Wright, Chell Crick, Fiona Longmuir and Elena Bjørn – I could fill volumes on what phenomenal writers and humans you are, but I'm running out of space, so I'll just say: Jesus, you all really are terrific.

And to Georgia Sanders, who thought I'd forgotten her, lol. All the above soup salutations apply, plus an extra thank you for being my chaos twin, for listening to every single thought that goes through my head, and for letting me know when I tip over into being fully ludicrous. Which is often. You deserve a medal, quite frankly.

Finally, to the dorky little weirdo who constantly felt out of step with everyone else, spent their lunchtimes in the library and bought a new notebook every time they left the house because *this* one was going to be their great novel – thanks, kid. You got us here.

About the Author

Becki Jayne Crossley (she/they) has had a book in her hands since before she could actually read, and since mastering the art of holding a pencil they've been writing down stories. As a bisexual author, Becki is passionate about queer YA stories that portray the realities of coming out and discovering your sexuality – especially considering the lack of stories they had like this while growing up. When not writing, Becki can be found reading at her favourite coffee shops around Nottingham, playing too much *The Sims 4* and occasionally painting things with questionable skill.